The Revolutionary War

*Book V
of the Royal Sorceress series*

The Revolutionary War

*Book V
of the Royal Sorceress series*

Christopher G. Nuttall

Elsewhen Press

To Aisha

Prologue

imone prided herself on never being afraid of men.

She was a Talker, with the ability to read thoughts and emotions, and incredible insight into the male psyche even when she wasn't using her talents. She knew what buttons to press to make a man think or say whatever she wanted, to spill his secrets or pledge himself to her life and defence even without any pledges from her in return. She'd used her talents on behalf of the empire and her adopted father, Ambassador Talleyrand, long enough to know precisely what she was doing. She wasn't fool enough to think herself immune from consequences, in the ever more faction-ridden Bourbon Court, but she knew that, as long as she was useful, she'd be relatively safe from harm.

And yet, Duke Philippe scared her.

He strode beside her, his arm resting on hers in a manner that might have seemed affectionate under other circumstances, his presence overshadowing her thoughts. She couldn't read *his* thoughts, or even pick up a sense of his emotions, and it bothered her. No one had said anything bad about him, as far as she knew, and yet their thoughts – when they thought about him, which was as little as possible – were coloured with apprehension, even fear. Duke Philippe was a close confidant of the king, yet very few people knew anything about him beyond his rank and title. It wasn't even clear what he *did* for the king.

Simone titled her head just slightly, enough to study him. He was a handsome man in his late thirties, wearing surprisingly modest dress for a courtier at Versailles, yet there was something about his appearance that made her feel uneasy. She couldn't put it into words. She was used to seeing men and women who dressed themselves to draw the eye, or to shock, and yet ... there was just something *off* about him. She tried, once again, to extend her magic and read him, but there was nothing. It was worrying. She knew people with the mental discipline to keep her out, or keep their thoughts spinning to prevent her from following the mental strands, but this ... it was almost as if he wasn't there. If he hadn't had his arm on hers, holding her tightly enough to make it clear she couldn't break free, she would have thought he really *wasn't*.

Her mind raced as they passed a pair of sentries and walked down a flight of stairs. She'd never been to the very lowest levels, but she'd heard the rumours. It was an open secret that the king had prisoners here, men and women arrested by *lettres de cachet* and held in the dungeons by the king's personal authority ... held without any hope of freedom unless the king decided to let them go. Others ... there were all sorts of whispers, from secret brothels for pleasures denied even to the courtiers, to private meeting rooms where the king met with foreign ambassadors away from prying eyes. Her blood ran cold as they passed a pair of Royal Guardsmen, wearing combat uniforms rather than the peacock finery of the sentries above; proof, if she needed it, that the normal rules didn't apply below the ground. If she'd realised where she was going ...

She swallowed, hard. She'd hadn't been in any position to argue, when the message had arrived at the suite she shared with her adopted father. She'd been summoned ... and Duke Philippe himself had arrived to escort her. It wasn't the first time she'd been invited to the palace – she *was* the adopted daughter of a great nobleman – but it was by far the strangest and the most dangerous. The war wasn't going well. The failed invasion of Britain, the defeat in America, the chaos to the east … she'd caught a handful of officers bemoaning the war, arguing that the empire should seek peace with the British so they could make territorial gains in Russia while the Russians fought their civil war. If the factions had turned murderous … it wouldn't be the first time. She tried not to shiver in fear. Every Frenchman dreaded a return to the Unrest of 1789, where revolutionaries had almost taken Paris, or the Wars of Religion between Catholics and Protestants. And yet, with the war going poorly, who knew what would happen?

People are starving, she reflected, grimly. She wasn't a well-dressed princess whose life was a constant whirl of parties, romantic relationships and little else. She *knew* the public mood was darkening. One didn't need to read minds to know *that*. *And when people are starving and desperate, they do desperate things.*

Duke Philippe tightened his grip, just enough to make her wince. "Beyond this door, keep your thoughts to yourself," he said. His tone was curiously flat, as if he cared nothing for her. Simone knew men who were enraptured by her beauty and men who disdained her for being a woman and yet, Duke Philippe – somehow – was worse. She had the impression he'd break her neck in an instant if it suited him, without even a flicker of emotion. "There are secrets here that must not be spoken."

Simone gritted her teeth, fighting not to pull away. It was hard, even as he loosened his grip. There would be marks on her bare skin … she knew, all too well, the dark underside of the fairy tale palace, the aristocratic women who used makeup to hide their bruises and the serving girls too poor or powerless to do the same. She controlled her thoughts with an effort as the doors swung open, revealing a simple chamber. Her heart seemed to skip a beat as she was guided into the room, the four men already present not even deigning to look at her. The room was completely unfurnished, save for a simple stone block. Fear ran through her as she realised where she was, where she had to be. It was the king's judgement hall.

"Stay quiet," Duke Philippe ordered. "Say nothing."

The other set of doors opened. Two guards entered, dragging a beaten and bound man between them. Simone's thoughts darted towards him, despite the warning, and stopped – dead – as she tasted his mind aura. It was almost as familiar to her as her own … Talleyrand, Ambassador Talleyrand, her adopted father and guardian and master and … she staggered, nearly fainting, as her father was pushed to the block. If Duke Philippe hadn't been holding her arm, she feared she *would* have collapsed.

A man stepped forward. He wore royal livery, but she didn't recognise him. The king had many servants, some kept in the shadows. There was no shortage of rumours about them either.

"Talleyrand," he said. "You have been judged guilty of …"

Simone didn't listen to the charges. She'd always known her adopted father was venal in almost every sense of the word, with an insatiable appetite for titles, money and women, but … they didn't matter. The simple fact he'd been brought here and treated as a rebel, rather than as a man of aristocratic blood, spoke volumes. The specific charges were nothing more than a thin veneer of legality, spread over a judicial murder to conceal the simple fact the victim had been sacrificed to appease the victorious faction. Simone knew no one would be fooled. One faction had gained ascendency and marked Talleyrand for death, proving their supremacy in a way no one could deny.

Duke Philippe's grip tightened, again. "Watch."

Simone blinked away tears as her adopted father was hauled to the block and shoved into place. There were no speeches, no final chance to sway the crowd … what crowd? Simone was powerless and everyone else agreed Talleyrand had to die. She forced herself to stand tall and watch, silently grateful he didn't look at her, as the axe came down. It was over so quickly she barely had a second to say a prayer for him. Talleyrand hadn't been perfect – she knew that all too well – but he'd been far from the worst of guardians. She didn't have to read minds all day to know *that*, either.

"It is done," Duke Philippe said, pulling her away from the scene. "Come."

Simone found her voice, the moment they were back outside. "Why …?"

"These are dangerous times for the empire," Duke Philippe said. There was still no emotion in his voice. "His Majesty has determined that a new policy is needed, to win the war and ensure Bourbon Supremacy for the rest of time. I, his Master of Magic, have been ordered to carry out the policy. You will assist me."

"I …" Simone caught herself. Talleyrand had been one of the most powerful courtiers at Versailles. His execution was clear proof the balance of power had shifted. She was mildly surprised she hadn't been executed too, or sent to the breeding farms. She wasn't meant to know they existed, but she did. "I serve His Majesty."

"Quite," Duke Philippe agreed. "And don't you forget it."

He let go of her and turned, walking back up the corridor. Simone *knew* he expected her to follow him – and knew he was right. What else could she do? She reached for her power as she started to walk, making one final attempt to reach into his mind and read his thoughts. This time, there was something … a jarring series of images, all tangled together into a single horrific mass. Simone had to bite her lip to keep from gasping. If he realised what she'd done, she'd never leave the court alive.

God, she asked herself. Her adopted father was dead … who else could she ask for help? She hadn't precisely been kept isolated from the rest of the courtiers, but they hadn't been very welcoming either … no, they'd be completely unwelcoming now Talleyrand had been executed. No one would give her so much as a smile, for fear it would draw entirely the wrong type of attention. *What do I do now?*

Something crystallised in her mind as she studied his back. She'd loved Talleyrand, regardless of his flaws, and he'd served his king loyally. She wanted to make the court pay for what they'd done to him. And besides, whatever the cost, Duke Philippe had to be stopped.

And Simone would have her revenge.

Chapter One
London, England

ondon *stank*.

Bruce floated above the city and breathed in the air, wondering – not for the first time – how people managed to *live* in such a nightmare. New York was cramped and unpleasant in places, but the wide open world beyond the colonies had all the living space anyone could possibly want. London, by contrast, sprawled for miles, a tangled nightmare of government buildings and aristocratic districts surrounded by circles of lower and lower class housing that eventually ended in slums and shanty housing owned by distant uncaring landlords and ruled by criminal gangs. London was the greatest city of the greatest empire the world had ever known and yet, looking at the capital from above, it was hard not to see the city as the rotten core of a rotten empire. He had no idea, he really didn't, why so many people were allowed to waste their lives in the slums. It would be so much kinder to ship them to North America, Australia, or even to Africa.

And this is when the city is shrouded in night, he thought, dully. *It looks worse during the day.*

He sucked in his breath, shaking his head. His father had told him tales of London and he wished, almost, he'd never seen the reality. It was a shining city on a river and also a hellhole resting on a bog. The population were great and noble and yet also sullen and murderous. It was hard to believe *Gwen* had been born and raised in London, but then … he only had to look beyond the edge of the city to see aristocratic enclaves, islands of greenery threatened by the ever-advancing tidal wave of civilisation. The great mansions weren't castles, not by any stretch of the imagination, but they might as well be, given how they protected the inhabitants from the reality of the world surrounding them. There'd been changes, he'd been told, after the Swing …

… And yet, from high above, it seemed nothing had changed in years.

Something moved, below him. Bruce darted to one side, gritting his teeth as he felt magic trying to envelop him. Two – no, *three* – figures were flying towards him, their hands raised as they steered magical force in a bid to grab and crush *his* magic. The spikes of raw power were meant to panic him, hinting it was a matter of seconds before his power failed and he plunged to the ground. Bruce refused to allow himself to be intimidated as he called on his own magic, snatching a fireball out of nowhere and hurling it at the lead figure. It should have forced the man to concentrate on his own defence, to wrap himself in power rather than try to snatch Bruce out of the air, but instead the fireball exploded harmlessly against an invisible wall. Bruce felt a flicker of wry amusement. It was hard not to be impressed at how well the three magicians – all Movers – worked together. One to carry the three into the air, one to defend them, one to attack. It might just work.

Bruce took a breath and dissolved his magic. They expect him to either go on the offensive himself or try to flee. Instead, gravity took effect and he plummeted downwards. The magicians seemed to hesitate, unsure if they'd done more than they'd intended or if he was trying to con them. Bruce took full advantage, wrapping his power around him to ensure he fell faster and further. They'd be after him in a moment – he was surprised they weren't already giving chase – but he had a few seconds. He dropped into the alleyway, gritting his teeth as he channelled all his power into a dead stop. He would have survived the landing if he'd come down hard, but the impact would have been impossible for even a blind man to miss. The rest of the magicians were out there somewhere, hunting him … he kept moving, keeping his head down as he flew through the alleyways. A handful of homeless people scattered as he kept moving … he felt a twinge of guilt, combined with the grim awareness they could easily have signed up to sail abroad instead. British North America was always looking for new colonists, particularly ones hungry for land and money of their own. He hoped they'd think about it, as he darted through an even darker alleyway. The ladies of the night waved at him …

He sensed the spike of power, an instant before the bolt impacted on his magic. For a second, the darkened alleyway was as brightly lit as the Royal College. He caught sight of two magicians ahead of him, both aiming their fingers … he ducked instinctively as they directed streams of raw power at him, trying to batter down his defences by naked force. It was surprisingly inelegant, but it might just work … he reached out with his magic and yanked on nearby pieces of debris, picking them up and throwing them at the magicians. His lips quirked as they hastily started shooting the debris out of the air instead, rather than trying to duck. He had to admit it made a certain degree of sense. There was no way to be *sure* he wouldn't steer the debris directly into someone's chest. Perhaps it wouldn't kill them, but they'd be bruised enough to make them regret tangling with him.

The air twisted, a second later, as a swarm of … *something* brushed against him. His mind blanked – bees or wasps or … *something* – before he realised it was animated dust. It didn't seem dangerous, certainly not when compared to the more powerful magicians hunting him, but it made it difficult to see and he dreaded to think what it would do if it got into his mouth and lungs. Gritting his teeth, he ducked and put all his power into pushing the dust away from him. A wind rushed through the alleyway, knocking down one of the Blazers who'd been fool enough to stand up again. Bruce barely noticed. He couldn't see the Changer who'd animated the dust, nor the Infuser who'd probably assisted the bastard, and that meant there was no way to stop him doing the same thing again. Worse, the bright light had probably brought the Movers down on him too. If they hadn't known where he was before, they sure as hell did now.

No point in trying to hide, he thought. *And that gives me options ...*

He closed his eyes and drew on his magic, generating a blinding light. Someone cried out ... it wouldn't blind them permanently, he hoped, but they'd be blinking away tears long enough for him to get moving. The light vanished ... he opened his eyes and looked forward, wincing in sympathy as he saw a magician rubbing his eyelids frantically. His partner raised a hand, directing a bolt of magic towards Bruce. Quick-witted enough to close his eyes, Bruce reflected, or simply lucky enough to be looking away from the light before it had snapped out of existence. It didn't matter. The rest of the magicians were briefly stunned, long enough for Bruce to fly straight at the Blazer and knock him down. Again.

There was no time to savour his brief victory. Bruce kept moving, staying low rather than risk the skies. There would be too great a risk of being spotted, even though the darkness and smog should have hidden him perfectly. And yet ... he ducked, sharply, as the world seemed to explode around him. The three Movers dropped down, their power lashing out like a hurricane. Bruce barely had a second to keep his head down as they threw enough bricks and stone to make an entire house at him, chunks of debris slamming into his magic and making him wince in pain. In theory, his defences were impregnable. In practice, enough hammering could and would bring them down.

Damn it, he thought. It was hard to see clearly in the semi-darkness, but it looked as if the Movers were fighting blind. They shouldn't be able to see him, let alone actually fight. There was something weirdly unfocused about their power, but ... they were still fighting with surprising effectiveness. If he stood still, they'd zero in on his position and take him down. *How are they doing it?*

His mind raced, considering the options. Were they Masters? Bruce would have bet his inheritance they were nothing of the sort, not when the Royal Sorcerers Corps had spent years trying to avoid making the decision to recruit Lady Gwen. They would have happily left her to rot if they'd had any alternative. Hell, Bruce *knew* there were quite a few magicians who chafed at the thought of taking orders from a woman, and a mere *girl* at that. The only other Master was Bruce himself and the senior magicians were still trying to decide if the disadvantages of him being American outweighed the advantages of having a penis. He rolled his eyes at the thought. Bastards. If they'd known precisely how Gwen and Bruce had met, they'd have had a collective heart attack. They really didn't think ...

Understanding clicked as the Movers kept coming, their power reaching out to grab him. They were a team! The heavy hitters might have taken the lead in the bid to catch him, but their supporters weren't far away. There'd be a Seer and a Talker – perhaps more than one – watching from a safe distance, coordinating the battle. The idea of surrendering control of his body and magic to *anyone* was unpleasant, and he doubted he could do it for anything, but the team had probably practiced long enough to overcome the instinctive reluctance to do anything of the sort. That they were using it in battle ... they'd had to have spent months practicing. Bruce had to admit it was clever, and not something anyone would have reasonably expected.

He tossed a handful of debris at them – he'd be astonished if it slowed them down for more than a few moments, but every second counted – and reached out with his mind. *Gwen* was the expert, when it came to the mental talents. She had a precision he could only admire, a degree of control he'd thought impossible before meeting her. Bruce suspected it had something to do with their upbringing. He'd been raised as a young man – and it had been expected he'd inherit his father's title and lands – while she'd been raised as a young woman, someone who'd be married off for best advantage after she was introduced to High Society. She'd never been supposed to use her powers openly …

Got you, he thought. The Talkers hadn't tried to latch onto Bruce's mind directly – he was sure he would have felt them reading his thoughts, even if he was in the middle of a battle – but he could still feel them, right on the edge of his awareness. They were closer than he'd expected or at least they felt that way. The mental magics behaved oddly where distance was involved, in ways that didn't quite make sense. *Did you come to share the danger or do you have to be close to use your powers effectively?*

It didn't matter. He drew on his power, broadcasting a disruptive thought into the air. No normal person, magician or no, would so much as notice its presence, but a Talker would be sent reeling by the sheer *wrongness* of the thought. It was like … he wasn't sure how to put it into words … perhaps being hit in the face by human faeces, only worse. The blowback made him gag, even as the Movers staggered, their coordination gone. Bruce could do nothing about the Seer, if there really *was* a Seer, but it didn't matter. There was no way for the Seer to keep the Movers informed, not now the Talkers were out of the game.

Keep moving, he told himself. It wasn't that long until daybreak. *Don't let them get a solid idea of where you are.*

He dropped to the ground and started to run, picking his way through the shadows with practiced ease. They'd be looking for someone flying, or wrapped in magic, rather than someone showing no visible signs of power. The confrontation had sent hundreds of people running in all directions, further confusing the searchers. It was quite possible he'd be able to walk right out of the cordon, as long as he kept his head down and tugged his forelock when he saw the searchers. His lips quirked at the thought. The hunters were proud men who considered themselves touched by God, even if they hadn't been born to the very highest levels of the aristocracy. They'd have trouble wrapping their heads around someone pretending to be a powerless commoner.

Which is a mistake on their part, he thought. The Sons of Liberty had had plenty of sources amongst the American aristocracy and almost all of them had been resentful servants. *A commoner might pass unnoticed in a place an aristocrat would be spotted effortlessly.*

He slowed his movements as he felt questing mental probes rippling the air, trying to pose as a cripple. There was a decent chance he'd simply be overlooked in the confusion ... perhaps. It was impossible to be sure. Seers tended to be dangerously unpredictable and a Talker might latch onto his mental aura without ever realising their thoughts were brushing against a cripple's mind. His thoughts hardened in disgust. It was technically illegal to read someone's mind without their consent, or a court order, but the rule was honoured more in the breach than the observance. Gwen had told him, bitterly, that aristos who loudly proclaimed female magicians should never be trained to use their powers had few qualms about using their mind-reading daughters to give them an edge in negotiations, particularly when no one knew their children had magic. And ...

The world seemed to explode around him. Bruce hurled himself into the air as two waves of magic slammed together, where he'd been an instant ago. He realised his mistake a second later. There was no reason for a vagrant, someone down on his luck and sleeping on the streets, to have such tight mental discipline, particularly when he had no reason to think he'd need it. Perhaps he should have tried to put together a better cover story, but it wouldn't have fooled the questing minds for long. He twisted his magic as the Movers closed in, sending a blast of raw power directly towards them while using a stream – almost a thread – of magic to yank him backwards, swinging from building to building. His old teacher hadn't been strong in magic, unlike his charge, but he'd made up for it in ingenuity. Who needed to fly when you could swing through the air.

He glanced at the sky. The first hints of dawn could be seen, although it was hard to be sure of anything in perpetually gloomy London. He pushed out another mental broadcast, hopefully knocking the Talkers back down again. It wouldn't take long for the Movers to realise they'd been conned … if they didn't already know it, he'd be astonished. But as long as he stayed ahead of them, he should be fine. The flying magicians could catch up with him quickly – they could probably move faster than him – but everyone else would be restricted to shanks's pony. They couldn't get into position unless the Movers slowed him down. And …

Something struck him, hard. Bruce barely had a second to realise what was happening before he – *they* – were plummeting to the ground. There was hardly any time to cushion the impact as the paving stones came up and hit him. The landing jarred him so violently it knocked the wind from his lungs. His attacker's magic was tearing into his, shredding his defences and brushing against his bare skin. He tried to summon his power to counterattack, but it wasn't enough. All he managed was to knock the hat from her head. Blonde hair spilled down and brushed against his hands.

"Got you," Gwen said.

Bruce looked up at her. She was beautiful, despite her rather severe clothing carefully cut to hide as much of her figure as possible. His heart raced, his body suddenly very aware of hers pressing against his. His magic thrummed … he raised his head, their lips touching without conscious thought. It was hard, very hard, to break the kiss. And yet, he had no choice. If someone saw them kissing openly, before their marriage, it would ruin her. Bruce would take a terrible revenge, if he ever figured out who'd done it, but the damage would be beyond repair. They weren't even allowed to hold hands in public.

"You got me," Bruce said. There was no point in denying it. "Are you going to let me breathe now?"

Gwen rolled off him and stood, brushing down her dark outfit. "You did well," she said, picking up her hat and putting it on her head. "There aren't many people who can stay ahead of us for long."

"Thanks," Bruce said. It was hard not to wonder if there really was an *us*. She didn't normally fight as part of a team, let alone the first and greatest team of magicians in the known world. Merlin should have recruited her long ago and yet they hadn't, while they'd extended an offer to Bruce with insulting speed. "What now?"

"Now?" Gwen shrugged, then composed herself as the sound of running footsteps echoed towards them. "Now, we go over the chase, and then you and I have an appointment at the hall."

Bruce swallowed. "Do I really *have* to meet your parents?"

Gwen laughed, but there was an edge to it. "I'm afraid so," she said. "It won't be easy to marry without their permission."

"Charming," Bruce said. It was going to be a disaster. He knew it. "But anything for you."

Chapter Two
Versailles, France

aechel Slater-Standish had thought, without irony, that she was a bad girl. Her parents had died when she'd been a child, leaving her in the care of a pair of guardians who cared more about propriety than the well-being of a young girl, never hesitating to punish her for failing to live up to their expectations. Raechel had rebelled, of course, as she grew into her teenage years, attending social clubs and dances properly brought up young women weren't supposed to know existed. She'd been courted by everyone – her beauty and inheritance drawing men to her like flies – and she'd had few qualms about pushing the limits as far as they would go. The more her aunt lectured and punished, the more Raechel had been determined to be a free-thinking young woman ...

She knew, now, she'd been a child playing at being bad. In London, High Society was stodgy and dull and merciless to anyone caught breaking the rules, particularly if they were young women. In Versailles, High Society was an endless series of entertainments and social crazes and activities that would have given her aunt a heart attack, if she'd walked into the ballroom and gazed upon the youngsters enjoying themselves. Raechel wore a dress that exposed the tops of her breasts, and had a slit to reveal brief flashes of her shapely legs as she walked, but she was easily one of the more modest young women in the ballroom. She could see women practically topless, to all intents and purposes, and others who looked as if their dresses were about to fall off at any moment. Perhaps they were, part of her mind reflected wryly. It didn't look as if they needed any encouragement.

The young – and not so young – men weren't any better. They wore fancy wigs and fancier uniforms, some carefully cut to reveal their muscles and others tailored to hide their paunches. Raechel had quietly decided, although it was hard to be sure, that anyone who had a chest covered in medals was only pretending to be a soldier …at least, they'd probably never seen any real action. The Franco-Spanish aristocracy was supposed to supply the great captains of tomorrow, the young men who'd lead their troops to victory over the enemies of their empire, but it wasn't easy to balance the quest for glory with the risk of being killed in combat. There was no shortage of volunteers for safe postings, fewer willing to go into commands that might get them killed. Her lips twisted in disgust. An army didn't *just* need generals and other high-ranking officers. It needed junior officers too and aristos willing to take on those roles were few and far between.

Her lips twitched in cold amusement. The Bourbons didn't make their own lives any easier when it came to filling out their armies. Technically, anyone who could claim aristocratic descent could demand a place at court; practically, many were too poor to buy commissions or simply too far from the main aristocratic bloodlines to command postings of real authority. They just couldn't be trusted. It was hard, sometimes, not to look around the court and see quiet desperation under the painted smiles. The men and women in front of her clung to their aristocratic descent because it was all they had. They were nothing without it.

And there are so many aristos out there that it is easy to insert one or two more into the lists, she thought, her lips twitching as she nodded politely to an older woman. *They didn't even notice!*

She smiled. She'd doubted her cover story would stand up to strict scrutiny when she reached Versailles, but no one had batted an eyelid when she'd presented her papers and explained she was the daughter of an aristo who'd left court under a cloud and died without ever regaining his position. She knew that wouldn't last, if she got too close to someone actually important, but that was unlikely too. There was no shortage of young women with aristo backgrounds coming to court in the hopes of making a good match, only to discover the best they could hope for was becoming a powerful man's mistress. They just didn't have the money to overcome the simple fact they hadn't been raised at Versailles and didn't have anything to offer those who *had*.

And just paying them all pensions is a major drain on the empire's funds, Raechel thought, wryly. She'd been taught as little as possible about money – her guardians had clearly envisaged continuing to handle her affairs, even after she was married off to a young man of their choosing – but even *she* could tell that thousands of relatively small pensions added up to a hell of a lot of money. *The Bourbons would be better off telling them to go seek their fortune overseas ...*

A hand grabbed her arm. "Raechel," a voice said. "That's where you are!"

Raechel kept her face under tight control. Louis – he had claimed a title others argued he had no right to – was a mid-ranking cavalry officer who seemed to spend most of his time at court, rather than leading his men into combat. He was handsome enough, she supposed, but his behaviour made the great rakes back home look like the stodgiest of men. His hand pressed against her back as he pulled her into the dance, drifting downwards until it was practically touching her buttocks. Raechel found it hard not to react. They were in public and ... she shook her head. There were couples practically making love on the dance floor.

She kept her mouth shut and her ears open as they moved around the room. People talked openly, sharing rumours that veered from the possible to the downright insane. The French armies had taken London and were marching on Edinburgh. No, the armies had taken Edinburgh and were marching on London. Russian troops were passing through Afghanistan to invade India … no, Afghanistan had swallowed the Russian army as effortlessly as it had swallowed every other invasion force since Alexander the Great. Raechel doubted *that* one was even remotely true. She'd *been* in Russia, before the war, and seen how the country had collapsed into anarchy. It was unlikely the country had much hope of invading anyone in a hurry.

"My unit might be going to Spain soon," Louis said, softly. "Do you want to wish me well?"

Raechel shrugged. She suspected Louis would not be accompanying his unit, no matter where it went. He was just trying to get her to sleep with him … hardly a mortal sin in the court, unlike High Society back home, but she knew his type. He'd pay court to her until she gave him what he wanted, then she'd never see him again. And if he got her pregnant … sure, there were ways to avoid pregnancy, but none of them were particularly reliable. And there was no way in hell she could *marry* him.

She pretended not to hear as her eyes swept the giant ballroom. A handful of familiar faces were gathered at the head of the room, talking in low voices. There was a gulf between them and the rest of the grandees, between the ones with true power and ones who had nothing but names and bloodlines. She saw a handful of men and women eying them with envious eyes, clearly unable or unwilling to hide their desperation. They wanted something solid, something they could rely on, and yet they'd never get it. Their time was running out and what did they have to show for it? Nothing.

Louis tightened his grip. "I said …"

A loud *BANG* echoed through the ballroom. Raechel spun around as the crowd rustled in front of her, the first clue the explosion wasn't part of the planned entertainments. A man – so beaten down by life it was hard to tell how old he was – stood at the top of the stairs, staring down at them with wild eyes. Smoke billowed behind him, the last remnants of something he'd done to distract the guards. Raechel braced herself, half expecting the menfolk to charge the anarchist while the women made their escape. The powerful people were already slipping to the rear.

"THE PEOPLE WANT BREAD," the anarchist screamed. His voice echoed louder than Raechel would have considered humanly possible. Magic? The Bourbons claimed that there were no lower-class magicians, but Rachel knew for a fact they were lying. They'd helped Jack in his mad plan to topple the British Government, over a year ago. "THE PEOPLE WANT PEACE! THE PEOPLE WANT FREEDOM!"

He stood taller, his coat opening to reveal the gunpowder bags wrapped around his chest. Raechel sensed, more than saw, the crowd starting to back away. The ballroom was vast, but the doors were small. It was impossible for more than a handful of people to get out before the anarchist blew them all to hell. She felt Louis freeze beside her, unable to decide if he should shield her from the blast or simply run for his life. His first real brush with danger, she suspected. God knew, she hadn't handled her first encounter with actual danger so well.

Her mind raced. How much gunpowder had he packed into those bags? How many metal fragments had he added, to make sure they were blasted right across the room? The guards could shoot him at any moment, but would that trigger the blast? She didn't know … she feared the worst. Her eyes flickered to the floor … could she get down in time? At least *her* dress wouldn't get in the way. There were ladies with dresses so complex they couldn't take them off without help, so widespread they were practically holding the wearer upright. She doubted they could tear them off before it was too late.

"AND MOST OF ALL," the anarchist boomed, "THEY WANT TO BE RID OF YOU! DEATH TO THE ARISTOS!"

His hands slapped against his chest. His form exploded, the blast roaring outwards … and stopping, dead. Raechel heard people fainting behind her … for a moment, her own legs buckled before her mind caught up with what was happening. There was a Mover in the audience, a magician who'd wrapped the anarchist in an invisible sphere of magic. The blast hadn't got very far at all. Louis shivered beside her as the blast faded and vanished, the bloody remains of the mad bomber falling to the stone floor. The cleaners would mop it up – they had practice in removing blood and vomit from the floor – and then it would be gone, along with all evidence of the man's existence. By tomorrow, the story would probably have grown to the point no one believed it. And then …

"Well," Louis said. "That was exciting, wasn't it?"

Raechel felt a surge of naked hatred as the crowd started to chatter, sharing tales about the whole incident that were already growing in the telling. If he'd thrown her to the ground and shielded her, she would have appreciated it … instead, he'd just stood there like an idiot until it had been too late to do anything. The aristos around her were already dismissing the threat, laughing at the idiot of an anarchist who'd blown himself up. They were pretending the threat hadn't been real – had *never* been real. Didn't they realise how close many of them had come to death?

"He was a fool," Louis said. His lips pressed far too close to her ear. "What would have happened to the country if he'd actually blown us all up?"

It would run a lot smoother, Raechel thought nastily, *and have a lot more money*.

She bit her lip to keep from saying it out loud. The Franco-Spanish Bourbon Empire was the single greatest threat to the British Empire, now the Russians were fighting a multisided civil war. They'd already landed one army on English soil and no one expected them to be deterred by the invasion's failure, not now they didn't have to worry about being stabbed in the back by the

Russians. There were already new ironclads taking shape in the shipyards – Raechel had gathered the details from a dockyard owner trying to impress a pretty girl – and she dreaded to think what would happen if they set sail. The French would need a lot of luck to get a second army over the channel, but they'd only have to be lucky once.

Her eyes wandered back towards the stairwell. The servants were nearly finished mopping away the remains, the aristos studiously ignoring them. Raechel wondered, idly, how many of them were spies, paid by the king and his court to keep a close eye on the aristocrats as they partied their lives away. It wasn't impossible. She knew from experience no one paid attention to servants and even when the risk was pointed out to them, tended to dismiss it. And yet ... her heart seemed to skip a beat as she spotted a tanned man watching the servants, his expression unreadable. He looked like a *don* and yet ... there was something about him that wasn't quite right.

She nudged Louis. "Who's that?"

"That's Duke Philippe," Louis said. There was a hint of envy in his voice. "Kinsman to the king, they say. He's a very important man."

I have no doubt of it, Raechel thought, darkly. It was irritating she couldn't pump Louis for more precise answers, but it was better he thought of her as a silly little girl rather than an intelligent woman. She was sure half the simpering women on the ballroom floor were doing the same thing, hiding their intelligence to make themselves seem less of a threat to the men. *And what does he do for the king?*

She contemplated it for a long moment. French aristocratic politics had been hard enough to follow, she'd been told, even before the Spanish and Latin American aristos had been added to the mix. Being close to the king was very much a mixed blessing. On one hand, you had the best choice of assignments and military commands; on the other, you'd be regarded as a potential usurper, someone with the bloodline to take the throne if the king appeared to be weak or vulnerable. She wondered if Duke Philippe had any designs on the throne. If he was a magician, and *someone* had clearly stopped the anarchist from blowing up the entire ballroom, he'd have one hell of an edge. Who knew what he'd do with it?

"Come," Louis said. "My room isn't that far away."

Raechel groaned inwardly. Louis was pulling at her and she couldn't break free, not without causing a scene. She had some tricks up her sleeve, if he insisted on a private party, but none of them were guaranteed to work. Once they were alone, he'd get much more insistent on finally going all the way ... Raechel tried not to shudder. She was no virgin – she'd given her maidenhead up out of pure spite, after a particularly sharp lecture from her aunt – but the thought of sleeping with a cowardly fop bothered her.

"Raechel!" A hand caught hers and yanked her away from Louis. "I've been looking for you all night!"

Raechel blinked, then hastily organised her thoughts into disciplined rows as she recognised her unexpected saviour. Lady Simone ... they'd met before, in Russia. And she was a mind-reading magician. Raechel tried not to cringe as Simone led her away, ignoring Louis's muted protests. Simone was head and shoulders above him and ... Raechel snorted inwardly. Louis wouldn't be in any real trouble. She, on the other hand ... if Simone had recognised her, or started listening to her thoughts, Raechel might be in very deep trouble indeed. Her tutors had made it clear, months ago, that if she was caught she'd be lucky to be merely arrested and thrown out of the country.

"I know the oaf," Simone said, tightly. "I thought you could use a hand."

"Thank you," Raechel managed. If things had been different, she could have believed Simone was just a girl helping out another girl who'd managed to get herself into hot water. But she knew better. "I ..."

Simone tapped her lips. "No need to thank me," she said. "Just do me the honour of listening."

Raechel braced herself, steeling her thoughts as best she could. She was as intensely focussed as they came, or so she'd been assured, and yet she had no magic. There were limits to how much she could do to keep Simone out of her thoughts … she glowered at the girl's back, wondering if she should knock Simone out and run. There *were* contingency plans … besides, young women fleeing the court in varying levels of undress were hardly unknown.

"This room is private," Simone said, as they entered a bedroom. "And they'll be expecting us to make good use of the bed."

"Oh," Raechel said. She knew it was possible for a woman to make love to another woman, or a man to make love to a man, but she'd never seen it. The whole concept was regarded with muted horror back home, even though some of England's kings had been more fond of their male companions than their queens. "Why did you …?"

Simone sat on the bed and met Raechel's eyes. For the first time, Raechel saw a hint of desperation within the other girl's dark orbs. Simone wanted – needed – her to listen. And that meant … Raechel had met her fair share of battered wives, women pretending everything was fine even as the bruises were clearly visible on their skins, and Simone reminded her far too much of them. And that meant … what?

"I know you're a spy," Simone said. "And …"

"And what?" Raechel had been almost certain her cover had been blown – Simone really had met her before she'd become an intelligence agent – but it still felt like a slap to hear it said so boldly. "What do you want?"

"I want you to send a message to London," Simone said. "I need your help."

Chapter Three
London, England

wen sat, resting her hands on her lap, and kept her thoughts to herself.

It would have been easier to simply *fly* to Crichton Hall. Easier, perhaps, but ... it would have been quicker. Much quicker. In truth, she wasn't looking forward to the coming discussion at all. She was a young woman who really shouldn't have accepted a man's offer of marriage without consulting her parents – hell, Bruce shouldn't have offered to marry her without asking her father first. She'd bent propriety into a twisted mess by not heading straight to the hall, as soon as they returned to England. Sure, she had her duties to attend to, but she could have made time for her family ...

Her hands toyed with her trousers. She stilled them with an effort. There was no point in revealing her nervousness. Her parents weren't *bad*, not compared to some others in High Society, but they'd find ways to object to the marriage if they took a dislike to her prospective husband. God alone knew what the lawyers would say. The marital settlement would be a nightmare, not least because Gwen had money and property of her own *and* the legal right to use it as she pleased. She was legally a man, in many ways, and her detractors hadn't hesitated to point it out. It wouldn't be long before someone started hinting Bruce was legally a woman. Her lips twisted in disgust. The Trouser Brigade had the right idea. It was high time women had the legal right to own property and keep their own money.

Bruce caught her eye. "There's always Gretna Green."

Gwen smiled, wanly. They *could* fly north to Scotland and get married there ... but there would be hell to pay. Probably. There was no way she could be cut off from her own property – it didn't matter what her parents would settle on her, not when she was already wealthy – but people would talk. She rubbed her forehead in irritation. People always talked. It hadn't taken her long to realise that the most bellicose of men – and women – were the ones in no personal danger. The worst of society's ladies were always the ones who couldn't be knocked down a peg or two.

"They'll love you," she said, although she feared the worst. Bruce came from decent stock – his father *was* the Governor-General of America – and yet, he was more American than British. Gwen found it refreshing, but her parents might simply not know what to make of him. "And we have to give them a chance to accept you."

She felt the butterflies in her stomach grow worse as the carriage turned into the driveway and headed up to the hall. Properly brought up young women did *not* travel alone with young men, let alone ... her stomach twisted as she remembered the moment they'd made love after fighting the enemy magicians. She didn't regret it, not really, but it could easily have had dangerous repercussions. If she'd got pregnant ... she thought she was safe, yet it was hard to be sure. Her periods had always been so faint she'd been surprised to be told other women cramped so badly they had to stay in bed. But then, she *was* a Master Magician. She might easily have been healing herself without knowing what she was doing.

The carriage rattled to a halt. Gwen heard someone shouting outside and braced herself. She'd fought enemy magicians. She'd flown into the path of enemy guns. Why was facing her parents so ... so terrifying? It wasn't as if their disapproval really mattered, in the long run?

There was no point in threatening to settle *nothing* on her when she had money of her own. And yet … she stood as the coachman opened the door and stepped back, allowing her to descend. She wanted her parents to approve and that was all there was to it.

And they'll turn the wedding into the social event of the year, she thought, morbidly. *It won't be about us …*

Crichton Hall rose up in front of her, the butler standing on the steps to welcome her home. She heard Bruce suck in his breath behind her … she tried, just for a moment, to see the mansion through his eyes. It was surprisingly big, for a relatively small family, but Gwen's parents had been reluctant to try for a third child. The rumours about *her* had made it hard for them to risk bringing another baby into the world, or so she'd been told. Perhaps their marriage was sexless, now they'd done their duty … she cut *that* train of thought off before it could go any further. She knew her parents must have had sex twice, but she didn't want to think about it.

"Impressive," Bruce said. "How old *is* the hall?"

Gwen hesitated. "The hall has been in existence, in one form or another, for over five hundred years," she said. "It was rebuilt twice, the second time by Bess of Hardwick, and there weren't many additions since then."

She forced her legs to move and walked up the steps. The butler bowed deeply – she couldn't help noticing there were more streaks of grey in his hair – and nodded to the maids behind him, who eyed Gwen warily as they hurried to the carriage to collect the bags. Gwen didn't recognise them, unsurprisingly. Crichton Hall had always had problems attracting maids, after the rumours about the family's witchy daughter had started to spread. Gwen had never turned a maid into a toad – that wasn't even *possible* – but when had rumours needed a basis in truth? There was a girl who'd been exiled from High Society for something she'd supposedly done two years before her *birth*.

"My Lady," the butler said. "Lord and Lady Crichton are waiting in the drawing room."

"Thank you, Woodstown," Gwen said. She felt a twinge of unease as she stepped into the hallway. It didn't feel like *home* any longer. "We can find our own way."

The butler nodded and stepped back. Gwen suspected he was privately relieved. Servants saw and heard everything and the prospect of being caught between a pair of parents and their daughter had to worry him. Woodstown had been with the family for only a few short months – far too many servants had refused to stay for long, for fear of her – and if the hall changed hands, he might be cast out as easily as a piece of rotting meat. He was dependent on them and yet …

Gwen kept walking, feeling the hall humming around her. The drawing room was neutral territory, neither her father's study nor the more intimate chambers further into the hall. She hoped that was a good sign. If they'd wanted to meet in more formal surroundings, or even somewhere outside the hall, it would have been a very bad sign indeed. She paused outside the door, taking a deep breath to calm her nerves, and looked at Bruce. His face was so calm and composed Gwen *knew* he was nervous. She'd met enough young aristocrats, desperate not to let the side down, to know what nervousness looked like.

And Bruce really did go into battle, she reminded herself. There was no need to worry her family with *all* the details, particularly his ties to the Sons of Liberty. *That's more than can be said for quite a few other potential suitors.*

She pushed the door open. The drawing room hadn't changed at all. There were two comfortable sofas, a simple yet elegant table, a writing desk pressed against the far wall and – looming over the room – a portrait of the first Lord Crichton, a man who'd been born in the reign of Henry V and died after the rise of Henry VI. Reading between the lines in the family archives, Gwen suspected he'd been a trimmer who'd been careful to keep his options open to make sure he could switch sides, when the time came, without being forced to pay by his former allies. He wasn't the only one, she reflected. A surprising number of noble families from that era had made a habit out of turning their coats, whenever one side appeared to be in the ascendant, and then turning them back again whenever the tide turned.

"Gwen," Lord Rudolf Crichton said. "Welcome home."

"Thank you, Father," Gwen said. Lord Rudolf *was* a decent father, if stuffy and boring and somewhat unimaginative. "Please, allow me to introduce Bruce Rochester, my fiancé."

Her mother stood. Gwen braced herself, again. Lady Mary Crichton could be … difficult, at times, veering between enough formality to make her husband seem a rake and a zany enthusiasm that made it impossible to follow her thoughts. Gwen still cringed at the memory of her mother trying to arrange her marriage when she'd been *eight*, although thankfully *that* hadn't managed to get far enough for papers to be signed before the prospective husband's family had had second thoughts and pulled out. The marriage wouldn't have been *real* until they'd matured, of course, but it could have become a legal nightmare if the final documents had been signed and sealed. And then her mother had thought she should set her cap at Master Thomas …

"Well," Lady Mary said, looking Bruce up and down. "Your father is Marquess of Swanhaven, is he not?"

"Indeed he is," Bruce said. Gwen thought she detected a hint of pompous amusement in his tone. "And Governor-General of British America."

Lady Mary nodded. "And your mother?"

"She was American, but of good colonial stock," Bruce said. "My father never spoke an ill word about her."

"That is always good to hear," Lady Mary said. She motioned for Gwen and Bruce to sit, then sat herself. "And yourself …?"

"I am first in line to inherit my father's lands and titles," Bruce said. "I already hold several thousand in the funds, as I am sure you are aware."

Lady Mary didn't bother to deny it. The moment she'd received word Gwen had engaged herself to Bruce, without even bothering to consult her parents, she would have hired agents to look into Bruce's background, finances and general health. Gwen wondered, idly, what they'd reported back to their mistress. Bruce's father was of very good stock, as far as the nobility were concerned, but his mother was the daughter of Benjamin Franklin. He might have been officially pardoned, after the defeat of the American rebels, and taken up a role in the post-war government, yet … her lips twitched in cold amusement. Bruce took after his grandfather more than anyone would care to admit.

"We are aware," Lord Rudolf said. Gwen suspected her father felt a little blindsided. He'd normally have more time to consider his response to his daughter's planned marriage. "You are aware, of course, that Gwen has an older brother?"

Gwen stiffened. Bruce showed no visible reaction. "Yes, My Lord."

"There are limits, of course, to what we can settle on her," Lord Rudolf continued. "The hall itself, and many of our other properties, are entailed and must remain with the family, passed down to our oldest son. It isn't quite clear what will happen if David dies without issue, given Gwen's curious legal status, and there is no guarantee the matter will be resolved in a hurry."

Bruce leaned forward. "I quite understand," he said. "I do have, as you know, sufficient monies to maintain your daughter in a reasonable manner. I am not given to gambling or drinking, nor do I or my father have significant debts that require constant servicing. As a government servant, I am paid a reasonable salary and, when my father passes on, as I said, I will inherit his lands and titles. In short, I am not marrying your daughter for your money – or hers – and I have no intention of laying claim to her marriage settlement."

His lips twisted into a smile. "Does that address all your concerns?"

Gwen saw her mother smile, just for a second before she hid it behind her hand. Bruce had cut right through the nonsense, right though the delicate questioning to determine if Bruce was, in some ways, utterly unsuitable for marriage. She found it hard to hide her own amusement, even though she knew her father meant well. There were too many rakes who sought to marry money and to hell with the girl, who often found herself effectively abandoned when the money ran out. It was a little insulting – she could take care of herself – but it came from a good place. Really.

Lord Rudolf stiffened. "Gwen is my daughter," he said. "It is important to me that she is happy in her marriage."

"Thank you, Father," Gwen said. Only a very sharp ear would have detected a hint of sarcasm in her tone. The faint twitch crossing her mother's face suggested she *had* heard it. "I appreciate your concern for me."

"It is important that you be happy," Lord Rudolf repeated. "And all the more so given your ... position."

Gwen kept her thoughts to herself. Her father would have married her off without a second thought, if she'd had the courtesy to be born without magic. Not through malice, she knew, but the results would have been much the same. Her husband might have been staid and boring or cruel and abusive ... it wouldn't have mattered, as long as the marriage delivered what her father wanted. There were times when she envied the freedom Irene Adler and her peers knew, even though it came with a high price. They didn't have to worry about getting married off to a near-stranger.

Or not getting married at all, she thought. *Father would have worried about that too.*

She cleared her throat. "We will be happy," she said. "And there is very little else at stake."

Her father nodded, shortly. David would inherit nearly everything. There was no real need to draw up a detailed marriage settlement, not when Gwen didn't stand to get anything beyond a few thousand pounds. Not that that would stop him, of course. He'd want to make sure the families were tied closely together. Bruce's father was actually higher up the social ladder than Gwen's, even though he'd married an American. And that would raise her father's status too.

"Very good," Lady Mary said. She reached for the silver bell and rang it once. "Perhaps we should have some tea."

Gwen nodded, leaning back against the sofa cushions. She was tempted to reach out and squeeze Bruce's hand, but her mother would have fainted or … Gwen sighed inwardly, telling herself she wouldn't have to wait long. They might have problems being alone together without someone noticing – if they weren't being watched constantly, she'd eat her hat – but once they were married no one would say a word. Probably. She forced herself to wait as the maid entered, carrying a tray of tea and cakes. The poor girl had probably been waiting for the bell. Gwen hoped her mother was paying the maid well.

"The fighting in America has calmed down a little," Lord Rudolf said, as the tea brewed. "Are you still planning to return to Mexico?"

"I've been told I'll be going with the army," Bruce said. It was an open secret an army was being prepared for departure. Its destination was supposed to be a secret, but everyone knew it was going to the Americas. "The French are apparently reeling from the defeat we gave them in the Americas and the Duke of India wants to hit them before they can recover."

"We intend to marry shortly before the army departs," Gwen put in. "I trust that meets with your approval?"

Lady Mary poured the tea, then handed it out. "There'll be less time than I would hope to plan a proper wedding," she said. "Is there a reason for such haste?"

Gwen felt her cheeks heat at the unsubtle implication. "Mother, our duties will keep us apart from time to time," she said. The idea of *her* staying at home, waiting for her husband to come home, was just absurd. "We do not need a big wedding."

"But it may serve a purpose beyond your marriage," Lord Rudolf said. "Do you not want to make it a society event?"

Gwen resisted the urge to point out that High Society had done its level best to pretend she didn't exist for *years*. There was nothing to be gained from hosting a wedding that had to be open to everyone who considered themselves important, from her closest friends to her worst enemies. Her father might see it as a networking opportunity, a chance to have private chats with ministers he couldn't be seen with elsewhere, but her ... she sighed, inwardly, as she realised her mother would remain adamant. She wanted – needed – her chance to be the mother of the bride. And if David never got married ...

"I would prefer a simple wedding," she said, finally. It was going to be a pain. She could justify excluding her detractors if she restricted the guest list to friends and family alone, but otherwise ... "And I see no reason to allow my wedding to be turned into a political football."

"You are a political figure," Lord Rudolf pointed out, calmly. "And so is your future husband."

Gwen tried not to make a face. He had a point. She *was* the Royal Sorceress and Bruce *was* next in line to Swanhaven, as well as being a magician in his own right. There'd be people feeling slighted if she declined to invite them, damn it. And yet ...

"We can hold a ball later, after the war," she said, although she suspected she was going to lose the argument. "But now, we shouldn't make a big show of it."

"People will talk," Lady Mary said, flatly. "And you know it."

"Yes," Gwen agreed. She thought she knew, now, why so many women threw fits over their weddings. There were just too many people offering *advice* that was nothing of the sort and suggestions that were nothing more than orders. "They do nothing else."

Chapter Four
Versailles, France

It was a misnomer, Raechel Slater-Standish had discovered years ago, to think of Versailles as just another palace. Buckingham Palace was a *palace*, a large building in the centre of the city; Versailles was practically a small town, with *the* palace surrounded by a handful of other palaces, mansions, army barracks, servant quarters and parklands, the latter veering from beautiful gardens to a mock peasant village that was about as realistic as her cover. Raechel had *seen* peasant villages, during her journey to Versailles, and none of them looked anything like as fanciful. Or as clean. It was proof, if she'd needed it, that the monarchy and aristocracy of the Bourbon Empire had long since lost touch with their people. They didn't even have the wit to live in Paris!

She walked through the gardens, keeping her eyes open for signs she was being watched or followed. There were more guards everywhere, from finely-dressed guardsmen in ceremonial dress to soldiers in combat uniforms. Horsemen galloped up and down, so intent on protecting the royal complex – and making sure a second anarchist didn't get through the defences – that they didn't even look twice at her. Raechel suspected someone in authority had lit a fire under their rears. The next anarchist might be lucky enough to take out a bunch of dancing aristocrats.

And someone probably had their head cut off for their failure. Raechel thought. It wasn't *that* hard to get through the outer defences, but into the palace itself? *Their replacement must be determined not to let the same thing happen on his watch.*

She sobered as she circumvented the gardens and made her way down to the residential suites. They were small grey buildings, designed to remind the common-born guests that, no matter how much money they had, they would never be nobility. Raechel kept her thoughts to herself as she spotted a pair of noblemen ahead of her, sneaking into the district so obviously it was unlikely they hadn't been spotted a long time ago. She wondered, idly, what they were doing. Perhaps they were going to the brothel. It was supposed to be easy to find a willing partner at court, but some people had tastes that would revolt even a courtier. Or maybe they were keeping an eye on her ...

Her eyes flickered from side to side. The vast majority of the female courtiers were in the gardens, enjoying a pleasant summer day. Their menfolk were with their regiments, playing at being soldiers, or heading to the gambling dens before returning to the palaces. There weren't many people within eyeshot, although that was meaningless. She'd been taught how to shadow someone without making it obvious and she dared not assume her French counterparts hadn't had the same training. They controlled the entire complex. They certainly had enough manpower to rotate watchers so she never realised she was being watched.

I could be making a mistake, she thought, as she turned into the dressmakers avenue. *If Simone was lying to me ...*

She swallowed, hard. Simone had certainly sounded as if she were telling the truth ... but she might just be a very good liar. Mind-readers were extremely capable liars, not least because they could pluck the right answer from the target's mind or simply adapt their approach to suit the target's prejudices. Raechel thought her mental defences had kept her thoughts private, but it was impossible to be sure. Simone was probably very good at reading people even without her magic. She'd been trained by one of the wiliest men in Europe and then given a chance to show what she could do.

The dressmaker's shop was unmarked. Raechel bowed her head, trying to look as though she was sneaking into the shop, as if anyone spotting her would be the end of the world. It might, this time. In London, the very best dressmakers never advertised. Their clientele liked the thought of exclusivity, of never having to share their dressmaker with anyone else. Here … the dressmakers were cheap, by local standards, and only patronised by financially embarrassed aristocratic women. Raechel's lips quirked in grim amusement. If someone saw her in the shop, they'd deny it till their dying day.

They'd have to admit they were patronising the shop too, she thought. *And that would mean they were too poor to afford full-priced dresses.*

She took a long breath as she closed the door behind her and looked around, drinking in the sight of piles upon piles of dresses and dressmaking material, the former sold or donated by the wealthy aristocrats to help their impoverished brethren. It seemed a sick joke to her – the dresses in front of her, even the tattered, torn and strained garments, could have fed a poor family for weeks – but it was courtly life, a façade of wealth and power concealing a reality of poverty and powerlessness. She supposed that explained why so many noblemen and women came to court to leech off the king, no matter the cost to the kingdom. They simply couldn't afford to support themselves back home.

"My Lady," Irene Adler said, stepping out of the shadows. Raechel felt a questing mind touch hers, just enough to confirm her identity. "I trust you enjoyed wearing the previous gown?"

Raechel smiled, looking her mentor up and down. Irene Adler was a social chameleon, someone who could don a noblewoman's clothes one day and a washerwoman's the next and assume the role as easily, as effortlessly, as she put on the clothes. She made a very convincing dressmaker, even though the role was incredibly challenging. Raechel had heard teenage aristos throwing fits because their dresses weren't perfect or didn't have enough tassels or gold lace or ... she refused to consider she'd been a little like them, once upon a time. If she hadn't found something to do with her life, who knew what would have become of her?

"It was divine," she said. "Do we have time to do a proper fitting?"

Irene nodded and stepped past her to put the CLOSED sign into place. No one would think anything of it. They'd know the shop wasn't really closed, but they'd also know the customer didn't want to be seen inside the shop. Raechel sighed, although she knew it made more sense than she'd thought, the first time she'd been told how she was going to keep in touch with her superior. One had to keep up appearances, if one was of noble blood.

"We should be safe to talk," Irene said. "I have an appointment at two, however."

"And I need to be gone beforehand," Raechel agreed. Whoever was coming *really* wouldn't want to be seen. "We have a problem."

She took a breath, then outlined everything that had happened the previous night. "I think she's telling the truth," she said, finally. "But it's hard to be sure."

Irene looked, just for a moment, as if she'd bitten into something sour. "Can you confirm Ambassador Talleyrand was actually executed?"

"There was no formal announcement," Raechel said. "But everyone knows he had his head cut off."

"Odd," Irene said. "He wasn't exactly popular. The king could easily have blamed everything that happened, over the last two years, on the ambassador and used his death as an excuse to change course."

Raechel wasn't so sure. The Bourbons were facing a nightmarish dilemma. They'd demanded huge sacrifices from their people, first to build up an army and navy to challenge Britain and then to fight a war on multiple fronts. If they lost the war, or even came to terms short of total victory, who knew how their people would react? And if the various nationalist and ethnic fractures within the empire started to crack …

"They need to win," she said, finally. "And if Simone is right, they're getting desperate."

"If," Irene said. "Do you trust her?"

"I think she was telling the truth, as she knew it," Raechel said. "But she could have been lying to me, or she could have been lied to herself …"

"True." Irene picked up a dress and frowned at the shoddy patchwork, "If she knew about you, she could have come after me. That she didn't is … indicative."

Raechel shivered. It wasn't *fair* dealing with mind-readers. Simone could have been shadowing Raechel, reading her thoughts as they passed through her head … if she'd picked up one hint about Irene, she could have unravelled the rest of the network very quickly and then … Raechel swallowed, wondering if Simone and her backers were just waiting for the rest of the network to be exposed before they swooped down and rolled it up. She had no illusions about her fate, if she was caught. The odds of her ever getting home would be very low.

"She asked for help, on behalf of her allies," Raechel said. "Do we pass the word to our superiors?"

Irene said nothing for a long moment. "It would be very much in character – would have been – for Talleyrand to be perfectly aware of who was plotting rebellion in Paris," she said, slowly. "He was just the sort of person who'd keep communications links open, just to make sure he'd come out on top if the rebels turned into revolutionaries and took control of the entire country. It's also possible he told her what he knew, or she read it from his mind. But we cannot be sure."

"No," Raechel agreed, waspishly. "What do you want me to do?"

"I need to pass the message up the chain," Irene said. "Our superiors will have to make the final decision.

We'll be left in the dark until we need to know."

"What we don't know we can't tell," Raechel said. She liked to think she could stand up to interrogation, but she'd been cautioned everyone broke eventually. "What do you want me to do now?"

Irene frowned. "Have you heard any other rumours?"

"The anarchists are getting bolder," Raechel said. "That was true even before the attack last night. Lots of rumours about food riots, men deserting their regiments or escaping the recruiters before they can be conscripted into the army. Plus ... there's at least some suggestion the empire should seek peace with Britain so it can expand east, but I don't know if that's anything more than angry grumbling. I don't know if any of it will become something more serious."

"It depends on just what happens," Irene told her. "I take it your latest conquest was useless?"

"He couldn't tell me anything of great value," Raechel said. "But Simone interrupted before we could get anywhere."

"See what he can tell you, but otherwise just keep your eyes open," Irene said. She picked up a pad and scribbled out a receipt. "This'll be your excuse to come back in a couple of days."

Raechel took the receipt and shook her head in amused disbelief. To a peasant, the listed price for an aristocratic dress would be eye-wateringly high. To a noblewoman, it would be far too *low*. It was an excuse to keep it hidden, she thought, as she tucked it safely into her underwear. Anyone who found it would understand perfectly why she didn't want it seen by prying eyes. Bad enough she was reduced to buying recycled dresses, worse that she wasn't even paying *half* price for them.

"I'll be back," she said. "Watch yourself, alright?"

Irene nodded, drawing the dressmaker persona around her like a shroud as Raechel headed for the door. She'd be fine, Raechel thought. She'd been a trained agent for longer than Raechel had been alive and her magic would give her at least *some* warning if the guardsmen swooped on the shop. Raechel had seen Irene pass for a man, more than once. She could knock out a guard, steal his uniform and simply walk out of the complex before anyone realised what she'd done and raised the alarm. Raechel would have a far harder time of it.

She made a show of sneaking through the avenues, passing slightly more upmarket shops and residences before turning to head back to her residence. She'd had to argue hard to get a room in the lodge, something that had made her fear she'd blown her cover before she realised how bad some of the other women were. They were getting free lodging – and food and drink – and yet they were complaining, as if they could convince the king's servants to get them better rooms by sheer force of personality. Raechel had heard whispering from her fellows that some really *had* jumped up the ladder, by starting relationships with powerful men that might – or might not – lead to marriage. It might not matter. A woman who saved the rewards of a relationship might be set for life, if it lasted long enough.

"Raechel," a woman called. Raechel sighed inwardly as she spotted Marie … Marie of a set of names and titles that were almost as fictitious as Raechel's own. She did have aristocratic blood, according to the court records, but hardly enough to count in any real sense of the word. "I hear you were walking out with Louis!"

"Perhaps," Raechel said. She pushed a fake smile onto her face. "Which Louis?"

Marie giggled, as if Raechel had just cracked a joke. Louis was one of, if not *the*, most popular male names in France. There were so many men called Louis, including the king himself, that it wasn't easy to separate them. And … Raechel tried not to roll her eyes at Marie's enthusiasm. She was hardly an old woman, not by any reasonable standard, but her time was running out. If she didn't make it soon, she wouldn't make it at all.

"A dashing horseman," Marie said. "Is it true he rides you like a horse?"

Raechel kept her smile in place as Marie giggled again.

"I wouldn't know," she said, trying to sound conspiratorial. "We haven't been alone together, not yet."

"Dear me," Marie said. She lowered her voice until she was pretending to whisper. "Is there something wrong with him?"

"I'm sure he's just waiting for the right woman to marry," Raechel said, purposely misunderstanding. Better to have Marie think she was naive than calculating. She had a nasty suspicion, at times, that Marie was a little smarter than she let on. "Besides, he hasn't made a formal suit for my hand."

Marie giggled, once again. "I hear he's off to the wars," she said. She made a kissing sound. "Are you going to give him a proper farewell?"

"Perhaps I'll give him a proper welcome home," Raechel countered. She probably wouldn't have to worry about it. By the time Louis returned, she'd be seeing another potential source. "Or ..."

She looked up as Jeanne, another lodger, burst through the door. "The news," she said, practically gasping for breath. "Have you heard the news?"

Raechel and Marie exchanged glances. Information was power at court. It was rare for anyone to share something they, and only they, knew ... even if they knew it wouldn't remain a secret for long. Jeanne was a lot smarter than Marie. She'd keep secrets ... Raechel felt cold, wondering just *what* had happened. If it was something big enough to make Jeanne act like a child ...

"There's a revolt," Jeanne gasped. "In Spain!"

"In Spain?" Marie made a sound that might – charitably – have been called a snicker. "And what does Don Cortes make of it?"

"I don't know," Jeanne said. "I just heard the news. There are uprisings in a dozen cities and all is chaos!"

Raechel said nothing, leaving Marie to probe Jeanne for details she didn't have as she thought fast. Spain was linked to France through dynastic marriage, and she knew French and Spanish troops had fought together against the British in America, but she doubted the Spanish cared *that* much for the French. Spain had once ruled much of the known world. Now, she was a client state of France and, no matter how hard the rulers worked to integrate the two countries, it was unlikely the Spanish *liked* being subordinates. They were a proud people, with much to be proud of.

"Don Cortes will act fast, I am sure," Marie said. "He's always saying he is the rightful heir to Spain."

"He'll have been arrested by now," Raechel said. Don Cortes was a fool. She'd never been sure why the Bourbon Court tolerated him, or the rest of his circle. It might have been better to quietly kill him and blame it on the British. "They won't let him leave court."

Jeanne smirked. "You want to go see the show?"

"I need to find Louis," Raechel said. It wasn't wholly faked. Louis had told her his regiment would be going to Spain ... and now, it looked as if they'd be headed right into the fire. Had someone known the revolt was coming? Or ... she wondered, suddenly, if the French could find enough regiments to put down the rebels before it was too late. What if they didn't? "If he's on his way to Spain ..."

"Use your mouth," Marie advised. She grinned at the flash of disgust that crossed Raechel's face. "It's always the safest way."

Raechel pretended not to hear her. Her mind was racing. She needed to know what was going on, and quickly, before she returned to Irene. Her mentor would hear the news quickly, Raechel was sure, but not whatever rumours were flooding the court. Irene would have to send word back to England and then ... who knew? If Spain left the empire, could the French continue the war alone?

"Come on," Marie said. The urgency in her voice would have made Raechel smile, if the situation wasn't so dire. But then, she'd never met an aristocrat who thought France might lose the war. "We have to hurry."

"Coming," Raechel said.

Chapter Five
London, England

ou've been oddly quiet," Lady Mary said, when Lord Rudolf and Bruce had retired to the study. "Should I be concerned?"

Gwen tried to keep her face impassive. It was hard to engender respect and obedience as a young women, commanding men old enough to be her father, but it was harder still to command anything from the woman who'd given birth to her. Lady Mary was, and would always be, her mother ... and yet, she'd always been hard to handle. Gwen knew she'd been lucky in so many ways – she knew girls who were still ruled by their mothers and mothers-in-law – but it was difficult to believe it. And part of her, she admitted sourly, resented her mother's reluctance to allow her to enter High Society as a young woman.

"I don't know what to say," she admitted, finally. Cold logic told her that her mother had gone through the same experience, when she'd been engaged to be married, but she found it hard to believe. The woman who'd given birth to her could *not* have been a little girl, then a young woman ... could she? It was impossible and yet she knew it was true. "Was it so hard, when you were a young woman?"

"My parents arranged the match, but they did want me to consent," Lady Mary said, glancing at the door. Gwen wondered how many servants were within earshot – and hoped they'd have the sense to leave, now the conversation was growing more intimate. "They insisted I spent some time with your father, and other prospective husbands, so I'd know what I was getting into. And what was getting into me."

For a moment, Gwen thought she'd misheard. "Mother!"

Lady Mary smiled, but there was a twinge of sadness to it. "Your grandmother, may she rest in peace, was quite blunt about the realities of married life once I was properly engaged," she said. "She was adamant a young woman should be protected, even from herself, but also that she should know the facts of life before the wedding night. The books, alas, are quite useless even when you can find a copy."

Gwen nodded curtly. The medical textbooks she'd read had either skipped over the realities of sex and reproduction or actively misled anyone unfortunate enough to study them. It was bad enough that *she* could look at her body and *know* the writers were either wrong or lying, harder still for a young man who couldn't know the truth until his wedding night. She wondered, rather snidely, if the writers had ever actually met a woman, let alone seen one naked. It wouldn't be that hard. There were no shortage of whores in London and they'd probably be happy to undress for an examination, rather than something more intimate. But then, the writers seemed more intent on discouraging experimentation than informing their readers.

She remembered something she would have preferred to forget. "You had marital relationships before you married, didn't you?"

Her mother flinched. "Yes," she said, tersely. "And I don't want you to repeat my mistakes."

"It would have been easier to avoid some of them if you'd had an honest conversation about your own past," Gwen said, feeling the old bitterness welling up within her. Her mother was a steadfast member of Polite Society, one of the older women who judged younger girls when they stepped out of line. And yet, she'd done things in the past that made her more than a little hypocritical. "I never thought I could discuss such matters with you."

"I was ashamed," Lady Mary said, simply.

"And that wasn't enough to keep you from penalising others for making the same mistakes as yourself," Gwen pointed out. "Was it?"

Her mother's face smoothed into a mask. "One must keep up appearances," she said. "You know it as well as I do."

"And so you feared I would cross the line because *you* had already crossed it yourself," Gwen said, tartly. Perhaps it would have been unthinkable if her mother hadn't had experiences of her own. God knew *Gwen* had seen people do things no decent person would ever consider thinkable, until the evidence was rubbed in their face. "Right?"

"And I suppose I have to ask," Lady Mary said, ignoring Gwen's sharp remark. "Gwen, are you pregnant?"

"No." Gwen put as much certainty into her voice as she could. "And I have reason to know."

"Good." Lady Mary made a very visible attempt to bite down the next question. "And how far have you gone with him?"

Gwen flushed. "A handful of kisses, nothing more," she lied. There was no way in hell she'd confess the truth to her mother, not as long as she had a choice. "We are waiting for the wedding night."

Lady Mary cocked an eyebrow. "It is very easy to get into trouble, when your emotions are driving you into the arms of young men," she said, as if she hadn't done it herself. "When you get into that sort of trouble, it is very difficult to get out of it."

"So you told me, when you were explaining why I couldn't leave the house without a chaperone," Gwen snarled. It had hurt, back then, to know she couldn't go anywhere alone. It would have been worse if she'd known about her mother's early life. "It isn't fair."

"The world isn't fair," Lady Mary told her, curtly. "If a young man gets a young woman into trouble, he can drop a few hundred pounds on her and ensure his prospects are not ruined by an unwanted child. No one knows he is no longer a virgin and no one much cares if they work out the truth. A young woman, by contrast, will have her life ruined. The best she can do is convince her mother to present the newborn child as *hers*, maintaining a veneer of respectability that could be destroyed in an instant. Even then … the fact she is no longer a virgin can and will make it impossible to find a good match …"

"Even though men can sleep with whores and no one bat an eyelid," Gwen snapped. She *knew* half the magicians under her command patronised brothels whenever they weren't on duty. "Why is it so important?"

"There must be no question over who fathered the child," Lady Mary said. Her face twisted in disgust. "Believe me, when your magic started to appear there were questions over precisely *who* had fathered you. It was not easy to dismiss them, at least until you were older and started to develop your father's nose. I was lucky your father never paid heed to the rumours. It might have ended badly."

Gwen swallowed. "I never knew."

"Probably for the best," Lady Mary told her. "But yes, it is important to guard your reputation carefully. Once gone, it can never be regained."

She paused. "And that is why you shouldn't be aiming for a quick and simple marriage. People will talk."

"So you said, repeatedly," Gwen said. Her mother had been saying that for *years*. "They do nothing else."

"And your reputation is already overshadowed by your magic," Lady Mary warned. "Do you really want to make it worse?"

Gwen laughed, humourlessly. "Do you think it *can* get worse?"

She went on before her mother could say a word. "I have men under my command refusing to follow my orders – or claiming they're following the orders I would have issued, if I'd been born a man. I have men who think I should sit in my office and do nothing while they do all the work and others who think I should step down and let someone else take up the job while I … go out of sight and out of mind. What does it matter, if they think I married too early or too late?"

"If you have a child shortly after your wedding, people will talk," Lady Mary said, flatly. "We were lucky it took us several years to have David."

"Lucky," Gwen repeated. She didn't want to think about her parents having marital relationships. She'd sooner fight another Null, with her clothes stripped from her and her hands bound behind her back. "I'm not pregnant."

"And it is never easy to tell when you will *get* pregnant," Lady Mary said. "Laura Winters got pregnant on her wedding night, but the child was premature. If she hadn't been kept under tight supervision, in the months before her wedding, it would have been easy for her detractors to destroy her reputation. If you get pregnant …"

She paused, dramatically. "We should have had this talk earlier, but better late than never."

Gwen wanted to cover her ears as her mother started outlining the facts of life. She wasn't wholly ignorant – she'd listened to Irene and the handful of other woman in the Royal College well before she'd met Bruce – but it was still embarrassing, very embarrassing, to hear her mother talk about such matters. She really *didn't* want to think about her mother and father doing such things, or … some of the advice was good, she supposed, but other bits simply didn't apply to her. *She* was not going to stay at home like a good little wife while her husband went drinking and whoring … Lady Mary had been lucky, she supposed, that her husband was so staid and boring. Gwen doubted her father had the imagination to even consider finding a whore.

"Ruth's – you know Ruth – husband went to India," Lady Mary told her. "He wrote to his wife and asked permission to take a heathen lover, claiming the heat inflamed his lusts and demanded release. She gave him permission, of course, as long as he was good to the girl."

"And she didn't want to go to India herself?" Gwen knew the answer even as she asked the question. A properly brought up young women was not supposed to be interested in sex. It was something to endure, not to enjoy. And yet, she couldn't deny she'd enjoyed the first tryst ... she scowled inwardly as she recalled how their emotions had run away with them, leaving them in no state to say no. "Did he take care of the girl?"

"Perhaps he did," Lady Mary said. "Ruth studiously refrained from asking."

Gwen nodded. The older woman would have a considerable degree of freedom and independence while her husband was on the other side of the world. Her family – both sides – would probably try to meddle, but there'd be limits to how far they could push her as long as her husband was away. Why rock the boat?

"Others have a harder time of it," Lady Mary added. "Their husbands are wild and beat them and they have to keep smiling."

"I won't tolerate it," Gwen said, curtly. She knew girls who used makeup to hide the bruises – and others who were too beaten down to try. In theory, the girl's family was supposed to step in if her husband was mistreating her; in practice, it didn't often happen. The wife was the husband's property and he had the final say in how she was treated. Her magic sparkled at the thought. Bruce wasn't like that, but if he was ... striking her would be the last thing he did. No one would ever find the body. "I won't!"

"You wouldn't be the first person to say that," Lady Mary said. "That's why a proper marriage settlement is so important. Your father is already discussing the details with your ... *prospective* ... husband."

Gwen met her eyes. "Bruce's family is superior to ours," she said, flatly. "If I didn't have magic, you'd be over the moon about him trying to court me."

"Yes," Lady Mary agreed. "And I'd be worried about *why* he was courting you too."

"Why ...?" Gwen shook her head. Her mother would be right to be concerned. Bruce's father wouldn't pass the viceroyalty down to his son, but everything else ... "Why is High Society so ... *judgemental*?"

Lady Mary looked back at her. "High Society is a ladder," she said, slowly. "You get onto the ladder and start your climb to the top, but other people are in the way. If you can push them off the ladder, it makes it easier for *you* to get to the top."

"Except it isn't like that," Gwen said. "If you are born into a decent family, you start out on a higher level than everyone below you."

She scowled. She wouldn't have hated it so much if it really *had* been a meritocratic climb to the top. But it wasn't. A commoner might not even be able to get on the ladder – and if she did, through money or marriage, she'd never be able to climb very high. The Great Ladies of High Society guarded their perches jealously, closing ranks against interlopers. She wondered, suddenly, how many of them had hoped for a better life – or at least more independence – before finding themselves hemmed in by social laws and convention. The sour-faced old women who made disapproving sounds at young women who dared show their ankles had been young too once, as hard as it was to believe. And they'd been warped and twisted to the point they no longer had any empathy for the young.

"No," Lady Mary agreed. "But it is the only way to rise."

Gwen nodded, slowly. She'd been lucky in so many ways. If she hadn't had magic ... her father's position would have ensured she entered society at a high rung, but hardly the highest. Gwen loved her father, yet she had to admit he wasn't *that* high in the hierarchy and there were limits to what he could do for her. And her mother ... she wondered, not for the first time, if her mother was disappointed in her husband's lack of overt ambition. If he'd climbed higher, she would have risen with him.

"There is much else I can tell you about married life," Lady Mary said. "But, in the end, the choice is yours. My parents gave me a choice and I will offer the same to you."

"Really?" Gwen met her eyes. "And how much of a choice *was* it?"

"I rejected four prospective suitors before I was introduced to your father," Lady Mary said, simply. "My parents didn't try to force me into the match."

Gwen considered it. Her mother's choices might have been more limited than she was saying. She wouldn't have been introduced to anyone unless her parents approved beforehand. If a known rake – or cad – came calling, her parents would have told the wretched man to peddle his wares elsewhere. They certainly wouldn't have arranged a match between their aristocratic daughter and a commoner. Her lips twitched. Perhaps they would, if the commoner had money. There were quite a few matches, these days, that traded aristocratic names for money. She wasn't against it. One Swing had been quite enough.

"I'm glad they gave you a choice," she said, finally. "And Bruce is *my* choice."

"He seems a nice young man," Lady Mary said. "But I wish I could speak to his family."

And the women of the American Viceroy's Court, Gwen added, silently.

She scowled. There were always rumours about the great and the good – everyone loved to hear stories that painted them in a bad light – but if someone really was a bad egg the rumours would be passed from woman to woman in a manner that could not be ignored. If Gwen had wanted a Londoner, her mother could have made sure there were no worrying rumours about him, but Bruce had been raised in America. Her mother had no contacts there.

"His mother died when he was young," she said. "Don't you trust me to make good decisions?"

"When I was a little younger than you, there was a man who charmed me," her mother said, bluntly. "He was older and more glamorous and had an air … oh, I liked him. I wanted him. He would kiss me and …"

Gwen stared in disbelief. "Mother!"

"Your grandmother put a stop to it," Lady Mary said. "I was *mad*. I was madly in love with him. I came up with all sorts of mad plans to escape the hall and run to him and … I didn't know the details, back then, but I was sure it was going to be good. We were going to be husband and wife and do everything husbands and wives did and …"

She stared down at her hands. "It was lucky I never had the nerve to go to him. I discovered, later, that he was nothing more than a rake. He deflowered three girls – that I know of – before he was driven out of High Society and sent overseas. His family sent him money on condition he never returned to Britain, or so I was told. The girls he deflowered? Ruined, each and every one of them."

Gwen swallowed, remembering how close she'd been to Sir Charles Bellingham. The man had kissed her and come very near to taking her maidenhead …

"I never knew," she said. A properly brought up young woman should denounce her mother for even thinking about allowing a rake anywhere near her. The woman she'd become had to admit it was an easy mistake to make. "Mother …"

"I wanted him," Lady Mary said, flatly. "I was young. I didn't know what I really wanted. I didn't even know the facts of life. I was so much in love – in *lust* – with him that I overlooked all the warning signs. The flashes of anger whenever things didn't quite go his way. His tendency to slip his hand where it didn't belong. The fact none of the maids would stay in his presence any longer than they absolutely had to … a couple of older girls tried to warn me, in hindsight, but I didn't understand what they were trying to tell me.

"And then I found someone else and nearly had a child out of wedlock …"

She looked up. "I have never told anyone this, Gwen. Your father doesn't know. Your grandfather never knew. Your grandmother took the secret to her grave. The only reason I am telling you, here and now, is to warn you not to let your feelings blind you to a man's true personality. Because once you get married, you are committed. It is very difficult to escape a marriage, particularly if you have children. You must be careful to avoid making a mistake."

"I wish …" Gwen swallowed, hard. "I wish you'd told me this before."

Lady Mary met her eyes. "I was ashamed," she admitted. "Like I said, I was ashamed of my own foolishness. If he'd held me down and had his way with me, it would have been easier to bear. Instead … I nearly trapped myself, because my feelings blinded me to the truth."

"Bruce isn't like that," Gwen said. He'd certainly respected her reluctance to have sex a second time, before marriage. If she had got pregnant, it would have been disastrous. "Do you like him?"

"There's a lot to like about him," Lady Mary said. "But you're the one getting married. And the one who'll have to bear the burden of a bad match."

Gwen nodded. "I won't let him push me around."

"They all say that," Lady Mary warned. "But once you are married, you are married for life."

Chapter Six
London, England

ruce wasn't sure what to make of Lord and Lady Crichton.

Lord Rudolf was old in bearing, although he wasn't anything like as old as Bruce's father. Gwen had described him as staid and stuffy and, looking at him, Bruce understood precisely what she meant. He was a grey man, a simple bureaucratic civil servant without the ambition or ability to become a grey eminence ruling the world from behind the scenes. He would serve his government and king faithfully, without regard for his personal feelings. His wife, Lady Mary, looked like an older version of Gwen, although she held herself so proudly Bruce suspected she came from lesser stock. The higher one was, the less one needed to proclaim one's status to the world.

He listened to their questions, torn between amusement and irritation. His father had made it clear he *was* a good catch for anyone, socially superior to everyone save for the king and his immediate family. Being American would be held against him by small-minded society matrons who thought travelling to Manchester greatly daring, but everyone else would respect his family's title and wealth. He wasn't particularly concerned with just how much money Gwen's father offered to give her, as part of the marriage settlement. His family had enough money to keep themselves comfortable for the next few generations. And yet …

They mean well, he told himself. He'd been raised in America, and his grasp of social protocol was somewhat limited, but he knew Gwen had pushed the rules as far as they would go by accepting his suit before asking her parents. If he'd been in Britain, he'd have had to ask her father first and if her father had said no … they'd have had to go to Gretna Green or simply give up. *They're looking out for their daughter.*

He looked around with interest as Lord Rudolf led him to his study, leaving the womenfolk behind. Crichton Hall was old, old in a way no building in Colonial America would ever be. Even the great mansions of New York were relatively new. Bruce had hoped to visit Mexico, and see what remained of the old empires, but it had never happened. Perhaps that would change, once the army reached Mexico. Or perhaps not. He might simply not have the time.

"Please, take a seat," Lord Rudolf said. He walked around his desk and sat down. "Tea?"

"Please," Bruce said. He didn't want to drink too much, but it was socially unacceptable to refuse. "It would be my pleasure."

He leaned back in his chair and studied the room, trying to glean something of Lord Rudolf's personality from his private chambers. It was neat and tidy, so perfectly organised Bruce was tempted to wonder if he'd been taken to a decoy chamber rather than the older man's private study. The books and files on the shelves were arranged neatly – he made a bet with himself they were in perfect order – while the walls were clean, rather than covered with paintings or maps. The only hint of actual character was a simple portrait on the far wall, depicting a loving couple with two small children. It took him a moment to realise it showed Gwen as a little girl. It was hard to reconcile the grown woman he knew with the child in the painting.

Lord Rudolf said nothing until the maid arrived, served

them both tea and then retreated as silently as she'd come. Bruce appreciated the lack of any power games, although it was an open question which of them was really in a position to play games. He considered the issue for a moment, then shrugged. His father had always got on well with his father-in-law and Bruce wanted the same, if only for Gwen's sake. She wouldn't be happy if her husband picked a fight with her father. Or vice versa.

"It's good to meet you," Lord Rudolf said. His tone was so neutral Bruce couldn't tell if he meant it. "Tell me, why do you want to marry my daughter?"

Bruce hesitated, unsure how to put his feelings into words. Gwen was ... *special*. He'd known hundreds of young ladies – there was nothing like being a Viceroy's son to draw the women – but they'd all been dull and boring, when they hadn't felt like putty in his hands. Some had been silly and prone to giggling, some had been concealing their intelligence behind a veneer of fake stupidity and incomprehension ... really, he had no idea why young women liked pretending to be dumb. He knew women who ran entire households or businesses ... they couldn't have done that, could they, if they hadn't been able to count past ten without taking off their shoes. Gwen was intelligent and driven and beautiful and powerful ...

... And he was not, in the slightest, *intimidated* by her.

"I love her," he said, finally. "We have much in common."

"You're both magicians," Lord Rudolf said. "Why did you hide your magic?"

"It wasn't meant to remain secret indefinitely," Bruce said. It wasn't wholly true, but it was a believable cover story. "My tutor felt it would be better if I were trained before I sailed to Britain to join the Sorcerers Corps. He was murdered before he had the chance to inform his superiors I existed."

"I see," Lord Rudolf said. Bruce wondered, suddenly, if someone had told him to ask the question. There were a *lot* of issues that had been carefully obscured, in the wake of the Sons of Liberty and Franco-Spanish invasion of America. "Does your father approve of the match?"

"Yes, sir," Bruce said. "I believe he wrote to you."

"Yes," Lord Rudolf confirmed. He sipped his tea, clearly preparing for the next question. "You are aware, of course, that Gwen is our second child, and stands to inherit very little?"

Bruce nodded, curtly. "It has been mentioned."

"Quite," Lord Rudolf agreed. "I can settle the sum of five thousand pounds on her, but little else."

His words hung in the air. Bruce frowned, certain he was missing something. Five thousand pounds was a *lot* of money. It wasn't as if he needed the cash. He had money of his own and so did Gwen ... hell, they didn't even need a settlement or a dowry or *anything*. And yet ... he cursed under his breath as he realised the problem. They had to offer him something that matched his status in society as best they could and yet, what could they offer? Clearly, being American hadn't knocked him as far down the ladder as he'd thought.

He took a breath. "May I talk bluntly?"

"Of course," Lord Rudolf said. His face told a different story. "You may speak freely."

"I don't need the money," Bruce said. "And nor does she. There is no need to try to make a monetary offer. We both have enough money to live."

"Quite," Lord Rudolf said, as if Bruce hadn't understated the matter considerably. "You do realise, whatever happens, you will not have access to her property? It is hers and it will remain hers until she dies, at which point it will be passed down to her heirs."

"I understand," Bruce said. It was an odd arrangement, one that probably wouldn't have stood up to a legal challenge, but who had standing to sue? Master Thomas hadn't had any children, nor any close family. "I am not marrying her for her money. I don't need it."

Lord Rudolf looked irked. "Be certain," he said. "There is no way you will be allowed to take possession of her property."

Bruce felt a hot flash of irritation, calmed by the grim realisation Lord Rudolf was trying to look out for his daughter. He supposed it spoke well of the man. He'd known fathers who'd happily do whatever they had to do to make sure their daughters married well, even if it meant signing over their rights, money and property to their husbands. And then, if the marriage hadn't worked out, the poor girls had been trapped in loveless matches while their husbands drunk or whored or did whatever the hell they wanted.

And Gwen's property does make her one hell of a catch, he thought, sourly. Her family might not be able to settle much on her, but it hardly mattered when she had property of her own. *Her father needs to look out for her interests.*

He met the older man's eyes. "I understand," he said. "And, as I have said, I do not need her property. I have money of my own – I have a job, no debts, no family obligations that require me to send money elsewhere. We will be man and wife and that will be all there is to it."

"Legally, you will be man and man," Lord Rudolf said. "I trust that will not cause problems?"

Bruce snorted. "A legal fiction," he said. "And one that has no bearing on me."

"I hope it stays that way," Lord Rudolf said. He finished his tea and set the cup back on the desk. "My lawyer will be in touch. The marriage settlement will be five thousand pounds, and a small house in the country. There will be legal protections for Gwen in the event of something unfortunate happening, with provisions for children – including, I might add, the child she legally adopted. I suggest you speak with a lawyer of your own before signing the paperwork. It may keep you from being blindsided later."

"You move quickly," Bruce observed.

"My daughter is determined to marry you before you depart for Mexico," Lord Rudolf said, dryly. "And given her legal position, it would be difficult to stop her if she chose to go against our will."

He stood. "Welcome to the family," he added. "I hope you and Gwen have a very long and happy life together."

Bruce nodded, following the older man as he led the way back to the drawing room. Gwen and her mother were talking quietly, falling silent when the menfolk returned. Bruce felt a stab of sympathy. It couldn't be easy being both a daughter *and* a prospective bride. He'd had problems when his father had treated him as a child, even though he'd been a legal adult for years. But then, his father was old enough to be his *grandfather*. Their marriage hadn't borne fruit until it had been almost too late.

"We have come to an agreement," Lord Rudolf said. "The lawyer will look at it shortly and then finalise the documents."

Gwen nodded, visibly biting her lip. Bruce suspected she was concerned about what would happen to her role, once she was a married woman. Officers were expected to marry, but female officers … save for Gwen herself, there were *no* female officers. Would she be expected to defer to her husband? Or … Bruce wasn't a history expert, but even *he* knew how dangerous it could be for a ruling queen to marry. Mary Tudor and Mary Queen of Scots had both suffered badly, for poor choices of partners … and, from what he'd been told, no partner would have been acceptable.

"Good," Gwen said. Bruce wondered suddenly what the women had been discussing while the men had been away. Men? It wasn't impossible. God knew men talked about women when there were none within earshot. "I think …"

There was a sharp rap on the door, which burst open before anyone could say a word. A maid practically fell through the door, gasping for breath. "My Lady," she managed. "My Lady, we just received a message from London. Lady Gwen and Lord Bruce have been summoned to Whitehall at once!"

"But …" Bruce was relieved to see Lady Mary didn't rebuke the poor maid. "We planned dinner …!"

"Duty calls," Gwen said. She stood, brushing down her suit and trousers. "Bruce?"

Bruce stood, shaking hands with Lord Rudolf and nodding politely to Lady Mary before following Gwen back to the driveway. The maid had had the presence of mind to summon the carriage from the gatehouse, he noted; it was already rattling up as they left the hall and paused in the doorway. Bruce glanced at Gwen – her face was grim, but he thought he detected a hint of relief – and then shrugged to himself as they scrambled into the coach and closed the door. The driver cracked the whip and the coach rattled away.

He took a breath. "What happened?"

"Lord Mycroft knew where we were going," Gwen said. "He wouldn't have recalled us unless it was urgent, something that couldn't wait more than an hour or two."

Bruce frowned. "How do you know the message was from him?"

Gwen smiled. "Who do you know who could send such a message and expect it to be obeyed?"

Her lips tightened. "Something must have gone badly wrong."

Bruce felt his heart start to race. "An invasion?"

"It's possible," Gwen said. "The last invasion was beaten back, the invading army destroyed or forced to surrender, but the French have quite a few other armies. And ... we heard nothing, as far as I knew, yet they could easily have put a landing together on the fly."

Bruce met her eyes. "What else could it be?"

"I don't know," Gwen said. She made a visible attempt to change the subject. "Those were my parents. I hope they haven't put you off getting married."

Bruce reached out and squeezed her hand lightly. It was hard to see how *Gwen* had come from Lord Rudolf and Lady Mary, although Gwen did look like a younger version of her mother. Lord Rudolf was ... boring, even though he clearly was trying to do his best for his daughter. He'd probably be happier if Gwen had been a nice normal daughter without magic or property of her own, if only because it would be easier to work out the marriage settlement. The poor man had to make a *show* of matching whatever Bruce brought to the marriage, even though everyone knew it was impossible …

Gwen looked back at him. "Father didn't scare you too badly?"

"No." Bruce tried not to laugh at the thought. He was a Master Magician as well as Lord Rudolf's social superior. There was no way he'd be *intimidated* by a grey man in a grey position. "But he was looking out for you."

"That's good, I suppose," Gwen told him. "Mother had a few things to say about … married life."

Bruce raised his eyebrows. "Should I be worried?"

Gwen grinned, although there was a hard edge to the smile. "I never really thought about my parents being *people*," she said. "They are just my parents."

"The idea of my father doing anything with my mother is a *little* hard to grasp," Bruce agreed. "I don't know how they did it."

He snorted, as they shared a laugh. His father was a stately old aristocrat, not … he remembered the rush of pure lust and desire, after the battle with the enemy magicians, that had driven them to make love for the first time. They'd rutted like animals and … he met her eyes, suddenly aware they were sharing the same thought. Their lips were very close … he kissed her lightly, the kiss growing in power as she returned it. He inched closer, until his hands were brushing against her jacket. Her bare skin was buried under layer upon layer of clothing and yet he felt as if there was nothing between them, nothing to keep him from having her … his manhood stiffened, demanding attention. The kisses were growing ever stronger. It crossed his mind the driver might hear something, but who cared? If the man said a word, Bruce would kill him in cold blood and drop his remains into a cesspit. Gwen moaned, deep in her throat, as his hand inched inside her jacket, her nipple hard against his skin …

The coach rattled, sharply. Gwen drew back, her hair spilling down around her face. Bruce wanted her … God, he wanted her. He took a deep shuddering breath, trying to calm himself as Gwen fixed her hair and jacket. They didn't have time. The coach was heading straight to Whitehall, the driver shouting to clear the way … there'd be no time to clean up afterwards, after … he forced himself to straighten his own jacket. They might be engaged, but they dared not be caught being intimate until after the wedding. Hell, being caught together even after the wedding would be awkward.

"Later," Gwen managed. "There has to be somewhere …"

"There are hotels," Bruce said. "Aren't there?"

Gwen looked doubtful. "The staff can be nosy," she said. "Or … there was a big scandal when a newlywed couple went to a hotel for their wedding night, then the hotel staff tried to arrest them for adultery because there was a mix up with the wedding certificate. Or another one where the couple really were running away together. If we get caught …"

Bruce scowled, but calmed himself as best he could. Gwen was right. It would be hard for him if they got caught and worse for her. *He* could beat up anyone talking out of turn – no one would think anything of him calling out someone insulting his wife – but she couldn't … damn it. It wasn't fair. A normal husband could beat or kill a man who was rude to his wife, but if he did it he'd undermine her position. She'd never forgive him for it.

The carriage came to a halt. "We're here," Gwen said. She schooled her face into a blank mask. If he hadn't known they'd been kissing, he would never have believed it. "Behave yourself."

"Of course," Bruce said, with the private thought he could always ambush an insulter in an alleyway and leave him a broken wreck. "Don't I always?"

Chapter Seven
London, England

wen kept her face under tight control as they were escorted to the offices underneath Whitehall.

It wasn't easy. She'd wanted to go further, much further. She'd hated pouring cold water on Bruce's idea of finding a hotel, when her body had wanted him inside her and … hell, there was no reason they couldn't go to one of the properties Master Thomas had left her or even find a residence somewhere outside London. And yet, if they were seen together, it would be utterly disastrous. Bruce could get away with it, but *she* couldn't. It just wasn't fair.

Her lips tightened. She'd never considered her *mother* might have had an encounter with a rake. It was just … impossible. The idea of her mother … and yet, she had to admit it had been hard to steel herself to resist the urge to just tear off her clothes and make love to him. The driver would keep his mouth shut and if he didn't … she scowled, her mood darkening. She could do anything to the driver, anything at all, and yet it wouldn't make the slightest bit of difference. The genie would be loose and they'd be no hope of putting it back in the lamp and sealing it away. She'd just have to put up with it.

She allowed herself a smile as she was shown into the conference room, Lord Mycroft – the one and only person to treat her as an equal – sat at the head of the table. Field Marshal Arthur Wellesley, 1st Duke of India, sat next to him; Lord Liverpool, the Prime Minister, sat on the other side. Gwen was mildly surprised he wasn't chairing the meeting, but Whitehall *was* Lord Mycroft's territory. Sir Edmund Hellebore sat at the far end, his eyes flickering to Gwen and then back again. Gwen had barely exchanged a handful of words with him, but she knew he was one of Lord Mycroft's rivals. And he was a known magician.

"Lady Gwen, Lord Bruce," Lord Mycroft said. "Please, take a seat."

Gwen sat, resting her hands on the table. There was no point in pretending to be a properly demure young lady, not here. Proper young ladies weren't invited to meetings that were clearly intended to be deniable … her eyes darted to the Duke of India, who looked as if he hadn't slept for a week. He was an old man, and yet no one doubted his mind was as sharp as ever. Lord Liverpool had been wise to keep him in government, rather than accept his request for a field command or let him retire to the countryside.

"There has been an interesting development, two in fact," Lord Mycroft said. The fact *he* was giving the briefing was more proof, as if she needed it, that the entire meeting was off the record. "A pair of remarkable opportunities have landed in our lap."

"And we must act fast," the Duke of India rumbled. He'd been known as a quick and decisive commander in his day and, even though he'd slowed down a little, he still had the nerve to act without recourse to higher authority. Gwen could respect that, even if he had a habit of talking down to her at times. "This opportunity must not be allowed to slip through our fingers."

Lord Liverpool leaned forward. "Perhaps you could start from the beginning?"

Lord Mycroft indicated the map on the wall. "It has long been our belief that the union between France and Spain, and various smaller countries and societies, was unlikely to last more than a few years. While the leadership may be tightly united – and that is debatable – there remains the legacy of centuries of war, mistrust, religious conflict and outright racism, problems that have been largely insoluble. France took most of the key roles for itself and the other states within the union bitterly resented it. The early victories – against Prussia, Russia and Portugal – did not threaten the union's survival. However, defeat appears to have opened faultlines within their government that led to outright revolution."

He paused. "Reports are vague, and in a few cases somewhat contradictory, but it appears there was a rising in southern Spain, a region well known to be restive even at the very best of times. The local military forces attempted to squash the fighting, only to be defeated – some reports say the troops murdered their officers and switched sides – and the rising spread rapidly. This led directly to a second set of uprisings in Portugal, which have been largely successful. So far, the fighting hasn't spread into northern Spain, but we think it is only a matter of time."

"We have an army here, ready for Mexico," the Duke of India said. "But if we send it to Portugal and Spain instead, the French will be finished."

Gwen considered it thoughtfully. Portugal had been occupied for decades, after the French invaded, put a puppet king on the throne and stamped on any hint of rebellion with undisguised savagery. She knew hundreds of thousands of Portuguese had fled their country, some heading for Britain and others trying to make it to the old colonies on the other side of the Atlantic. If they'd revolted …

She leaned forward. "Who's in command of the rebellion?"

"We don't know," Lord Mycroft said. "The old aristocracy of Portugal was either driven away or assimilated into the Bourbon Family. It isn't clear, yet, if anyone will emerge from the rubble to take command. In Spain, the situation is a little more complex. Some of the local nobility have been attempting to assert control, but they've been challenged by town councils and communities that loathe the local nobles as much as they hate the French. It was always a snake pit, politically speaking. It may take time, again, for a clear leader to emerge and take command."

"And the French will be sending their own armies," the Duke of India said. "We have to support the rebels as quickly as possible."

Gwen nodded, slowly. Neither France nor Spain – alone – could challenge the British Empire. If their union of crowns could be broken in two, and if they started fighting each other, the war would be over. Britain would have all the time she needed to rebuild, raise new armies and lay claim to the New World. And then she'd become unchallengeable.

"It would also be risky, if your army were to be lost," Lord Liverpool said. "We have *one* army. A defeat would set the war effort back by years."

"The risk is smaller than you think," the Duke of India fired back. "We would enjoy complete naval supremacy. We'd also have magicians. We'd be able to pick and choose our landing sites, then withdraw the troops if it turns out the enemy is stronger than we thought. If their navy comes out to fight, we'll squash it; if it doesn't, their morale will plummet and victory will be within our grasp."

"Particularly if their navy is also feeling mutinous," Lord Liverpool said. "Are they?"

"Unknown," Lord Mycroft said, bluntly. "We know they took heavy losses during the invasion of England – their ships were poorly manned and poorly led – but we don't know how it affected their morale."

Gwen's lips twitched. "It's hard to imagine it did anything *good* for their morale."

Sir Edmund shot her a sharp look, but didn't reply directly. "And what happens if the rebels refuse to cooperate with us?"

"It is unthinkable the rebels in Portugal will refuse to work with us," Lord Mycroft said, calmly. "They have long resented their subordination and without our help, their rebellion will be quashed. Spain is a harder question, but if our officers on the spot are diplomatic it is at least *possible* they'll work with us against the common foe. We will be careful not to suggest, at any point, we have any territorial ambitions. Gibraltar will remain Spanish."

"That will be a political nightmare," Lord Liverpool pointed out. "The backbenchers will not be pleased."

Gwen nodded, coldly. Gibraltar had been captured during the last major war and the Bourbons had flatly refused to even *consider* returning it to Britain. She understood their thinking – the Spanish would have rebelled thirty years earlier if the French had suggested giving up the ruined town and fortress – but it was still galling. Gibraltar, in enemy hands, locked British ships out of the Mediterranean and kept British forces from intervening in Italy, Greece or North Africa. But it was unlikely the Spanish would willingly give it back.

"Perhaps not," Lord Mycroft agreed. "But we must avoid causing undue offense to our allies. Given time, the French will reassert themselves and resume control of Spain and Portugal – if we give them the time. Better to deal with the Spanish than face a reunited empire under a regime that has brutally put down an insurrection, and has trained and experienced troops to take the offensive against us."

He paused. "And that leads neatly to the second issue."

His eyes lingered on Gwen for a long moment. "We have received a message from a ... *dissident* ... faction in Paris. They inform us that the French have found a way to ... *enhance* ... magical ability, to the point they have been able to put together a whole new force of military sorcerers. Combined with an extensive building programme – both warships and airships – it poses a significant threat to our physical security. If the figures are accurate, and the ones we have been able to check appear so, the French may be able to land a second invasion force in just under a year."

Gwen sucked in her breath. "How do they enhance magical abilities?"

"The message didn't say," Lord Mycroft said. "However, we have some reason to believe the French were either involved with the Russian experiments or recovered information from the Russian scientists, the ones who fled west when all hell broke loose in Russia. The French have always been behind us, when it comes to pure magical research. They couldn't afford many scruples about how they catch up, if they are desperate."

"They are," Lord Liverpool said. "The war is a death match now. They win or they lose completely. No middle ground."

Gwen kept her face impassive. She'd seen the horrors the Russians had unleashed – and heard Olivia's nightmarish stories of what her captors had done to her, when she'd been their prisoner. She was uneasily aware Britain had a research programme too, one that pressed against the limits of the acceptable. And she wondered, sometimes, if there weren't programmes that had been kept from her. She'd made her opposition to immoral research very clear.

The French may think they don't have a choice, she mused. *And if they are prepared to gamble everything on a mad quest for victory ...*

She didn't want to think about it. The necromantic outbreak in Russia had killed millions and it would have been worse, much worse, if the maddened Tsar remained in control of his undead armies. Were the French walking down the same path? Or ... or what? There'd been quite a few experiments that hinted at possible results, if one discarded all moral and ethical principles. If the French were pushing ahead, she dreaded to think what they might have found and weaponised.

"The dissidents have requested our help," Lord Mycroft said. "In exchange for our assistance, they'll help us win the war."

"Odd," Lord Liverpool said. "Are they traitors to their own country?"

"Or is this a trap?" Sir Edmund tapped the table. "What do they want from us?"

"Magical training," Lord Mycroft said. "And little else."

"Still ..." Lord Liverpool's face twisted in disgust. "Traitors."

"One man's traitor is another man's patriot," Bruce said. "Do we have any other options for ending the war quickly?"

Gwen winced, inwardly. She was surprised no one had objected to Bruce attending the meeting ... she felt her mood darken as it dawned on her someone really *should* have raised an objection. His entire position was a little undefined. And yet, he'd been allowed to walk into the meeting and sit next to her ...

"No," Lord Mycroft said. "If the dissidents are on the level, they might be able to bring down the French Government. But if it is a trap, whoever we send to France will be in terrible danger."

"And that raises another question," Gwen said. *"Can we get someone into France?"*

"We think so," Lord Mycroft said. "Getting to France itself will be easy. Getting to Paris will be a great deal harder. The French have been tightening up their internal security and even with inside help, it won't be easy to get into the city."

Sir Edmund looked at Gwen. "You speak French, don't you?"

"Yes," Gwen said. It was an odd question. Most upper-class boys and girls were taught to speak French from a very early age. She couldn't pose as a native, she thought, but she could certainly communicate with them. "But I've never been to France."

She sighed, inwardly. It had been common, before the war, for noblemen – and some noblewomen – to travel to France, Italy and even Spain before returning home and assuming their positions in society. She'd never gone. Her father had been reluctant to leave the country when she'd been a child and, as she'd grown older, her magic had made it impossible to take her anywhere. And now it was too late.

Lord Mycroft held up a hand. "It might be a trap," he

said. "We will be dealing with people who have interests ... that will not always accord with our own, even if they are on the level. They may oppose the government without opposing the country. They may also be dangerous enemies in the long run, if peace is followed by another war. In truth, we don't know very much for sure. The handful of pieces of information we have been able to verify are far outweighed by the ones we can neither prove nor disprove."

"Whoever we send will have to be very capable," Sir Edmund said. "And also capable of escaping if this really *is* a trap."

Gwen closed her eyes for a long moment. She had a feeling she knew where this was heading. "You want me to go," she said. "Don't you?"

There was a glimmer of triumph in Sir Edmund's eyes. "You would be the best suited for the mission, for various reasons."

Bruce shifted beside her. Gwen tried to ignore him. "I have never been to Paris, or even to France," she said, as if that was in doubt. "My French is perfect, on paper, but I have no hope of fooling a native."

"The pen of your aunt is no longer in your garden," the Duke of India cracked. "And whatever other such nonsense you were taught to say."

Gwen hid her amusement. The old man was right. Her tutor had drilled her on complicated phrases and sentences she suspected were rarely, if ever, heard in France itself. She might speak the language, but not in a flowing manner that would hide her true origins. She'd have to practice, and fast, if she wanted to convince people she was a genuine Frenchwomen. She wasn't even sure she could get away with it ...

"I can go," she said. There was nothing else she could say, not if she wanted to keep their respect. They'd shun a *man* who declined a dangerous mission ... in some ways, it would be worse for him. He'd get called a coward. She'd merely get sneered at for being a weak and feeble woman, someone who naturally could not be expected to undertake a dangerous mission. "If it turns out to be a trap, I can fly away."

"I'll come with you," Bruce said. "Someone has to watch your back …"

"No," the Duke of India said. "You're needed with the army."

"There is an entire *corps* of sorcerers who can accompany the army," Bruce snapped. Gwen winced at the frantic desperation in his voice. He knew she could take care of herself and yet it would look bad, very bad, if he let her go alone. "You don't need me."

"We will, if we encounter more enemy sorcerers," the Duke of India told him. "There is no way to be sure of anything until we arrive."

"Perhaps not," Gwen said. There'd be Talkers with the army … perhaps Talkers already on their way, disguised as merchants or sailors. "How do you plan to get me into France?"

"We're still working on the details," Lord Mycroft said. "Give me a day or two to find a way that isn't too risky."

Gwen studied the map for a moment. It was a shame she couldn't simply fly across the English Channel and make her way directly to Paris, but it would be asking for trouble. The French were supposed to have a network of Seers watching for flying magicians and if she was spotted they'd be on her with terrifying speed. In theory, if she stayed on the ground, it would be easier to remain unnoticed unless she did something stupid.

They're probably watching for local common-born magicians, she thought. The French had been reluctant to risk recruiting commoners, at least at first, but that might have changed under the pressures of war. *And if I get detected in the open, I'll have to fight my way out.*

"Good," Lord Liverpool said. "We move to support Portugal and Spain against France, while offering covert help to the French underground. Does anyone have any significant objections?"

"I see no alternative," the Duke of India said. "Do you?"

"No." The Prime Minister leaned back in his chair. "We must move fast. This opportunity will not come again."

"No, My Lord," Lord Mycroft said. "This is how we should proceed …"

Chapter Eight
London, England.

ruce had never felt quite so …

In truth, he wasn't sure *how* he felt. Trapped, perhaps; trapped between two choices, both equally bad. The idea of being sent to war didn't bother him – he'd fought before, as a Son of Liberty, and he knew he could handle it – but the idea of letting Gwen go into horrendous danger on her own was … it was unthinkable. What sort of man would let his *fiancée* go into the dark heart of an evil empire? He'd be lucky if he wasn't mocked for the rest of his life for agreeing to let her go. And if she died … his heart twisted painfully as it dawned on him she might not survive the war. The French knew her. They wouldn't take chances if they captured her. They'd kill her and dump her body in a ditch.

The meeting droned on. It took all his self-control to keep from exploding at the men – the *men* – who proposed to send a young woman to enemy territory. There was no way to be sure it wasn't a trap, no way to be certain the French dissidents weren't being used by their government … no way to be sure the French dissidents were actually *real*. Bruce had been a Son of Liberty. He knew the risks in contacting foreigners and asking for aid … risks that would be magnified, impossibly so, when asking for help from the old enemy. England and France had been at war, on and off, for centuries. The French dissidents had to know what it would cost them to accept help from the British, if it became public. And it would.

Their government might not know the dissidents are accepting help, he thought, with a flicker of gallows humour. *But that won't stop them from accusing the dissidents of doing it anyway.*

"I trust you can discuss the specifics with Lady Gwen," Lord Liverpool said, finally. Bruce allowed himself a moment of relief. He'd thought his father's meetings were long, but he hadn't had to sit through them. "Master Bruce, the army will be enriched by your presence."

"Thank you," Bruce said. It was hard to keep his voice under control. "I live to serve."

Lord Liverpool seemed to miss the sarcasm. The Duke of India shot him a sharp look. Bruce stared back at him, torn between admiration for a man who was clearly still a force even though age had taken its toll on his body and resentment for someone who was taking him away from his *fiancée*. The Duke *was* the greatest living soldier, of that there was no doubt, and yet ... Bruce wondered, sourly, if his glory days were over. He'd mastered his trade in the days of rifles and cannon, not steam-powered ironclads and airships. Was he still up to the job? Or was he trapped in the past?

He kept his face under tight control as he looked at Lord Mycroft. The man was immensely fat – the nasty party of Bruce's mind whispered he was a danger to shipping – his strong cheekbones and chin marred by all the signs of good living. His hair was receding rapidly, to the point it was a surprise he hadn't donned a wig. Bruce wanted to dislike him, for steering Gwen towards the mission, and yet there was something about the man that made him difficult to dislike. Gwen had said he was one of the finest minds in the world, if not *the* finest. And yet ... Bruce felt a wave of resentment. *This* was the man who was sending his *fiancée* into terrible danger.

"The basic concept is sound," Lord Mycroft said, once the rest of the ministers had left the room. "There are still trading ships operating between London and Amsterdam. We'll send you on one, attached to a trading mission that'll eventually get you into Paris. Your cover story should stand up to close inspection."

Gwen's lips twitched. "We are still trading with the enemy?"

Lord Mycroft snorted. "It would be more accurate to say we're trading with the Dutch, who are trading with the French," he said. "They're caught between two powerful enemies and have to chart a careful course betwixt them, just to ensure they don't find themselves beholden to one and facing a nasty little war with the other. We've been keeping an eye on the trade without making any overt attempts to shut it down, not least because it lets us have considerable insight into continental politics. The trading networks are often more aware of what is going on than the secret service."

"I see," Bruce said. His voice hardened, revealing too much of his inner feelings. "And you are prepared to tolerate their double-dealing?"

"They have no choice." Lord Mycroft didn't seem annoyed, but his eyes rested on Bruce thoughtfully. "The French can invade if they wish, although it would be a very hard campaign and they'd take immense losses for very little return. We would find it harder to invade and occupy the republic, but we could shut down their foreign trade and take over their colonies. They have to steer a course between us, as I said, or risk losing everything no matter who wins the greater war."

"And you are trusting them with Gwen's safety," Bruce snapped. He was aware, suddenly, of Gwen bristling beside him. "You cannot trust *any* of them. For all you know, this is a trap."

"There are no certainties," Lord Mycroft agreed. "But we cannot afford to let this opportunity go by."

"If you trust them," Bruce said. "Can you be sure the dissidents won't turn on us?"

"There are no certainties," Lord Mycroft repeated. "We don't know what, if anything, the French have discovered. They claim they can boost magic … we simply don't know. We do know that there *is* an uprising in Spain, and that there are Frenchmen who think their empire needs a change of course."

"And you are sending Gwen into a snake pit," Bruce said. He'd been a revolutionary. He knew how quickly allegiances could shift, if something – anything – changed. "Send me instead."

Gwen leaned forward. "Do you speak French?"

"Yes," Bruce said. His father's tutors had drilled it into him, with book and cane. "My French is acceptable."

"Are you sure?" Gwen's voice was hard. "If your accent gives you away …"

Lord Mycroft cleared his throat. "I have urgent business in another room," he said. He stood, with remarkable agility for a man of his bulk. "I shall return shortly."

Bruce blinked. Urgent business? What could be more urgent than *this*? There hadn't even been a message … unless Lord Mycroft was a Talker, with all that implied. But he hadn't sensed any attempt to read his mind … not, he supposed, that a *smart* Talker would try. Lord Mycroft knew Bruce was a Master Magician. Why try something that would not only fail, but turn Bruce into a formidable enemy?

He watched the older man leave, trying to calm his thoughts. Lord Mycroft's tailors had made no attempt to disguise his size, something that would have been impossible but still … Bruce would have expected it. He knew men who preferred tailoring their clothes to healthy exercise, although very few of them could make it work. And yet … the door closed, surprisingly quietly. The room suddenly felt very small.

Gwen's voice was practically a snarl. "And what has got into you?"

Bruce gritted his teeth, feeling his temper boil. No one spoke to him like that … no one, not even his father. And yet … he controlled himself with an effort, all too aware his anger was covering for worry and fear. He didn't want to risk losing her … no, he didn't want her to go alone. She was his *fiancée.* He couldn't let her go.

"I have worked for years to earn a little respect," Gwen snapped. "And you threaten it by trying to go in my place!"

"You could die," Bruce said. It was hard to conceal his anger … not, he suspected, that she was fooled. She'd always been better at the mental arts than him. "If you get caught, do you know what could happen to you?"

"Yes!" Gwen leaned forward until they were practically touching. "I know. But that isn't going to stop me."

"You've never even been to France," Bruce pointed out. "If you stick out …"

"Neither have you," Gwen interrupted. "Or did you manage to sneak from New York to Paris and return in time for tea?"

"No," Bruce said. "But I'll draw a hell of a lot less attention than a pretty girl."

Gwen's temper flared. Bruce could *sense* her anger pulsing against her self-control. He cursed himself under his breath. It had been the worst possible thing to say. She'd spent far too long trying to convince people she could do her job, despite being a young woman … hell, she was young enough for most of the government ministers to see her as a child. And yet … he didn't want her to go.

"I went to Russia undercover," Gwen snapped. "Do you think I can't handle France?"

"The French know you," Bruce countered. "What happens if they get their hands on you?"

"I am aware of the risks," Gwen said, stiffly. "But some risks have to be taken."

"Then let me come with you," Bruce said. "The army doesn't need me!"

"It does," Gwen said, flatly. "It needs a Master Magician. It also needs someone with natural authority" – her lips twisted into a bitter grimace – "who can bond with the officers and men. I can't, as you know. And I would be happier with someone I trust out there too."

Bruce blinked. "You don't trust your subordinates?"

"I trust them to be themselves," Gwen said, a little vaguely. "They have a nasty habit of ignoring my orders if they think they know better."

She took a breath, her anger pulsing on the air. "Go back to the Royal College. Get ready to depart. The Duke does not let the grass grow under his feet. I'll be along after I finish discussing matters with Lord Mycroft."

Bruce blinked. "You're sending me away?"

Gwen met his eyes. "I cannot have someone – anyone – undermining me in front of the government ministers," she said. "I have worked too long to convince them I need to be taken seriously ..."

"They're sending you to Paris!" Bruce was too shocked to muster a more coherent response. "Gwen, they're sending you to ..."

Gwen cut him off. "I may be your *fiancée*, but I am also a person of considerable power and authority. I am not – I cannot be – the kind of wife who stays at home and never speaks when her husband is present. I will not submit wordlessly to your authority and I will not let you push me into the backroom when the *men* are talking. And I will not let you beat me, verbally or physically, if you think I am misbehaving."

She kept her eyes steady. "If you have a problem with that, let me know now and we can go our separate ways."

Bruce felt his emotions shift so rapidly he couldn't keep up ... anger and fear and worry and despair and ... he knew he was no coward, no fool, and yet he had no idea what to say. He wanted to reassure her and he wanted to yell at her and ... he gritted his teeth, clamping down on his feelings. He'd thought he understood what her position implied, but ... he kicked himself. Stupid. He'd considered her something akin to a female shopkeeper, or a housekeeper, not a government official in her own right. And ...

"I'm sorry," he said. It was never easy to apologise, but ... it had to be said. "I just ... I just want you to be safe."

"Life isn't safe, even for young women who stay at home and never go outside," Gwen said. "Do you know how many women die in childbirth?

She shook her head. "Go back to the college," she said. "I'll see you there."

Bruce nodded stiffly, then stood. They were alone and yet … were they unobserved? There might be prying eyes watching them … he touched his lips gently, the closest he could come to blowing a kiss, and turned and hurried out the door. A young man was already waiting for him, ready to show him back to the carriage. Bruce left it in Whitehall and took to the air, flying back to Cavendish Hall. London might be a smoggy nightmare of a city, but it wasn't that hard to pick out the important buildings from overhead. Besides, it gave him time to think.

His mind churned. He'd never really considered what getting married would be like. His mother had died when he was very young and his father had never remarried. He'd known other married couples, of course, but he'd never seen how they interacted in private. Of course not. The very idea was absurd. His friends had rarely talked about it either. It was funny, he reflected sourly, that they'd boasted about things they'd done with various young women – most of which he suspected to be nothing more than blatant lies – and yet they'd never talked about how their fathers treated their mothers. The only time anyone had ever talked about anything of the sort had been when a particularly amusing scandal had broken into the public eye.

He dropped down and through the open skylight, landing neatly in the barracks. It was galling to sleep so far from Gwen's suite, but propriety demanded they keep their distance until the wedding night. He snorted in annoyance – he didn't really care who talked about them – and pushed the thought aside. Their first argument had been vicious. She wasn't going to want to do anything *intimate* with him for a while. And if they were setting off within a day or two, the plans for a quick wedding had been disrupted beyond repair.

The barracks felt weird as he made his way down the corridor. It had little in common with an army barracks, beyond the name, yet it was almost empty. The majority of the Royal Sorcerers Corps was on deployment, dozens of rooms left unoccupied until their return, leaving only a handful of magicians in London. Official magicians, at least. Gwen had told him there was a surprisingly high number of female magicians, their existence officially denied even as their families made use of their talents. His lips twitched in cold amusement. How would their future husbands cope with magical wives? Would it solve all their problems or create new ones?

"My Lord," a voice said, as he reached his suite. "A word?"

Bruce gritted his teeth. He'd slipped. He'd been too lost in his own thoughts to notice the man standing near the door. His eyes narrowed as he recognised the speaker. Pinfold was a Blazer, a man with enough power to make a name for himself, yet he'd always struck Bruce as something of a coward. He certainly hadn't done any military duty, beyond guarding London against probing airships. *That* hadn't happened for a while. The first bombing raids had been so costly both sides had decided there was no point in trying again.

"If you must," he said. He was damned if he was inviting Pinfold into his rooms. "What do you want?"

Pinfold seemed surprised at his curt voice, but pressed on. "I need to discuss a matter of some delicacy with you," he said. "Can we discuss it in your chambers?"

"No." Bruce rested his hands on his hips, not bothering to try to hide his irritation. It had been a long day. "Get to the point."

"Many of us feel the demands of war dictate the corps be led by an experienced fighting man," Pinfold said. "Lady Gwen, despite her many good qualities, does not have the talent for …"

"You are aware, are you not, that Gwen is my *fiancée*?" Bruce clenched his fists. Blazer or no, he was sure he could break the man's nose before he could react.

"Choose your next words carefully."

Pinfold hesitated, but didn't back down. "We feel she is better suited to running the corps here, rather than leading it into battle," he said. "We think …"

Bruce interrupted. "Who's *we*?"

"Some of us," Pinfold said. Bruce wasn't sure if he was concealing the names or if he was speaking for himself, rather than a handful of others. "We would like to nominate you as her replacement. We think …"

"Really?" Bruce darted forward and shoved Pinfold against the wall. "And you think I would betray her just like that?"

Pinfold stared at him. "But …?"

"But what?" Bruce pushed harder. It would be easy, so easy, to summon his magic and smash Pinfold into a bloody mess. Or snap his neck and drop the body in the river. Or something … cold anger burned through him, mocking his earlier thoughts. He loved Gwen. He might have argued with her, but he loved her. "You thought I would betray her?"

"But …" Pinfold stuttered and gathered himself. "It's for her own good."

"No, it bloody isn't," Bruce snarled. He sniffed, then rolled his eyes in disgust. The toad had wet himself. Disgusting. "You go back to your friends, if they even exist, and tell them I won't betray her. And if I hear you doing this again, I'll tear you to pieces."

He turned and stepped into his room, closing the door behind him. Pinfold didn't even have the nerve to blast him in the back … he scowled, bitterly, as he headed to his bed. Gwen had told him she had enemies, but he hadn't thought they'd try something so blatant. Clearly, even being an American trumped being a young woman.

If he's operating on his own, that's one thing, he thought. Pinfold was a coward. It was unlikely he'd have the nerve to do anything alone. *If he is part of a group, though, they could cause real trouble.*

He scowled. *And I have to talk to her about this, as quickly as possible.*

Chapter Nine
London, England

wen gathered herself.

It wasn't easy. She'd heard all sorts of horror stories from married women about how their husbands could turn from being nice acceptable prospects to bullying monsters as soon as they put the ring on their wife's finger. Her own mother had been remarkably lucky compared to some of the others, from the women who talked openly about their problems to the silent little mites who, no matter how they tried, couldn't hide the bruises. It was a reality of life for wives that their husbands were not only superior to them by law, but also physically strong enough to impose themselves on their wives. It wasn't true of her, she knew, yet she was unique. And Bruce ...

He means well, she thought. She'd tasted his feelings during the brief argument. The worry, the fear ... the awareness, despite everything, that she might go to Paris and never come back. Gwen wasn't blind to the risks, but they could be managed. *And he really can't come with me.*

She sighed. She was uneasily aware she really *wasn't* the best choice for a military deployment. She would find it difficult, if not impossible, to bond with the rest of the commanding officers, even though she was hardly inexperienced. A young officer who'd bought his commission without a shred of experience would find it easier to make ties with his seniors, although they'd be careful to keep an eye on him until they were sure he knew what he was doing. It would be difficult for her, even with the Duke's open support. Hell, his support would probably make things worse.

The door opened. Lord Mycroft stepped back into the chamber, closing the door behind him. Gwen felt a rush of gratitude. Lord Mycroft had been perceptive enough, thankfully, to let them have the argument in private. One of Lady Mary's better pieces of advice had been to never disagree with your husband, or *fiancé*, in public. Gwen suspected, from her own experience, that it made it harder for someone to back down and consider her arguments logically. Master Thomas had said the same, a few short years ago.

Praise in public, punish in private, he'd said. *The more public the punishment, the more they'll resent it.*

"It is never easy, to have one set of plans and then have to switch at short notice," Lord Mycroft said. "But I am sure you will cope."

"We will," Gwen said. She understood Bruce's feelings, and his position, but did he understand hers? "Do you really think you can get me to Paris without problems?"

"We believe so," Lord Mycroft told her. "The great trading families have few qualms about allowing their daughters to accompany them to Paris and Versailles. You'll be posing as one of them until you reach the city, whereupon you'll be handed over to the local agent on the ground. There are some safe houses and suchlike within Paris itself, which you'll be briefed upon before you leave. Naturally, this information is to go no further."

"Naturally," Gwen echoed. She wouldn't be told everything. What she didn't know she couldn't be made to tell. "And once we're there?"

Lord Mycroft frowned. "Your contact will be Simone," he said. "I believe you know her."

Gwen's eyebrows shot up? "Simone? Ambassador Talleyrand's daughter?"

"Adopted daughter," Lord Mycroft corrected, mildly. "And yes, it's the same person."

"And *she* is a dissident." Gwen didn't know if she should laugh or cry. "Is she really …?"

Lord Mycroft said nothing for a long moment. "Ambassador Talleyrand was executed a week ago," he said. "It wasn't formally announced, and his head wasn't put on a spike as an example to others, but – from what we've heard – no one is in any doubt what happened. His death marks a major shift in Franco-Spanish policy."

Gwen frowned. "Is that tied to the rebellion in Spain?"

"It may be," Lord Mycroft said. "Ambassador Talleyrand was definitely a member of the peace faction, and his execution is a clear warning to the rest that peace is no longer on the table. He certainly was involved in trying to smooth out the differences between France, Spain and the rest of the Bourbon Empire. But … it may also be a coincidence. We don't think anyone in Versailles plotted to induce the Spanish to rebel."

His lips twisted into a brief smile. "Not intentionally, anyway."

"No," Gwen agreed.

Lord Mycroft met her eyes. "Simone got in touch with one of our agents at Versailles," he said, "and requested to pass on a message. The dissidents want our help."

Gwen said nothing for a long moment, then frowned. "Simone is a *dissident*?"

"It isn't clear," Lord Mycroft said. "It's quite possible there were – are – ties between the peace faction at Versailles and the dissidents in Paris. The Bourbon Government is something of a hodgepodge grafted onto a far older state and the links between them are not always easy to understand. Loyalists, dissidents and opportunists rub shoulders openly, I believe. And there are links between shopkeepers in the city and farmers outside the walls and …"

He met her eyes. "My office has been predicting a major revolution in France for the last four decades. They came very close to an open breakdown of law and order in 1789 and a crisis was only just averted through emergency spending and a certain display of naked force, both of which left scars on the French psyche. There have been some attempts to address the problems undermining the French state, but most of them have failed because Versailles is unwilling to demand sacrifice from the nobility and the clergy. If they'd avoided war, or won quickly, disaster might have been averted for quite some time. Instead, they are on very thin ice."

"Because the war bogged down," Gwen said.

"Yes." Lord Mycroft raised his eyes to look at the map. "There are too many faultlines within their empire, not all of which can be papered over. And if they explode …"

He looked back at her. "Can we trust Simone?"

Gwen hesitated. They'd met twice and, in both cases, Simone had struck her as being loyal to her adopted father, if not the state itself. And now Talleyrand was dead …

"I don't know," she said, finally. Her father was a government minister. What would *she* do if he was executed by the government he'd served loyally for his entire adult life? Her magic pulsed in response, reminding her she could take revenge. Simone had much less power and yet, with a little effort, who knew what she could do? "But do we have a choice?"

"No." Lord Mycroft shifted, uncomfortably. "There have been some … political changes here too. The war should have been short and victorious – they thought, once we defeated the French in England and America, the end would come quickly. Some think we need to push harder, others that we should seek peace now while the French are weak and unable to continue the fight. Lord Liverpool's position is nowhere near as strong as he would prefer."

"And so he's willing to gamble on supporting the rebels in Spain," Gwen said. "If he's wrong …"

"A failure would make his position untenable," Lord Mycroft agreed. "But that's far from the only problem. The stresses and strains of war are causing our own system to buckle. If the government falls, there'll be an election at the worst possible time."

"So we need to win," Gwen said. "And quickly."

"Yes." Lord Mycroft looked back at the map. "There have been some very quiet peace talks – talks about talks, more accurately – but they've gone nowhere. That's worrying. The French know they're on the back foot. They should be trying to talk peace – or, at the very least, trying to stall for time. That they've done neither …"

"They think they can still win," Gwen said. "What do they have up their sleeve?"

"I wish I knew," Lord Mycroft said. "If the war rested on cold economics and logistics, our ultimate victory would be assured. The French have always been behind us, magically, and they haven't been able to catch up. But … they may have found something they think will give them an edge. We simply don't know."

Gwen took a breath. "I'll go to Paris," she said. "And see what happens from there."

"I can't give you more specific orders," Lord Mycroft agreed. "But anything you can do to cause trouble for the French would be very helpful."

"The army will probably cause a lot of trouble on its own," Gwen commented, wryly. She was no logistics expert, but she'd read accounts of campaigning in France and Spain. The landscape made logistics difficult, to the point the French would have very real trouble keeping their forces supplied if the British had control of the seas. "How badly will it hurt the Bourbons if the Spanish drop out of the empire – and the war?"

"Hard to say," Lord Mycroft said. "Spain is no longer the unchallenged master of South America. But I can't imagine the results will be *good* for the enemy."

"No," Gwen said. It was hard to say if Latin America would follow Spain out of the war – the Bourbons, to give them due credit, had worked hard to give the locals a stake in their empire – but even if Latin America stayed in the war the effects would be profound. "It wouldn't be remotely good for them."

Lord Mycroft nodded. "And Gwen, watch your back."

Gwen's eyes narrowed. "What do you mean?"

"You have enemies," Lord Mycroft said. "Some dismissed you because you were – are – a girl. Others, now, dislike and resent you because of your involvement in political affairs. They see it as meddling and regard the American intervention as the very last straw."

Gwen felt a hot flash of anger. "Did I have a choice?"

"No," Lord Mycroft said. "But it is not given to us to make a mistake, then learn from it and rewind history to avoid making it in the first place. They think you did the wrong thing because they don't know what would – might – have happened if you hadn't interfered in American affairs. And others ..."

He shook his head. "Lord Liverpool and the Duke are in your corner," he said. "Others are not. Watch yourself."

"I will." Gwen stood. "And you watch your back too."

Lord Mycroft chuckled. "Anyone who takes a shot at me is bound to hit *something*," he said, mischievously. "Luckily, I can stand to lose a few pounds."

Gwen smiled, then turned and left the room. Her thoughts churned as she made her way back to the carriage. She'd done the right thing – she knew it – and yet, as she clambered into the carriage and told the driver to take her back to the hall, she suspected it was going to come back to haunt her. No good deed went unpunished ... she wished, suddenly, she'd kept hold of the blackmail material she'd destroyed years ago. It might have kept her enemies from plotting against her.

Bastards, she thought. *What are they thinking?*

She glowered into the darkening sky. She'd done her duty. More than that, really; she'd saved England from an uprising, she'd eliminated a spy ring, she'd prevented Russia from turning the entire world into a charnel house, she'd beaten a French invasion of England and another in America. And yet, it wasn't enough? What did she have to do to earn even half the trust and respect that had been extended to Master Thomas? Defeat King Louis in single combat? Or smash a French army with a wave of her hand? Or … or what?

The carriage rattled to a halt. "My Lady," the driver said. "We have arrived."

Gwen nodded, then opened the door and levitated into the air. She had no desire to walk through the hall, not when it would mean talking to whoever she met on the way. The more sensible magicians were gone, either standing watch near Dover or heading to Portsmouth to link up with the Duke of India's fleet. They were lucky they'd made most of the preparations to deploy an army ahead of time, even though they'd planned to send it to Mexico. A few weeks either way and they'd have real problems getting troops to Spain in time to make a difference. If the French didn't have plans to deal with a Spanish revolt, she'd be astonished.

She dropped through the skylight and landed neatly on the floor, then straightened. It had been a long – long – day and all she wanted to do was sleep. She had no idea how she was going to talk to Bruce, when she saw him again … *would* she see him again? She knew one husband who had a habit of walking off for days, when his wife upset him, and another who was called away so often his wife never knew if he'd be coming home until he walked through the door. Bruce wasn't that sort of bastard, but … she shook her head. They weren't used to being engaged, let alone married. And while they'd been together on the boat, they hadn't exactly been under any real stress.

Her lips thinned as she spotted the pile of paperwork on the desk. Her subordinates could and did make a lot of decisions for themselves, but there were matters only she could handle. And … she wondered, suddenly, if allowing her subordinates so much latitude had been a mistake. It was one thing when she was in the colonies, and there was no time for a message to reach her before a decision had to be made one way or the other, but quite another when she was in London. She scowled as the pile seemed to grow larger, then sighed inwardly. She'd have to see to it that, when she returned, she knew exactly what was being done under her name.

She put the thought aside as she headed to bed, wishing – not for the first time – that Bruce could join her. It would be nice to sleep with his arms around her ... no, it wasn't possible, not until the wedding. Even then ... she scowled. There were few wives living in the hall and barracks, even though most of the senior magicians were married. It might be better if Bruce and she lived elsewhere ...

There was a knock on the door. Gwen tensed. Bruce? No, Bruce wouldn't come sneaking through the hall to her. Someone would see him, draw the right conclusion and all hell would break lose. He wasn't that dumb. He'd be smart and fly from the barracks to the skylight and ... even that would be risky, with so many watching eyes. She ground her teeth in silent frustration as she stepped back into the living room, reaching out with her mind to open the door. Who could she ask for advice? Her mother? Lord Mycroft ... he might have some insights, but she didn't want to show weakness in front of him. Who else? She didn't know.

"My Lady," Martha said. The maid looked as calm and composed as always. She'd been with Gwen long enough to take everything, including magic and magicians, in her stride. "I have two messages from the War Office."

Gwen nodded curtly as she popped the seal and opened the first envelope. Lord Mycroft really didn't believe in letting the grass grow under his feet. The formal orders for Bruce to report to Portsmouth had already been written, as had a very vague set of instructions for her. She wondered, sourly, if Lord Mycroft had known she'd volunteer for the mission. Probably. He was one of the smartest and most insightful people she knew and he'd *never* made the mistake of treating her as something lesser, just because she was a woman. He'd probably assumed she'd go and ordered everything prepared, even before telling her what he had in mind. And if she'd said no, someone else would have gone in her place.

Bruce can't go, she thought. She knew Bruce was good at playing roles – he'd certainly convinced her he was a useless fop – but he was needed elsewhere. *And there are no other Master Magicians to send.*

Martha cleared her throat. "Will that be all, My Lady?"

"Please take this letter to Master Bruce's rooms and slip it under his door," Gwen said, holding out the first set of orders. She thought he'd have been sent a copy of his own, but it was good to be careful. "If he's awake, tell him I'll see him at breakfast."

"Yes, My Lady." Martha dropped a curtsey, then straightened. "It will be done."

Gwen nodded, dismissing the maid. There'd be no time to arrange a private meeting, not if they had to depart so quickly. She dared not invite Bruce to her suite – not alone – nor could she go to his rooms. And … she ground her teeth in frustration. They needed to talk. They needed to discuss everything and … it wasn't going to happen, not in time. And … she was tempted to ask the maid – Martha had seen far more of the dark underside of humanity than her – but she dared not. She trusted Martha and yet … who knew?

If I was courting someone who lived here, he'd probably know just where to go, she thought, with a flicker of disquiet. There were hotels that looked the other way, as long as they were tipped heavily and the guests were discreet. She was almost tempted to find one. They could spare a few hours, couldn't they? But what was tolerable in a man was intolerable in a woman. *And I'd never hear the end of it.*

She closed and locked the door, then headed for bed. There was no point in worrying about it now. All she could do was rest, and hope tomorrow would bring better news.

Chapter Ten
London, England

ruce had never felt quite so frustrated in his life.

It wasn't the training he'd done over the last two days that bothered him. Under other circumstances, the chance to train beside Merlin – and a number of other experienced magicians – would have been a dream come true, once he'd convinced them that being American didn't mean he was incompetent, stupid or otherwise unworthy to fight beside the best of the best. He would even have enjoyed himself, if he hadn't been worrying so much about Gwen. Pinfold, the little rodent, hadn't dared show his face again, but he wasn't brave enough to make his suggestion so brazenly unless he was sure he wasn't alone. Bruce wondered, between bouts of training, which of the senior magicians were planning to stab Gwen in the back. He hadn't even had a chance to tell her what had happened.

His mind churned as the carriage rattled its way back towards London. He'd threatened Pinfold in a place there was little true privacy and yet, no one had said anything about it? That was odd. Pinfold would probably have aimed to have the discussion as covertly as possible and yet … surely, he would have gone whining to his supporters after Bruce had threatened him, unless someone had told him to keep his mouth firmly shut. Or … Bruce wanted to believe Pinfold was alone, that he was jealous of Gwen and trying to put her down, but it was impossible to convince himself. Pinfold simply didn't have the nerve. Someone else was behind him, someone with enough nerve and power to stiffen Pinfold's spine.

Damn it, he thought. It was bad enough they hadn't had a chance to talk, after they'd calmed down. It was worse to think she was going into danger, without him by her side. He'd follow orders, he'd do whatever she said … he shook his head crossly, knowing it wouldn't happen. Gwen was so determined to prove she was as good as any man that she *wasn't* going to do everything she could to tip the odds in her favour. *What do I do if she dies?*

The thought was nightmarish. He loved Gwen. He … knew there'd never be anyone like her. Other girls appeared silly and foolish, all coy and giggling in a bid to draw his eye as they hinted at marriage … marriage not to him, but to his titles and bank account. His lips quirked into a bitter smile as the carriage rattled again. If there were a way to separate him from his title, the girls would chase the title and reject him. It was the way of the world. A man might lust and even love – and a woman too, although polite society insisted otherwise – but marriages were between families. Bruce liked to think he was a handsome soul, yet it mattered not. Everyone knew what happened to women who married penniless men.

He shoved the thought out of his mind. It didn't matter. Gwen would be fine, he told himself. She really *had* gone into danger, time and time again. And while he'd posed as a useless young man, he'd never tried to pretend to be anything other than American. Passing as a Frenchman might be beyond him, no matter how well he spoke the language. And yet, he feared for her. He didn't want to let her go again.

The carriage rattled to a halt. Bruce heard voices outside, demanding papers. The driver answered, his words too low for Bruce to make them out. They must have satisfied the guards, for the carriage shuddered back into life and headed onwards. Bruce sighed inwardly and gathered himself. It wouldn't be long now.

Sure, his thoughts mocked. *And then it will be a very long time before you see her again.*

His heart twisted as the carriage stopped one final time. The driver jumped down and opened the door, revealing a simple port. A trading ship – sail rather than steam – floated at the dockside, even though it was quite some distance from the river mouth. Bruce didn't like the implications. He knew from his old life just how easy it was to smuggle arms and ammunition by water, even into the heart of a giant city. He wasn't sure how close they were to Whitehall, but if they were in London they were too close for comfort. He took a long breath, tasting the air. The stench of London assaulted him once again.

We need to live out in the countryside, he thought, coldly. *Growing up here can't be healthy.*

He jumped down and made his way to the dockyard. The ship rose and fell as the water flowed down to the sea. He glanced into a warehouse and frowned as he saw crates upon crates of goods, each one carefully labelled in English and French. It really didn't seem a good idea to be trading with the enemy, even by proxy. He had no idea if the secret intelligence network remained undetected or if the Bourbons were just biding their time, monitoring who and what passed through the network before rolling it up. There was no way to be sure, he reflected. Intelligence and counter-intelligence work was all smoke and mirrors and the *real* successes – and failures – often went unnoticed, at least by everyone outside the field. It was quite possible they'd all been taken for fools.

The small party waved to him as they stood, just inside the warehouse. Bruce headed towards them, silently gauging the location. The dockyard was carefully designed to make it hard for anyone, even a flying magician, to see inside the compound. If he was any judge, the guards on the gate were soldiers rather than commercial guardsmen or policemen. And that meant … he wondered, suddenly, just what would happen if the London mob thought the dockyard was trading with the enemy. It wouldn't be pleasant.

"Bruce," Gwen said. "I'm glad you could make it."

Bruce nodded, wishing – again – for some private time. There were too many witnesses; Lord Mycroft, Sir Edmund, a man he didn't recognise. He wanted to tell her what had happened, what Pinfold had said to him, but how could he in front of strangers? And there were too many docksmen walking around, carrying crates onto the sailing ship. What would happen if they saw something and spread the word?

He sucked in his breath as he looked at Gwen. She'd ditched her uniform, trading it for a simple dress and shirt that made her look like a prosperous trader, or the daughter of one. Her hair was hanging down in a neat little ponytail … he wondered why she hadn't braided it, then remembered she'd need a maid to assist her. It wouldn't be possible, not when a travelling woman wealthy enough to have a maid would draw attention. He felt a twinge of something as he looked at her, something he didn't care to look at too closely in front of witnesses. Gwen might be wearing strange clothes, but she was still *Gwen*. She hadn't changed at all.

"You look demure," he said, finally. He'd wondered how she'd intended to convince the French she wasn't the Royal Sorceress, but looking at her he knew the answer. Gwen was blonde and blue eyed and … there were thousands upon thousands of young women who matched that description. The French wouldn't try to arrest them all – how could they? The very thought was absurd. "No one would know you."

Gwen smiled. "My mother certainly would not," she said. "I know how to play the role."

Bruce let out a breath. "She'd certainly be shocked," he agreed. He mentally cursed the onlookers. There was so much he wanted to say, but … he dared not. "Will you be careful?"

"I always am," Gwen said. "And you?"

"I'll come back with my shield or on it," Bruce promised. He didn't want to be thought a coward – or someone who'd be unmanned by his first taste of European war. "And you …"

Sir Edmund cleared his throat. "I believe we are on a schedule," he said, as the last of the crates were loaded onto the ship. "Sir Sander?"

"Right you are," the stranger said. He had an odd accent, one Bruce couldn't place. He had a feeling it was an affectation. "Lady Gwen, with your permission …?"

Gwen met Bruce's eyes. He saw a hint of love and regret and affection in her gaze, there and gone in seconds. It would be so much easier if they could talk mind to mind – he kicked himself, mentally, for not suggesting they practice – rather than out loud. There really were too many listening ears. And watching eyes … he wanted to reach out and take her in his arms, but he dared not. People would talk.

"I'll be back," Gwen said. "Don't let the Duke do anything stupid."

"I'll do my best," Bruce said. "Good luck."

He stepped back and gritted his teeth as Gwen and Sir Sander walked up the gangplank and onto the ship. He had no idea what sort of cover story had been created to explain her presence – Sir Sander hadn't looked old enough to have a grown daughter – but it hardly mattered. Part of him was bitterly jealous at watching the man stand so close to his *fiancée*, the rest of him feared what could happen to her, alone on the high seas. Everyone knew what sailors did, even if they had trouble putting it into words. And the traders weren't even naval officers.

Not that naval officers are that much better, he thought, tartly. *Lord Nelson seduced a married woman and carried on with her, long after the war ended in stalemate.*

"She is a very capable young woman," Lord Mycroft said, as if he'd read Bruce's thoughts. "She can handle herself."

"I should be with her," Bruce said. He felt like a failure, even though orders were orders. The gangplank was being withdrawn, the lines unlocked one by one ... he glanced into the darkening sky, wondering why the ship hadn't left earlier. They'd have to be careful to make it down the Thames in the semi-darkness. The river pilots were experienced men, and the river had been carefully charted over the years, but one uncharted sandbank would slow the voyage even if it didn't bring it to a humiliating end. "She shouldn't be alone."

"She won't be alone," Lord Mycroft assured him. "She has friends in Paris."

"Frenchmen," Sir Edmund said, coldly. "And traitors to their own people."

Bruce scowled at him. "You are taking a hell of a risk with her life."

"She is sworn to the crown, as are we all," Sir Edmund said. "We all do what we can. Lady Gwen is best suited for Paris and so she'll go to Paris. You are best suited for the army and so you'll go to Spain. Wave goodbye, then head back to Portsmouth. The army will be on the move shortly."

He turned and strode away. Bruce scowled at his back. It would be easy, so easy, to put a blast of magic in the man's back. If he had magic, whatever it was, it wouldn't be enough to stop him. There was no way in hell Sir Edmund was a Master Magician. He'd be in Gwen's place if he was and ... Bruce turned away, looking at the ship. It was already gliding away from the dock, a pair of lights burning brightly as darkness fell. A gust of cold wind blew over the river, sending shivers down his spine. He wanted to fly to her and yet ... it was already too late.

It isn't too late, his thoughts argued. He was a fast flyer and the ship was hardly out of range. He could be on the deck before anyone even noticed his coming. *I could get to her and ...*

He glanced at Lord Mycroft. The man was making no attempt to move, even though Gwen was gone. What was he even doing on the dockside? Bruce doubted he'd come for the good of his health. Gwen had said Lord Mycroft spent most of his time moving between his office, his club and his rooms, somewhere in Whitehall. It spoke well of him, Bruce supposed, that he'd come to say goodbye. And yet, if he stayed there, Bruce couldn't move without being instantly spotted …

"She has enemies," Lord Mycroft said. His voice was calm and composed, but there was a hint of something cold lurking behind the bland tone. "Some of them put her name forward for the mission."

Bruce stared at him. "She volunteered …"

"There was never any doubt of it," Lord Mycroft said, sharply. It was suddenly very hard to think of him as anything but an elder statesman of no small renown. Bruce was suddenly reminded of his father … no, of a version of his father with all the dross burned away to reveal a cold calculating mind determined to do whatever it had to. It made him wonder just how far Lord Mycroft would go, to accomplish his goals. "Her enemies counted on it."

"Then I'm going with her," Bruce said. He could fly to the boat now and to hell with what Sir Sander had to say about it. "She needs me."

"She needs a covert bodyguard," Lord Mycroft said. He stuck a hand into his pocket and produced a wallet, which he passed to Bruce. "Take this, then fly to the boat and stowaway. Stay out of sight – don't let anyone see you, not if it can be avoided. If she remains unaware of your presence, stay and protect her from a distance. Do you understand me?"

"Yes, My Lord," Bruce said, automatically. There were few people who commanded that sort of respect from him, but Lord Mycroft definitely qualified. Now. "What about the Duke?"

"I'll speak to him," Lord Mycroft assured him. "He will not be pleased, but he'll cope."

Bruce took a breath. "Why are you doing this? And why … why didn't you tell me earlier?"

"Because I don't want anyone to know she has a bodyguard," Lord Mycroft told him. "And because you'll go anyway, with or without permission. Won't you?"

Bruce coloured. He'd been through a dozen crazy plans, each one more insane than the last, ever since he'd been sent to Portsmouth. He could have risked flying directly to Paris – it wouldn't be that hard – or taken a boat to the French coast and flown from there. There might be watching magicians, but he was sure he could have evaded them. He might even have been able to get to the coast without using magic, then bribe someone to take him to Paris. It would hardly have been that difficult.

"Yes, My Lord," he said, finally. He tucked the wallet in his belt. "I won't let you down."

"Worry more about her," Lord Mycroft said, bluntly. His voice was very hard. "And don't let yourself be seen unless there's no other choice."

Bruce nodded, then turned away. The ship was almost lost in the gathering gloom, the only sign of its presence a single light glowing on the stern. The famed London fog was closing in … he grinned at Lord Mycroft, then hurled himself into the air and flew over the choppy waters. The river seemed to splash around him, the waters filthy beyond words, as he darted towards the ship. It rose up in front of him, seemingly both huge and incredibly flimsy. Bruce had to admire the sailors for risking their lives in the toy … he told himself, firmly, that Christopher Columbus had opened up the new world with ships no larger than the Dutch vessel in front of him. She was as safe as possible, in a world with rough seas and magicians …

He held himself by the deck as his eyes searched for a porthole. It was smaller than he'd expected, and locked besides, but he could cope. He drew on his magic, studying the lock and cabin through his mind's eye, before unpicking it and levitating himself through the porthole. The sailors would have trouble believing anyone could have sneaked through the hole, but it was child's play for him. There was no one between him and the hold, also locked. He had no difficulty getting inside and locking the hatch behind him. The air was stuffy and unpleasant, but it was better than London's ghastly stench.

And now, all I have to do is wait, he told himself. It wouldn't be that hard to avoid detection as long as he was careful, although he'd need to go look for food shortly. He hadn't had time to get anything beyond the wallet and a quick check revealed nothing save for money and a set of false papers. *It'll only take two days to reach the Dutch Republic and then ...*

He sighed inwardly as he sat down to wait. There were too many things that could go wrong. The English Channel and North Sea were notoriously dangerous bodies of water. The French Navy might spot them coming and insist on searching the ship ... hell, the Royal Navy might do the same. The naval officers on both sides wouldn't be happy at the semi-legal trade, even if their governments tolerated it for reasons of their own. And Gwen might sense his presence ... Bruce tried not to think about what she'd say, if she knew he was shadowing her from a distance. Lord Mycroft had told him to go, but still ... she'd be furious.

But I couldn't let her go alone, he thought. It was tempting to think he should go back to London and wring Pinfold's neck until he talked, but Gwen came first. *And as long as she's alive, the rest doesn't matter.*

Chapter Eleven
Ostend, Dutch Republic

wen felt … uneasy.

It wasn't something she could put into words, but … it was there. A vague sense of disquiet, a feeling something wasn't quite right, something … she paced the cabin repeatedly, checking and rechecking for peepholes and other unpleasant surprises. The cabin was tiny and smelly and generally unpleasant, yet it seemed to be private. And yet …

I don't know if Sander has a real daughter or niece or whatever, she thought, *but I feel sorry for her.*

She scowled as she sat on the bunk and waited. It wasn't the first time she'd travelled by sea – she'd sailed to America and back only a few short months ago – but she hadn't been practically kept prisoner in her cabin. It didn't matter that she could have picked the lock effortlessly with a hairpin, or simply blasted her way through the wood with magic; she was a prisoner, to all intents and purposes, and all the talk of safety merely grated on her. And yet … she scowled, remembering all the stories of what sailors did when confronted with something female, young and apparently defenceless. Sander had a point. It was better to keep temptation out of their way. Damn him.

The ship rocked again, the sailors shouting outside as they steered her into the estuary. The crossing had been rough, the ship shifting so violently under her feet that she'd wondered if they were on the verge of capsizing. If the ship keeled over … she wasn't sure if she could get out before it was too late, if water slammed into the cabin while the ship sank to the bottom of the sea. She certainly couldn't breathe underwater. She'd have to wrap herself in magic and fly up, hoping for the best. And if her oxygen ran out before she reached the surface …

She heard someone rattling at the door and forced herself to stand on wobbly legs, looking down to make sure she was decent. She'd heard women had far more rights and freedoms in the Dutch Republic, and yet Sander had insisted she wore an outfit so demure she blended into the background. She supposed it wasn't a bad choice on his part. She was meant to go unnoticed, either by watchful magicians or – more likely – guards and soldiers hunting for smugglers and criminals. There were horror stories about them too.

And a couple of people tested the lock, she reminded herself. She'd heard the lock rattle in the middle of the night. Sailors, testing their luck? Or Sander making sure she hadn't left the cabin? *If this is someone else …*

The door opened. Sander entered, his face grim. "We have arrived," he said, stiffly. "Are you ready?"

Gwen nodded, curtly. She didn't have much with her, save for a single bag she picked up and slung over her shoulder. There'd been no point in bringing much else. Her bags would probably be searched at one point, she'd been cautioned, and bringing anything obviously English would lead to questions she didn't want to answer. It was a shame she hadn't even been able to bring anything to read … she sighed inwardly, eyeing the bible on the table. It wasn't the one she'd grown up with, when she'd been a little girl. But it had been all she'd had to distract herself from the rough seas and the task ahead of her.

Sander beckoned her to follow him as he turned and walked back through the door. Gwen looked around, just to make sure she hadn't left anything behind, then walked after him as he led the way through a pair of wooden doors and out onto the deck. The stench of a coastal town slapped her in the face, so similar and yet so different to London … she looked around, interested, as they made their way to the gangplank. Ostend was … odd. There were row upon row of drab grey buildings, broken by a handful of odder designs that seemed a little out of place. A pair of churches and a synagogue sat next to a mosque and a building she didn't recognise, streams of people flowing in and out to pray for good weather and safe voyages before they set out on their travels. They seemed very diverse, she noted; men in drab clothes rubbed shoulders with men in courtly outfits and women in dresses that would scandalise High Society, men from Africa and the Ottoman Empire brushing up against men from China, Japan, India and a handful of other places Gwen had read about, but never seen. It was rare to see so much diversity in London, outside the docks, yet here …

This is a coastal city, she reminded herself, as they made their way down the gangplank and onto the street. *They trade with the entire world here.*

She kept her eyes open as they were walking. There didn't seem to be any police or customs agents checking the passengers as they disembarked, let alone searching the cargo for prohibited goods. She wondered at it, then remembered the Dutch Republic was practically *run* by its merchants, none of whom would be remotely happy with a government that impeded free trade. They had to keep the trade links open, come what may. Without them, the Dutch Republic would be nothing more than a tiny state on the edge of the Bourbon Empire. They'd be gobbled up whenever the French felt the need for a short victorious war to remind everyone they were the leading state in Europe, if not the world.

Her eyes narrowed as she spotted the gunnery positions on the edge of the harbour, covering the approaches. The Dutch weren't taking chances. The Spanish had tried to crush them, in the days of Imperial Spain, and the long and brutal war had left vast swathes of the republic in ruins. They'd fought the British and French later, barely preserving their independence against extremely powerful foes. Gwen had to admire their determination. She wondered, idly, if Britain would do so well, if she hadn't been protected by the English Channel.

The sense of unease refused to fade as they left the harbour and walked into the town itself. It felt strikingly compact, as if the population was crammed into a tiny space, yet there was no sense of oppression or disharmony. The people looked and sounded free ... her lips twitched, briefly, as she spotted a number of women walking the streets alone, without even a hint of a male guardian. Rare, in London, but here ... others manned shops, or spoke at street corners, or just seemed to enjoy life. Their outfits veered between the staid and unquestionable to the striking and stunning, some even revealing their shapely legs or the tops of their breasts. Gwen shook her head in disbelief. Anyone who walked into High Society like that, back home, would be the talk of the town. And not in a good way.

Sander reached a large warehouse complex on the edge of town and stopped. "The convoy should be ready to depart," he said, shortly. "Are you ready?"

Gwen nodded, feeling uncomfortably like a package being handed from person to person. "Yes."

"Good," Sander said. "Remember the cover story, and say as little as possible. Your French is not good."

Gwen scowled at his back as he turned away and headed into the warehouse, although she knew he had a point. She could make herself understood, but her accent was too *English* for anyone's peace of mind. There were limits to how far she could disguise herself. She'd spent some time, before departure, working with a French tutor who spoke with a southern accent, but he'd cautioned her she didn't sound anything like as countrified as she needed to be. Gwen's lips twitched sourly at the thought. It might be better to seem like a country mouse than a city lion, in a world where countryfolk were often looked down upon by their city relatives, but it was still annoying. And if her accent wasn't perfect – or too perfect – someone might start asking questions.

Better to be thought an idiot than a spy, she told herself. Paris – like London – was a melting pot. The young and eager – or desperate – flocked in droves to the capital city, hoping to make better lives for themselves and largely failing. *If they don't take me seriously ...*

She pushed the thought aside and watched as the convoy assembled. It was bigger than she'd expected – nine passenger coaches, fourteen wagons loaded with cargo – but she supposed it didn't matter. Sander had given her a crash course in the underground economy – a fancy term, she'd thought, for smuggling networks – and he'd noted that, as the formal economy staggered and collapsed, the underground was coming more and more into the open. She'd thought it was just rare and expensive products, but apparently it was food and drink as well as silks, satins and quite a few other things. It made her wonder how bad things had become in France, if smugglers were making money by sneaking *food* into the country. Couldn't France feed itself?

Sander motioned for her to clamber into a carriage, then followed her. Two older woman joined them, their eyes flickering with cold disapproval – Gwen had no trouble recognising it – that seemed to be directed more at Sander than herself. It took her a moment to realise they didn't think he should be supervising her so closely, even though her cover story insisted she was a distant relative accompanying him to learn the trade. Or perhaps they were just annoyed at having to share a carriage with a man. They could hardly talk freely with him sitting right next to them.

She peered through the window, watching as the last of the smugglers moved into position. She'd always had the impression smugglers sneaked around – there was no shortage of folk legends about heroic smugglers outwitting customs and exercise men – but the Dutch didn't seem to be making any attempt to hide. Sander had sworn blind it was safe ... she gritted her teeth as the carriage rattled into life, the drive surprisingly smooth as they made their way through the streets. That changed, the moment they passed through the gates. The Dutch roads were worse than the roads outside London, something she would have considered impossible. But then, the Dutch had a vested interest in making it difficult to drive from the French border to the cities.

A handful of horsemen – clearly French – joined them as they drove down the road, passing fortifications from simple trenches to massive fortresses bristling with guns. She was surprised the Frenchmen were being allowed to see the defences, then decided it was probably an attempt to remind them that any attempt to invade the republic would be costly even if the invaders occupied the entire country. The Dutch had plans to blow the dykes – the dams – and flood vast swathes of their own country, perhaps even drowning an invading army as it marched west into the heart of Dutch territory. Gwen had no idea how well it would work out, but she had to agree it was a reasonable deterrent. The cost of cleaning up the mess would be staggering. And if the floods destroyed an entire army …

She tried to relax as the convoy – growing larger all the time – drove onwards, the landscape shifting constantly between patches of farmland and clumps of rocky wilderness that looked tough territory for armies. Sander said nothing – she wondered if he wished they were alone, so he could talk to her – and the two women kept their thoughts to themselves. Gwen yearned for a book – for something, anything, to do – as time ticked on and on. Sander had said they'd be in France by the end of the day, but … it felt as if they were barely moving. She would have preferred a railway carriage. The French were behind England, when it came to using railways to link the disparate regions into one, but they weren't *that* far behind. Surely there'd be a rail line to the Dutch Republic or two.

But the Dutch don't want the French that close to their border, she thought. *And the French might feel very much the same way.*

The landscape continued to change as they headed

towards the border, the farms becoming larger and seemingly more prosperous. Gwen tried not to yawn, unwilling to sleep so close to Sander and two women she didn't know. The disapproving looks they kept shooting her reminded her of society matrons back home, although she didn't know what they found so annoying. Compared to some of the girls in Ostend, she was practically covered from head to toe. Perhaps they suspected she wasn't quite what she seemed. It wasn't uncommon for a wealthy man to hide an affair by claiming his mistress was actually a relative …

And yet, there'd be no need to hide it if that was the case, she reflected. *The Dutch aren't as priggish as the English.*

The carriages rattled to a halt. Gwen leaned forward to peer out the window. A handful of guards stood in front of a small building … she couldn't help thinking, looking at it, that it looked like an absurdly tiny castle. She smiled as Sander stepped past her and clambered to the ground, then held out a hand to help her follow him down. The women tut-tutted in disapproval, just loud enough to be heard. Gwen ignored them, choosing instead to look around as they walked to the guardhouse. She'd half-expected the French border to be walled solid, but there was nothing beyond the guardhouse and a handful of boundary markers that flowed into the distance and vanished in the haze. Gwen snorted at herself a moment later. France was a big country. It would be fantastically expensive to build a wall around the Dutch Republic and, if they did, it would be as pointless as Hadrian's Wall. The Romans might have expected the Scots to stay on the far side, although Gwen doubted it. They'd learnt better. So had the French.

"Stay here," Sander ordered.

Gwen nodded as Sander went forward to talk to the officer in charge. The French troops were odd. They were finely dressed – they stood out so clearly she *knew* they weren't expecting trouble – and yet, they managed to look sullen and slovenly. They didn't look anything like as tough as the Franco-Spanish troops she'd faced in America ... she had the feeling that, despite their uniforms, their morale was in the pits. She frowned. Had they even been paid? Sander certainly didn't seem to have any trouble convincing them to take a bribe ...

Sander rejoined her. "We're good," he said, as he led the way back to the carriage. The leading wagons were already driving forward, passing the guardhouse and heading into France. "No trouble at all."

Gwen blinked. "They just took the money?"

"That, and a few other things," Sander said, vaguely. "The border guards are supposed to be well paid, for their service, but their pay is often weeks or months delayed. Even when they get it ... prices are rising constantly, so the money is worth less and less and they can't feed their families. We come along and offer a bribe for safe passage, without any attempt at a search, and they leap at the chance."

"I see," Gwen said, remembering her earlier thoughts. Fancy uniforms were meaningless if you didn't get paid. "Doesn't anyone check up on them?"

Sander laughed, harshly. "There isn't an officer in the borderlands who doesn't have at least some ties to the smugglers, or the republic, or both. People have been going back and forth across the border for centuries, no matter who's in charge. To hell with religion or politics or whatever, there's money to be made. No one wants to rock the boat. And if they did, they wouldn't last long."

His expression darkened. "A couple of years ago, a senior official was sent out to clean up the mess. A wealthy man, with courtly connections and everything else he needed to ensure he didn't have to take bribes. And he committed suicide by stabbing himself in the back repeatedly. It was very tragic."

Gwen said nothing as they scrambled back into the carriage, the driver cracking the whip as soon as the door was firmly closed. A shiver ran down her spine as they passed the guardhouse, crossing the line into France. Enemy territory ... she was almost disappointed, as they rattled down the road, that it looked no different to the land on the far side of the border. The handful of farmers – all male – could have passed for Dutchmen. If she hadn't already known she'd crossed the border she wouldn't have known at all. There was nothing in view to suggest she was in a foreign country.

Her lips tightened. France was enemy territory. There were no shortage of utterly absurd stories about the evils lurking in France, ranging from monstrous people to outright monkeys. An English town had even hanged a monkey on the grounds he *had* to be a Frenchman. And yet, France looked surprisingly like England. The buildings were a little different, she had to admit, but otherwise … she shook her head in irritation. She'd read the canards they said about her. She knew very well they were nothing but lies.

Everyone demonises their enemies, she thought, ruefully. *It's easier to slander them than address their points.*

"We'll be stopping shortly for the night," Sander told her. He sounded relieved, as if he'd been more worried about the border crossing than he'd been prepared to admit. "And we'll resume our journey in the morning."

Gwen nodded, shortly. It had been a very long day.

Chapter Twelve
Border Region, France

ruce was reluctant to admit it, as he rode beside the carriages, but it had been disturbingly easy to attach himself to the convoy. He'd expected to find it hard, if not impossible, and yet they'd accepted it without a second thought. There were quite a few different groups of traders, smugglers and travellers, all heading in the same general direction, and no one had objected to another horseman. Perhaps it made a certain kind of sense – there was strength in numbers, after all – but it still bothered him. If he'd joined the convoy, who else had done the same?

The feeling of unease grew stronger as they crossed the border and headed into France itself. It was no surprise they'd bribed their way past the guards – Bruce had been a Son of Liberty long enough to know customs and excise men were mindlessly corrupt and venal – but the landscape beyond was strikingly poor. Bruce had travelled up to Canada – it had been New France, before British and Colonial American troops had conquered it – and the Frenchmen had been happy, prosperous and relatively peaceful. France itself ... Bruce wasn't a farming expert, but he had the sense the farmers were producing less and less with every passing year. A surprising number of farms seemed poor, or abandoned, or ... it boded ill, he thought, for the future. If France really couldn't feed itself ...

He'd expected the convoy to stop at a traveller's inn, as would have happened in Britain, but instead they came to a halt in a clearing, a few miles inside the border. Bruce clambered off his horse and stretched, keeping a wary eye out for Gwen. It might have been smarter to follow the convoy at a safe distance, and he intended to put some distance between them as soon as he could, but a lone horseman would inevitably draw more attention when he crossed the border. Bruce didn't want to risk it. Lord Mycroft had given him some money, but nowhere near enough to convince the guards to look the other way. They'd be a great deal more suspicious of a man on his own.

There was no grumbling, he was surprised to note, as the convoy prepared a hasty meal, then settled down to rest. The womenfolk – including Gwen – were kept separate from the men, something Bruce knew would annoy her even though it would ensure she didn't stick out too much. He accepted a request to join the guards for a few hours, then sat back and waited as the remainder of the convoy headed to bed. Some would sleep under the wagons, but others would rest their weary heads under the stars. Bruce felt a twinge of pain as he forced himself to stay awake. There were four guards and if they all fell asleep …

The very fact they need to establish a guard rota is bad news, he thought, as he concentrated on smoothing his aches and pains. *Do they expect to be attacked?*

It wasn't a pleasant thought. Highwaymen weren't unknown in Britain, but they rarely attacked anything bigger than a single carriage or two. There might be patches of extreme violence up in the north of Scotland and Ireland, from what he'd heard, but England was relatively safe. France felt more like the wilderness to the east of the colonies, back in America. Patches of civilisation, tiny outposts of European civilisation surrounded by unexplored and untamed lands … no one dared travel alone, outside the stockades, unless they were very brave or very stupid. Bruce was a powerful magician, perhaps one of the most powerful in the world, and yet even *he* wouldn't go alone. Not there.

He gritted his teeth. He was a skilled horseman – he'd been learning to ride almost as soon as he'd learnt to walk – but he had his limits. The horse he'd hired at staggering expense didn't seem to like him either. He was going to be sore tomorrow, no matter what he did. He was almost tempted to try to stay awake all night, although he knew it was a very bad idea. He'd be in no shape for anything the following morning.

The night air seemed cool, yet there was an edge of *threat* to the wind that made it hard to relax. He closed his eyes, opening his mind gingerly. There was no way to be sure there were no enemy sorcerers watching for invaders, and Gwen herself wasn't that far away, but as long as he was careful there'd be nothing for them to detect. The real danger was a mind-reader insisting on checking each and every person in the convoy … not, he supposed, that even the French would dare risk *that*. Talkers were the most feared and hated magicians, even though they were far less destructive than Movers or Blazers. But then, no one liked the thought of having their mind read …

Something *brushed* against his mind, a flicker that was gone almost as soon as he detected it. Bruce bit his lip hard to keep from reacting. A questing mind ...? Someone taking the risk of reaching out with their mind, in hopes of detecting another responding to the probe? Or … it didn't feel like a provocation. It felt more like a flicker of magic far too close for comfort. It wasn't Gwen. Her magic was far more controlled.

Bruce stood, drawing on all his stealth to slip away without making a sound. The other guards would think he was going to relieve himself, somewhere in the trees. Bruce's lips twisted in disgust. They wouldn't expect him to go that far, not when there could be *anything* lurking in the shadows. He'd grown up on stories of the men who opened up vast tracts of America to settlement … and what happened to those men when they went too far from the campfire, when they were caught and killed by the Indians. There weren't any Indians here, he was sure, but someone was far too close for comfort. The pulse of magic was closer now – and stronger. He didn't like it.

His eyes seemed to sharpen as he drew on his magic. He'd never been anything like as precise as Gwen, when it came to the mental arts, but he knew enough to be dangerous. The darkness faded, as if it were broad daylight. He saw – sensed – a handful of people inching towards the camp, at least one of them a magician. An unpleasant sensation ran down his spine, as if someone had brushed their hands against his body without his permission. A charmer, he realised dully. And a very powerful one too.

The men came into sharp focus as he paused, careful to hide within the shadows. A couple looked like deserters – they wore military uniforms, tattered and torn – but the remainder were just bandits. They seemed famished, as if they hadn't had a decent meal for years. Bruce shuddered in disgust. They'd be desperate, which would make them dangerous. He'd overheard someone claiming the French had resorted to cannibalism, something he'd dismissed the moment he'd heard it. Now, he wondered if he'd been wrong. If the French really were that desperate …

He pushed the thought aside. He could sneak back to the camp and raise the alarm and … and then what? Some of the smugglers were armed, but there was no guarantee they could beat the bandits. Even if they did, the fighting might draw attention from the border guards … particularly if Gwen used her magic. The bandits had remained undetected for quite some time – Bruce suspected that meant the French didn't have magicians to spare for bandit hunting – but that didn't mean someone wouldn't take notice. Better to deal with them himself and hope for the best.

And they will loot the convoy, rape the women and then kill everyone, he thought, as he scooped up a rock and captured it with his mind's eye. The bandits wouldn't want to leave any witnesses. *They don't deserve to live.*

He pushed the rock forward with his mind. It hissed silently through the air and struck a bandit with terrifying force, cracking his skull so hard he couldn't make a sound before he died. Bruce felt the man's mind snap out of existence, but had no time to consider the enormity of what he'd done. He caught the man's body with his magic and lowered it gingerly to the ground, then steered the rock into the second bandit. His skull shattered, droplets of blood and gore flying everywhere. The other bandits tensed, hands snapping to weapons. They had surprisingly good discipline, Bruce noted coldly. They didn't make a sound, even though they knew something had gone wrong.

For all they know, he tripped and hurt himself, he thought, as he reached out with his magic once more. The forest was a surprisingly noisy place, even at night. He'd actually thought it was quieter than it should be, although he wasn't sure why. The bandits didn't know they'd been spotted, not yet, and if they were quiet they might still be able to get into position to attack the convoy or back off without confirming their presence to the guards. *But it is too late for them.*

The closest bandit had no warning as Bruce's magic tightened on his skull and crushed it to a pulp. The further ones started to move backwards, their eyes searching for threats, but it was too late. Bruce killed them all, one by one, as he searched for the magician. A man broke and ran, heading into the distance. Bruce guessed he was the magician – most Charmers were cowards – and reached out to catch the man's leg, sending him crashing headfirst into the ground. His senses swept the forest for more threats and confirmed there were no more bandits save for the leader, then relaxed. Bruce walked calmly to the fallen man and stared down at him, then turned him over. The man was a sinewy weakling, surprising for someone who worked on the farm. His face was pockmarked with traces of smallpox …

"Let me go," the man hissed. His voice dripped magic, despite his pain. "Let me go …"

Bruce felt the magic batter against his mental defences, then fade to nothingness. Charmers could be very dangerous, particularly if their victim had no idea he was being influenced, but they had their limits. One didn't *need* magic to resist, just a tight grip on one's own thoughts and feelings. He reached down and pressed the man's lips closed. Actually tearing out the man's tongue might not be enough to still his power – Charm worked in ways no one quite understood – but it would cripple it. He'd certainly need time to relearn how to use his power and Bruce doubted he'd have the time. A man leading a mob of bandits – and given how poorly they'd acted, he suspected he knew how the Charmer had taken control – was pretty much always on the edge.

"I have questions," he whispered, pitching his voice as low as he could. Sound could travel surprisingly far in the darkness and if the guards had heard anything, they'd be on the alert for more. "Come with me and answer them and I'll let you go. Refuse to answer and I'll hurt you."

He yanked the bandit to his feet and pushed him further into the forest. It wasn't easy to guess a safe distance, so he walked further than he thought necessary. The bandit didn't try to struggle. Bruce was almost disappointed. Charmers tended not to engage in fisticuffs – and the bandit knew Bruce was stronger even if he didn't know Bruce had magic – but still he should have tried to fight. Or run. Or something …

They reached a small clearing, illuminated by moonlight. Bruce shoved the bandit to the ground and bent over him. Dark eyes stared back, full of fright. The bandit probably wasn't used to losing control, particularly with his magic. Bruce had heard stories of Charmers – including a handful who never realised they actually *had* magic – taking control so effortlessly resistance was utterly futile. Like most bullies, they crumbled when challenged by someone more powerful.

"Pathetic," he said. "Why did you attack us?"

"We're starving," the bandit said. Bruce tasted the truth in his words … and more besides, a disgusting pulse of lust and bitterness that boded ill for anyone who fell into his hands. "We need food."

"And you thought to rob us," Bruce said. There'd only been twenty bandits, nineteen of whom were dead. The convoy outnumbered them … although, if the bandits managed to take out the guards, they might just manage to get the drop on everyone else. One could go quite some distance through bluff, bluster and a willingness to be absolutely ruthless if push came to shove. "Why?"

"We need food," the bandit repeated.

Bruce frowned. It was hard to be sure, but the man sounded a little more educated than he'd expected. "How did you become a bandit anyway?"

The bandit glared at him. "Who are you?"

"I'm asking the questions," Bruce said. He rested his foot on the man's chest, daring him to resist. "You're an educated man, aren't you? Why are you a bandit?"

"I …" The bandit sagged noticeably. "I went to school. I was going to be a schoolmaster. They discovered I had magic. They were going to kill me, just for existing, and so I fled and became the leader of a gang and …"

"You compelled them to follow you," Bruce said. He couldn't imagine the bandits following their leader willingly. He was too much of a wimp in a land where strength came first. "Why were they trying to kill you? Who did you Charm?"

"No one," the man protested. Bruce suspected that wasn't entirely true. It would be quite easy to seduce a wife, or a daughter, or … who knew? Perhaps he'd tried to charm a tax inspector and discovered, too late, the man was trained to resist charm. "They wanted to kill me for existing!"

Bruce frowned. He'd been told the French had banned magic, to the point of executing every magician who fell into their hands, but that policy had fallen by the wayside as soon as they'd realised how much magic helped their British enemies. They'd still crippled themselves, killing hundreds of magicians and convincing others to keep their powers secret as long as possible … or to flee, either to England or the New World or somewhere else that wouldn't try to murder them. And yet … he scowled down at the man. He might have been forced to flee – Bruce had his doubts, knowing how much damage a Charmer could do if he didn't realise he had magic – but that didn't excuse his crimes. Bruce had grown up in America. He didn't coddle men who preyed on their fellows …

And I can't leave him alive, he thought, coldly. He had no doubt the bandit, lacking any faith in his magic and all too aware his gang had been slaughtered, wouldn't hesitate to sell him out. *He could tell the government about me.*

He bounced a handful of questions off the bandit, although the man knew little useful and cared less. Yes, farming was growing less and less profitable. Yes, taxes were getting higher and higher. Yes, the nobles and the clergy and the well-connected weren't paying their fair share … they were even being coddled by the government, whilst the poor were taxed out of house and home. The entire countryside was simmering with anger and rebellion, the bandits merely the tip of a growing iceberg heading straight for the ship of state. Bruce was surprised the countryside hadn't exploded already. But then, it was never easy to predict when sullen anger would turn to violence.

"Let me go," the bandit pleaded. His magic leaked into his voice, to no avail. "Please …"

Bruce reached out with his magic and crushed the bandit's skull. The man went limp. Bruce sighed inwardly. The man was no Robin Hood, no Ethan Allen … no heroic warrior who stole from the rich and gave to the poor, as if such figures really existed. He might have been driven out of house and home, but – since then – he'd looted and raped and killed his way across the countryside. His band of cutthroats would have slaughtered the entire convoy if they'd been given a chance. The man had died relatively peacefully – and painlessly – and that was all Bruce would do for him.

Rest in peace, he thought, as he searched the man's clothes. There was nothing; no coins, no maps, not even a weapon or two. Proof, if he'd needed it, that pickings had been very slim indeed. There was no point in trying to steal from people who didn't have anything worth the risk. *Goodbye.*

He turned and made his way slowly back to the campsite. It hadn't been that long since he'd left, but … he allowed himself a sigh of relief as the guards paid no heed to him. If they'd heard something … he scowled as he remembered something else the bandit had said, something that matched his own observations. There was much less wildlife in the region than he'd expected, not even small animals scurrying through the undergrowth. He didn't like it. If the locals were hunting so desperately they didn't leave a breeding population behind …

Good god, he thought, as the guard shift finally came to an end. Crop failures were hardly unknown – he'd heard of farmers losing everything they'd planted to locusts or unexpected weather – but this was on an impossible scale. It was almost too big to comprehend. *The entire country might be on the verge of total famine.*

Chapter Thirteen
Paris, France

aris," Sander said. He'd grown more willing to speak, once the two women had departed … not without a final sniff. "Once we're through the gates, we'll be there."

Gwen nodded. It had been an eye-opening trip in many ways, even as the convoy had started to split up, the various groups heading to their separate destinations. She'd seen the lands and farms around London and noted how they seemed to flow into the city, but the region around Paris was worse. It was hard to be sure – she was no expert – but the small farms appeared to be on their very last legs, while the larger fields looked as if they were being worked to death. There were signs of trouble everywhere, from armed guards patrolling the roads to burnt-out houses, farms and churches, the latter apparently desecrated as well. Gwen understood, better than she cared to admit. The Bourbons had forced the Pope to bend the knee to them long ago, putting the Catholic Church at their service and ordering the clergy to keep the commoners in line. It hadn't taken long for dissidents to start popping up in previously peaceful regions.

And for the church to be seen as just another oppressor, she reflected. The French Church was one of the greatest landholders in the country, snapping up lands with a passion that far exceeded any sense of prudence.

Worse, it didn't pay taxes. Gwen had always found it maddening to be lectured on social propriety by women who clearly didn't practice it themselves and she assumed the average Frenchman, when told about his duty to pay taxes to his king, felt much the same way. *No wonder so many churches are being attacked.*

The landscape seemed to grow darker as they crossed a river and headed down to Paris itself. The city was surrounded by slums, rows upon rows of shanty housing and shacks that were grim and dirty and crammed with the poor and the desperate. The hopelessness was stifling ... she shuddered as she saw a handful of women selling themselves, their children sitting next to them, as listless as the rest. The guards patrolled in small groups, where they patrolled at all. She tried not to be sick as the wind shifted, blowing an unspeakable stench into her face. The French knew how to boil water and wash thoroughly to keep their population healthy, but it stank as if they'd forgotten basic hygiene. She turned away as she saw a young child lapping from a pool of brackish water. If the poor child lasted a year in the slums ...

Her stomach twisted painfully. She wasn't sure – yet – if she wanted children. She'd never discussed it with Bruce – the thought reminded her there were a lot of *other* things they'd never discussed – and yet, she was sure he'd feel an obligation to have at least one or two children. Gwen wasn't her father's only child – and she wouldn't even carry the family name after she married – but Bruce was an only child. He'd need to have children to carry on the family name. And ... she tried not to think about it. She knew how dangerous it could be to carry a child to term, even in the best of places. Here ... she didn't want to contemplate it for a moment. Any pregnant woman in the slums was unlikely to survive giving birth.

No wonder the French moved their court out of the city, she thought, as they neared the walls. Paris was supposed to be beautiful, but – to her – it looked like just another city. The walls seemed to come from another era, in which the city might come under siege at any moment, yet the shacks and slums pressed so close to the walls she had no doubt they were effectively useless. *The king wouldn't want to be so close to this ... this nightmare.*

She sucked in her breath and forced herself to wait as they joined a long line of wagons, carts and carriages trying to get through the gates. A stream of people on foot walked past them, mainly farmers and other countryfolk ... she guessed they were looking for work in the big city. Anyone who was anyone would ride, on a horse or in a carriage, and the poor ... she cursed under her breath as the line inched forward, painfully slow. Why didn't they just open up the gates and let everyone come and go as they pleased?

Because the city is already bursting with people, she thought, answering her own question. *And they want to know who's coming into their capital before they let them pass.*

It felt like hours before the carriage finally reached the towering gatehouse. The guards were more alert than the border guards, she noted, although they paid little attention to her. She relaxed, slightly, even though they'd expect her to be annoyed at how they were pawing their way through her bag. It wasn't as if she'd brought dozens of dresses and expensive pantaloons ... how could she, when she was pretending to be a trader's distant relative? She certainly couldn't be expected to dress to the nines, let alone ... she shook her head and waited, keeping her mouth shut as the guards bombarded Sander with questions. He answered them all calmly, even when they turned insulting. It was a relief when they were finally allowed to drive through the gates and into the city itself.

"Better to let them find a small problem, than wonder why they can't find anything," Sander commented. "As long as they think we're not up to something really bad ..."

Gwen nodded, studying the streets of Paris with a cold critical eye. Paris had been a favoured destination of the Grand Tourists, before the war, and their descriptions had imbued the city with a brilliance and a glamour she considered sorely lacking. There were streets of remarkable elegance, she noted, but the majority were as dark and grimy as any London could boast. The alleyways were crammed with shacks, just like the slums outside the walls, while the inns were crowded with men drinking away their sorrows. Tension hung in the air, a promise of violence and death to come. She hadn't felt anything like it, not even during the worst of the Swing. London's poor had the opportunity to emigrate to the New World. Paris didn't seem to have that option.

She kept her thoughts to herself as a military patrol strode past, the officer on horseback and his men on foot. Bastard. She understood the importance of projecting authority, but she doubted the officer was trying anything of the sort. Being on a horse while his men walked just made him look insecure, if not a coward planning to gallop away if the crowd turned and attacked them. Horses were fantastic beasts of war, she knew, but they could be very vulnerable in confined spaces. The officer might be an idiot as well as a coward.

The carriage drove into a courtyard and rattled to a halt. "Home away from home," Sander said, cheerfully. He opened the hatch and jumped down, then helped her to step after him. "And your friend should already be on the way."

Gwen nodded. They'd stopped beside a building that looked like a cross between an inn and a warehouse. Teams of men were already walking towards the remains of the convoy, hurrying to unload so the legal goods could be sold and the semi-legal and flat-out illicit goods smuggled further into the city. Gwen suspected they didn't need to move so quickly, but who knew? Paris wasn't the borderlands. It was a great deal harder to bribe the local police and guardsmen, from what she'd been told. The military patrols, in particular, were drawn from the fancier regiments. They were often too wealthy to bribe.

Sander showed her into a small room and told her to

wait. Gwen sat down and picked up a newspaper, her eye running down the articles. She'd been told the French press was heavily censored, when it wasn't controlled – directly or indirectly – by the government, but she hadn't realised how much was kept from the population until she read the newspaper for herself. There was no mention of anything from America, no hint of revolution in Spain, no suggestion a French invasion force had stormed British beaches, only to be driven back into the sea. And nothing, nothing at all, about food shortages and all the other problems she'd noted during the trip from Ostend to Paris. The writing was so bland it was easy to see why so few people believed it.

She leaned back in her chair, opening her mind slightly. There were no magicians – no *active* magicians – near her, at least as far as she could tell. There were no suspicious minds either, although that was meaningless. She couldn't passively read someone's mind, not without reaching out and ... she shook her head. Right now, it would be dangerous to risk opening her mind any further. God alone knew what might crawl into her thoughts.

A mind brushed against hers, lightly. She started, gathering her power. If she was caught ... she'd have to fight her way out and hope she could make it clear of the city before she ran out of magic. If there was anywhere, anywhere at all, where the French would concentrate their magicians ... she breathed a sigh of relief as Irene Adler stepped into the room, wearing a dress that made her look like just another poor woman working desperately to keep food on the table and a roof above her head. Her old friend and tutor looked Gwen up and down, then grinned. Their minds touched again, a subtle warning to be quiet as Irene unslung her bag and opened it to reveal another dress. Gwen took it and the hat, then pulled them on and followed Irene through the door. Sander knew she was going. Anyone else shouldn't notice them at all.

She kept her eyes open as they left the warehouse and made their way through the streets, carefully avoiding the city centre. The people on the streets looked drab and sullen, although there were flashes of colour and bright display that drew the eye for a few brief seconds. The whores waved and beckoned, even to two women … Irene ignored them and Gwen followed her lead. It felt like she was adrift in a dreamlike world, everything ever-so-slightly out of place, by the time they stepped into a simple dressmaker's shop. Irene closed the door and slid the bolt. Gwen sagged, feeling safe for the first time in days.

Safe, her thoughts mocked. *You're not that far from the Bastille.*

"It's been a while," Irene said, as she turned to lead Gwen further into the shop. She spoke perfect French, with a surprisingly formal accent. Gwen wasn't surprised. Irene changed her personas as easily as Gwen changed her dresses. "I hear you're getting married."

"Yes," Gwen said, in English. "I …"

"French," Irene snapped. "You speak that tongue here, someone will overhear and report it."

Gwen flushed, cursing herself. It had been a stupid mistake. "Sorry," she said, in French. "It's been a long day."

"For everyone," Irene said. "We were lucky we had this place organised ahead of time. Even so, when *she* turned up, we had to scramble to deal with her."

Simone, Gwen thought. *Does Irene trust her?*

She leaned forward, putting the question into words. "Can we trust her?"

"She guards her thoughts well, that one," Irene said. "Not that I wouldn't do the same, if I was in her place. We owe her nothing and she knows it. But I've picked up enough hints from around here" – she waved a hand in the air – "to think *something* is going to change and change fast. They're not dispatching a major force to Spain."

Gwen frowned. Bruce was going to Spain … he might be there already, if he'd been assigned to the lead elements. The Duke of India had talked about using rebel-held ports to unload his army ... if the ports remained in rebel hands, when the Royal Navy arrived. It was odd the French weren't taking the crisis seriously. If the British landed an army and took control of Portugal, and secured the borders between Portugal and Spain, it would be extremely difficult to dislodge them.

"Why?" Gwen found it hard to believe. "Don't they know the risks?"

"Yes, or so I assume," Irene agreed. "A number of courtiers have very private doubts ... never said out loud, of course. They assume, rightly or wrongly, that expressing their doubts will get them beheaded. They might be right. Versailles has done a lot of clamping down over the last few days, after an anarchist broke into a ballroom and tried to blow up the guests. If anyone really has raised objections, I haven't heard about it."

Gwen nodded. "Would you?"

"It's hard to say," Irene said. "The French aristocracy is a mess. Anyone who can prove they have aristocratic blood is legally entitled to a pension, a room and a place at court. The cost is staggering, even though most aristos aren't really entitled to *that* much. The bigger aristos, the landholders and a handful of military officers as well as the blood royal, are the ones who are really important, and – of those – the ones with *real* influence are the ones the king keeps close. They are smart enough to keep their mouths shut, at least when they don't know who's listening."

"It sounds like a nightmare," Gwen observed.

"It is." Irene shot her a mischievous look. "King Louis – every third Frenchman is named Louis – has real power. His wife has very little, at least in public. Even so, they can't change protocol. They have almost no privacy, surrounded by aristos dancing attendance on them while trying to get the king to agree to ... to anything. Half the aristos have claims on property and titles held by the other half, which means they're constantly suing for the return of ... of anything. The other half are determined to keep whatever they've got ..."

She shook her head. "It's no surprise to *me* that very little gets done. They need to reform just about everything, from land ownership to the tax system and religious settlements, before the country explodes, but every time someone proposes a change everyone else gangs up on him and the suggestion is firmly buried. So yes ... I do think that anyone with doubts would have kept his mouth shut. There's nothing to be gained by getting one's head lopped off for nothing."

Gwen nodded. "And to think I used to imagine being presented at court."

Irene snorted. "You should be glad you're not a young woman living here," she said. "It's a whole different world. The majority of the aristos have nothing better to do, but chase women – or men – and plot against their peers. You can't wave a hand without hitting someone plotting against someone else, often for the smallest of stakes. The queen is a particularly enthusiastic plotter, I'm sorry to report. She has little else to do with her life."

"Poor woman," Gwen said. It felt odd to feel sympathy for a French queen, but ... she knew what it was like to be trapped in a goldfish bowl. "What now?"

"I have deliveries to make," Irene said. "As far as anyone is concerned, you're my new apprentice from the south. Your mother was English which will explain your accent, if anyone bothers to ask. That'll give us a chance to explore the city, letting you get your bearings before we make contact with *her* and decide how to proceed. I was ... discouraged ... from making any contacts with the underground, at least until now. And we might walk into very real trouble."

Gwen frowned. "How so?"

"Paris is on the edge," Irene said, bluntly. "The police are doing what they can to break up any revolutionary circles, but ... there are more revolutionaries than policemen and a hell of a lot more angry and frustrated people on the streets, keen to take their rage out on any passing policemen. There are parts of the city that are simply too dangerous for the police now, or for anything less than a cavalry regiment. Even the upper-class districts aren't exactly safe now. Half of them are revolutionaries themselves or think the coming revolt will end with *them* on the top ... Gwen, it makes the anger and ambition that drove the Swing seem like nothing."

"Ambition?"

"Oh, yes," Irene confirmed. "You want to be a high-class lawyer? You'd better have good connections or you'll never get anywhere. The ones who don't ...? They're hungry and smart and very resentful at being unable to use their education. They want to climb through merit and they can't, because merit is a feather compared to the stone of having the right connections or the right bloodline or whatever. And they're not even the worst of the problems facing the country. Everyone is angry and everyone wants to fight."

Gwen swallowed. "How long do we have?"

"I don't know," Irene said. "The king is either unaware of the problem or unable to do anything about it. The aristos – and the church – would sooner die than give up a tiny fragment of their power, possessions and prestige. And there's a war on ... some commoners are patriotic enough to think they should remain quiet as long as the fighting is going on, while others are starting to think the demands of the war will force the king to grant concessions ..."

She paused significantly. Gwen nodded. "Concessions he might not be able to grant."

"No," Irene agreed. "Gwen, one way or another, all hell is going to break loose soon. And when it does, we have to be ready."

Chapter Fourteen
Paris, France

ruce had thought the countryside was bad. Paris was worse.

He fell back as the remnants of the convoy approached the gates, choosing to abandon the horse rather than try to take him into the city. He had no suitable papers, no way to convince the guards he was allowed to pass through without further ado ... he considered, briefly, trying to charm his way through before dismissing the thought as too reckless even for him. The guardsmen on the gates would probably have been trained to detect and resist Charm and even if they weren't, there were too many of them to be sure he could convince them all to believe he had every right to be there. He needed to find another way into the city.

The stench assaulted his nostrils as he strolled through the slums, cloaking himself in an illusion that would make him hard to spot. It was hard to keep his mind focused on the magic when, everywhere he looked, he saw poverty and deprivation on an unimaginable scale. He'd seen Indian camps after traders had sold them their fill of alcohol; and slave ships crammed with their human cargo; and yet, neither of them came close to the horror surrounding the city of lights. Paris was supposed to be the greatest city in Europe, a favoured destination for British tourists and American dissidents, but ... he wondered, sourly, if the nightmare surrounding him was why so many Sons of Liberty had gone to Paris and simply vanished. The reality of Paris might have convinced them they were on the wrong side.

Or the French decided they were no longer useful and executed them, he thought, as he tried to breathe through his mouth. The stench, incredibly, was growing worse as he neared the river. The waters were sluggish with waste, from human piss and shit to effluent from factories on the other side of the city. The French had been caught by surprise by the industrial revolution, as well as magic, but they'd been making up for lost time with all the desperation of men who knew they had to catch up or be left behind. *The American guests probably made the mistake of talking frankly to their autocratic hosts.*

His stomach twisted, painfully, as he surveyed the river. The French had built a bridge across the river and turned it into a checkpoint, searching every boat that tried to make its way into the city. Guardsmen – in surprisingly fancy uniforms – inspected every passing vessel with dismaying competence, ignoring protests from the crews. They looked ready to slap down any troublemakers with extreme force, Bruce noted; they certainly didn't seem inclined to tolerate much of anything. He wondered why the crowd hadn't overwhelmed them by sheer force of numbers, then spotted the fortifications and turrets resting just inside the city. The idea of the Royal Navy forcing its way up the river to attack Paris was absurd, but that hadn't stopped the French turning their city into a fortress. They were more paranoid about their own people than their traditional enemies.

He turned away, heading back into the slums. The guards on the bridge were too alert to challenge and he'd bet good money there were magicians behind them, ready to deal with any magical threats. He wondered if he'd made a mistake by not trying to slip through the gates, then dismissed the thought. He still didn't have papers. He briefly considered trying to waylay a traveller and stealing his papers, before deciding he wouldn't know enough to fool the guards. They weren't just looking at papers and internal passports. They were asking questions and making careful note of the answers. And if the answers were wrong ...

Bruce mentally kicked himself as he wandered, unwilling to risk stopping and waiting for nightfall. The poverty brushed closer, from men desperately cooking what little they could find over open fires to women selling themselves and their children ... his stomach twisted in utter disgust as he saw a woman offering her young daughter to men who clearly had at least *some* money. Bruce had thought himself used to horror – he'd seen more than he'd wished, even in genteel New York – but this was beyond anything he'd ever envisaged. Men, women and children caught rats ... he saw a child catch a rat, only to have it yanked out of his hand by an older boy who ran into the slums and vanished before anyone could give chase. The hopelessness surrounded him, a listlessness that made him wonder how many people had just lain down and died. There were no bodies within view, as far as he could tell. He dared not think about what their absence might mean.

His heart sank, again, as he spotted a handful of clergymen. One was preaching the importance of obedience to authority, to King Louis – God's regent on Earth – and to the Royal Family ... and, of course, to the aristocracy. The others handed out bowls of soup and mugs of water, after speaking quickly to each visitor to determine their faith. Bruce shuddered. France had been racked by religious conflict for years and yet, surely it didn't matter in the face of such deprivation. He looked at the clergymen, wearing decent clothes and looking down on the people they were trying to help, and felt a surge of hatred. He'd never thought much of the independent preachers who preached to the poor and downtrodden in London and New York, but at least they were trying to help. The French priests seemed more inclined to lecture the poor than try to help.

Nightfall came rapidly, but not rapidly enough. Bruce

kept himself out of sight as everyone who could scurried into makeshift shacks and shanties, leaving the night to criminals and rebels. There were no visible guards on patrol – he was amused to note the priests had vanished with the sunlight – and no one trying to take their place, save for a handful of criminal gangs. The population was too poor to be worth robbing. He scowled as he slipped past a ragged tent, noticing a man trying to sweet-talk a young woman who couldn't be older than Gwen ... the hell of it, he thought, was that life in a brothel would be far – far – kinder than life in the slums. And yet ... he bit down, hard, on the urge to intervene. He needed to get into the city and hide before daybreak.

The walls rose up in front of him, a solid stone barrier that wouldn't have stopped an army for more than a minute or two. A volley from a battery of modern artillery would smash it down effortlessly. He wondered, idly, just how many tunnels had been dug under the wall, then decided it was probably pointless. The slums pressed against the walls so solidly there were no shortage of places for someone to climb up and over the walls. He found a suitable clambering spot and slipped upwards, silently grateful his magic let him see in the dark. The guards overhead didn't have lights or magic. The air seemed to grow lighter as he lifted himself onto a rickety roof and scrabbled onto the wall. Something creaked below him, cautioning him he needed to move fast. New York's rooftops were reasonably solid. The slums were so fragile a man climbing on the roof might fall through into the nightmare below.

He paused as soon as he got onto the wall, looking into Paris itself. The city of lights was shrouded in darkness. A handful of government buildings were lit up, and he could see some streetlights, but the remainder of the city was dark and cold. He shuddered in disgust, then cursed himself – again – as he realised his second and greatest mistake. Paris was huge ... where was Gwen? Sander had been supposed to take her to his warehouse and hand her over to ... someone. Who? And where? Bruce gritted his teeth in frustration. He really hadn't thought it through very well. Gwen could be anywhere within the city and as long as she didn't make herself obvious, he'd never find her.

A sound caught his ear and he froze. A scraping sound, behind him … he turned, slowly, to see a gang of workers – smugglers – carefully scrambling over the wall. They carried heavy bags, crammed with … Bruce had no idea, but they clearly knew what they were doing. They didn't seem to have any difficulty navigating in the dark …

They'd know where to find the rebel underground, he thought. If there'd been rebels in New York and Boston, there'd be rebels in Paris. *They might be able to help me.*

He inched forward, keeping his eyes open. The smugglers had shoved ladders into position on the inner side of the wall, allowing them to scramble to the ground. Bruce wasn't surprised. The wall wasn't intended to defend the city from invaders, but to keep the poor and dispossessed out. He hesitated, trying to think what to say. Smuggler rings tended to be paranoid at the best of times, from what he'd learnt when he'd been a Son of Liberty, and rarely trusted anyone who wasn't part of their family. They were often family businesses …

A crack ran through the air, so loud he thought it was a gunshot. A ladder was breaking … he acted instinctively, reaching out with his magic to catch the two men clambering down before they fell. One of them cried out as he was lowered to the ground, the other – with more presence of mind – drew a dagger the moment his feet touched the muddy pavement, his eyes flickering from side to side. Bruce wondered, as he levitated himself down too, if he'd made another mistake. The vast majority of local magicians were government servants … but then, why would a government servant save a falling smuggler? The government wouldn't hesitate to execute them if – when – they were caught.

He stepped forward, suddenly unsure what to say. "Greetings," he said, in careful French. Gwen had been right about that too. His French was good, but far from perfect. He'd just have to claim to be a sailor who worked with men from all over the world and hope no one tried to poke holes in his tale. "I need your help and …"

The smuggler muttered a word in a language Bruce didn't recognise. His mind churned. The British Government had worked hard to convince the Welsh, Scots and Irish to stop using their own languages and speak English exclusively … had the French done the same? He doubted they could have excluded Spanish, given how many people spoke Spanish over French across the Bourbon Empire, but everything else …? Did France have languages other than French? He had no time to figure it out.

"Magician," one of the men said, sullenly. "What do you want?"

"A place to stay for the night," Bruce said. He'd discuss the rest later. "That's all."

The smugglers muttered together, what little he could hear in the same unknown language. His mind churned, wondering if he'd made a mistake. If they betrayed him …

The sound of running footsteps assaulted his ears. Bruce cursed under his breath. He'd wondered why there were no visible guards … they weren't on the battlements, he noted, but lurking in the shadows underneath. The broken ladder had called them as definitely as … he shook his head and reached for his magic, bracing himself. The guards needed to be stopped without killing them …

"Close your eyes," he said, sharply. "Now!"

He turned and generated the brightest light he could. It flared for a second – he didn't dare hold it any longer – but it was long enough. The guards staggered back, dropping their weapons and rubbing their eyes. He doubted he'd blinded them permanently, but it didn't matter. He'd used so little magic to generate the light that it was quite possible it had gone unnoticed, that the French would look for a more scientific explanation …

A hand grabbed his arm. "This way," the smuggler snapped. "And quickly!"

Bruce gritted his teeth, keeping his eyes open as the smugglers led him through a maze of backstreets and alleyways. He'd half-expected the roads to be empty, but there were people sleeping in doorways or slipping up and down under cover of darkness … someone shouted behind them, but the sound was swallowed by the immensity of the city. Paris was … he shook his head. Some streets seemed dangerously hot, others so cold he shivered helplessly.

The smugglers stopped by a darkened building and opened a hatch. Bruce watched the first two jump down, then catch the sacks as they were lowered into the darkness and placed carefully out of sight. The remainder dropped down, motioning for him to follow before pulling the hatch back into place and lighting a lantern. Bruce looked around, then nodded in understanding. He'd seen something like it, back in New York. The innkeepers preferred to lower barrels of beer into a basement, rather than roll them through the inn and down the stairs …

"Well," a droll voice said. "My name is Jean-Luc. Who are you?"

"A friend," Bruce said, vaguely. He hadn't had time to come up with a cover story, let alone a false name. Was *Bruce* a common name in France? He had no idea. *Gwen* could pass unnoticed, but *Bruce?* "And a runaway magician."

Jean-Luc – if that was the man's real name, Bruce would eat his hat – studied Bruce thoughtfully. Bruce looked back at him, trying to assess the man. Jean-Luc was short, with curly black hair, dark eyes and an unshaven face. His clothes were dark and drab … not, Bruce reflected, that a smuggler would wear something particularly noticeable. There were traces of hard work clearly visible on his hands, scars that suggested he'd been working from a very early age. He wondered, idly, what Jean-Luc made of him.

"A runaway," Jean-Luc repeated. "From whom?"

"I came into my magic back home," Bruce said,

carefully. It wasn't an uncommon story, from what he'd heard. A great many magicians remained undiscovered until they used their magic for the first time. "I killed an aristo who wanted to rape my sister and had to go on the run. I came here to see what work I could find ..."

Jean-Luc snorted. "A bad place to hide from the aristos, my friend."

Bruce smiled. "Would they *expect* to look for me here?"

He waited, bracing himself. Jean-Luc might not buy the story. It was plausible – it had happened – and there was certainly no way it could be easily disproved, but the smuggler hadn't lasted so long by being trusting. He might think he owed Bruce a favour or two, yet he might also wonder if he was being conned. And if he knew enough about magic to realise Bruce had shown two different kinds of power ...

"You're a Mover," Jean-Luc said. Oddly, he used the English word. Bruce did his best to show as little reaction as possible. "How did you make the flash?"

"A magnesium grenade and a great deal of luck," Bruce said. It would be difficult to disprove – and, if rumours spread, would distract attention from him. "I only had one."

Jean-Luc smiled. "Of course," he said. "And what do you want to do now?"

Bruce shrugged. "Can you give me a place to rest, for the night? I'll leave tomorrow."

"You can also stay and work with me, at least for a while," Jean-Luc said. "If you want a job ..."

"Yes, please," Bruce said. Jean-Luc would be suspicious if Bruce turned him down flat. He might even start thinking about killing Bruce, rather than risk him walking away with enough information to betray Jean-Luc and the rest of his gang. Bruce already knew too much for anyone's peace of mind. And yet, Bruce had also saved their lives. "It'll be something to do."

"Of course," Jean-Luc agreed. "Come with me."

He turned and clambered up a wooden staircase. Bruce

followed him up and into a simple pub. It looked very much like its British and American counterparts, right down to the beer-stained tabletops and stools that looked as if they were on the verge of collapsing under their own weight. The air stank of cheap alcohol ... Bruce was tempted to ask just *what* Jean-Luc had been smuggling into the city, but dismissed the thought before he could take the risk. It would be far too dangerous to ask, not yet. Perhaps not ever.

"You can sleep on the floor," Jean-Luc said. He opened a concealed cupboard and tossed a pair of blankets at Bruce. "There's a privy in the next room" – he pointed – "and some water in the bucket. We'll be opening in the morning, so you have to be up and about before then – I'll show you the ropes when you get up."

Bruce nodded. It was a gesture of trust, but ... he'd bet good money it was also a secret test of character. Would he take advantage of the opportunity to search the pub for money and booze? Or would he sleep like a baby, safe in the knowledge he wouldn't be harmed? He shrugged as he found a place to lie down that wasn't too grimy, reminding himself he'd slept in worse places. Jean-Luc might be considering cutting Bruce's throat while he was asleep ... he drew on his magic, weaving a tissue-thin shroud of power around him. It wouldn't stop a determined attacker, but it would slow him down long enough for Bruce to wake and lash out with the rest of his magic.

Tomorrow, I have to find Gwen, he thought. It wasn't going to be easy, even if Jean-Luc let him wander the city long enough to get his bearings. *And when I find her, I have to look out for her.*

On that note, he fell asleep.

Chapter Fifteen
Paris, France

 *our days*, Gwen thought as she paced the dressmaker's shop, uneasily aware she was acting like a girl waiting for her *beau* to present himself to her parents. *It took four days to set up the meeting.*

The time hadn't been entirely wasted, she supposed. Irene had shown her around Paris, from the proud buildings that dominated the islands in the river to the poorhouses and slums that made London look a very paradise, and she'd managed to get her bearings. Paris was a confusing city, the streets so jumbled she thought the designers and builders had operated on radically different ideas of how a city should look, but it wasn't completely devoid of logic and reason. She'd also practiced her French, talking with Irene's contacts – in her role as Irene's apprentice – until her accent was almost flawless. And yet …

She forced herself to sit down, resting her hands in her lap. She'd walked all around the district, noting ways she could sneak out of the shop and others she could use to run, if enemy magicians tracked her down, but she was uneasily aware she was deep in the heart of unfriendly territory. The French could rain magicians on her like stones … and they would, if they knew she was there. Gwen knew she was a capable fighter, and her command of mixed magics would give her an edge, but there were limits. She could be beaten. And the French wouldn't hesitate to slit her throat if they worked out who she was.

The door rattled. Gwen twitched, bracing herself. Simone had been an opponent if not an outright enemy and she was dangerous, not least because she was a very skilled mind reader indeed. Gwen tightened her mental shields, all too aware they might not be enough if Simone went probing. She could ooze through Gwen's defences, if she was willing to take the risk ... Gwen gritted her teeth, then pasted a smile on her face as she heard someone opening the inner door. Irene stepped into the room, wearing the same bland dressmaker's outfit she'd worn over the last few days. And Simone ...

Gwen studied the other girl thoughtfully. Simone had always been enchantingly pretty, to a degree she'd made Gwen feel positively dowdy by comparison, and there was a hard look to her eyes that suggested she'd grown up a hell of a lot since they'd last seen each other. She was a delicate little thing, her features so fragile it was easy to believe they were made of fine bone china, and yet ... Simone had donned a drab dress without complaint, hiding her fine black hair under an oddly masculine hat that cast a shadow over her face. Gwen had to admit she wouldn't have recognised her, if she hadn't known who was coming. Simone looked, very much, like a poor girl from a family one rung – just one – above absolute poverty. Poor, yet proud. And very reluctant to do anything that might send them falling down the final rung.

"Lady Gwen," Simone said. Her voice, too was enchanting. Gwen had been told she was a wonderful singer as well as everything else, something she had in common with Irene. It wasn't uncommon for the aristocracy to encourage its daughters to dance and play music – Gwen herself was something of an exception to the rule – but the French took it much further than anyone in Britain. "It's good to see you again."

Gwen swallowed the sharp response that came to mind. Simone sounded sincere, but that was meaningless. She would be a good judge of human reaction even when she wasn't reading her target's mind, allowing her to adapt her approach to overcome their doubts and convince them she was telling the truth. Gwen had encountered a con artist who'd talked a dozen wealthy men into investing in a colony that existed only on paper, in a country that didn't exist at all. It still astonished her, sometimes, that he'd managed to get away with it for so long. He wouldn't have got caught if he hadn't made the mistake of trying to con a man with an extremely sharp wife. She'd looked up the colony, discovered the truth and reported him. And even after that, it had been hard to convince his targets that they'd been fooled ...

"And you," she said, curtly. She knew how to be flowery, but Simone wouldn't be fooled by pretences of friendship. "What have your new superiors discovered about magic?"

"They claim they have a way to boost magic," Simone said, curtly. "I can confirm they have *something*. There's a number of people at court whose minds are effectively unreadable."

Gwen's eyes narrowed. "Nulls?"

"I don't think so," Simone said. "A null ... a null doesn't exist, to my magic. These people exist – I know they're there, even if I can't see them – but I can't read their minds."

"How terrible," Gwen said, dryly. She had no illusions about what Simone had been doing for her adopted father. She'd read minds for him, giving him an unfair advantage in negotiations ... even when she hadn't used her powers, she was still astonishingly insightful and perceptive. "Do they have anything else?"

"I believe so, from the rumours I've heard, but nothing definite," Simone told her. "They don't seem inclined to make use of me."

"Odd," Gwen said. If Talleyrand was dead, she'd expect Simone to be executed shortly afterwards. She was good at her job, but she was by no means unique. "Why not?"

"I don't know," Simone said. "They haven't even bothered to confine me to my rooms."

Gwen looked at Irene, who frowned. "There was no attempt to follow us to Paris," she said, simply. "But that could be meaningless."

"They could have snatched me at any moment," Simone said, "Why let me come *here*?"

Gwen said nothing, her thoughts racing. She'd been taught how to spot a tail – how to keep an eye on who was behind her, without making it obvious – but the French had absolute control over Paris. They could keep swapping tails, ensuring they had an agent with eyes on Simone at all times without tipping her off. Her magic might tip her off, if someone paid too much attention to her, but would she be able to tell the difference between a man admiring a pretty girl and a government agent? She'd need to read his mind and that would betray her in an instant if he caught her peeking at his thoughts?

"Good question," she said, finally. "What are they saying in court?"

"There's a lot of chatter about Spain, but very little action," Simone said, confirming Irene's earlier report. "A number of regiments are marching south, from what I've picked up, yet they're ordered to hold a number of strongpoints rather than crush the rebels or push the British army back into the sea. I don't know what the king is thinking."

Gwen smiled, despite herself. "The army landed safety?"

"Apparently so," Simone said. "But there are so many rumours flying around that I know very little for sure, beyond the bare fact the army landed."

"If the army had been defeated, they'd be shouting that to the skies," Irene put in. "I think we can safely assume it landed, took up defensible positions and is currently preparing to resume the advance."

And Bruce is down there, Gwen thought. She was torn between relief and fear. Every analysis she'd read had stated the French *had* to deploy their army south or risk losing everything. If Spain went, Spanish America might go too. And yet, the French themselves evidently disagreed with that assessment. *What are they thinking?*

She leaned forward as a thought crossed her mind. "Does King Louis *have* armies to send?"

Simone looked discomforted. "Yes," she said, flatly. "He could easily send a much bigger force without weakening his defences here. Or so I have been told."

Gwen nodded, slowly. The armchair admirals had come up with grand plans for massed landings in Normandy and the armchair generals had devised schemes for a march to Paris, but the Duke of India had quashed all the plans before they got off the drawing board. They looked good on paper, yet they were completely impractical in real life. The French could mass enough troops, within days, to utterly smash an invasion force and push it back into the sea. The logistics were terrible. She was fairly sure the duke was right.

Her lips twitched. *Not that anyone bothered to ask my opinion anyway ...*

She met Simone's dark eyes. It was easy to see how many young men had been lost in them. Simone extruded a childlike vulnerability that made men want to protect her – Gwen felt it too – even though she was a grown woman. And ... Gwen kept her face blank with an effort, tightening her defences again. She dared not assume she could keep Simone out of her mind indefinitely.

"You claim to speak for the dissidents," she said, carefully. "Why? And what do you have to offer us?"

"The Court has been hunting down magicians ever since magic was proved to be more than gibbering nonsense from the dark ages," Simone said. "They were tolerant of aristocratic magicians, when they realised magic wasn't going to go away, but they rarely extended such tolerance to commoners. I ... my family sold me to my father so I'd share his bloodline ... on paper."

Gwen took a moment to work through what she'd been told. "You're a commoner?"

"I was," Simone said, flatly. "Legally, the moment I was adopted, I became an aristocrat."

"Charming," Irene commented.

"I see," Gwen said. She supposed she'd done the same, with Olivia. That was something else she had to discuss with Bruce. Olivia was hardly a child of her body – Gwen wasn't old enough to have given birth to her – but there was little legal difference. "And you kept in touch with your birth family?"

"Yes," Simone said. "And some of them have ties to the magical underground. The underground would be a potent force, if they had proper training. If."

"I see," Gwen said, again. "And what do you have to offer?"

"An end to the war," Simone said. "If you help us, we'll help you."

Gwen guarded her thoughts carefully. She doubted Simone had *that* much influence within the magical underground. Until recently, she'd had no reason to open what few ties she had to her family. It would have been risky to try, even if Talleyrand had offered no objections to the occasional letter. Legally, he was her father and she had an obligation to do nothing that might spoil the illusion. And Gwen had no idea if the underground could coordinate an uprising that would bring down the government and put an end to the war. The Swing had been bad, she recalled, but it hadn't brought down the entire government.

But a French Civil War would work out in our favour, she told herself. *If the French are too busy fighting each other, as the Bourbon Empire comes apart, the British Empire will be supreme.*

Her lips thinned. *Besides, we need to know what they're doing with magic ...*

"I'll do my best," she promised. It wasn't going to be easy to hide their training from questing minds. She'd sensed a couple of magical sweeps over the city and she suspected there'd be others, others she'd missed. Another good reason to send her, she supposed. She could conceal the training as well as carry it out. "And what do we do when we're ready?"

Simone's eyes were cold and hard. "Whatever we have to."

Gwen looked at her for a long moment. "Why are *you* doing this?"

"He was a good man." Simone's voice was cold, more convincing – in a way – than tears would have been. "He treated me well. He always had the best interests of the empire at heart. He ... yes, he was venal. He had a string of lovers, from young women who wanted favours to older women who wanted a little more stability, and his appetite for money and titles was unquenchable, but he meant well. The empire benefited from his advice. And then they killed him, because he told them truths they didn't want to hear."

She scowled, her anger and bitterness clearly visible on her face. "I want them dead," she said. "I want them to pay!"

"We'll do what we can," Gwen said. What would she do, she asked herself, if her father was executed? Or Lord Mycroft? She knew she wouldn't take it very calmly. "And now ..."

Someone knocked on the door. Irene stood and slipped out of the room, moving so quietly Gwen couldn't hear anything beyond her rustling skirts. Simone looked alarmed, her fists clenching even though she wasn't a physical fighter; Gwen shot her a reassuring look, trying to remind her the police would have smashed down the door rather than simply knocking. A police spy was a more likely possibility, but Irene wouldn't let a spy into the backroom without a loud argument. And yet ...

Irene returned, looking grim. "There's a gathering crowd at the shops two streets from here," she said, tartly. "Someone is riling them up."

Gwen stood, her mind racing. Paris had so many revolutionary groups, according to Irene, that it was just a matter of time before one of them tried to step out of the shadows. And then ... she shuddered as she pulled her cloak over her dress, then headed to the door. She needed to know what was going on and why, particularly if it did lead straight to an uprising. Was it possible? She didn't know. There was so much anger and frustration on the streets that the entire city was a powder keg, just waiting to explode.

"If we go ..." Simone swallowed. "Who are they?"

"Unknown," Irene said, tersely. "You can stay here if you like."

Simone hesitated, then joined them. Gwen allowed herself a moment to feel impressed before they hurried onto the streets. Simone might be able to read minds, but knowing someone was going to hit her wouldn't be enough to stop him from punching her. She had no doubt the local police – or the army – would hit a girl. She'd seen so much brutality on the streets she'd be more surprised if they didn't.

She kept her face under tight control as they joined the throng heading towards the growing crowd. The shops were closing, the shopkeepers slamming their shutters, barring their windows and locking their doors. A handful of young men – clearly pickpockets – ran past, looking for prospective targets. An older man pinched a woman's rear and she swung around and socked him with astonishing force. The crowd roared with laughter as he staggered away. Gwen hid her amusement with an effort. That never happened in London.

"They say we should go to war," the speaker proclaimed. He stood on a cart, his voice barely audible over the roar of the crowd. "Why should we go to war? For what?"

Irene nudged Gwen. "They've been trying to conscript as many young men as possible since the war began," she said. "It's been very unpopular. For every man who reported to his depot for training, there are ten who go on the run or injure themselves to escape military service. That man is probably someone who ran all the way to Paris."

Gwen nodded, keeping a wary eye on Simone. She

looked unsteady, as if someone had slapped her hard enough to stun. Her mind was locked down – Gwen hoped – and yet, the crowd's roiling emotions would be battering her defences. If Gwen could feel it, Simone definitely could. It was a nightmare.

"Stay back," Irene muttered, pulling at Gwen's sleeve. "The horsemen are on their way."

"I see them," Gwen said. The cavalry wore fancy uniforms and carried sabres as well as rifles. If they charged the crowd … she frowned, her eyes narrowing as she spotted a handful of men who looked unsteady in the saddle. Aristocratic boys were taught to ride from a very early age. It was rare to find one who wasn't perfectly comfortable on a horse, even if they rode as little as possible. "What …?"

She let Irene pull her and Simone back as the crowd's mood darkened. It might have been wiser, part of her mind reflected, for the police and military to let the crowd shout itself out, rather than move to break it up. And yet … she frowned as they inched past the crowd as the racket got louder, a flicker of movement overhead suggesting a magician hovering high overhead. What was happening …?

A wave of *something* pulsed through the air. She staggered, feeling sick. It was all she could do to keep from throwing up. Behind her, she heard people – hundreds of people – vomiting loudly, or losing control of their bladders and bowels. The tainted magic pulsed on the air … it was Charm, part of her mind noted, but *tainted*. She'd never felt anything like it, even when she'd tracked down and arrested a serial killer with enough magic to make his grisly fantasies a reality …

Irene looked pale. "Run!"

Gwen barely heard her as a second wave of magic washed over them. It felt as if she'd gone to the toilet and hadn't washed her hands … no, as if she'd fallen in the cesspit … as if someone had taken disgust and pared it down to the bare essentials, then pulsed it at the crowd. Her stomach heaved again, so violently she thought she was going to throw up everything she'd eaten in her entire life. The dry retching was painful …

Well, her mind whispered as she battened down her shields desperately, *you wanted proof they'd come up with something new, didn't you?*

Somehow, it was no consolation.

Chapter Sixteen
Paris, France

ruce hadn't originally meant to investigate the riot.

He'd spent the last four days working for Jean-Luc, all the while exploring the city to get his bearings and keeping his eyes open for Gwen. It had rapidly proven impossible. He'd had no trouble tracking down Sander's warehouse, but by the time he got there Gwen had moved elsewhere and Sander himself was back on the road. Bruce had thought about interrogating the staff, only to realise they would have been told as little as possible. If the whole affair had gone off as planned, no one in the warehouse would know Gwen had even stayed in the city. They'd think she'd left with her guardian.

It had been a lesson in patience, and in thinking ahead. He walked the city, delivering goods for Jean-Luc, all the while hoping for a lucky break. There was nothing. Paris was huge and Gwen was tiny, certainly on such a scale. Bruce hoped he'd be able to get an introduction to the magical underground, but Jean-Luc had cautioned him it might be a while before they'd speak to him. Bruce understood – the Sons of Liberty had been careful when dealing with new recruits, for fear one might be a police spy – yet it was deeply frustrating. He hated to admit it, even to himself, but he might have made a mistake.

He kept himself to himself as he wandered the city, noting the deep and spreading discontent. The shops were practically empty – the long lines of women waiting for food boded ill – and far too many people were constantly on the verge of starvation. The police patrolled the upper and middle-class sections of the city in force, backed up by army patrols, but rarely came into the lower-class districts. When they did, they came in force. Bruce had disliked the redcoats in America, but the French troops made them look like saints. The rumours about them were far worse than anything he'd heard, let alone seen, in America. It was hard to tell how much, if any, of them were true, but it hardly mattered. What mattered was that the rumours were believed …

The rustle running through the crowd caught his attention as he started to walk back to the inn. Someone was shouting ahead … it sounded like a riot. He heard horses behind him and darted into a side street, then scrambled up the building and onto the roof. A magician darted through the air above him, the arrogant git confident no one could blast him out of the sky. Bruce wanted to reach out and challenge him, but … he shook his head as he hurried forward, leaping from rooftop to rooftop. The French really shouldn't have built the giant apartment blocks so close together.

He frowned as he found a vantage point and peered down. The crowd was immense. Hundreds – perhaps thousands – of people, crowded together in front of a row of shops. A young man was haranguing the crowd, his voice barely audible over the racket … Bruce couldn't make out the words, but it sounded convincing. The crowd certainly thought so … he scowled as he saw the horsemen massing further down the street, preparing themselves for a charge. Bruce felt a flash of cold anticipation. The cavalry were tough, even if modern weapons had limited their use on the field of battle, but they'd be doomed if they charged the crowd. There were so many people crammed into the street that they'd crush the horsemen by sheer weight of numbers, pulling them from their mounts and tearing them to shreds. And yet, the cavalry seemed to disagree …

Magic spiked. Bruce retched, gagging helplessly. It was hard, so hard, to keep himself from throwing up the piece of bread and cheese he'd eaten for breakfast. His legs buckled, so badly he nearly fell off the edge and plummeted to his death. He had to drop to his knees to keep himself steady as a second wave of magic washed through the air, blasting the crowd with pure unadulterated disgust. He saw men vomiting helplessly, women stumbling away in wet skirts and trousers and …

The cavalry cantered forward. It wasn't a full charge, at pell-mell speed, but it didn't have to be. The crowd scattered, hundreds of people running for their lives. The horsemen lashed out with their whips, pushing the crowd further and further … Bruce stared, honestly shocked. His father had never had any qualms about correcting his behaviour with a belt, and he knew criminals were sometimes lashed in lieu of jail or indentured service, but whipping someone's face … he cursed out loud as he saw a young boy fall to the ground, blood streaming from his eyes. The cavalryman had struck him right across the face!

He looked up, trying to find the hovering magician, but saw nothing. The man had either flown away or had dropped down to aid the cavalry as they scattered the crowd. Bruce didn't hesitate. There was so much magic in the air his magic should go unnoticed … it crossed his mind to wonder if the French had accidentally killed their own magician, before he concentrated and focused his own magic on the side of the rooftop. The wall disintegrated, pieces of brick and chunks of stone falling on the cavalrymen below. It was hard to know if he'd hit anything, but there was no time to check. He turned and fled, jumping from building to building. The crowd below kept running too. He winced in sympathy as he saw a young man, staggering away like a drunkard who'd been thrown out of the pub for not paying his debts, then paused as he spotted a trio of young women behind him.

They looked drab and dull and yet, compared to the rest of the crowd, they were practically unaffected by the tainted magic. Their dresses weren't stained with their own vomit.

His eyes narrowed. Had they been out of range? It didn't seem likely. The blast of magic had covered several city blocks. Did they have magic themselves? It wasn't impossible and yet, unless it was very powerful magic, they should have been affected too. And yet …

Bruce blinked, his heart skipping a beat. That was *Gwen*.

He stared, almost not believing his own mind. Gwen looked like a shopgirl, a quiet mousy apprentice who did as she was told and nothing else, and yet … he knew her. He'd been close to her. He'd … he forced that thought aside as he dropped back, watching the trio from a safe distance. It was her. She might look different, and she'd drawn down her magic as much as possible, but it was her. Once he saw it, he couldn't convince himself it was anyone else. Even in a drab outfit, she was something else.

Gwen hurried away, her two friends beside her. Bruce eyed them thoughtfully. One was older than Gwen and her other friend, he'd wager; the other was probably about the same age as Gwen herself, although – judging from the way she moved – she wasn't used to the drab outfit. An aristo? Or … Bruce wished, again, he knew more about Gwen's plans when she reached Paris. There'd been no time to demand a detailed recounting from Lord Mycroft before he left. Getting onto the ship had been quite hard enough …

He watched, from a distance, as the three women reached a dressmaker's shop – marked only by the handful of outfits in the window – and rushed inside, closing the door behind them. Bruce moved closer, his mind alert for possible traps or tripwires. There were none, as far as he could tell. He couldn't tell, either, if whoever owned the shop owned the rest of the apartment block too, or if the floors above the shop were apartments crammed with complete strangers. Or both. Jean-Luc had told him nearly every apartment in Paris was crammed to busting, with the landlords dividing and sub-dividing each property and the tenants, often, doing it again. Gwen might be surrounded by potential enemies, ready to rat her out to the police for three meals a day.

Which wouldn't surprise me in the slightest, Bruce thought. It was easy to talk of points of honour and codes of silence when one had a full stomach and a safe place to sleep, harder to stick to your principles when your children were starving and begging for something – anything – to eat. *The smugglers have to be careful and so do the rebels and spies.*

He frowned, studying the shop for a long moment before turning away. It would make a good base for a spy, he thought. Plenty of people from all walks of life would have an excuse to step in and out of the building, making life difficult for any watching eyes. The shop was close enough to the upper-class districts to allow them to visit, while not close enough to draw too much attention. Who knew what else might be happening in the shop? Who cared?

The thought nagged him as he returned past the scene of the crime. A few dozen prisoners – scooped up from the running crowd or simply dragged out of the nearest jail – had been shackled and put to work, cleaning up the mess. Bruce gritted his teeth as he saw a pile of dead bodies, dumped at the edge of the scene. God alone knew what'd happen to them after the clean up was complete. Dumped in the ghastly river, perhaps, or simply thrown into a mass grave. Or ... he didn't want to think about the alternatives. Their families would probably never be told what had happened to them, let alone be given a body to bury. It was far more likely no one would bother trying to figure out who they were.

His stomach clenched, painfully, as he slipped away. The crowd hadn't been scattered. It had been crushed. The shock would make it harder, if not impossible, for another crowd to gather in a hurry ... and if it did, what was to stop the cavalry from doing it again? And again? Bruce shook his head in bitter disbelief. He'd often wondered why his grandfather had been so quick to rise with so little cause, while the French peasants and Russian serfs remained submissive despite far greater reasons for anger. He thought he knew now. The British, for all their flaws, hadn't been so quick to stamp down on prospective uprisings. The French and Russians had different ideas.

And that means Gwen's mission might have become impossible, he thought, as he dropped down to the ground and hurried back onto the streets. There was a nasty feeling in the air, a sense everyone was trying to pretend everything was normal even though it wasn't. *If she can't convince the Parisians to stand up for themselves, who can?*

***

"What ...?" Simone swallowed hard and started again. "What was *that*?"

"I don't know," Gwen said. Her stomach hurt. She hadn't thrown up, but it had been a near run thing. Her shoes were stained with someone else's vomit and she'd come very close to kicking them off completely as they made their escape. "Tainted magic ... Charm, perhaps."

She forced herself to think. She'd dealt with some powerful Charmers in her time. Some had been subtle, so light with their magic it was very hard to stop and think about what she was doing and why; some had been so heavy-handed she'd had no trouble understanding they were trying to force her to do something, even though it was hard to keep her limbs from marching to their tune. And yet, whatever the French had unleashed had been worse. Far worse. Could it be ...

Maybe they found a Talker who could broadcast thoughts and feelings into someone's mind, she thought. Talkers could talk to each other, easily, but it was hard – almost impossible – to send thoughts to unmagical minds.

If they really do have a way of enhancing magical power, they might have found a way to do it on a reliable basis and use it to stop a riot in its tracks.

"I'll have to think about it," she said, finally. Her ignorance gnawed at her. If she knew what the French were doing, she might be able to come up with a way to counter or negate it. "I think we have to proceed to contact the underground as quickly as possible."

Simone's eyes were wide. "After *this*?"

"If you let them silence you now, they'll win," Gwen said, wondering what had happened to the girl who wanted revenge for her adopted father. "They'll do worse shortly."

"If they're not already doing it," Irene said. She poured three glasses of water and passed two to Gwen and Simone. "How far did the effect spread?"

Gwen shook her head. Talking was one of the trickiest of the talents to understand. The limits appeared to have been devised by a lunatic, rather than the God of Reason. They just didn't make sense. The French could have blanketed their own capital city or just a single apartment block or anything in between. She made a mental note to find out just how far the effect had spread. Given she'd heard nothing – not even rumours – of the French doing anything like it earlier, it might well have been the first time. The French themselves might have been surprised by their success.

As well they should be, her thoughts whispered. *If they didn't know what they were doing ...*

She glanced at Irene. "Are the streets safe?"

"No," Irene said, flatly. "We should stay inside for the rest of the day and night."

Simone started. "I have to get back to court!"

"Why?" Irene cocked her head. "Who's waiting for you?"

"They'll notice if I don't go back to my room," Simone said. She sounded so badly shaken she'd lost her nerve. "They will!"

Irene shook her head. "The streets are very far from

safe," she said. "I saw teams of horsemen cantering back. At a guess, anyone caught on the streets near here will be in some trouble. And it'll be curfew soon. If you get caught then …"

"I …" Simone sighed. "What if you're wrong?"

"If you go back now, you might be fine," Irene said. "If you get caught, you will have to tell them who you are, which will lead to questions you don't want to have to answer, or risk them treating you like a helpless young girl completely at their mercy. You will not be able to escape. Stay here tonight – tomorrow, Raechel and I will put together a cover story to conceal your absence. It would not be the first time."

Simone sagged. "I'm sorry," she said. "I hope you're right."

Gwen sighed inwardly. She'd almost have preferred to send Simone back to Versailles. But Irene was right. The risks were too high. And yet, so too were the risks of Simone worming her way through Gwen's defences while she was asleep. She considered, briefly, suggesting Simone took a soporific before she went to sleep, before dismissing the idea. She had no idea if Irene had anything suitable and it would be a clear sign to Simone that Gwen didn't trust her. The thought almost made her smile. Simone didn't need to be a Talker to know *that*.

"She's very good at her job," Gwen said. She glanced down at her dress. It was clean, but she still felt the urge to get changed as quickly as possible. "How did they find you? I mean, when they discovered you were a magician?"

Simone blushed. "I was ten," she said. "I started picking up thoughts. I didn't know what they were, at the time. I honestly thought they were speaking to me and so I started responding to them. And they knew there was something strange about me … luckily, my father had *some* connections. One thing led to another and they sold me to my adopted father."

"At ten," Gwen repeated. She'd thought she'd had a hard time. It must have been worse for a young girl, being told she'd had to leave her family and embrace a new man as her legal father. The cruelty of the system left her shaken. Master Thomas had never insisted *he* was her father, or forbidden her to see her family … "And then … what?"

"There was some training," Simone said. "They taught me how to sharpen my powers, how to follow threadlines of thought and … other things. They trained me how to act when I was at court, then told everyone I was a distant relative who'd been adopted so I could have the best possible start in life. As I grew older, they added other things to the lessons. I also learned just how lucky I was, compared to others."

"Maybe you were," Gwen said, quietly. It was easy to feel sorry for Simone. Her adopted father – her master – could easily have done far worse than just use her as a private mind-reader. Gwen knew more than her mother would have liked about the seedy side of London Town. "Did you never have any doubts?"

"About what?" Simone shrugged. "I was never born to power. There was never any sense I'd marry well, or wield power on my own, or anything. I was content, or so I thought, until they killed him. Did you have any doubts?"

"Sometimes," Gwen said, slowly. There'd been times when she'd wondered if there was any point, when far too many of her subordinates would push her aside in a heartbeat if they thought they could get away with it. And yet, she was loyal to her country. "But that doesn't mean I can't do my duty."

"You were born to power," Simone said. "For all my talent, I was not."

And that, Gwen supposed, was all too true.

Chapter Seventeen
Versailles, France

omething had happened.

Raechel could feel it in the air, a sense something had changed. The court was as lively as ever – men dancing around women in a manner that would never be tolerated in London – and yet there was something different, a strange sharp edge she could feel bristling at the limits of her awareness. The news from Spain had forced the court into ever more tasteless displays of confidence – the heavily-bedecked men slated for deployment south had their pick of the ladies – but this … this was different. It felt as if it was closer to home. Raechel kept her ears open, catching snatches of conversation as she was whirled around the dance floor by a succession of different men, but none of the conversations made any sense. She had the nasty feeling none of the courtiers *really* knew what had happened.

"They thought they could riot," one man pretended to whisper, pitching his voice so everyone within earshot could hear it. "And we taught them a lesson."

"They were no match for our blood," another man said. His face was florid from too much alcohol and good food. Raechel was surprised his companion hadn't pushed him to drink himself to death. His slobbering was disgraceful even by local standards. She made a mental note to see if the poor girl could be turned into a source.

She certainly had excellent reason to loathe her unwanted companion. "We ran them down like rats."

You didn't, Raechel thought, coldly. The man looked as if he ate, drank, slept and nothing else. Whatever had happened, she'd bet her entire fortune he hadn't been involved. *You just heard something and repeated it in hopes it would make you sound important.*

"They were vomiting in the streets," a haughty woman put in. It sounded as if she were trying to undercut the florid man. "That's what happens if you drink too much cheap wine."

"You whine," the man said, and brayed like a mule. Everyone else smiled politely. "It really was quite something."

Raechel turned away, steeling her face into a pleasant mask as she found another partner and another. They didn't seem to know much; one spoke so vaguely she was sure he was making it up, the other's eyes never left her breasts even while swinging her around the dance floor. Raechel tried not to roll her eyes in disgust. She knew how to pick a man's pocket and she was tempted to do it, relieving the idiot of his money pouch and whatever else he'd crammed into his trousers. It would serve him right. There were so many people bustling around that no one would notice ... she put the thought out of her head as the man started bragging about his estate somewhere in the north. If it really existed, he'd be one hell of a catch for a young noblewoman without two coins to rub together. If.

She was almost relieved when Louis, appearing out of the throng, swung her away. She hadn't seen anything of him over the last two days, something that alternately pleased and worried her. She'd spent too long cultivating him as a source for her to be entirely pleased if he was sent elsewhere, and yet he was a deeply unpleasant person. Her eyes narrowed as she smelled the alcohol on his breath. Why had he been drinking so heavily? Didn't he know strong drink gave the desire, but took away the ability?

"I was there," Louis muttered. "It was ..."

Raechel kept her face under tight control. The courtiers were fond of bragging. There wasn't a man in the hall who hadn't loudly insisted he'd killed a hundred enemies with a single stroke, or owned so many estates he held title to all of France and beyond … it was sad, in a way. The men gathered in the hall might have titles, but little else. Their pensions were all they had and they were rarely large enough to meet their needs, not if they stayed at court. And yet, who'd leave? It was the hub of a mighty empire. It wasn't impossible a particularly adroit courtier would be able to parley his name into real power and responsibility.

Not impossible, she thought. *Just very unlikely.*

Her eyes narrowed. Louis was fond of bragging too, and yet he was speaking quietly … *that* was out of character. There were few secrets in court because everyone who had a secret used it ruthlessly to boost their own prestige and position, even if they'd been told to keep their mouths firmly shut. If Louis was being quiet … could it be he was telling the truth? She doubted it – everything he'd told her, ever since she'd started to get to know him, had been exaggerated at best – but his behaviour was odd. It made little sense.

She risked a question. "What happened?"

Louis hesitated, noticeably. Raechel felt the hairs on the back of her neck stand on end. Louis was smart enough to know he was tipsy, that he might say something he shouldn't … what? What could he know – what could he have done – that prompted such a reaction? It was enough to make her think he really did know something …

"I was there," he said. "It was awful. It was …"

A low gong echoed through the room. Raechel looked up. A herald, wearing the formal livery of the king's inner circle, stood at the top of the stairs. "Ladies and Gentlemen," he said. "Duke Philippe, Victor of Paris."

Raechel frowned as Duke Philippe descended the stairs. It wasn't the first time she'd seen him – he was an occasional face around court – but she knew very little about him, beyond rumours that grew more and more absurd with every telling. The king's kinsman was one of the most important people in the country, the target of every woman and the subject of nearly every rumour … and yet, very little had been confirmed. They were missing something. The French Court was far more open than its British counterpart, to the point the monarch rarely had a moment's peace. The fact that so little was known about a man so close to the throne bothered her.

Duke Philippe moved through the crowd, a shark amongst minnows. Raechel kept a wary eye on him as he glided around the room, dozens of men and women surrounding him and dozens more watching from a safe distance. Her disquiet grew as she watched their reactions. The king and queen would be mobbed if they set foot on the floor, hundreds of penniless aristocrats trying to get their attention so they could discuss their hereditary rights and properties, but Duke Philippe had far fewer petitioners. It was odd. The duke sat firmly in the line of succession, a person who couldn't be discounted because he might sit on the throne one day. He should be orbited by far more men and women, trying to get his attention by whatever means necessary.

She needed to get closer. Her instincts told her it was a bad idea, but … she tugged at Louis, carefully angling their dance until it intersected with the crowd surrounding the duke. Duke Philippe wasn't dancing himself, but … she had the nasty feeling, suddenly, that he was showing off his power in a manner few could ignore. The crowd ebbed and flowed around him without ever quite *touching* him. And …

For an instant, their eyes met.

Raechel nearly froze. It took every last ounce of mental discipline to keep moving. The Duke … Raechel knew men who saw her as nothing more than an attractive piece of meat and others who saw marrying her as the key to wealth and power beyond the dreams of avarice, but the Duke was different. His face was handsome, almost classically so; his eyes were so soulless they flickered over her for an instant before dismissing her. She felt alone and vulnerable, even though she was in the midst of the crowd. Duke Philippe … to him, she was nothing. She wasn't even a portfolio with a pretty young girl attached. Raechel had few illusions – there was no shortage of men who would marry her for her money, even if she was the ugliest girl in the world – but the duke was just … different. Cool, clinical and terrifying.

Louis seemed to feel it too, tugging at her to bring her out of the circle and straight towards the doors. Raechel didn't try to fight. Duke Philippe had scared her and she wasn't even sure *why*. She was a practically penniless aristocrat, as far as the French Court was concerned, but she *was* a beautiful young girl, precisely the type who'd make a good mistress for a senior nobleman. And the Duke hadn't shown any interest at all. His eyes had been so cold she doubted he was more interested in men, or anyone. He'd been so cold …

Her mind raced, even as Louis pulled her right out of the ballroom. Had Duke Philippe seen through her cover story? He hadn't tried to read her mind, as far as she could tell, but he could be an expert in reading body language instead. Her cover story accounted for her limited grasp of courtly manners – better to have the high-ranking women sneering at her for being countrified than have them asking dangerous questions – yet there was no guarantee it would stand up to careful examination. Might the duke suspect she'd come from further afield? Or … she hesitated, unsure if she should be making plans to run. If she left now, she could be well away by the time someone raised the alarm.

You're panicking over nothing, she told herself, sharply. *The Duke just wasn't interested in you.*

Her thoughts kept churning as Louis led her into his rooms and closed the door behind them. Raechel cursed her own mistake as she snapped back to reality. Louis had taken her home and now … it would be difficult, if not impossible, to escape if he'd decided they were going to have sex. Or something … she knew how to fight, particularly if her target thought she was a weak and feeble woman who couldn't lift anything heavier than a wine glass, but her trainers had left her with no illusions. The average man was stronger than the average woman and if he managed to pin her down, there'd be little stopping him from doing whatever he wanted. And Louis already felt entitled to her …

She blinked as Louis poured himself a glass of something alcoholic – it smelt like strong brandy – and tossed it back as if it were cheap rotgut instead. The French prided themselves on their wine – she'd endured endless wine-tasting sessions when trying to get close to potential sources – and it was rare for them to quaff expensive wine like beer. Louis didn't even seem aware of her presence as he poured himself a second glass and drank it, then a third. Raechel wasn't sure if she should be relieved or annoyed. It would have been amusing if it wasn't so serious.

Louis finished the bottle and glared at it, as if it had personally offended him. "I …"

Raechel leaned forward. Louis was used to drink, and she'd seen him drink heavily before, but … he'd been tipsy before he started quaffing brandy like water. The alcohol had to be hitting him pretty hard by now, making it harder for him to think clearly. She didn't like the look of it. Louis wasn't one of the old sots whose glory days were well past them, the sad men who came to court to drink and wouldn't leave until their bodies were carried out and buried in unmarked graves. He wasn't that much older than her.

"Louis," she whispered. "What happened?"

Louis didn't answer for a long moment, his eyes on the empty glass in his hand. "I was with the regiment," he said, finally. "We were supposed to be going to Spain. We were …"

He broke off and swallowed hard, his voice starting to slur. "Messenger arrived, told us there was a riot. Had to put it down. Took swords and whips and everything else and headed off, then the magics turned up. Men who'd never ridden a day in their lives" – he giggled like a schoolgirl – "on horseback, constantly on the verge of falling off. It was funny and yet no one dared laugh."

You're laughing now, Raechel thought. *What happened?*

"Big crowd," Louis slurred. His words came in fits and starts. "Traitors, one and all. Screaming for something … don't know what. Magics went to work. I felt it … they made them all sick, made them all run. We charged. We thrashed everyone. Everyone who didn't run. Everyone … it was bloody and terrible and all the time, the magics were smirking like … smirking things. It was …"

He swallowed, again. "More wine."

Raechel stood, opened the cabinet and picked a bottle at random. Louis snatched it out of her hand, yanked the cork out with surprising force and put the bottle to his lips. Raechel tried not to recoil as he drank heavily, dribbles of yellowish liquid running down his neck and staining his clothes. An expensive whiskey, she thought. The war had interrupted trade between Scotland and France, which meant the bottle was pretty much irreplaceable until the fighting came to an end. And Louis was drinking it like water …

"They made them sick," Louis said. "They made them sick."

He staggered, dropping the bottle. Raechel caught it before it could hit the floor and shatter. She had no idea if the maids cleaned the rooms or not and, after pretending to be a maid a couple of times, she had enough sympathy for the poor women not to want to make their jobs any harder. Besides, any maid who entered a nobleman's rooms put her virtue at risk. It had been true in London, even though everyone denied it, and truer in France.

"They used magic on the crowd," Louis said. "They did …"

He staggered again, falling against her. His hands twitched towards her breasts – she tensed, unwilling to allow him to fondle her and yet aware she couldn't stop him – and then fell as he started to collapse with painful slowness. Raechel gritted her teeth and gently led him to the sofa, helping him to get onto the cushions before his body gave out. He belched loudly as consciousness fled, his eyes closing. Raechel stared down at him for a long moment, torn between disgust and an odd kind of pity. Versailles tolerated all sorts of things London wouldn't allow for a moment. What could be so terrible it would shock even a hardened denizen of the French Court?

They used magic to break up a riot, she thought, remembering some of the earlier whispers. She'd never heard of it happening in England, although she supposed it wasn't impossible. *And whatever happened was bad enough to shock even Louis ...*

She stood and looked around. She'd never had a chance to search his rooms before and she had no intention of letting it pass. She locked the door – it was unlikely anyone would come, but there was no point in taking chances – and then slipped into the bedroom. He'd spent so much time trying to lure her inside, she reflected, that he'd probably be pleased to think she'd done as he wished even if he hadn't been there. She went through the room quickly, noting the unmade bed, pile of unwashed clothes and very little else. She shook her head in irritation and slipped back into the living room. The writing desk was covered in papers, mostly military orders. It looked as if the French Court didn't know what to do with Louis.

Her lips twitched as she parsed the formal script and phrasing. They'd ordered him to Prussia, then to Paris, then to Spain and then – the most recent set of orders – to Paris again. She sat on his stool and skimmed the rest of the paperwork, looking for an explanation. She'd assumed he'd argued and cajoled not to be sent away from Versailles, although she had no idea if he had enough contacts to get his orders changed. If he'd had that sort of clout, he could have written his own orders ... she frowned as she read the final set of deployment orders. There was something curiously impersonal about it, as if Louis was just one of a multitude of officers receiving the same orders. It wasn't impossible. The French had too many fires and not enough firemen.

She went through the rest of the papers – confirming, to her amusement, that Louis was even more penniless than her cover *persona* – then carefully put them back into place. It was hard not to feel she was wasting her time. Louis had nothing beyond a name. He hadn't even distinguished himself in battle. The *really* important aristocrats – the ones with money and power – didn't spend their time at court, bragging to anyone willing to listen. They certainly didn't run up so many debts their great-grandchildren would still be paying them off. It made her wonder just what Louis would do for money.

And yet, if I offered to bribe him, he'd start wondering about my cover story, Raechel said. She had a pension and nothing else ... on paper. *Perhaps someone else should try to approach him.*

She stood and walked back to the sofa. Louis looked ... disgusting. It was hard to believe the wreck of a man below her was the same person who'd swung her around on the dance floor, wearing a uniform so crisp and new it had clearly never seen active service. And yet ... she felt a twinge of something she didn't care to look at too closely. She might have turned out just like him, or worse, if she hadn't met Gwen. She'd certainly been on the path to self-destruction.

We are all prisoners of our societies, she thought, as she turned and left the room. *And there is no escape for any of us.*

Chapter Eighteen
Paris, France

It took two days for the streets to calm down and two more for Simone to arrange the meeting.

Gwen didn't blame her – or Irene – for the delay, although she couldn't escape the sense time was pressing. The French seemed unsure if they wanted to send troops south, to Spain, or keep them on the streets of Paris, but she suspected it wouldn't be long before they reinforced the formations already heading south. Bruce was down there, fighting beside an army that hadn't faced an enemy on equal terms for quite some time. Gwen respected the Duke of India – Field Marshal Arthur Wellesley hadn't earned his rank and title by sitting on his backside and leaving the conquest of India to his subordinates – but he hadn't commanded an army in battle for years. He hadn't even directed the counterattack that had smashed the French invasion force, back when the war started. She worried, despite herself, about what would happen when the British encountered the French.

It was a relief, beyond words, when the time came to head to the dissident base. Or one of them. The French dissidents had been vague, to say the least, about quite who or what she was dealing with. Gwen rather thought Bruce would have made a better choice of representative. He was used to cloak and dagger meetings, rather than open discussions and outright combat. But she had to admit Lord Mycroft might have had a point. The police and military patrolling the streets paid more attention to young men than young women. They clearly expected the former to prove more dangerous than the latter.

Her lips quirked, then thinned as they made their way deeper into the slums. There was a nasty edge to the air that promised imminent violence, a sense that the slightest incident would start a fire that would burn the entire city to the ground. She kept her eyes open, noting how many political slogans and antimonarchical insults had been daubed on the walls, even in the upper class districts. A handful of youngsters had been caught and marched off to an unknown fate – two more had been gutted on the spot – but it hadn't been enough to stop others taking their place. The police seemed to be having problems washing the graffiti away or hiding it beneath newer layers of paint. Gwen had no idea if that meant the police secretly supported the artists or if they simply didn't have the manpower to tackle the problem effectively.

"Charming," Irene muttered. "Look."

Gwen followed her nod. The graffiti was growing sharper – and nastier. KING LOUIS HAS TEN PIGLETS WITH THE ROYAL HOG. QUEEN CATHERINE HAS FIFTY CHILDREN BY THE KEEPER OF THE ROYAL PRIVIES. TO HELL WITH BURGUNDY! She didn't understand the last one, unless it was a reference to the closest duke to the throne. The Duke of Burgundy was extremely unpopular, from what she'd heard, both with the commoners and the aristocracy. But he was too close to the throne to be safely ignored.

She put the thought out of her mind as they neared a small warehouse, half-concealed within the towering apartment blocks and makeshift shanty towns. It looked deserted, but she spotted a handful of concealed guards watching the approaches, ready to give the alarm if unwelcome guests came too close. She suspected no police or military force could enter the district without being spotted, perhaps even attacked. Irene had told her the commoners were stockpiling everything they needed to put up a fight, save for magic. Gwen hoped she could do something about *that* before it was too late.

Simone showed no visible nerves as she pushed open the door and led the way into the warehouse, even though she had to be feeling strikingly out of place. She'd never been anywhere like it before, not as a young girl nor as an adopted noblewoman. The only source of light was a single lantern, illuminating an empty chamber. Gwen followed, reaching out gingerly with her senses. The warehouse was surprisingly quiet, with only two minds within range. She hoped that was a good sign. The magical underground was at a grave disadvantage. If they used magic too close to a guardhouse, the magician was all too likely to be detected and caught before he could escape.

"Sir," Simone said. "I brought our teacher."

Gwen did her best to look respectable as two men appeared from the shadows. One looked poor and slovenly, his shirt stained with alcohol, although the hard glint in his eyes suggested he hadn't actually been drinking. The other looked more like a prosperous merchant than a rebel, his clothes fine enough to brush against the local sumptuary laws. Gwen was surprised he'd made it through the streets without being robbed or murdered, although he could easily have hidden his clothes under a cloak. Or enough people knew him to be certain that any attempt to attack him would bring dire consequences in its wake. There was no shortage of idiotic noblemen, back home, who dropped hints of roguish dealings to make the ladies giggle and blush ... hints, Gwen was sure, that were little more than blatant lies.

Or it's a disguise, she reflected. *To mislead me ... and whoever interrogates me.*

"You're our teacher," the merchantman said. He made no attempt to introduce himself. "Can you be trusted?"

"She's one of the best," Simone said. "And we need her."

"Do we?" The merchantman looked Gwen up and down. "Is she trustworthy?"

Simone spoke calmly, but firmly. "You need a teacher," she said, simply. "And I promised you the best."

"And every attempt to learn to use our powers has ended badly," the poor man said. His accent was different, suggesting he wasn't native to Paris. "They always track us down."

"You're not blocking the magical emanations," Gwen said, simply. How much did the magical underground know about its own powers? There were so many absurd stories about magic – and magicians – that the truth was buried under a mountain of nonsense. She'd been credited with turning a French spy into a frog and eating him, a concept that was both effectively impossible *and* disgusting. "If you keep using magic in one place, they will eventually detect and track you down."

She paused, waiting. How much did *Simone* know about her powers? She might have been taught by the best, or by people as blind as her. It has taken decades for the Royal College to put together even a simple picture of how magic actually worked and even *that* was very far from complete or conclusive. There were just too many questions that had never been answered, too many types of magic that had never been identified and catalogued. It was hard to believe the French had come up with something new, but it was impossible to be certain. The French themselves might not know what they'd done.

They learnt a great deal from Jack, she thought, recalling the English rebel who'd done so much to trigger the Swing. *And how much could they have inferred from what he told them?*

The merchant scowled. "And you know how to shield us from detection?"

"You infuse magic into the walls and ceiling to block

the emanations," Gwen said. It was one of the simplest tricks, all an infuser had to master to be sure of a job for life. "And then you can train in peace, without being detected. I can do it for you, then teach others."

"I see." The merchant said nothing for a long moment. "Show me."

Gwen glanced at Simone, who nodded. "Watch carefully," she said, walking over to the wall and resting her hand against the wood. "If you can sense what I'm doing, it might be useful…"

She would have preferred to touch the ceiling, but it was out of reach. Her magic slipped into the wood and spread out, sensing the warehouse and the world beyond. It felt alarmingly flimsy to her mental touch, but it didn't matter. She infused a simple layer of magic into the wood, locking it firmly in place. It wouldn't last forever, but it should last long enough for her to train a handful of local infusers so they could replenish the magic.

"Done," she said. "What did you sense?"

"Nothing," the merchant snapped. "Are you sure it's safe?"

"Yes," Simone said, simply. "I sensed it."

"I sensed … something," the poor man said. "What now?"

Gwen held out a hand and summoned a ball of light. "Now I start teaching you some *real* magic," she said. It was a gamble – she didn't dare mislead them, which meant there was a very real risk someone would realise she was using more than one type of magic – but she didn't have time to argue. "Are you ready to learn?"

The poor man stared at her, his eyes wide. It was … men had stared at her many times over the years, before and after they'd worked out who she was, but … he wasn't staring at *her*. He was staring at the light, at the proof of her power floating in the air … he wanted it desperately, wanted it enough to take horrendous risks. Gwen understood, better than she cared to admit. It was bad enough being an aristocratic daughter – given everything save freedom – but far worse to be a poor man on the streets of an uncaring city, someone whose life and death would pass unnoticed and unmourned. She knew how easily an unskilled worker could be discarded if he were to be crippled …

"Yes," the poor man said. "Show me."

"Give me your hand," Gwen said. She'd sense what sort of magic he had, then tailor her training to match. "Let me sense your magic."

The merchant scowled. "Why do you need to sense our power?"

Gwen took the poor man's hand and ran her finger across his skin, feeling the life and power crackling underneath. "Magicians have different talents," she said, carefully. She really didn't want to lie openly. She had no idea how much they knew – or what they might deduce, from what she told them and what she left unanswered. "If the training is devoted to a certain kind of talent, it brings the power out quicker."

She frowned, closing her eyes for a second. "I think you're a Mover," she said, to the poor man. "Watch – sense – what I do and try to follow it."

Her magic twisted, producing a stream of force. It was blatantly overpowered – Master Thomas would have scolded her for wasting so much magic – but it was easy for someone else to sense. It wasn't easy to put magical instructions into words. It was like trying to explain to a young man how female bodies really worked, a difficult task at the best of times and one Gwen privately dreaded. How did one explain how to use a muscle? Sure, you could tell someone to stand up and walk to the far side of the room and back, but it was impossible to tell them how to do it.

The Mover stared, then tried to follow her. The air rippled as a wave of magic shot out in all directions, shaking the entire building. Gwen silently thanked Master Thomas for teaching her how to use magic to conceal the training centre, all too aware the magic would have been detectable right across the city. She glanced at the walls, reaching out to check the infused magic remained in place, then allowed herself a smile. The newborn Mover stared back at her.

"It worked?" He sounded stunned, as if he didn't believe himself. "It worked?"

"Yes," Gwen said, mischievously. "It worked."

She didn't give him time to relax. She'd never been able to resist using her magic as a young girl and the worst *she'd* had to deal with were scoldings from her mother and maids hastily leaving the hall to find employment elsewhere. If the new magicians used their magic outside a shielded warehouse – or somewhere – they were going to be caught and interrogated. And then, probably, executed. The French might be short of magicians, but they'd be reluctant to trust a known rebel, no matter how much they offered in exchange for his services …

"Keep going," she said. "I want you *used* to it."

The Mover did as he was told, his magic flailing around like an invisible octopus as he struggled to get it under control. It would be some time, Gwen thought, before he learned how to shield himself and fly, but he'd get there. His powers weren't weak, merely unpractised. She offered a few words of advice, then pushed him into a corner to keep practicing. The merchant hesitated, before offering her his hand. Gwen took it without comment and frowned. The man was probably a Blazer.

She met his eyes. "Didn't you ever lose control of your magic?"

The merchant flinched, as if she'd hit him. "Once," he said. "I had to leave in a hurry."

Gwen nodded. It wasn't an uncommon story. "And then?"

"I kept it under tight control," the merchant told her. "I came here, to Paris, and apprenticed myself to my old master. It's astonishing what people will overlook when you wave money under their noses. I kept having little flashes of magic, so I drifted into the underground in hopes they could teach me how to use it. They couldn't, but …"

"Watch me," Gwen said. Perversely, it was easier to train Blazers than Movers. "And do as I do."

The merchant learned slowly, too slowly. Gwen suspected he'd been repressing his powers for so long he found it impossible to use them easily. That wasn't an uncommon story either. She knew too many girls in England who'd been ordered to keep their magic hidden, as if it was something shameful, and ... she put the thought aside as she showed him what she could do with the same powers. She doubted he'd be as powerful as Peter Wise or even Pinfold – a man who practiced as little as he could get away with – but that didn't mean he wouldn't be effective. A little magic in the right place could be more effective than a great deal of magic thrown around at random.

"You just need to keep practicing," Gwen said, finally. "Magic is a muscle and you need to exercise it if you want to build your power."

"Here, you mean," the poor man said. "Where else can we practice?"

"I can safeguard other places for you," Gwen told him. "But practicing anywhere outside a shield is asking for trouble."

Simone cleared her throat. "How so?"

Gwen hesitated, unsure how to put it into words. "Magic requires an incredible degree of precision," she said. "The less precise your magic, the greater the overspill ... which can be detected by another magician. Once it is detected, they can zero in on you and even look at you though their magic. And then they hunt you down."

The merchant frowned. "They can spy on you?"

"Yes." Gwen didn't dare try to sugar-coat it. "A Seer cannot see the future. That's nonsense. But they can peek on you from a distance and it is very hard to detect the probes, let alone stop them."

"They could peek on me in the bath." The poor man snickered. "They'll go blind."

Irene snorted. "You have a bath?"

Gwen ignored the snide remark. The poor man was right. It was quite possible for someone to spy on someone else's private moments … no wonder, she reflected, that there was no shortage of work for infusers. It wasn't as easy to spy on a given person as rumour suggested, but it could be done. Lord Mycroft had an entire team of Seers trying to keep an eye on his French counterparts.

"It isn't that easy," she said. "If they don't know who you are, or where, it isn't easy to follow you. Think of them as … birds, flying in the sky. They may spot a field mouse from high overhead, or the mouse might be concealed and thus impossible to see."

"It isn't very reassuring," the merchantman said. "What happens if they are following us and we walk into a place they can't see?"

"They'd know something was wrong," Gwen admitted, bluntly. "Of course, they might also lose track of you in other ways. The mental talents are poorly understood. It isn't always easy to follow someone if they go into a building, even if there's nothing stopping you."

The merchant cocked an eyebrow. "Can *you* do it?"

"Not as effectively as others," Gwen said. It was true. She was no Seer. "It isn't one of my talents."

"But why can't you follow me home?" The merchantman sounded worried. "Or someone else do the same?"

Gwen hesitated, trying to put it into words. "Think of yourself as a ghost," she said, finally. "You are invisible. Practically undetectable. You can walk through walls and levitate through floors and ceilings … you can go anywhere. Except … you can't, because your mind doesn't really believe you can. You have to convince yourself to walk through a wall and by the time you do, your target might have escaped, without ever knowing it was what he'd done. And …"

She shrugged. "Someone has to take care of your body in the meantime," she added. Her eyes narrowed thoughtfully. "Actually, if we know where the Seers are, that might make a good first target."

The merchantman said nothing for a long moment, then shrugged. "Let's not get ahead of ourselves," he said. Gwen couldn't tell if he was taking her idea under advisement or not. "Right now, we need more training."

"And food," his companion said. "Right?"

Gwen looked at Irene and Simone, then nodded. "Please," she said. "We have a lot of work to do."

Chapter Nineteen
Paris, France

"You're a magician," Jean-Luc said, four days after the riot. "Do you want to get in touch with the magical underground?"

Bruce hesitated. Jean-Luc's offer was sincere, of that he had no doubt. The smuggler was a hard man, concealing a certain degree of ruthlessness and calculation behind a genial bonhomie that would have fooled Bruce if he hadn't spent so much time in his father's court. Maybe not a bad man, not in any real sense, but not entirely trustworthy either. Bruce knew it would be a long time before he was welcomed as one of the gang, something that would have bothered him if he'd genuinely wanted to join. As it was, he'd gone back and forth between staying in the pub and using it as a home base and slipping away to hide somewhere near Gwen.

"Maybe," he said, finally. "What are they offering?"

"Training, apparently," Jean-Luc said. "Or so I heard."

Bruce frowned, contemplating the question. If someone was offering training ... Gwen? It had to be, unless someone else had been sent with the same mission. Or ... he'd heard hundreds of rumours over the last few days, from the Duke of Burgundy leading troops to overthrow the king to a revived Huguenot uprising threatening to plunge France into a bloody civil war. The fact that none of the rumours were particularly believable was neither here nor there, but it wasn't impossible that a court-trained French magician would set out to raise a private army. Or … something else, something equally insane.

"I can try," he said. "But I do like to remain in the shadows."

Jean-Luc shrugged. "You came to Paris to find work," he said. "But what work is there?"

"Point," Bruce conceded. There was no work to be found, not for a young lad from the countryside. He'd been lucky to find Jean-Luc and the smugglers, people who wanted someone who'd keep his mouth shut … someone who had ample reason to avoid attention from the authorities. And even so … he suspected Jean-Luc had his own reasons to want Bruce to join the underground. The smugglers stood to gain if there was more demand for their services. "I can take a look."

He listened as Jean-Luc briefed him, cursing under his breath. Word was already out and spreading … sure, there were any number of insane rumours, but there was no way *this* story would be dismissed out of hand. The police would take note and investigate and if they found Gwen … Bruce wasn't even sure how the story had got out in the first place. Someone talking out of turn? Or a deliberate attempt to bury the truth under a pile of crazy stories? Or … he shook his head, inwardly, as he donned his cloak. He couldn't get very close or Gwen would sense him. And then …?

"Don't get too close to any of the young ladies," Jean-Luc advised, as he waved farewell. "They're deadly."

Bruce shrugged, his mind elsewhere. Jean-Luc was a smuggler, not a traitor. If he had any dealings with anyone outside France, Bruce didn't know anything about them. It was unlikely he had any direct contacts in the Dutch Republic, let alone Britain or Austria or the Ottoman Empire. Whatever links he had to traders like Sander – and the trading networks that linked Europe together – were kept quiet and deniable. He might be opposed to his government, but that was a far cry from being an outright traitor. What would he do if he knew the truth? Bruce didn't want to find out the hard way.

The slums of Paris surrounded him as he made his way through the streets to the contact point, the stench a grim reminder something had to change and fast. The anger on the streets was almost a physical force, but as long as the government retained the whip hand it wasn't going to be enough to change the world. Jean-Luc had laughed when he'd heard the story of the riot – and so had most of his legal customers, who drank themselves senseless every evening and slept on the floor every night – but there'd been an edge of fear to the laughter. It would only grow worse, Bruce suspected. The stories were already wild enough to daunt even the stoutest heart.

His thoughts spun in circles. If he'd been alone, meeting the underground – such as it was – would have been desirable. He'd enough experience of rebel groups to know how to handle them, to offer support without arousing their suspicions. But here … he didn't dare let himself be introduced to Gwen. And that meant … he cursed under his breath. Jean-Luc would be pissed if he returned without a good excuse, which would lead to … what? The smuggler wouldn't betray him – the code of silence in the slums made the Sons of Liberty look like tattletales – but he might not let Bruce stay either. And that meant he'd probably wind up with a cut throat. He knew too much for Jean-Luc's peace of mind too.

The streets seemed to darken as he turned the corner, heading down to a pub that was dire even by the standards of London Town. The whores lining the alley looked terrible, as if they were in their dotage even though they couldn't be much older than Bruce himself. Their pimps didn't look much better. Bruce wanted to reach out with his powers and crush their skulls, to do something – anything – for the poor girls, but it wouldn't make any difference. Even if he got them off the streets, they'd be replaced within the day. Paris was crammed with desperate young women, ready to hear promises from a pimp … or just to be carried off, kicking and screaming.

No, he corrected himself. *The pimps don't need to bother kidnapping anyone.*

He felt sick as he approached the pub. The gutter stank … the older man lying on the pavement, completely unmoving, was almost worse. A pair of bravos stood outside, ostentatiously ignoring the drunkard. Bruce couldn't tell if the man was alive or dead, then decided it didn't matter. If he was alive, he'd be reasonably safe. He had nothing to steal.

The bravos stepped forward, their hands on their daggers. They looked Spanish, rather than French, although they spoke French with Parisian accents. "Yes?"

"I was told to ask for Milou," Bruce said. "Where is he?"

"Inside," the lead bravo said. He exchanged glances with his comrade before turning away. "Follow me."

Bruce braced himself. If this was a trap, he'd fight his way clear and leave the pub in ruins. If not … his skin prickled as he sensed the magic infused into the walls. It was crude, by English standards, but more than enough to keep out unwilling eyes. He hoped the fact the pub was hidden from magical probes didn't draw attention in its own right. The only source of light was a single lantern, but it revealed enough to make him glad he couldn't see the rest. The floor stank of cheap and rotting beer. At least, he hoped it was beer. He stepped over a pair of bodies and followed the bravo into a backroom. It was better lit, but still dark and shadowy. A single figure sat on a chair, cloaked and masked. The cloak was so all-encompassing that he couldn't even tell if he was looking at a man or a woman. If Milou was the cloaked person's real name, he'd eat his hat.

"Greetings," Milou said. The voice was carefully bland, devoid of almost all emotion. "Why are you here?"

"Jean-Luc sent me," Bruce said. He tensed as he felt the first mental probe, brushing against his defences. It was hard to keep his face under control. There was more logic to the cloak and dagger rigmarole than he'd realised. Anyone wanted to join the underground had their mind read, before they were allowed to get any closer. Anyone who failed the test or refused to submit … "He said the underground might be interested in me."

The mental probe got sharper. Bruce cursed under his breath. The cloaked person wasn't a half-trained street magician, whatever else they were. There was little hope of letting them see a façade … hell, if they realised he'd shown them a façade masking his innermost thoughts, they'd know he was more than he seemed. He answered a couple of questions with vague half-truths, suspecting he'd already blown his chances. What would the underground do, with someone whose mind was hard to read? Would they suspect he'd been trained to resist mental probes? Or … or what?

Milou leaned forward. There was a hint, just a hint, of femininity in the movement. The mind probe withdrew. "We'll be in touch," she said. "Go to the girls outside and tell them I sent you. They'll give you a good time."

Bruce nodded, allowing himself a moment of relief. He'd failed the interview in a manner that couldn't be fairly blamed on him. Probably. Some people's minds were harder to read than others. The underground had every reason not to want to take the risk … he shook his head as he turned and left the room, silently impressed the bravo had returned to his post without him noticing. Impressive, and disturbing. He said nothing as he passed the two men at the door, his back prickling as if they were on the verge of drawing their daggers and plunging them into his back. No one would notice another body, not here. He kept walking, ignoring the girls, until he was in a shadowy alleyway where he could wrap his magic around himself. No one saw him when he returned to watch the pub.

It was nearly an hour, more or less, before a handful of people were escorted out of the pub and through a tangled maze of streets. Bruce followed, eying their backs thoughtfully. It was impossible to determine which of them was the mind-reader, if indeed she was there at all. The group moved in silence, not even exchanging brief words, until they reached a simple warehouse. It looked harmless, but the handful of concealed guards within the mishmash of shanties suggested otherwise. Bruce kept his distance and reached out, gingerly, with his mind. The entire warehouse was a blank space, as if it was nothing more than an illusion.

Clever, he thought. It would be a dead giveaway if someone happened to notice, but the odds of *that* were very low. In fact, given how few policemen came so far into the slums, it was unlikely anyone would come close enough to notice. *Gwen could be in there and I'd never know.*

He forced himself to wander the streets, as listlessly as any of the other homeless and jobless men sitting in the alleyways. None seemed to pay any attention to him, although he suspected some were a little more alert than they looked. Most people didn't pay close attention to the down and out, no matter how loudly they begged, unless they made a terrible nuisance of themselves. And then they called the police to send the homeless away ...

Hours passed, slowly. Bruce noted a handful of people entering the warehouse and leaving, an hour or so later, with renewed confidence. They were taking lessons, he thought, recalling how the Sons of Liberty had trained their magicians. Gwen would be training new magicians, who in turn would train others ...it wouldn't be long, he thought, before the underground was well on the way to branching out and opening up new training bases. The police would catch wind of it sooner or later – he knew from grim experience that bringing in more and more people would increase the odds of detection – but by then Gwen would have faded into the background, ensuring the police couldn't catch her. Or so he hoped ...

It takes time to become an effective magical warrior, he thought, crossly. He'd been capable of doing quite some damage from the start, as had Gwen, but he'd had to train hard before he was ready to take on other magicians.

Gwen had been at a disadvantage for quite some time, from what she'd said, although her mastery of all magics had evened the odds. *How long will it take to get the underground ready to face the government's magicians?*

He frowned as one of the homeless men stood and wandered away, staggering like a drunkard or drug addict. Bruce's eyes narrowed. There'd been nothing to eat or drink … nothing he'd seen. The church didn't try to feed the homeless in the slums, not unless they went to church and even then … ice congealed in his chest. A spy? It wasn't impossible. There were so many people moving around that a stranger might have gone unnoticed, just like Bruce himself. He stood and followed, trying to remain unnoticed. Perhaps the man was just trying to find a place to relieve himself, although it seemed unlikely. He'd seen women squatting in the gutter in full view of everyone who cared to look.

His heart twisted. *How can people live like this?*

The thought haunted him as he shadowed the homeless man. He wasn't looking for a pub or a church or anything, anything at all, that might have made sense. Bruce had walked around the district enough, over the last few days, to realise there was no reason for a homeless and desperate man to walk so far, unless he was going to the police guardhouse. His blood ran cold. The man was a spy. God alone knew how much he'd learnt, in the last few hours …

Too much, Bruce thought. The man walked like a drunkard, staggering along as if one good breeze would blow him over, but there was something a little too precise about his movements. It wouldn't have been noticeable if Bruce hadn't watched him for so long. *And if he gets to the guardhouse, Gwen will be in deep shit.*

He forced himself to think. There were too many people around to risk grabbing the spy and trying to interrogate him. They might mind their own business or they might not … the police, if they realised what had happened, would hand out money and food to the witnesses to get them to talk. And if he used magic … a very little magic would probably pass undetected. Probably.

Better not to risk it, Bruce thought, crossly. He sped up, walking after the spy. The man was still swaying as he walked, but there was a twinge of alertness in his movements that warned Bruce the man was more than he seemed. He'd feared he might be wrong, that he was about to kill an innocent man, but no drunkard could walk like *that*. *Let them think it was just a random knifing.*

He slipped the knife from his belt and plunged it into the back of the spy's neck, thrusting the blade into the man's brain. The spy staggered, then collapsed as Bruce withdrew the blade and walked on. It had been messy – he'd been taught to aim for the heart or the lungs if coming at someone from the rear – but he dared not risk the man reaching a healer, or gasping something before he died. Someone shouted behind him … Bruce ignored it as he turned the corner and slipped back into the shadows, hoping the spy hadn't had a chance to send any sort of report to his masters. A random murder might go unnoticed – Paris apparently had quite a high murder rate – but if the man had reported he was on to something his masters would suspect he'd found something and been killed for it.

Nothing to be done, he thought, tiredly. He didn't like killing, not like that, but there'd been no choice. *If he reported back to his masters …*

The thought haunted him as he made his way back to the pub. Jean-Luc nodded as soon as Bruce entered and set him to carrying barrels of beer up from the cellars and installing them behind the counter. The scent of desperation in the air was stronger, somehow; the men, only a rung or two above the very bottom, were drinking beer as if there were no tomorrow. There might not be, not for them. Bruce suspected half of them would do anything for one more bottle of beer, even break the code of silence. If they knew who he was, would they report him?

It might be time to move on, he thought. It wouldn't be impossible to stay closer to Gwen and her allies. As long as he kept his magic under tight control, she shouldn't know he was there. *The longer I stay here, the greater the risk.*

Jean-Luc didn't say anything until nightfall, when they helped the drinkers who could still walk onto the streets and left the comatose to sleep it off. "What happened?"

Bruce shrugged. "They said they'd be in touch, and sent me to the girls," he said. It was true enough, just incomplete. Better Jean-Luc thought he'd been fooling around than shadowing a spy. "They weren't as bad as you said."

Jean-Luc leered. "Did they use their mouths?"

"Yeah." Bruce had been told that only Frenchwomen went down on their men. He also knew it to be a lie, one of the many pieces of arrant nonsense High Society told itself. He had no idea why, nor did he particularly care. "It was great."

"Make sure you wash, properly," Jean-Luc said. If he doubted Bruce's story, he didn't show it. Bruce was mildly surprised he didn't ask more questions. The French seemed more willing to discuss such matters than the British. "And then get some sleep. Tomorrow will be a very busy day."

Bruce nodded. "Yes, boss."

Chapter Twenty
Paris, France

 think this is it," Simone said, tapping the map. "But it's hard to be sure."

Gwen eyed her, sharply. "How sure *are* you?"

Irene cleared her throat. "She just said she wasn't sure."

"Yes," Gwen said. "If this goes wrong …"

She rubbed her forehead. She'd spent the last two weeks training the magical underground as best she could, ensuring her most talented students were sent onwards to train others so as to minimise the number of rebels who met her in person, and she *knew* her students were growing competitive. They'd had very little power in their lives until now and that meant … she sighed inwardly. On one hand, they had magic now; on the other, they had friends and comrades and allies, which made it harder to cold-bloodedly consider their position and determine if they were really *ready* to take to the streets. Gwen had never really understood how a sense of camaraderie could undermine critical thinking, not until now. But then, it had never really been extended to her.

Bruce is probably having an easier time of it, she reflected, with a twinge of jealousy. There'd be no question about inviting *him* to the mess, to dine with the officers, nor seeking his opinion on everything from expensive wine to military tactics. *And if the French really are reluctant to send entire armies down south, he's probably taking fortified cities and unravelling their entire position by now.*

Simone spoke quietly, but urgently. "I know a handful of people – Seers – who use their talents to serve the government," she said. "I read their minds. That place" – she tapped the map – "is where they're stationed, when they watch the city. That's where they find new magicians and send troops to round them up, before they can realise the danger and vanish into the underground. It has to be shut down and fast."

"I don't disagree," Gwen said. "It's just that … something about it feels *wrong*."

She stared down at the map, her thoughts churning. The French would have been wiser to position the magicians outside the city. It would certainly have made planning and executing an attack a great deal harder. And yet … was it a trap? Or … did they think they needed to keep the Seers within the city? It would make it easier, she supposed, to coordinate a snatch-and-grab raid, when a new magician was detected. The underground leaders had made it clear the government worked hard to arrest new magicians and take them off the streets …

And what, Gwen asked herself, *happens to them afterwards?*

The underground, as far as she'd been able to determine, didn't know. Some magicians probably went to work for the government, accepting high salaries and promises of other rewards in exchange for their services. Others … she didn't know and that bothered her more than she dared admit to their allies. She would have understood them all going into government service, but if they had the French should have deployed a hell of a lot more magicians during the early days of the war. Instead, a number seemed to have simply vanished. Had they been murdered? Or … she was sure she wouldn't like the answer when she found out.

"We need to move," Irene said, simply. "Or someone else will jump the gun."

Gwen nodded. Paris seemed peaceful enough, for a city with a crime rate that dwarfed London's, but even a blind man wouldn't have missed the anger simmering under the placid surface. The only thing holding the city's rage in check was the threat of overwhelming force, be it physical or magical, and even that wouldn't hold forever. There were endless rumours of rebel cells stockpiling weapons and readying themselves to act, some of which were quite possibly based on reality. It was just a matter of time before someone – one of her students, perhaps, or someone who didn't even know she existed – decided to act. Her ability to control events was very limited.

And if we don't take out their Seers as quickly as possible, she reflected, *they're going to be able to bring overwhelming power to bear against us*.

Her eyes lingered on the map for a long moment. Paris was a heavily-garrisoned city. There were major troop and police concentrations in the upper and middle-class districts, as well as a small army based outside the walls. She didn't have any figures for how many magicians were amongst them, but ... she shook her head. There'd be enough to cause real problems if they joined the fight. And that meant ...

"Right," she said, finally. "I'll lead the operation myself."

Irene shot her a sharp look. "Do you not think it would be better to lurk in the shadows?"

"No," Gwen said. She folded up the map and stuck it in her pocket. "I'm the only experienced combat sorcerer they have. I have to be there."

It was more than that, she reflected as she sent Simone to rally the troops and prepare for the mission. She was a person of action and she hated the idea of sitting around doing nothing – or watching from a safe distance as others put her plan into action. And ... she knew what her enemies would say, when she returned home, if she stayed safely in the rear. They'd say a *man* would take the lead, putting his life at risk for the cause. They'd be sweet and polite and they'd make it clear she was a frail woman … she shook her head, tamping down her anger before it affected her magic. She owed it to herself, and to the women who'd come after her, to prove she could do the job.

And they'll start complaining I put myself in danger instead, she thought, as she collected her cloak and pulled it over her shoulders. *No matter what I do, they'll find a way to turn it against me.*

"Stay here," she told Irene. "If something happens, make sure London knows."

Irene nodded, curtly. Gwen felt a stab of sympathy mingled with envy. Irene might exist on the fringes of polite society – singers and adventuresses were barely tolerated, even when they weren't spies for one government or another – but she had a kind of freedom Gwen couldn't help wishing for herself. And yet, if the operation went spectacularly wrong, Irene might be forced to flee. She was tougher than she looked, but she couldn't fight a gaggle of policemen. The entire intelligence ring in Paris and Versailles might come apart at the seams.

There'll be others, she told herself, as she left the shop and made her way back to the concealed warehouse. *Lord Mycroft wouldn't put all his eggs in one basket.*

The streets felt darker somehow, cold eyes following her as she walked. Paris was drawing in on itself, bracing for the coming storm. It was hard not to feel as though she'd been spotted and identified, although she knew that couldn't possibly be true. If the French had known who and where she was, they'd have sent every magician they could find to arrest or kill her. She had no illusions about how she'd be treated. She'd be lucky if they just slit her throat.

"My Lady," the lead magician said. "We are ready."

Gwen took a moment to survey the assault force. Ten men and five women, all Movers and Blazers, all dressed like lower middle class workers on their way to work. She didn't know their names. The dissidents had made it clear she never would, a precaution she found irritating as well as understandable. The pendants dangling from their necks had been infused with magic that should – in theory – make them impossible to detect and track. Gwen didn't know if they would work in practice. The enemy Seers might just spot a place they couldn't See and react accordingly.

No way to test them either, she thought, as she unfolded the map. The underground didn't have any Seers, as far as she knew. The talent wasn't exactly rare, but – unlike the more physical talents – it was harder to detect and train. *We may not know something is wrong until they come boiling out to kill us.*

"This is the target," she said. "You'll note it's too close to the enemy garrisons for comfort, so we're going to get in, destroy everything we can and get out again. We are not going to stick around long enough for them to mass their troops and come after us. We do not want to be caught."

"We can take them," a young man said. "We have the power."

"So do they," Gwen said, sharply. She bit down hard on her irritation. Honestly! What was it with young men constantly underestimating their abilities? She knew the speaker was a strong magician, with remarkable potential, but he lacked the training he needed to be a real threat. He'd be in trouble if he faced a government magician one-on-one, let alone an entire team. "Our first mission *must* be a success. We will not risk everything on a mindless quest for glory."

She chose to ignore the man's muttered response as she inspected the rest of the team, then led the way onto the streets. They probably wouldn't arouse any suspicion, at least at first ... her lips quirked in dark amusement. Paris was hardly a safe city and the population had a tendency to seek safety in numbers, families and workmen alike. The police would probably try to crack down on it, when they realised what had happened, further alienating the population from the monarchy. Judging by the ever-growing number of political slogans painted on walls, too many for the police to even begin to remove, it wouldn't be long before the population gave up on the monarchy completely.

The streets grew wider as they crossed the invisible boundary line and walked into the upper middle-class district nearer the heart of the city. The population still looked sullen, even though most of them could make a good living if they tried. But ... there were limits to how far commoners could rise. Gwen had been told many educated middle class men – and women too – had become revolutionaries, purely because they'd been denied a chance to rise to the top. Why should they respect an accident of birth? It made her wonder, despite herself, if the same might happen in Britain? She knew what would have happened to her, if she'd been born into a poor family, or her brother. It was unlikely either of them would have bettered themselves.

A problem for another time, she told herself. There was at least *some* social mobility in Britain. There was none in France. It was vanishingly rare for a man without magic to be ennobled and, even if he was, he wouldn't be taken seriously. *Right now, we have to bring the empire down from within.*

She put the thought aside as she peered at the target building. It looked like a middle-class office block, the kind of place government ministers and bureaucrats might do the paperwork while keeping their distance from the men who did the *real* work. She'd visited similar offices in London, all of which were designed more to impress visitors and lobby politicians rather than anything important. The only sign there was anything interesting – and dangerous – about the building was a pair of guards on the door, both looking surprisingly professional despite their fancy uniforms. Gwen suspected there were others further inside the office block. It was what *she* would have done.

"Two minutes," she muttered. "When I start, follow my lead."

Her eyes flickered up and down the street. There were too many people outside the buildings for her group to be picked out easily, but a pair of dangerously aware guards might notice something – anything – out of place and react accordingly. The longer they loitered, the greater the chance ... there were a handful of beggars in view, she noted, but no homeless sleeping in the alleyways. The police had probably moved them on long ago. It was the same in London. The rich could order the police to move the homeless somewhere else and often did. The poorer parts of the city tended to be a little more sympathetic.

She raised her hand, summoned her magic and blasted the nearest guard. He staggered and fell, dead before he hit the ground. The second reacted with commendable speed, lifting his rifle to firing position. Gwen snorted – he'd have been wiser to duck inside the building – and reached out with her magic, yanking the rifle out of his hand before grabbing the man himself and hurling him across the street. The crowd started to scatter, panic spreading like wildfire, as Gwen led the way into the building itself. A force of armed guards were sprinting down the corridor towards them. Gwen shaped her magic into invisible daggers and lashed out at them, cutting through their bodies as easily as a hot knife would cut through butter. She heard someone being sick behind her as she kept moving, picking her way through the blood and gore, and gritted her teeth. She'd seen much worse things in her short career.

"Block the exits," she snapped, as they crashed through a set of doors. The office in front of them looked like any government office, so much so she wondered if they'd made a mistake and shown their hand for nothing. "Burn everything!"

A rebel whooped as he summoned fire and lashed out at the clerks and their filing cabinets. Gwen felt a twinge of sympathy for the bureaucrats, which she ruthlessly suppressed. They might be individually innocent, but France had perfected the art of government by desks, converting something meant to make the country easier to run into an instrument of tyranny. The men running for their lives had probably taken bribes and …

She swore under her breath as the roof fell in, a pair of magicians dropping down and lashing out with their magic. They moved in harmony, balancing their powers in a manner Gwen had to admire. A Mover and a Blazer … her team struck back, raw magic smashing into the Mover's shield and boiling into nothingness, without harming the Blazer behind him. She was a woman … Gwen blinked, honestly surprised. As far as she knew – had known – she was the only female magician to take on a combat role. Most women with physical powers were advised to stay at the rear, leaving everything to the men.

Not that she can do anything else, not now, Gwen thought. *We brought the war to her.*

She shaped her powers, combining them into a single needle that pricked the Mover's bubble and burned through his skull before he could react. His body dropped like a stone. The Blazer stared at Gwen in shock, then started to raise her hands. It was too late. The rebels blasted her apart, ripping her body to shreds. Gwen bit down hard on the urge to shout at them. She could have learned a great deal from interrogating a prisoner … she shook her head. Keeping a magician prisoner wasn't easy and she doubted the rebels had the facilities to do it. And yet …

"Get upstairs," she snapped. She hoped they'd noticed how easily their attacks had been deflected. The enemy magicians had known how to work together, something the rebels lacked. They needed to practice – and quickly. "Hurry!"

She levitated through the hole in the ceiling, gritting her teeth as a sickly-sweet stench brushed against her nostrils. Opium, she thought, or something like it. She'd visited a pair of opium dens in London, in the line of duty, and … she felt her stomach churn as she looked at the men and women lying on mattresses, smoking the drug to expand their minds and magic. They appeared completely unaware of her presence, just like the opium fiends she'd seen back home, but she could *feel* them looking at her through their mind's eye. Behind her, someone swore. They could feel it too.

The air seemed to sparkle with magic, a deadly potential slowly taking shape. Gwen gritted her teeth. Master Thomas had told her that using drugs to unlock the mental powers brought immense risks, from a magician losing control of his powers to a magician finding himself unable to return to his body. Or worse … there were horror stories, from the early days, that she would have thought had grown in the telling if she hadn't known her former master wasn't given to exaggerating. A Talker, given the right sort of drug, could broadcast his thoughts and feelings into someone's head …

Her entire body felt lethargic, as if she was on the verge of falling asleep. She bit her lip, hard, and drew on the pain to centre herself. She didn't know if they were trying to compel her to fall asleep or if there was enough drug in the air to make her dizzy and it didn't matter. Her power boiled through the air, setting fire to the entire building. The Seers were too drugged to move. She felt another pang of guilt – most of the poor bastards were about to be roasted to death – and pushed it aside. The walls started to creak as the other magicians added their power to hers. It was just a matter of time before the entire building came tumbling down.

"Move," she snapped. The creaking was getting louder. She thought she'd survive – she'd been through worse – but she wasn't sure the rebels would make it out alive. Besides, the enemy troops were on their way or their commander was a complete idiot. "It's time to go."

Gritting her teeth, she took one last look at the dying men – none of them were even trying to save themselves – and then turned and ran.

Chapter Twenty-One
Paris, France

ruce was surprised, very surprised, that the rebel underground hadn't been wiped out long ago.

The only advantage it had, he supposed, was the code of silence. Very few amongst the poor and downtrodden would willingly betray the rebels, or the smugglers, or almost anyone within the poorest parts of the city. Their hatred and distrust of the authorities, married to a certain lack of faith in their willingness and ability to keep their promises, ensured the rebels were shielded even though they didn't deserve it. Bruce hadn't found it too hard to keep track of their activities, or to monitor the expanding number of makeshift training camps and barracks within the city. If he'd been a police spy, he reflected ruefully, he could have captured Gwen and most of the rebel leadership in one fell swoop.

It was a tangled mess. There were middle-class leaders and activists rubbing shoulders with poor and hopeless magicians and street toughs – and criminals. Bruce could understand their motives, without thinking they were the good guys. The majority of the rebels and their allies wanted something, from freedom and opportunity to chaos to cover their criminal activities. He had no illusions about just what would happen, if the government offered to bribe a real criminal, paying vast sums of money in exchange for actionable intelligence. And yet …

He'd had no trouble keeping an eye on the training programme and monitoring discussion as more and more rebels wanted – demanded – action. Gwen was a good teacher, he knew through experience, but she'd want action too. It hadn't been that hard to tell something was in the wind, nor to realise when a handful of magicians were called into the warehouse to prepare for something special. Bruce had shadowed them from a distance, keeping the group in his sight at all times. Their target didn't quite make sense – he would have expected them to go after a police station or troop garrison, not an anonymous office block – but he was sure Gwen knew what she was doing. If nothing else, proving the rebels could and would strike so close to the Bastille was a clear warning they had to be taken seriously.

He took up a vantage point near the office block and watched as the crowd scattered and ran for their lives. It was mildly disappointing none took the opportunity to pick up bricks and lash out at their tormentors, but most of the locals would be middle-class citizens who had something to lose. Bruce's lips twisted in disapproval. They'd always been the worst, as far as the Sons of Liberty had been concerned; they'd had enough, just enough, to be afraid of losing it. And they were also educated enough to know what had happened to the last rebellion. He snorted at his own hypocrisy – his father was a government servant, his grandfather had made his peace with the government – then leaned back to watch as a dull roar split the air. The office block was starting to collapse.

Gwen, he thought, feeling a twinge of alarm. He hadn't seen her go. Would she be safe, inside the falling debris, or …? *Where are …?*

A handful of figures ran out of the collapsing building, an instant before the office block crumbled in on itself and fell into a pile of dust. Bruce thought he recognised Gwen snapping orders, directing the rebels to run. The police and military – and magicians – would be on their way shortly, if they weren't already charging to the scene. Bruce had no idea how alert the Frenchmen were, but they had to be aware the rebels were planning something. Or that something would happen. The word on the streets was clearly audible. If the police hadn't heard it, they were too incompetent to survive …

He smiled, coldly, as he heard galloping hooves. The cavalry were on their way, charging through the suddenly-empty streets as if they thought they could run down the rebels and bring them to justice – or simply kill them – before they made their escape. They might have been right, Bruce reflected, under other circumstances. The horsemen could move with astonishing speed and, given how far they were from the poorer parts of the city, they might just run the rebels down before they were too late. And yet, trying to capture Gwen would end badly. If they knew what they were facing, they'd have sent magicians first.

A shame I dare not use my full power, he thought, as he shaped a strand of razor-thin magic and pushed it out of his mind. *But it will be enough.*

The horses seemed to hesitate – he heard them whinnying in protest – as they galloped towards the trap. Animals were sometimes able to sense magic, for no apparent reason, and a wise rider would listen to his steed … the Frenchmen, clearly, weren't wise. Bruce blinked in surprise as they whipped their horses, pushing them to keep moving … it was odd. He'd seen aristos think nothing of striking men in the streets, or beating children, or raping kitchen maids and then kicking them out of the house for daring to get pregnant, but they tended to lavish care and attention on their horses. And yet … the horses staggered and fell as they ran into the magic, their bodies collapsing as their legs were sliced free. Bruce saw a rider thrown forward, flying through the air and striking the ground hard enough to break his neck. Bruce hoped he was dead. His horse had done nothing to deserve such a rider.

But he'll have to explain what happened to his superiors, if he survives the day, Bruce thought, sardonically. Someone would have to take the blame for the whole affair – and for getting so many horses crippled or killed. *It isn't a harmless little prank like cutting a man's head off because you're having a bad day.*

He took a moment to appreciate the chaos as the cavalry charge came to an abrupt end. A dozen horses and men were either dead or seriously injured, the horses almost certainly going to be put down by the end of the day. The remainder were staggering around, unsure what had happened. Bruce glanced around, noting a handful of eyes peeking from behind curtains or from the rooftops. Yesterday, the cavalry had been feared by all. Today, they were a joke.

His eyes narrowed as a line of troops came into view, moving with remarkable speed for soldiers who might not have wanted to don the uniform. They didn't hesitate as they saw the remains of the cavalry, just spread out and kept coming. Bruce had to admit they were well trained. A certain degree of training and acclimatisation could keep men from panicking, when they ran into the unexpected – and the unknown. They might not know for sure what had happened, and they might never work it out, but they weren't reacting badly. They might even start chasing the rebels …

And we can't have that, Bruce thought. He reached out with his magic, taking hold of the rooftops and pulling as hard as he could. *If they want an enemy, I'll give them one.*

The soldiers didn't panic as pieces of stone and debris crashed down on them. Some sought cover, others raised their rifles and fired at imaginary enemies. A commanding officer started to bark orders as the men swept the rooftops, trying to take command; Bruce grabbed another piece of debris and aimed it at the CO's head, cracking his skull and probably killing him outright. It was a little too revealing – the soldiers might suspect one or two magicians attacking from a safe distance – but by the time they realised the truth it would be too late. He hoped. Right now, they were in such disarray it would take them quite some time to give chase.

He smirked, then turned and sauntered off. It was important not to run. The streets were largely empty, which meant a running man would draw the eye like nothing else. He looked up, wondering if someone was already watching him through magic. It wasn't impossible. He'd used enough magic – so had Gwen and her allies – to set off alarms right across the city. The French Seers might be triangulating on him even now. And if they did …

They'll start locating the training bases soon, he thought. The infused magic wouldn't be that hard to find … Gwen, he was sure, would make certain to set up a number of decoy bases as soon as possible. She might have already done it. *If there are too many bases to search properly, they'll never find the real base or Gwen herself.*

Something wrapped around his ankle. He barely had a second to react before he was hoisted into the air and hauled upwards – upside down – until he was facing a flying magician. The Frenchman looked at him as if he was a particularly unimpressive personage – the kind of person who'd normally be found drinking himself senseless, or lying in the gutter – rather than a suspected magician. Bruce was almost disappointed, although it was also something of a relief. If the man *had* suspected him, it would suggest he had more than one type of magic. And that would mean …

The Mover blinked. Bruce frowned in puzzlement, then realised his own mistake. Most people would be upset, if not panicking, if they were yanked into the air and held upside down. It would be worse for the local women, given the dresses they wore … he kicked himself, mentally, for not pretending to panic. He could fly. He wasn't in any real danger if the magician dropped him. And that was far too revealing for anyone's peace of mind.

Bruce closed his eyes, then summoned the brightest

light he could. The magician screamed as the light stabbed deep into his eyes, letting go of Bruce a second later. Bruce opened his eyes and landed safely, feeling a twinge of guilt as the magician drifted to the ground, his hands pressed against his eyes. Blood was leaking from between his fingers, his entire body twitching ... he was whimpering, the sound oddly disturbing even to someone who'd seen the worst of humanity. Bruce put a pulse of magic through the man's head, then turned and ran as the body hit the ground. It was a mercy kill. He'd done far more damage than he'd expected.

Odd, he thought, as he sped up. *What did I do to him?*

The streets were buzzing as he kept moving, running into the poorer parts of the city and then slowing to walk in circles, just in case he was being watched. There were already rumours, ranging from the plausible to the utterly absurd. Bruce wondered how many of the latter were being spread by police spies. If someone was exposed to an insane story, one that couldn't possibly be true, it was harder for them to believe the truth. Not, he supposed, that the police needed to bother. In his experience, stories grew and grew until they were completely unrecognisable. There was nothing that could be done about it.

He slowed, reaching out carefully with his mind to ensure he wasn't being watched through magic before making his way back to his base. There didn't seem to be anyone following him, but he made sure to walk through a handful of crowded pubs and apartment blocks before heading to the pub. Jean-Luc gave him a sharp look as he entered, but said nothing. Bruce hoped that was a good sign. He knew Jean-Luc had been involved with smuggling weapons and explosives into the city. Perhaps the man had more sympathy with the rebels than he'd admitted.

And he'd be a free trader if he could, Bruce thought, tiredly. The French seemed intent on strangling their own economy, in a manner that would cause a civil war if it were tried in Britain. There were so many monopolies preventing competition – and bureaucratic nonsense – that there was little hope of reform. Jean-Luc and his peers wanted to be legal, to be free to run their businesses without interference, but it wasn't going to happen. *If the rebels really do take power, will they make life better for everyone by terminating monopolies and wiping out the bureaucrats?*

He shrugged. Right now, it wasn't his problem.

***

Gwen didn't relax – she didn't dare – until she got the team back to the warehouse, then slipped back into the streets and made her way to Irene's shop. There appeared to be a great deal of confusion – the underground had hinted there might be other strikes, carried out to distract attention from her activities – but more and more police and soldiers were taking up positions on the streets. She breathed a sigh of relief as she stepped into the shop and closed the door behind her. It wasn't perfectly safe, but it was better than nothing.

"You stink," Irene said. "What have you been doing?"

"I need to wash." Gwen said. Her clothes stank of opium. She hoped the rest of the team had the sense to wash and change their clothes too. "We got in, did the deed and got out again."

"Don't waste water," Irene advised. "We don't know if they'll keep the water running or not."

Gwen nodded stiffly as she stepped into the washroom, feeling the adrenaline slowly flowing out of her body. It had hardly been the first time she'd faced the enemy, and the unknown, but there'd been too much that could have gone spectacularly wrong. She dreaded to think what would have happened if there'd been more guards and magicians defending the office block, or if the Seers had been more capable of defending themselves. The opium fog had been quite bad enough and *that* had been a largely passive defence. She stripped off her clothes one by one and dumped them in a basket, reflecting ruefully she'd have to wash them later. The thought made her snort in cold amusement. The idea of a lady of *her* class washing her own clothes … her mother would sooner go to a house of ill repute than do domestic chores, certainly not where anyone could see her. It would be a clear sign the family finances had collapsed quite some time ago.

We'd be expected to quietly withdraw to the countryside and pretend we were going into retirement, rather than hanging around and embarrassing everyone, she thought. *And I'd be expected to marry someone with money …*

She sobered, feeling a twinge of regret. She missed Bruce dreadfully. His kisses, his strong arms, his hands touching her in places no girl was supposed to know existed … she snorted, rolling her eyes at the absurdity of her own world. It was one thing to be ignorant of the details of male anatomy, but to wilfully ignore what she saw when she looked at herself in the mirror …? Absurd.

He's probably having a grand time with the army, she told herself. It wasn't that bad. She could cope. She'd hardly be the first wife to have to wait behind while her man went off to war. She even had the advantage of a mission of her own, rather than staying in the house and doing nothing. *And when he comes home we can get married.*

She put the thought aside as she washed herself thoroughly, taking care to run water through her hair, and then dried and dressed herself before stepping back into the tiny kitchen. Irene was nowhere to be seen, but Simone was sitting at the table, drinking a cup of coffee. Gwen hesitated, her magic starting to crackle around her fingertips before she calmed herself. They were allies now, even if they'd never be precisely friends. They had to work together.

"You have to work on your shields," Simone said, sardonically. "I could feel your emotions from over here."

Gwen flushed, embarrassment rapidly shading to anger. "And you went peeping?"

"I didn't read your thoughts," Simone said. "But I had no trouble sensing your feelings. Boy trouble?"

"None of your business," Gwen snarled. She'd known Simone was good at her work. She didn't need more proof. "Keep your thoughts to yourself."

"It's not a good idea to get too close to someone," Simone said. There was something reflective in her tone that made Gwen wonder who she was *really* thinking about. "It just makes it hurt more when they betray you."

"He isn't going to be betray me," Gwen said, icily. "Who betrayed you?"

"I read thoughts and emotions all day," Simone said. "I know men who loudly promise their eternal love to their mistresses, all the while planning their next conquest. I know women who say they pledge their hearts to men, aware even as they speak that their affection will last only as long as the money holds out. I know aristos who keep their distant cousins on strings, endlessly pledging royal introductions and offices without ever being able or willing to keep their word. And others who ..."

"That doesn't prove *Bruce* will betray me," Gwen snapped. "Does it?"

"Better to keep it cold and simple and matter-of-fact," Simone said. "The truly long-lasting matches are built on shared understanding, not lust and love. And no illusions about your partner."

Gwen opened her mouth to retort, but stopped herself as Irene returned home. "The mood on the streets is ugly," she said. "Simone, I'm afraid you'll have to be staying for a while longer."

Simone made a face. "Again? I do have a pass ..."

"I doubt they're organised enough to check passes before they throw you in the Bastille," Irene said. "Stay here. If things get worse, we might have to abandon the shop and hide somewhere else."

Simone muttered a word under her breath. "I can't afford to be caught!"

"Nor can any of us," Irene said. "We're just as committed as you."

Chapter Twenty-Two
Versailles, France

hey say the traitors blew up a whole office block," Lady Jeanne said, with a surprising amount of glee. They sat together in a small sitting room, the door hanging open. "They killed hundreds of desk workers and their staff."

Raechel frowned. Lady Jeanne was an incorrigible gossip, tattletale and a number of other things that stemmed – Raechel suspected – from her having little else to do with her life. She might be an aristo, with a claim to a pension and a room, but she lacked any formal power or influence. She compensated by bossing around anyone lower on the scale than herself and, more interestingly, gathering and spreading gossip without bothering to check if it was actually true, to the point hardly anyone took her seriously. And yet, everyone listened.

"I heard it from my latest," Lady Jeanne insisted. "He was very clear on what happened."

"The traitors must have missed their real target," Raechel said, more to keep the conversation going than anything else. She didn't really believe it. There'd been too much disruption in court, over the last two days, for her to think the incident had been something as minor as an anarchist bombing. Louis had been called away so quickly he hadn't had time to do more than leave a note for her. "What do you think they were trying to do?"

"Well ..."

Raechel sighed, inwardly, as Jeanne expounded on her theories, ranging from the plausible to the extremely unlikely. It was clear, at least to her, that Jeanne knew very little, which suggested someone was covering up the real details. Jeanne might be known for exaggerating the truth, or simply making stuff up, but others – who had better reputations – were keeping their mouths firmly shut. They didn't know anything either. She waited for a suitable moment to take her leave, bracing herself for a chance. Jeanne was incredibly clingy. If Raechel said she had to powder her nose, or visit the bathroom, Jeanne would insist on going with her.

Someone started shouting, outside. Jeanne stood and hurried to the door, moving with surprising speed. Raechel followed and peeked out, long enough to note the two men arguing loudly, then muttered a quick farewell as Jeanne drank in the sight. She'd be telling the entire world that the pair had had a lovers' quarrel or some such nonsense, if they didn't threaten her into keeping her mouth shut. Raechel's lips curved into a brief smile at the thought. Whatever else could be said about Jeanne, it was very hard to convince her to keep anything to herself.

She frowned, inwardly, as she walked down the corridor and onto the balcony. The mood had changed in the last two days, growing darker as more and more men were called to the colours and sent out to the war. Or something. Raechel knew there'd been an *incident* in Paris, although the details were lacking. Jeanne might insist a simple office block had been blown up, but Raechel doubted it. The court wouldn't give much of a damn unless it was something worse. She sucked in her breath as she stared down at the dance floor. There were fewer dancers now, as if the energy was slowly being sucked out of the court.

And everyone is gathering in small groups, she reflected, her heart growing cold. *What happened?*

Her eyes swept the floor below. Who could she ask?

The majority of the men on the floor were old, fat and pretty much useless, even if they could recite their ancestry back to the days of Roman Gaul. One man had insisted, loudly, that he was a descendent of Julius Caesar, but he'd clearly not inherited any of his famous ancestor's military skill. Raechel was pretty sure it wasn't true, although there was no way to be certain. The historical records of that period were pretty lacking.

"My," a quiet voice said. "You're still here?"

Raechel schooled her face into calm immobility as she turned to face Lady Francis. She was old, old and sour and – in her own way – as haughty as Queen Catherine herself. Raechel had heard Lady Francis had been the former king's mistress, which she found a little hard to believe. But then, Lady Francis had presumably not been an elderly woman for her entire life. She'd have been younger when the former king sat on the throne.

"I have nowhere to go," she said, shortly. It was pretty much true. She'd done her best to remain on friendly terms with everyone, but she'd been careful not to let herself get too close to any of them ... something that would have grated, if she'd been a *real* aristo. There'd been no invitations to summer estates, no hints of marriage, nothing that might suggest she was anything other than a pointless pensioner. "What can I do?"

Lady Francis peered down her long nose. "A country mouse such as yourself is truly ignorant of modern affairs," she said. Her London counterparts would have said much the same thing. "It would be wise for you to go home."

Raechel shrugged. "What's happening?"

"Trouble," Lady Francis said. "Unrest in the streets, unrest in the fields ... I heard tell of churches being burnt, right across the south."

And you told me to go home, Raechel thought. As far as Lady Francis knew, Raechel had grown up in a mid-sized southern town that might as well be on the other side of the world, for all the attention Versailles paid to it. *Charming.*

"I heard about something in Paris," Raechel said. "What happened?"

Lady Francis eyed her coldly. "As if I would discuss such matters with you," she said, stiffly. The contempt in her voice was enough to make Raechel's blood boil. The cold awareness Lady Francis wouldn't have dared speak to anyone with real power like that would have made it worse, if Raechel had been what she seemed. "You could not possibly understand them."

"You don't know," Raechel said. "Do you?"

"You ..." Lady Francis raised a hand, as if she were about to slap Raechel's face, then lowered it again. "You want to know? Ask your lover, if he isn't too busy getting his fun in Paris!"

She turned and stalked away. Raechel watched her go, unsure what had just happened. Lady Francis couldn't have lasted so long at court without knowing where some, if not all, of the bodies were buried. Royal mistresses tended to get sent into *de facto* exile as soon as their lover passed away, after being stripped of everything they'd been given over the years. And yet, if she didn't know what was happening ...

Raechel shook her head, then turned and made her way back to her room. It was unlikely she'd hear anything more, not the way the court had closed itself up. Too many men had been recalled to the colours, too many others – and their families – had started to decamp, something she couldn't help thinking was a worrying sign. Versailles was *the* place to be, as far as the aristocracy was concerned. If they were heading to the country estates or even further afield ... she thought it boded ill. But then, people had been projecting the fall of France for years. It hadn't happened yet.

She tensed as she reached her door. It was ever so slightly ajar ... ice ran down her spine, her instincts telling her to turn and run. A lady's room was supposed to be her kingdom. No one, but no one, was supposed to enter without permission. Her mind raced. Louis? It wasn't impossible he might be trying to surprise her, if he'd returned from Paris. Or …

The door opened. Simone peeked out. "In here," she hissed. "Quickly."

Raechel gaped at her, then slammed her mental shields into place as she stepped into the room. It wasn't much, although she knew most of the aristo pensioners wouldn't have traded a room at court for a palace on the other side of the country. A bed large enough for three, a washroom and walk-in closet …. she'd had little time to decorate and it showed, although Irene had cautioned her not to get too attached to the tiny suite. She might have to leave in a hurry.

"You shouldn't be here," she said, once the door was firmly closed. "Why have you come?"

"I need some help," Simone admitted. "The Duke has locked down the entire court. I can't even get close to my old contacts."

"I see." Raechel forced herself to sit on the bed. "And what do you want me to do about it?"

Simone shot her an angry look. Raechel calmed herself with an effort. Simone had taken one hell of a risk to come to her, particularly given the death of her adopted father. Raechel was surprised she'd been allowed to walk around freely, considering what secrets might be locked up in her pretty little head. A life spent reading minds for a man like Talleyrand had to have taught her a lot of secrets.

"General Lafarge is on the dance floor," Simone said. "I want you to bring him back here and distract him while I read his mind."

"Distract him," Raechel repeated. "And what, precisely, do you mean by *that*?"

"Whatever it takes," Simone said. "There isn't time to argue. Do it."

Raechel glared. "What happened in Paris?"

"We … the magical underground launched a strike," Simone said. "General Lafarge knows enough to be useful, if I can read his mind. But he needs to be distracted."

Raechel nodded, shortly. General Lafarge was old, yet stubbornly refused to retire. She had no idea why he'd been tolerated so long, or why he hadn't been called away with the rest of the military aristos. Not, she supposed, that it mattered. If Simone was right …

"Stay here," she said. "I'll see what can be done."

Her heart twisted. It wouldn't be the first time she'd distracted someone, although … she scowled, suspecting Simone had picked up more of her thoughts than she wished, then turned and made her way back to the ballroom. There were fewer dancers than before, mostly women … her eyes narrowed as she silently noted who was missing, either called up or heading into the countryside. It didn't bode well for the future. If nothing else, there'd be fewer people she could use for cover.

General Lafarge stood by the drinks table, sipping a glass of wine. Raechel studied him thoughtfully. He was old, yet he was still a presence … he was, she reminded herself, close enough to the king to be entrusted with a number of vital commands, as well as titles and other honours. She couldn't help thinking that, unlike Louis, he really had gone to war. And … her eyes narrowed. Why was he even in the ballroom? Surely, he should be assisting the king to handle the crisis?

"I take it you want something," he said, as she came up to him. He had been drinking, but his voice was surprisingly clear. "A post for your lover?"

Raechel blinked in surprise, then did her best to look *more* surprised. It wasn't a bad guess … God knew, Louis's only hope of making something of himself lay in being assigned to a general's staff or frontline command before it was too late. And if she helped him to accomplish it … she wondered, suddenly, how many times the general had gone through the same script. There were certain men who were so powerful, so prominent, that they could take whatever they wanted, if it was not offered to them on a silver platter before they could even ask.

"Yes." She'd take the misconception and run with it.

"If you could raise him to a post worthy of his skills …"

"I could," General Lafarge said. His eyes took the scenic route up and down her body, lingering on her breasts before rising to meet hers. "But would it be worth it?"

"Yes," Raechel said, flatly. "Shall we go to my room to discuss it?"

The general gave her a more considering look. Raechel wondered, grimly, if she'd blown it. Women weren't expected to be so forward in London, but France was a very different country. Had she been too forward for him? Had he smelled a rat? Or had she deprived him of the pleasure of the chase? She didn't know, and it didn't matter. She had to get him close to Simone and distracted before it was too late.

"Perhaps we could," General Lafarge said. "What does your lover want?"

"A post worthy of him," Raechel repeated. "Somewhere he can shine."

General Lafarge followed her as she led him out of the ballroom and down the corridor to her room. He was surprisingly focused, for a man who'd spent much of his time drinking. Raechel knew a pair of distant relatives who drank so heavily they could function even after drinking enough alcohol to float a battleship … or so she'd been told. She had met a man who'd drank and drank and never showed the slightest hint of tipsiness. And yet, something was nagging at her mind. Was it a simple business transaction, without even the slightest attempt to pretend it was something it wasn't, or was she missing something?

"I could do that, if you like," General Lafarge said. His hands brushed against her rear, surprisingly gently. "But it would cost you."

Raechel closed the door, then disassociated her mind as she knelt in front of him and went to work. It wasn't something she particularly enjoyed doing, even though it was common at Versailles. It certainly had the great advantage of preventing pregnancy. A woman who fell pregnant might be able to convince her lover to marry her or … she might find herself cast aside, abandoned to raise the child or risk her life on a semi-legal abortion. Raechel knew more than she wanted about such things – Irene had made sure she knew the basics – and the procedure seemed life-threatening. And yet, in a world where premarital sex and pregnancy could end badly …

The general lasted longer than she'd expected before he exploded, but she told herself it was a good thing. Simone was nearby, reading his thoughts. If he was distracted … she tried not to swallow as he exploded, her stomach churning in disgust. He pulled up his trousers, brushed himself down and left without a word. Raechel stood, hurried to the toilet and threw up. The whole experience had been vile. She would almost sooner have let him go inside her.

"Here," Simone said. Raechel wondered, numbly, where she'd been. "Drink this."

Raechel took the water and washed her mouth out, then sipped. "Please … please tell me it was worth it."

"I'm sure Louis will think so," Simone said. "The general was quite pleased."

"You …" Raechel drank more water, her stomach heaving. She hadn't felt so bad since the undead plague in Moscow, where the stench of dead bodies had filled the air. "What did you learn?"

"The government is planning to lock down the city," Simone said, curtly. "And that there's definitely something of interest below Versailles. You and I will have to go exploring."

"Thanks," Raechel said, sourly. The taste in her mouth refused to fade. "Did you find anything actually useful?"

"A few things," Simone said. "If it is any consolation, you're not the first person to be in such a state."

"You?" Raechel felt her head spin. "Why …?"

"I did a lot of things for the ambassador," Simone said. "And I read the minds of people who did similar things, sometimes with their partner's knowledge and sometimes without it … you might be surprised to know how many women in London have done the same thing, even though it would mean social death if they were caught. But then, your society is pretty buttoned up. You know it, don't you."

Raechel remembered her former self and shuddered. "Yeah …"

"Get a wash," Simone advised. "And then get some sleep. I'll be back soon."

"I have to report to Irene," Raechel said. "And then …"

"I'll deal with it," Simone said. "Keep your head down for a few days. You need to be sharp when the time comes for us to go exploring."

Raechel shrugged. She had no intention of *not* reporting to Irene. Her mentor needed to know what had happened and why, even if Raechel's report couldn't be complete. And then …

"The general …" Raechel swallowed and started again. "Do you think he'll keep his word?"

"I think he'll certainly try to," Simone said. "Men like that are crude and rude and entitled" – her lips twisted in disgust – "but they do have a certain animal cunning. They know a history of breaking their word will eventually come back to bite them, no matter what they say or do. The general is very fond of young girls offering themselves to him. He wouldn't want to convince his future partners that it won't be worth it."

"I'm starting to think it wouldn't be worth it even if Louis got promoted right to the top of the tree," Raechel muttered. "Why is he such a … a bastard?"

Simone took the question seriously. "He was raised as a close kinsman to the king, close enough to the throne to be important and yet distant enough to make any attempt to actually *take* the throne unlikely. He had pretty much everything he wanted right from birth, with attendants meeting his every whim … I doubt anyone ever said no to him, which meant he grew up with one hell of an entitlement complex. And he did well enough to ensure he kept his place even as he grew older."

"Charming," Raechel muttered.

"But useful," Simone agreed. "There are some other things you can offer him, if you like."

Raechel lifted a hand and made a rude gesture. "No. Just no."

Chapter Twenty-Three
Paris, France

wen stood on a rooftop and waited.

The rest of her team waited beside her, their faces either grimly resolved or excited. They'd been cooped up for so long, forced to swallow their rage and hatred and bitter helplessness, that the prospect of action was irresistible, even though they knew there was a very good chance some of them wouldn't survive the day. They'd been helpless to shape their lives, denied even the slightest control over their own destinies ... she wondered, suddenly, how many of High Society's problems stemmed from the simple fact very few aristocrats had any real control over their own lives. The women were denied any real agency ... and so, she reflected, were half the men. They might be bound in chains of gold and silver, rather than iron and steel, but they were bound none the less. And so they took it out on the nearest convenient target.

At least the men can leave without too much trouble, she reflected, wryly. There was no shortage of men flowing around the country, staying with friends or trading entertainment for hospitality, or simply heading out to the Americas or the East Indies to seek their fortune. *The women find it a little harder to leave without cutting ties so completely they can never return.*

She scowled as she caught sight of a young girl, perched so close to the edge a gust of wind might blow her over and send her plummeting to the cobblestones below. She'd been cautioned not to talk too openly to her charges, but she'd had no trouble picking up the girl had been a whore – sold into prostitution – before coming into her magic and accidentally killing a particularly unpleasant client. Gwen was surprised she'd escaped before the magic-hunters had tracked her down, although it was possible she'd had help. If the client had been that unpleasant … Gwen knew more than she wished of the seedy side of London Town, of the realities of life for the poor and deprived. She found it impossible to condemn the young girl for lashing out with magic she hadn't even known she had, or running when she'd realised what she'd done. And yet, how had she escaped the hunters?

Perhaps they decided to look the other way, after examining the whorehouse, she thought, coldly. It would be unusually humane of them, but humanity could be found in some of the oddest places. *Or they simply discovered the place was patronised by the upper classes and decided it would be better not to search the building too thoroughly.*

She dismissed the thought as she heard the advancing policemen, backed up by cavalry and – she assumed – magicians. The last two days had been disturbingly quiet as the enemy struggled to react to what had happened, the uneasy silence broken only by a handful of anarchist bombings and a leaflet campaign that had papered the city in revolutionary propaganda. Gwen had heard whispers the underground council was having problems as it fought to bring all the various smaller rebel groups under its banner; she wasn't, in truth, particularly surprised. The police had been surprisingly effective at sowing distrust between the different factions, trying hard to convince some revolutionaries that others had sold them out. Gwen suspected they didn't need to bother. There were so many different groups, with so many different aims, that keeping them all pointed in the same direction was pretty much impossible.

But as long as the government keeps up the pressure on

us, the groups will be forced to work together, she thought. *And that means they have to put off the debate about what happens after the revolution until after the revolution.*

Someone shouted a warning. Gwen leaned forward, peering down into the streets below. The policemen were advancing in force, carrying rifles as well as clubs and pistols; the cavalry, behind them, were inching forward in a manner that suggested they wanted to throw caution to the winds and charge. Gwen's lips twitched in dour amusement. She'd met plenty of cavalry officers back home and they'd all been determined to charge, even if it meant galloping into the teeth of enemy fire. And they'd thought they were the kings of the battlefield.

They're not even trying to flank the barricade, Gwen thought. The rebels had hastily thrown up a makeshift barricade, providing a target for the enemy force, then started work on throwing up one behind them. Paris was a maze of streets, side streets and alleyways, allowing the rebels to simply flow around the police and soldiers and take up position to seal them into a trap. *Didn't they bother to think before they came calling?*

She sighed inwardly. She'd met too many cavalry officers who didn't bother to think. It was rare for a wealthy merchant's son to enter a cavalry regiment and almost unknown for anyone below upper middle class to join. They tended to be entitled as hell, even though they should have been smart enough to understand their weaknesses. The cavalry might be king on the battlefield – modern weapons argued otherwise – but their advantages were diminished, if not lost completely, on the streets. They could barely dominate everything within sight and even *that* was questionable. The population was no longer afraid of them and it showed.

"Liberty!" A cry broke the air, picked up by dozens – hundreds – of voices. "Liberty!"

Gwen leaned forward, watching as a shower of stones, bricks and chamberpots rained down on the enemy force. A man stumbled and fell off his horse as something struck his head, others scattered or fired madly in all directions as they caught brief glimpses of their unknown tormentors. Horses whinnied in alarm as more pots crashed down, then started as they realised the pots were full of boiling water or other – nastier – substances. Gwen had flinched at the thought of bombarding horses with lye, but she had to admit it was effective. The enemy force was coming apart at the seams.

Her eyes narrowed as the enemy commander – an officer, bedecked in a uniform that made him a very obvious target – ordered a charge, the cavalry crashing forward and crushing the policemen under their hooves as they hurled themselves at the barricade. Gwen snorted in contempt, although she had to admit it was probably the only thing he could do. The enemy had no room to fall back, not without giving in to panic. A handful of men had already started to run, exposing themselves to more falling debris. Only one of them made it out of her sight before he could be knocked down and left for dead.

She braced herself as the cavalry neared the barricade, the riders firing desperately. They were going to try to get over the barricade ... she grinned, savagely, as the gunpowder underneath the barricade exploded, sending a hail of sharp debris flying right into the cavalry's face. The charge came apart, men flying in all directions as their steeds panicked or died. Gwen saw the commander's head ripped from his body and sent spinning through the air until it smashed against a wall and burst like an egg. His body was lost somewhere in the chaos. There hadn't been *that* much gunpowder packed into the barricade, but it had been enough – more than enough – to break a charge.

The air below shimmered – she braced herself, spotting the enemy magicians. They were good, she had to admit; one was clearly shielding his companions while they started to return fire. Bolts of magic slammed into the buildings and swept over the rooftops, forcing the rebels to cut and run. Her team didn't wait for orders. They stood and returned fire in unison, raining death on the enemy position. Gwen cursed under her breath as their magic splashed uselessly around the shield. They hadn't realised they were just wasting energy …

A rolling sensation of *something* washed through the air, a sensation so disgusting she felt her stomach heave. She staggered under the impact, hearing men throwing up behind her as the magic lashed into them. A man standing on the parapet fell, vanishing out of sight … she had no time to catch him before he was gone. Her team started to waver, their attacks losing their power as they stumbled back … she cursed under her breath. They'd had almost no time to prepare the troops for mental attack and now they were paying for it.

She grabbed her magic and threw herself off the rooftop, channelling a beam of raw magic ahead of her. The enemy sorcerer was tough – he'd shielded his entire team – but he hadn't trained for something like her. How could he? And he'd spread himself far too wide … she shaped her magic into a needle, stabbed right *through* his shield before he could tighten his defences, and drove death into his skull. The Blazers turned on her, bombarding her shield with magic of their own, but it was too late. She split her attention, yanking everything from stones to bodies from the ground and hurling them at her targets. They barely had time to blow them apart before it was too late.

Light flared. Gwen's lips twitched – the enemy had clearly learnt from their earlier experiences – and squeezed her eyes shut. The tactic would have worked on almost anyone else – except Bruce, her mind reminded her, if he'd kept up with his training – but on her it was almost useless. She could *sense* people moving near her, *feel* objects flying through the air. Her magic spun around her, a deadly cloud of raw power. The enemy magicians started to fall back in disarray. Their blinding light had been more dangerous to them than it had been to her.

Magic flared. An uppercut – a wave of raw magic – slammed into her shield. She let it hurl her upwards, channelling the power to send her spinning over the rooftops and down into the alleyway, well away from the enemy magicians. Her team should have scattered by now, if they'd followed orders ... she'd bet good money some of them had stayed to fight, even though it was futile. The rest of the French magicians would be on their way, flying over the rooftops to come down hard on the rebels. Gwen suspected they wouldn't hesitate to smash the entire street to dust, if they thought it was worth the effort. The rebels had made them panic.

She landed neatly on the damp ground and took a moment to compose herself. The fighting was still going on, but slowly starting to taper down. The rebels would have to break contact and quickly ... she prayed, to a God she wasn't entirely sure she believed in, that her team had the sense to retreat when more magicians arrived. If they got caught and interrogated ... Gwen had no illusions. The enemy would shortly know everything their prisoners knew.

The air shifted, behind her. Gwen ducked and span around, instinctively, as *something* flashed over her head. A young man stood behind her, wrapped in power. It was difficult to see his face. A Mover? Gwen dodged a second blow, her head spinning in confusion. She'd seen some magicians use magic to enhance their physical abilities, but this ... the man struck the stone wall, sending cracks spinning out in all directions. Gwen cursed under her breath and reached out with her power, trying to hurl him into the air. If he was enhancing himself, he didn't have the raw power to tackle her directly ...

She knew she'd made a mistake, an instant too late. His magic crashed down on her, a sheet of magic that nearly crushed her shield and tore her to pieces. She hadn't felt so helpless since ... since ever, even when she'd encountered her very first Null. Her legs buckled, threatening to collapse, as she forced herself to stumble back. Raw magic crackled around her, blurring into the nearby buildings. She realised, to her horror, they were going to collapse. If there was anyone still inside … she hoped – prayed – they had the sense to run.

The Frenchman growled, his face still hidden behind his magic, as he pressed down on her shield. Gwen found herself pushed back, unable to defend herself … unable even to hold the shield in place. He'd drawn her into a test of strength she couldn't win and … her mind raced, searching for options. If she … she reached out frantically, splitting her attention to tear at the falling buildings and draw the debris onto him. The Frenchman lashed out with a blast of raw magic, dangerously uncontrolled. The falling brickwork shattered into clouds of dust. Gwen hastily directed it towards him, dropping to the ground to avoid his retaliatory blast. It wouldn't get through his shield, but it would give her time to muster her defences and *think*. Escape was impossible. She'd have to kill him or …

She braced herself as the Frenchman walked forward, his power shimmering around him. Her magic hummed in response, brushing against his … a shudder ran down her spine, a sense she was about to cross the line in some manner she didn't quite understand. His power blurred into hers, allowing her to slip into his shield … she had an impression of him looking down at her, completely confused, before she caught hold of his ankle and reached out with her mind. His heart exploded in his chest. She grunted in pain as his power vanished, his body landing on hers a moment later. It was all she could do to muster the strength to push him aside and stagger to her knees. His dead eyes looked up at her, his face locked in a death mask.

Gwen stared. *What the …?*

She had thought herself used to horror. She'd seen men crippled by war, women ground down by life … she'd seen the inhumanity man could do to man, or the poor unfortunates born freaks of nature, and yet the Frenchman was something else. His head was a bulbous mass, his veins so prominent she couldn't help wondering if he was human; his arms and legs were disturbingly big, while his torso was uncomfortably small. Gwen felt sick, but forced herself to pull back his clothes to inspect his bare skin. It felt unpleasant to her touch, almost leathery. She swallowed, hard. What the hell had the French *done* to the poor man?

It took her all her nerve to inspect his arms and legs. They felt ... wrong. Gwen didn't know *that* much about anatomy, but she had lain with Bruce and *he'd* been nothing like the man she'd killed. He'd felt *right*, while the Frenchman looked like a crude mockery of the human condition. And he'd had enough raw power to come very close to killing her outright. It made no sense. On one hand, he'd had the power; on the other, he'd lacked the training to finish her off. And ...

Did they use magic to make him stronger, she asked herself, *or did he do it to himself?*

She stood, gritting her teeth. There was no time to take the body back to the underground base and ... even if she did, what could they do with it? She had no idea. Her medical staff were back in London ... she briefly considered trying to smuggle the body all the way back to the city, then dismissed the thought with a moment of irritation. She knew that wasn't going to work. Instead, she closed her eyes and summoned enough magic to burn the body to ash. The French would never know what had happened to their magician.

Her legs wobbled uneasily as she stumbled down the alleyway. The sound of fighting had died away, replaced by an eerie silence that chilled her to the bone. The police and soldiers were dead, she hoped, and a number of their magicians shocked out of their complacency. The underground had scored a major victory and yet ... she kept walking, drawing on her magic to keep herself going. She was in no state for a fight, if she was caught or if she simply ran into someone with bad intentions. She had few illusions about that either.

Simone wasn't wrong to sound the alarm, she thought, leaving the battleground behind. The streets felt edgy, people looking around as if they expected the sky to fall at any moment. It might, if the French government decided to raze the entire district. *What the hell are the French doing?*

"Gwen," Irene said, when Gwen finally stumbled into the shop. "What happened to you?"

"Good question," Gwen managed. It dawned on her she had to look absolutely nightmarish. Her cloak was in rags, her shirt and trousers were torn … her garments were stained with blood. She cursed under her breath. If someone had noticed she'd been in a fight and followed her … she'd been in no state to notice a shadow either. "Read my mind. Please."

Irene blinked. "What *was* he?"

"I don't know," Gwen said. Her head hurt, either through magical exhaustion or Irene's magic clashing with hers. She sagged into a chair, feeling utterly drained. "But if there's more than one of him …"

She shuddered. She'd faced magicians who knew their powers better than her, who'd turned themselves into masters through endless practice, but the Frenchman had been something else altogether. If he'd had better training, he might have bested her and then … she didn't want to think about it. Her thoughts raced, questions without answers spinning through her mind. What had they done to him? And were there more? The experiment, whatever it was, had clearly been a success.

And if there is more than one of him, she reflected as Irene passed her a glass of water, *the war might be within shouting distance of being lost.*

Chapter Twenty-Four
Paris, France

he trick to spreading rumours, Bruce had learnt when he was a child, was to speak with absolute confidence while keeping the rumour reasonably plausible. The wilder the story, the less likely it would be believed by anyone who wasn't already invested in the tale and the less they believed the whispers, the more they'd think critically about what they were being told. It might be amusing to listen to stories of satanic rites performed by Queen Catherine – to say nothing of tales of incest with her entire family – but relatively few people actually believed them. They were just used to mock someone the vast majority of the population had never seen in person and never would, someone it was easy to hate and resent ...

He stood in a bar, listening to the chatter amongst the patrons as they argued over the events of the last few days. They knew less than he did, but they were united in anger towards the government even if they weren't sure what to make of the rebel underground. Some thought the rebels would make things better, others thought they'd make them worse; others, still others, thought the government was bound to win and refused to take the risk of open opposition. Bruce understood, all too well. The men who had something to lose were reluctant to risk it for nothing.

The chatter went back and forth, chewing the fat about

grudges against the government that went back literally decades. Bruce was astonished the French hadn't had a revolution earlier. The American Colonies had been treated very kindly, by comparison, and *they'd* still tried to declare independence from the British Crown. The sheer level of wasteful spending, corruption and incompetence was daunting. Bruce had had little regard for his father's administration, but even *he* had to admit his father had done a better job than King Louis. The Frenchman wasn't even a capable tyrant.

"My master was told his daughter would have to give a few favours if he wanted his licence renewed," Bruce said, infusing a little magic into his words to make them convincing. The patrons had drunk enough to weaken their defences, but there was no point in taking chances. "If she went out with the bastard, he'd give her whatever she wanted."

The patrons muttered in outrage, several more chiming in with their own stories. Bruce allowed himself an inner smirk. The story was believable because nearly every Parisian bureaucrat was incredibly corrupt, demanding a bribe – or sexual favours – for even the smallest request. It wasn't even the most outrageous story Bruce had heard while walking the city, but it was a particularly nasty one. The French were more sexually open than the British, yet there were limits. Coercing an innkeeper's daughter to have sex with a bureaucrat very definitely crossed the line. And yet, what was the point in trying to complain? Everyone knew that trying to raise the alarm would only get you targeted by the bureaucrat and his pals, all of whom would happily close ranks to punish someone who got above his station.

"I heard the bank is refusing to pay out money," another patron offered. "They just offered useless paper!"

Bruce took the rumour and ran with it. "My sister's dressmaker said the aristos aren't paying their debts," he said. "Do they even have the money to pay?"

He smiled, again, as the rumour spread through the

pub, growing with each and every retelling. It wasn't untrue, either, although it was hard to be sure if it was just a handful of aristos trying to welsh on their debts or something indicative of a far larger problem. The aristos had always been reluctant to pay full price for anything purchased in Paris and it was hard, if not impossible, to legally *force* them to pay. And yet ... it was worrying that, from what he'd heard, nearly all of the debts had gone unpaid. If the banks really were refusing to hand out *real* money ...

That's something else we can do, he thought, as the discussion raged on. Paper money had never been popular in France, not when the French economy was constantly one bad day from collapse. No one had forgotten just what had happened when the French government had encouraged commoners to invest in a crazy financial scheme which had – of course – collapsed, nor how the government had forced the handful of commoners who'd actually managed to make money to surrender their gains. *If we undermine the economy, they'll all start demanding real money and the banks will simply run out.*

"I heard the shopkeepers are keeping back their bread to sell on the black market," he said, finally. It was true. He'd heard *that* from Jean-Luc personally. "They don't want to sell at government rates."

He grimaced, inwardly, as he made his farewells and slipped away. The French Government had imposed price controls, insisting the bakers – in particular – sold their wares at a fixed price, a price that bore no resemblance to the cost of actually obtaining the ingredients and baking bread. The farmers were having problems growing wheat, so their costs were rising and the bakers were caught between the devil of losing money or the deep blue sea of selling their bread to those prepared to pay a reasonable price. But when that price was well above the ability of most people to pay for it ...

His lips quirked into a cold smile as he made his way down the street. This part of the city had barely been touched by the rebels, although that hadn't stopped the government from stationing a small body of troops within the district. They stood on street corners, eyes flickering from side to side as if they expected to be jumped at any moment. Bruce had heard rumours they were eunuchs, because they weren't hooting and hollering at any young women who happened to be passing. He suspected it was more a case of their commanding officers laying down the law, making it absolutely clear the locals were not to be harassed unless they were on the verge of riot. The poorer districts being lost would be a headache, but not particularly fatal as long as the rioters remained confined to their districts. Losing the middle-class districts would be the beginning of the end.

Which means we need to keep pushing, he thought. He was tempted to attack the soldiers himself, but he had no idea what – if any – magicians they had backing them up. *And that means finding new ways to hurt the government.*

He kept walking, dropping into pubs long enough to fan the flames before resuming his walk. The signs of trouble were everywhere, if one had eyes to look; long lines of women waited outside bakeries and grocers, while their menfolk lined up outside banks to withdraw their money in coins, rather than paper. Bruce smiled as he saw a young child handing out leaflets, then making a hasty escape before he could be caught and beaten by the soldiers. The crowd muttered its anger, convincing the soldiers not to give chase. Bruce was surprised at their restraint. But then, if rumour was to be believed, any police or military force that ran into the darker parts of the city was never seen again.

There are just too many people willing to fight them, he reflected, as he kept moving. *And they can't afford another defeat.*

He stopped outside a large bakery and watched a sweating man try to tell the women – and the handful of men – that there was no more bread. His attitude wouldn't have been convincing even if the women hadn't been in a foul – and desperate – mood. They had no time for his excuses, no time for his plaintive explanations that he could no longer afford to bake vast amounts of bread. Their anger was driven by the grim awareness their children would be growing hungry …

"Give us bread," Bruce yelled. The rest of the crowd took up the cry. "Give us bread!"

The baker stumbled backwards, looking guilty. Bruce didn't see who threw the first stone, but it didn't matter. The baker was battered to the ground by a hail of stones, the crowd charging over his dead body and trampling him to death as they plunged into the bakery and searched it from top to bottom. A young woman fled for her life, carrying a baby in her arms, as the crowd ripped through the shop, finding a handful of loaves concealed behind a false wall. The crowd's rage spread as it flowed back out, a couple of women carrying the bread above their heads and calling for the rest of the shops to be searched. Bruce watched from a safe distance – the crowd no longer needed encouragement – as groceries were looted, what little they had pulled from their stores and shared out amongst the crowd.

He braced himself as the soldiers marched up, hastily fixing their bayonets as they prepared to disperse the crowd. No horsemen, he noted absently, and no magicians too … probably. The former wasn't really a surprise. The rebels had killed a number of cavalrymen and their horses – it said a great deal about the government they were more worried about the horses than the men – and the mob was no longer scared of them. Armed troops were likely to be a great deal more effective, if they were well-trained and well-led. Bruce eyed the men thoughtfully, assessing their chances. They looked alarmingly capable. They weren't even trying to pen the crowd in so they could be slaughtered.

Smart of them, he acknowledged. *If they give the mob room to retreat, it won't try to fight.*

The troop commander started barking orders, commanding the mob to disperse. Bruce didn't give the orders any chance to take effect. He reached out with his magic and threw chunks of stone and debris at the soldiers. They fired without waiting for orders, the bullets snapping into Bruce's hastily raised shield. The mob howled in outrage and charged, swarming and crushing the soldiers through sheer weight of numbers. Bruce turned and walked away, feeling a pang of guilt as he left the mob behind. It had to be done – he needed to keep the city boiling – but a great many people were about to die, simply because they were in the wrong place at the wrong time.

A line of troops hurried towards him, drawn to the racket. Bruce stepped aside to let them pass, noting how shopkeepers were chasing out customers and slamming down shutters in a desperate – and probably futile – attempt to save their shops. The mob knew, now, that some bread had been held back for sale on the black market, or – just as likely – to keep the baker's family fed. Bruce could hardly blame them, if it was the latter. The baker had every reason to want to ensure his family lived …

He felt another pang of guilt as he reached a bridge and stared down at the churning smelly river below. The woman he'd seen flee … the baker's wife or daughter or … what did it matter? Had she made it clear? Or … it was easy to plot rioting and uprisings and even outright war against people he didn't know, people who were nothing more than numbers, but harder when those numbers had names and faces. And yet … he scowled, remembering the constant disputes between the various colonial governments and the settlers along the frontiers. The former wanted to honour the treaties with the various Indian tribes, the latter saw the Indians as a deadly threat and wanted them gone, no matter what it took. He supposed the British Government felt much the same way about the French. It was one thing to have colonial contests, and genteel struggles for influence in places like India and China, but quite another to have an invasion force land in Britain itself. Lord Mycroft and his peers might have decided it was time to put an end to the threat …

His eyes narrowed as he spotted the barges being carefully navigated down the river, a handful of soldiers clearly visible on their decks. Troop convoys? It was possible, he supposed, although the French *did* have a reasonably well-developed road and rail network. There was no need to copy the American settlers and use the water for transport ... he smiled, suddenly, as he realised what had to be on the barges. Grain. Or food ... it would be shipped to the government-controlled harbours and parcelled out to government-controlled shops and churches and sold, the bureaucrats taking their cut at every opportunity. Bruce was *certain* a sizable number of men were profiting greatly from the scarcity, just as they'd done in America and Britain. A country's peril was always an opportunity for someone willing to take advantage of it.

Cold anger bubbled up within him, fuelling his magic. The French had invaded the American colonies, as well as Britain. They'd come far too close to killing Gwen. He hadn't even known her at the time, not properly, and the thought he might never have known her at all ... he jumped into the air and landed neatly on the barges, flames boiling around him and lashing out at the soldiers. They barely had any time to react before his fires washed over them. One man had the presence of mind to jump into the water, the remainder caught fire and died screaming. Bruce barely noticed as he blasted the barges themselves, the boatmen joining the lone soldier in the water as the flames spread from barge to barge. The stench of burning human flesh wafted through the air, making him choke. He turned, just in time to see a line of soldiers on the bridge, aiming their rifles at him. A pair of magicians hung in the air behind them, growing closer with every passing second.

Brave bastards, Bruce thought. He yanked at the river water with his magic and threw as much as he could at the soldiers. The magicians wouldn't be slowed for more than a few seconds – if he was lucky – but it would be enough time to make his escape. *Brave and too slow.*

He wrapped his magic around himself, took a deep breath and jumped into the water. The Seine was so polluted and dank it was unlikely anyone went swimming voluntarily, but his magic would keep him safe long enough to evade the magicians and get out. They'd have trouble following him too, given how badly he'd churned up the water. He felt bullets cracking into the dark waters as he pushed his way through the mire, holding his breath as long as he could. There were some magicians who boasted they could breath underwater, but he'd never seen it done. He had a feeling they'd just made it up.

And yet, we'd make them prove their claims, he thought, as he surfaced. *We wouldn't take them on faith.*

A pair of young children gaped at him, then ran. Bruce gasped for breath, then levitated his way into the air and landed neatly on the riverside, looking around for danger. He hadn't travelled that far – the plume of smoke was only three or four bridges away – but it was far enough to break contact. He hoped. He looked down at himself, dispelling the magic that had kept him dry, then started to walk. He'd be back with Jean-Luc shortly, then covertly check on Gwen. It wasn't easy to keep an eye on her. She was astonishingly perceptive herself and he was fairly sure she was training her students how to use the mental arts to guard their bases. It would only take a moment for one of them to sense him, conclude he was a police spy and sound the alarm. And then he'd have to fight or run or both.

She might be happy to see me, he thought. There'd been no news from Spain, save for newspaper bulletins pretending high confidence. They were so short on actual detail he knew no one who found them convincing. Bruce suspected the Duke of India was giving the French a very hard time. *But what'll she say if she sees me?*

He scowled as he passed a pair of guardposts, the guards paying no attention to him. He wanted to think she'd be pleased to see him, but he knew her well enough to know she'd say otherwise. She had her sense of duty, and felt more obligation – he admitted privately – to the government than himself. It was odd, he reflected. He'd been a child of privilege – his father a wealthy nobleman and viceroy – and yet he felt less regard for the government than a young girl who would have been married off by now, if she hadn't had enough magic to make her unmarriageable. It was very definitely odd.

"Welcome back," Jean-Luc said, as he entered the pub. His voice dripped sarcasm, a droll reminder Bruce had been meant to pass on a handful of messages and then return immediately. "How many whores did you meet?"

Bruce shrugged. "There was a bread riot," he said. "I thought it best to stay out of sight until things quietened down."

Jean-Luc nodded. "Demand for bread will be going up shortly," he said, as if the demand – and the prices – hadn't already been on the rise. "We must be ready."

"Of course," Bruce agreed. He wasn't quite sure what Jean-Luc saw in him, if indeed the smuggler believed his story about being a runaway magician, but he wasn't about to look a gift horse in the mouth. "I also heard stories about the government printing more paper money."

"That's probably true," Jean-Luc said. "Luckily, no one with any sense puts their money in the bank."

And he laughed.

Chapter Twenty-Five
Versailles, France

he rumours are true," Simone said, as she stepped up to join Raechel. "The government has ordered the banks to hold back gold and silver, and only allow customers to withdraw paper money."

Raechel gave her a sharp look. "And how do you know that?"

"The decree was published only a few short hours ago, but the nobility is already pressuring the banks to hand over their money – *real* money," Simone said. "It'll be interesting to see how it plays out."

"Right." Raechel finished her drink and put the glass aside for the servants. "Are they getting anywhere?"

Simone shrugged. "The richer aristos don't have to worry about their money in the bank, as long as they own their land," she said. "The poorer ones ... they'll be in real trouble."

"Their money will be worthless," Raechel agreed. "That won't go down well."

She'd listened, saying nothing, as courtiers grumbled openly about the sudden shift in government financial policy. It was rare to hear any sort of criticism, let alone veiled attacks on the king and his innermost circle, and yet the attacks had been relentless. She supposed it made a certain kind of sense. The courtiers were dependent on their pensions and if they were paid in money their creditors considered worthless … sure, the government might insist the creditors had to take paper money, but she doubted they could enforce it. The creditors might just defy the government openly, if money was at stake.

"No," Simone agreed. "But it does give us an opportunity."

Raechel nodded and allowed Simone to lead her out of the smaller ballroom and through a maze of corridors. They were surprisingly empty, for a palace that was normally buzzing with life. Versailles felt eerily deserted. It was a complex of palaces and apartment blocks, designed for thousands of residents and long-term guests, yet half the inhabitants had fled to the country and the remainder were talking in low voices, discussing the king and his government's latest decisions. They hadn't hidden their discontent. Raechel suspected it boded ill for the future.

"We're relatively safe here," Simone muttered. "But once we sneak through the guardpost we'll be dangerously exposed. If you don't want to come …"

"I have to," Raechel said. It wasn't entirely true – Irene had told her to embed herself within the court and listen to what the courtiers were saying, rather than risk being caught sneaking into somewhere forbidden – but she suspected they'd never have a better chance to take a look under the court. "Are *you* sure?

Simone grimaced. "They'll deal with me, sooner or later," she said. "I doubt I'll be allowed to leave freely, too."

Raechel nodded. Simone wasn't *just* Ambassador Talleyrand's adopted daughter. She might have been urged to leave the court and settle somewhere in the countryside if that was *all* she'd been. She was a mind-reader with enough insight into government politics to make her very dangerous, particularly when the dovish faction started to reform. They might even reach out to her, to see if she knew what had happened to her father's files. And who knew what might happen then?

"In here," Simone said. She pushed Raechel into a

room, shut the door and indicated the dresses on the bed. "Get yours on, quickly."

Raechel blinked. The dress was surprisingly demure, designed to make the wearer practically invisible. Simone donned hers with commendable speed, pulling it over her regular dress and covering her hair with a simple bonnet. Raechel followed suit, glancing at herself in the mirror. She looked so different from her regular appearance that she might as well be considered part of the furniture, when there were so many women strolling around in remarkable dresses or showing enough flesh to get them ostracised back home. It puzzled her for a moment, then realised the aristo women didn't want the competition. They had far more sexual freedom than their counterparts in Britain.

She scowled. "Are you sure you can get us past the guardpost?"

"Yes," Simone said. She took a sheet of paper out of her pocket and held it in front of her. "Let's go."

Raechel followed, feeling her heart begin to beat rapidly. The French treated their maids better than their English rivals – it was surprising, yet it was true – but she was pretty sure the French would not be pleased if they caught the maids poking around under the palace complex. She'd have to run and hope she could get out of sight long enough to ditch the maid's dress and pretend she'd been nowhere near the guardhouse. If Simone felt the same way, she showed no sign of it. She just strode up to the guard, showed him the paper and waited. He stepped aside to let them pass.

Impressive, Raechel thought, as they made their way through the door and down a long flight of stairs. *What was on that paper?*

Simone held up a hand to slow her as they reached the bottom and stepped into a long corridor, lit by flickering lanterns. The air was cold, a faint gust of wind suggesting the underground complex had a passageway that led to the open air. Raechel looked around, feeling cold as she saw the stone walls and bare floor. Versailles was known for staggering luxury, even for the lowest of the low, but this … it felt more a prison than anything else, somewhere unsafe and unwelcoming even to the country's king. She followed Simone onwards, eyes flickering from side to side. The corridor seemed never ending.

"Keep calm," Simone mouthed, so quietly Raechel could barely hear her. "Keep your eyes down. Don't react to them."

Raechel opened her mouth to ask who, an instant before the corridor twisted to reveal a pair of men walking towards them. She nearly froze, her legs tottering before following Simone as she stepped to one side to allow the men to stride past. They paid no attention to the two maids … Raechel blinked, feeling a hot flash of amusement. Irene had told her that, if someone managed to slip through the guards, people tended to assume they had a right to be there without bothering to check, as long as they didn't do anything too striking. She kept her eyes lowered as the men receded into the distance, careful not to look up until they were gone. It was important she pretended to be submissive to keep them from asking pointed questions.

Simone caught her eye and tapped her lips as they neared an open door. Three men were talking, their voices blurring together. She had trouble picking out individual voices, although she thought she recognised one from the endless dances in happier times. Another was as cold and hard as the grave.

"… Is very concerned," a Spanish-accented voice said. "We need more of your troops heading south."

"The trouble in Spain, although regrettable, is not lethal," a second – and oddly familiar – voice said. "The trouble here, in and around Paris, is far worse. We need to put it down and fast."

"The special troops are still being prepared," the cold voice said. "There are … *issues* … with their preparation."

"Issues," the second voice repeated. "You mean, the process is yet to be finalised."

"Yes," the cold voice said. "We and the British have been largely dependent on luck. Our process is harsher, and it comes with a price, but we have evaded the *luck* requirement. But we need time to finalise the process."

"We don't have time," the first voice snapped. "We have lost control of Portugal and too much of Spain! How long will it be until the British cross the mountains and invade France itself?"

"Quite some time," the familiar voice said. "The British are reliant on their navy to land and support troops. The further they advance into Spain, the harder it will be to supply and reinforce their troops. They will also have to reckon with Spanish factions that don't want to be beholden to anyone, even their fellow Spanish. And that will be quite bothersome. The Spanish have never been easy to rule."

"But far too many of them hate you more than the British," the accented voice said. "And so …"

Raechel nearly jumped as she heard a hand slap the table. "It is of no account," the cold voice said. "Our counterattack is nearly ready. We will move and obliterate the rebels, then turn our attention to the British army. They have only one. Once it is destroyed, they will have to seek peace or risk us landing on their shores. Again."

"Again," the accented voice echoed. "They drove you into the sea, last time."

"Yes," the cold voice said. "And now …"

Simone caught Raechel's eye and motioned for her to follow. Raechel did as she was bid, a moment before a handful of men in drab outfits walked out of a nearby door and strode past them. A chill ran down her spine. The men were …odd. They didn't seem to notice the two girls, let alone stare or do anything to them. She wondered, rather numbly, if they were drugged. It wasn't impossible. She'd visited opium dens in London a couple of years ago, with a male companion she preferred to forget, and she knew how easy it could be to lose track of everything but the drug. The men filed past them and walked into the distance.

They kept moving, passing a number of closed doors. Raechel was tempted to try to open them, but she knew better. There was no way to know what might be on the far side. She found herself looking around again and again, trying to determine just how large the complex actually was. Versailles was easily the size of a small town, bigger than any aristocratic or regal complex in Britain, and if it spread from one end to the other … she wondered, suddenly, if there were tunnels linking to each and every building overhead. It was quite possible. And that meant …

"In here," Simone whispered. She pulled a rag from her dress and tossed it to Raechel. "Try to look as though you're dusting.

Raechel nodded as they stepped into an empty office and looked around. It seemed more like a clerk's chamber than anything more formal, but there were still a surprisingly high number of papers on the desk. Or perhaps it wasn't a surprise … her uncle had had a small army of assistants, from his trusted secretaries to clerks who handled the paperwork while he set overall priorities and wormed his way into the confidence of a succession of government ministers. If she was any judge, the French aristos were no different. They adored the perks that came with being noblemen, but detested the hard work of government. She'd heard a story, once, about a town clerk who'd used his position to dissolve his own marriage. Looking at the papers around her, she wondered if the Frenchmen were doing the same.

She read fast, eyes jumping from paper to paper. It was confusing. The French were moving things to Paris and Versailles, but the paperwork wasn't clear on exactly *what* was being moved. Everything was referred to by code names, save for a single note informing the buyer that the king had used his authority to mandate that the matter had the very highest priority. The rules and regulations governing the import of … *whatever* … had been suspended. Raechel stared down at the final set of notes in bafflement. If whatever it was happened to be banned in France ... what was it? And why would the French King put his name to an order lifting the ban, for a single very specific case?

Her eyes narrowed. *Slaves?*

It was possible ... perhaps. The French had banned the slave trade years ago and, on paper at least, freed all their slaves. In practice, from what she'd heard, the slaves hadn't noticed any real difference. And yet ... what had they banned, and then decided they needed after all? She could name a hundred possibilities, but none of them seemed particularly likely.

Simone caught her eyes. "What is it?"

"They're moving things around the country, but I don't know what," Raechel said. It was impossible to come up with an answer. Slaves? Possible, but unlikely. "I think ..."

A rush of air touched her skin. She looked up. A young man stood in the doorway, staring at them. Raechel cursed, inwardly. They'd been caught ... Simone should have sensed his approach, shouldn't she? A flash of suspicion ran through her, driven away by the grim awareness Simone hadn't *needed* to lure Raechel below ground if she'd wanted to betray her. She could just have reported her true identity and traded it for ... for whatever she wanted.

"We were hoping to discuss matters with you, My Lord," Simone said, in a breathy voice that sent chills down Raechel's spine. "We have much to offer you, if you are interested."

The young man swallowed, hard. Raechel couldn't read his thoughts, but she could see his churning emotions. He could take advantage of them, yet ... if his superiors discovered he'd left his office unlocked he'd be in deep shit. Better to chase them out of the complex, or at least somewhere outside his bailiwick, and hope for the best. And yet ...

"Get out," he hissed. "Go!"

"My," a cold voice said. "Just what is going on here?"

Raechel glanced up and froze. Duke Philippe was

standing there, looking calm and composed and very dangerous. His hands were clasped behind his back … she wondered, suddenly, just what he was hiding. A second man stood behind him, wrapped in a shapeless robe and cowl that made him look like a monk. She lowered her eyes hastily, telling herself they could still get out of trouble. Better to be thought a pair of lazy or incompetent maids than spies.

"We hoped to discuss our assignments with your clerk, My Lord," Simone said, bowing so low it was impossible to see her face. Raechel hoped it was convincing. She could take a whipping. Being hanged would be much harder to survive. "We thought we could …"

Duke Philippe snorted. "Simone," he said. "Did you think I would not know you?"

Simone started. "I …"

"And who is your friend?" Duke Philippe gestured. Raechel felt an invisible force grab her chin and push it up. "And who might you be?"

"My maid," Simone said, quickly. There was a hint of panic in her tone. She was dependent on her talent, yet it had failed her. "She came on my orders."

"I think not." Duke Philippe gestured again. Raechel's bonnet flew off, allowing her hair to fall free. There was a hint of triumph in the duke's tone as he spoke again. "I thought there was something *fake* about you. A shame I didn't think to look beyond the country mouse. No matter. It will all come out shortly."

He nodded to his companion, who stepped forward and reached for Raechel's arm. Raechel cursed herself for her own stupidity – she should never have disobeyed Irene, she should never have listened to Simone – and brought her knee up as hard as she could, striking the man in the groin. He should have felt it, even if he wore a codpiece; instead, he didn't show any reaction at all. Raechel tried to dart back, but he was faster. He grabbed her arm, yanked her forward and peered down at her. His face was … *off*. Raechel couldn't put it into words, but it was there. His face was …

Her eyes skipped over it. His face just wasn't *right*.

"Interesting," Duke Philippe said. "And what are you?"

Raechel struggled, but it was futile. Irene had cautioned her never to pit herself directly against a man – men were often stronger and faster, if not smarter – and she was starting to think her mentor had been right. She kicked her captor's ankles, but – again – he showed no visible reaction. It made little sense. What *was* he?

Duke Philippe's hand lashed out, lightning quick. Simone collapsed. Raechel stared, icy fear trickling down her spine. She'd never seen anything like it, not … it was … it was unthinkable. It was precisely controlled violence, enough force to knock Simone out without doing permanent harm … she hoped. Duke Philippe stepped forward, his dark eyes meeting hers. She quailed at the ice she saw in them.

"Answer my questions," he said. His voice was cold and hard. "Who are you?"

Raechel gritted her teeth, keeping her mouth firmly shut. There was no point in giving him her cover story. He already knew it was a lie. Probably. He'd certainly investigate, sending his men to trace back her story to the point he could simply unravel it piece by piece … she thought she saw, for a second, something glinting within his eyes. She'd seen him use one kind of magic. Did he have more? Did he have them *all*?

"Fine," Duke Philippe said. There was no hint of anticipation in his voice, which made it all the more terrifying. "Let us see …"

His eyes seemed to grow even darker, until they became dark holes sucking in all light. Raechel fought to break eye contact, or to close her eyes, but her body refused to obey. Her will was crumbling, her body weakening with terrifying speed … her thoughts started to wander, flickering memories flashing across her mind and then vanishing again before she could focus on any of them. Irene had schooled her in resisting Charm, when it was applied by a Charmer, but this was different. Her legs buckled. She would have collapsed if it weren't for the man holding her upright. Her mind staggered under the pressure, her defences collapsing …

… And then the darkness reached out and swallowed her.

Chapter Twenty-Six
Paris, France

e need to decide how to proceed," the merchant said. "What do we do now?"

"We need to continue the fight," the poor man said. "They are moving more and more troops into the city."

Gwen kept her thoughts to herself. The underground council had expanded, then contracted, then expanded again as more and more revolutionary groups tried to join up. There were former soldiers, lawyers, teachers, farmers and so many others she was tempted to ask if the aristocrats were the *real* rebels. There were even a handful of penniless aristos trying to join the underground, although no one seemed quite sure if they had genuine conviction or if they simply hoped to ride the tide of rebellion to the top. The only ones who had no representation in the rebel underground were the clergy and that, from what she'd heard, was because the Pope had ordered the church hierarchy to stand solidly behind the king and his government.

She listened, keeping her mouth firmly closed as the debate washed around the room. The rebels needed to get organised and they had to do it themselves, both to ensure they could still claim to be patriotic Frenchmen – rather than British patsies – and to make certain they knew what they were fighting for. There was no vision of the post-revolutionary future, no sense of what the rebels wanted to achieve. Some wanted a democracy, with the population voting for ministers and the aristocracy being marginalised; some wanted to abolish the aristocracy, erase all traces of hereditary privilege and ensure that only true leaders rose to the top; some wanted to nationalise all the land and share it out on a communal basis, rather than have it held by a handful of noblemen and worked by farmers with little say in their affairs. The wish list of objectives was long, contradictory and included – she suspected – a great deal of wishful thinking. The rebels were growing stronger, but they were far from ready to overthrow the government.

"We should at least *try* to present our demands to the king," one of the moderates urged. He had something to lose, which was more than could be said for the poorer rebels. "Perhaps we can still get most of what we want …"

"And you think the king will just *give* it to you?" The hard-liners were united in opposition. "He'll refuse, or stall for time. We must strike now while we have the edge."

Gwen scowled, turning away to study the map. Paris was rapidly becoming a deeply-divided city, with troops and magicians garrisoning the governmental and upper class parts of the city and the rest effectively in rebel hands. The troops were keeping the roads open – she had to admit the French had made sure their garrisons couldn't be isolated easily – but they controlled little outside their line of sight. The rebels were moving around freely, harassing troops and magicians from a distance and retreating the moment reinforcements arrived. And yet … they might be winning by not losing, as one man had pointed out, but the government still had the edge. Gwen was mildly surprised the king hadn't evacuated Paris, then sealed the city off and left the rebels to starve.

He can't afford to lose his capital city, she reminded herself. *Versailles may be the core of the government, but Paris is the core of France itself.*

She studied the map thoughtfully. France was in

turmoil. Large swathes of the countryside were simmering with rage, ready to burst out at any moment. Brief bursts of violence were met with heavy repression, which provoked more violence; she was sure, looking at the numbers, that a general uprising would be impossible to contain once it spread beyond its birthplace. The stresses and strains – the government had overplayed its hand by introducing conscription and price controls – were threatening the integrity of the state, risking a collapse into complete chaos. There were already reports of small uprisings and peasant revolts right across the countryside.

Of course, not all of those reports might be remotely true, she reminded herself dryly. She'd heard reports of Christ Himself returning to strike down corrupt churchmen and aristocrats, then declare the land held in common by His true believers. *But the country is sliding towards chaos.*

Irene stepped into the room, looking grim. Gwen caught her eye and inclined her head towards the side room, leaving the underground's politicians to their argument. It didn't matter what they decided, she told herself, as long as they continued the revolution. France had to be plunged into chaos, ending the war with Britain before Britain broke under the strain. Being in Paris had been something of an eye-opener, showing her how the common people suffered in wartime. It made her wonder how her own people were coping …

"They locked down Versailles," Irene said, as soon as they were alone. "I wasn't allowed to enter. I was damn lucky not to be taken prisoner."

Gwen frowned. There was something in Irene's voice …

"The guards had orders to detain everyone who tried to enter," Irene said. "Luckily, I found one who could be talked into letting me go."

"That's good," Gwen said. She had a feeling there was more to the story than Irene had said. She also thought she didn't want to know. "What about Simone? And Racchel?"

Irene grimaced. "They were both inside when the lockdown happened," she said. "They're resourceful. They might manage to slip out, or keep their heads down until the restrictions are lifted again. I suspect they'll be seen as useless mouths and told to leave within a day or two."

"Unless they've been caught," Gwen said. She had a great deal of faith in Raechel, but she had to admit the other girl was impulsive and hot-headed. Gwen had been taught to think before she acted. Raechel had never felt the urge to think before doing something that – at best – could leave her reputation in ruins. "Why did they lock down the complex?"

"The guards didn't know," Irene said. "They were just following orders. No one enters and no one leaves, without permission from the king and his council. They were digging trenches and raising barricades when I left, so ..."

"They might expect an attack," Gwen finished. "From us? Or a dissident nobleman?"

Irene snorted. "There are rumours of noblemen assembling troops to put themselves on the throne, or crush the rebels, or both," she said. "How many of them are actually true? I couldn't say."

"No," Gwen agreed. The French Court was in a mess. It needed to prevent overmighty noblemen from raising their own private armies, then pressing their claims to the throne, but it was also unable to protect those noblemen from their subjects ... which provided all the impetus they needed to raise the armies that worried their king. She would have been more worried about the armies if she hadn't been fairly certain that not many noblemen could raise more than a few dozen men and none of them could be trusted. "We have been spreading a lot of nonsense in the past few days."

She stared down at her hands, all too aware the argument in the main room was still going on. The rebels had the government off-balance, but ... how long would it be until the government recovered? Or the growing food shortage started to bite? She suspected it already had, although it was hard to be sure. Some rebel cells were coming out into the open, requisitioning – stealing – what food they could and sharing it out. Others were trying to reserve food for the fighting units, rather than women and children. She suspected that policy would prove a mistake, in the long run, but for the moment it made a certain kind of sense.

We're already cooking and eating horses, she thought, numbly. *How long until we start eating people?*

Gwen met Irene's eyes. "Do you think they're safe?"

"Raechel and Simone?" Irene said nothing for a long moment. "It's hard to say. There's no hint the French Court had any idea of their true loyalties. Raechel is, as far as any of them know, a pretty and penniless aristo girl, hardly someone they need to take seriously. Simone … is a little more dangerous. They should have taken her off the board when they executed her father."

Adopted father, Gwen thought. Her thoughts ran in circles. Simone had had ample time to betray them, if she wished. She'd certainly figured out Raechel was a spy and kept her mouth shut … how had she done it? Had she caught a stray thought? Or had she recognised Raechel from Russia? They'd met … probably. They'd certainly been in the same general area. *If she's trapped inside the court, she might not even be able to get a message out.*

She scowled, rubbing her forehead. It might be nothing more than a coincidence. The French Government *knew* the rebels were building an army. They *knew* it was just a matter of time before the simmering rage burst into the open, the people's anger sweeping away the French state and replacing it with … what? Gwen didn't know if the government suspected British involvement, or if they thought a dissident aristo was pulling the strings, or … her lips twitched, humourlessly. The French Government didn't seem to believe the commoners could do something on their own, without an aristo telling them what to do. They were wasting their time hunting for men who didn't exist. And fortifying Versailles made sense. They couldn't afford to lose the palace complex or the entire nation would come apart …

And yet, the timing is worrying, she thought. *We are denied access to intelligence from Versailles at the exact moment we need it most.*

Irene cleared her throat. "What do you want me to do now?"

"Go back to the shop," Gwen said. "No, I'll come with you. They'll need to make up their minds on their own."

Her thoughts ran in circles as they walked downstairs and onto the streets. Simone had spotted Raechel … someone else could easily have done the same. There were uncounted thousands of people with legitimate claims to aristocracy – rebel propaganda insisted there were *millions*, parasites one and all – so many it was difficult to tell where the line between an aristocrat and a commoner could reasonably be drawn. Gwen had been told, although she found it hard to believe, that it was easy to insert a fake aristocrat as long as the fake wasn't too blatant. People would ask questions of someone claiming to be third in line to the throne, but not of someone insisting they were a very distant cousin of a poor and unimportant bloodline …

She's pretty, Gwen thought. *If someone decided he wanted to marry her, or make her his mistress, he might have looked into her background and discovered the fraud.*

"I'll keep my ears open," Irene said. "I still have clients in the court. They'll be demanding my return soon enough."

Gwen snorted. She knew what *she'd* say to any silly girl – or grown woman – who moaned about losing her dressmaker while the country was in the midst of a national crisis and she was pretty sure King Louis would say much the same. And yet … she sighed inwardly, remembering just how many silly women there *were* in High Society. They were denied roles beyond wives and mothers, treated as baubles rather than people in their own right ... no wonder, she supposed, that some grew silly and others grew poisonous. The French would be just the same, perhaps worse. There were too many of them.

"We'll see," she said, neutrally. It was hard to be sure of anything. If Raechel and Simone *had* been caught ... had they been made to talk? Or was she overthinking it? The government hadn't sent its super-magicians after her, the very first thing they should have done if they'd known she was in Paris. "Keep your ears open by all means, but don't compromise yourself."

"If I don't go back when ordered, I'll lose everything," Irene said. "Not fatal for me, of course, but ..."

Gwen nodded. On one hand, the French Court needed dressmakers like her; on the other, she was easy to replace. Probably. They needed someone who was both skilled and discreet, the latter a rarity in a court where knowledge was power. Knowing someone was calling on Irene – and making use of her services – was quite informative, if one drew the right conclusions. Gwen snorted inwardly. Half the aristocracy was impoverished by British standards ... and half of *them* would be reasonably wealthy, if they weren't spending frantically to keep up appearances. They were lucky they got free food and drink at court. She knew families that had gone hungry, back home, because they were pretending to be rich.

"Be careful," she said. "And don't let them catch you."

She braced herself as they reached a street and paused to let a line of marching soldiers walk past them. The men were alert and nervous, their rifles swinging from side to side as they watched for possible threats. The crowd stared at them, their anger and hatred pulsing on the air. Gwen felt a shiver run down her spine, a sense of nakedness and vulnerability despite her power. The crowd wanted to tear the men apart, limb from limb, and leave their bodies in the streets as a warning to others. She half-expected something to happen – a rebel to pick up and throw a stone, a soldier to shoot an imaginary threat – that would trigger a bloodbath, but nothing did. The soldiers kept marching until they turned a corner and stepped out of sight.

"They're not ready to go to war," Irene predicted. "They'll break if pressed hard enough."

Gwen hoped she was right. It was hard to tell.

She kept her eyes open as they made their way back to the shop. The walls were covered in graffiti, so many revolutionary slogans they were starting to blur together. Someone had shoved a handful of pamphlets under the door, ranging from a reasonably well thought out call to arms to an incoherent screed that insisted the aristocracy were the children of the devil, practitioners of black magic and deeds so vile the writer declined to put them into words. She sighed inwardly as she glanced at a string of accusations, then shoved the pamphlets in the stove. The police had been searching shops and houses, seemingly at random, and if they spotted the papers all hell would break loose.

Irene grinned at her. "What now?"

"Good question," Gwen agreed. She put the kettle on – her mother would have been shocked at seeing Gwen doing it herself – and frowned. "We need to keep the pressure on."

She dropped tea leaves into the cups – they were running short of those, as well as nearly everything else – and added water. "If I go after the enemy commander ..."

"They'll have him heavily guarded," Irene pointed out. "We still don't know how many super-magicians there are."

Gwen scowled. "Your contacts turned up nothing?"

"Nothing reliable," Irene said. "A lot of nonsense, a lot of suggestions about deals with the devil and suchlike ... really, I think there aren't many people who know the full story and none of them are inclined to come to my shop. I could try and get into the garrisons and see what they might know, but it would be risky."

"If they catch you reading their minds, you'll be dead," Gwen agreed. She wasn't looking forward to meeting a second super-magician. Whatever the French did to create them, it was effective. If she ran into two or three of them … she feared she'd come off worst. She'd done what she could to train the rebel magicians, but there were limits. She wasn't even sure they had numbers on their side. "Don't take any risks …"

Her mind churned. What *were* their options? Continue the insurgency, grinding down the government's forces? Or risk an uprising …? It would be a bloody fight to take Paris, she thought, and there was no guarantee of victory. The super-troopers were too dangerous, to say nothing of the thousands of soldiers who garrisoned the walls and strongpoints. Or … could they risk an attack on Versailles? She dismissed the thought almost as soon as she had it. In the open, they'd be slaughtered like bugs.

I could get into the court myself, she thought, although she wasn't sure it was true. The French hadn't managed to replace the Seers she'd killed … she thought. It was quite possible they simply didn't have the manpower to take advantage of them. *If I killed the king …*

Her heart twisted at the thought. The king was a king … part of her recoiled in disgust at the thought of killing him, of murdering a man of the blood royal. The rest of her was torn between the practicalities of getting in and out and concern over what would follow, if she killed the reigning monarch. Would his son take the throne and carry on? Or would there be chaos? Or … or what? She wasn't even sure how her own people would react, if they found out what she'd done. King Louis might be French, an unpardonable crime in the eyes of many British, but he was still a *king*. Assassinating him would set a terrible precedent. Lord Mycroft would not approve.

"I'm going to rest," she said, finally. The rebels needed time to hammer out a joint platform before they took the offensive. She could wait a few days – she hoped – before she had to force things. "Let me know if anything happens."

"Of course," Irene said, dryly. If she'd been following Gwen's thoughts, she kept it to herself. "Sleep well."

Chapter Twenty-Seven
Paris, France

ruce watched, coldly, as the spy fell to his death.

The man had been a spy, no doubt about it. He'd been watching the rebel headquarters from the rooftops, then shadowed Gwen and her companion back to the dressmaker's shop. Bruce had been lucky to spot him, given how many unfamiliar names and faces were flowing through the various rebel bases and checkpoints without any real attempt to verify their *bona fides*. It was careless, he reflected, although probably unavoidable. None of the rebel groups could hope to bring down the government on their own, even with Gwen's help. They had to work together and that meant a certain degree of openness, an openness that could easily be exploited by an enemy infiltrator. If there wasn't more than one, he'd eat his hat.

He checked to make sure the spy was dead – there was no point in taking chances – then turned and hurried away, hopping from rooftop to rooftop. The rebels had set up dozens of bridges and walkways, before the soldiers had started sweeping the roofs with bullets whenever the rocks started flying. Not a bad move on their part, he conceded, although it was also a sign of weakness. They were burning up their limited ammunition, for what? If the rumours were true, they hadn't killed more than a dozen people at most.

And then they get overwhelmed because they run out of ammunition, he thought. *They should be trying to divide the rebel forces, not crush them.*

Bruce kept moving, keeping his head low. A pair of street children – probably carrying messages for their elders – glanced at him, then looked away. A handful of older people eyed him warily, unsure who or what he was. Bruce did his best to ignore them as he headed further into the slums, then scrambled down a rope that would have daunted a sailor to get to the ground. It wasn't ideal, but what was? The Parisians had few qualms about risking their necks, not when the alternative was worse. He glanced from side to side, then hurried back to the pub. Jean-Luc had told him to be back for nightfall.

It might be wise not to go back at all, he told himself. Jean-Luc hadn't figured out the truth, as far as Bruce knew, but he knew too much for Bruce to be entirely comfortable with him. The smuggler didn't trust him completely either, which meant … Bruce suspected Jean-Luc saw him as a tool, rather than a person in his own right. He told himself, firmly, that it did have its advantages. *Better to be underestimated than seen as a very real threat.*

The pub was busy, yet something dark and nasty hung in the air. The crowd looked dangerous, drinking heavily while muttering quietly amongst themselves. Jean-Luc had hired two women to serve as waitresses and they looked tired and overworked, their eyes flickering from side to side as if they expected to be attacked at any moment. Perhaps they did. One of them had been groped only two days ago – and, when she'd slapped the groper, it had started a fight that had threatened to destroy the entire building. Bruce thought most of the fighters hadn't known what had happened, and wouldn't have cared if they had. It'd been nothing more than an excuse for violence.

Jean-Luc caught his eye and nodded to the backroom. Bruce followed, taking the time to see if anyone seemed unduly interested in him. It didn't seem so, although a handful of suspicious glances were thrown in his direction. Jean-Luc was reassuringly free of prejudice – everyone was welcome, as long as they could pay – but the same couldn't be said for many of his customers. Paris was a melting pot like New York, with communities from all over the Bourbon Empire, and they hated and resented each other. It was just a matter of time, he feared, before the unrest turned into something worse.

"You had some training," Jean-Luc said flatly, when the door was closed and they were alone. "Can you open a lock with magic?"

Bruce kept his expression as blank as possible. Jean-Luc was no fool. He'd seen enough to know Bruce was a far more experienced magician than the average rebel, which meant … Bruce had avoided saying anything definite, but he'd hinted he'd deserted rather than simply discovering his powers and running before the government could conscript him. Jean-Luc wouldn't have much to say about a runaway – the smugglers had been helping unwilling conscripts escape military service for years – yet he'd want to see what use he could make of him. And now the Seers were gone – if rumour were to be believed – unlicensed magicians had much more freedom to manoeuvre. Gwen had certainly trained enough infusers to make sure it was harder for anyone to track them.

"Perhaps," he said, finally. The hell of it was that he could pick a lock very easily, by drawing on two types of magic. A regular Mover would find it a little harder, although far from impossible. "It depends on the lock."

"I have a team ready to empty a warehouse," Jean-Luc said. "There's a way in from underground, but the door is locked. I can't imagine why."

Bruce had to smile at his dry tone. "Anyone would think they were afraid of thieves stealing the stuff."

"Quite." Jean-Luc met his eyes. "Do this for me, and you can ask for whatever you like in return."

I can ask, Bruce thought. *No guarantee I'm going to get it, is there?*

He shrugged, inwardly. He needed to sing for his supper or risk Jean-Luc telling him to get out – or, more likely, trying to slit his throat while he slept. The smugglers would view him as an asset, but also a potential threat. He knew too much. If he wanted to stay with them …

"Sure," he said. It was a small price to pay. Besides, looting a warehouse would help to undermine the government. "When do we leave?"

Jean-Luc glanced at his watch. "Two hours," he said. "Go freshen up, then change into something dark. The team will be ready by then. No names, remember."

Bruce nodded, stiffly. Jean-Luc had done his best to keep Bruce away from the rest of the smugglers, something Bruce could only admire. The fact he'd been asked to help now … he contemplated it as he washed his face and changed into a new outfit, then settled down to wait for the team. It felt longer – much longer – by the time Jean-Luc called him back down to the bar. Half the drinkers had left, the other half looked as if they were on the verge of collapsing at any moment. A grim-faced whore sat next to her client, her face torn between relief and dismay. Bruce felt a twinge of sympathy. The poor girl wouldn't be paid for services her client had been too drunk to demand …

"This way," Jean-Luc said. "Keep your mouth shut."

Bruce took a moment to assess the team as they made their way onto the streets. There were five men, wearing dark clothes and hats that – quite coincidentally – concealed much of their faces from casual view. Covering one's face was technically illegal, from what he'd heard, but most of the rebels did it anyway, or wore wigs to make themselves as hard to identify as possible. Bruce suspected they didn't need to bother. The government troops weren't trying to feel out rebel cells and chains of command, merely kill as many rebels as they could. It was rather self-defeating, he felt. Every time they killed someone for being in the wrong place at the wrong time, they created hundreds of new and deadly enemies.

He kept his mouth firmly closed as they walked through a maze of alleyways and darkened streets. The government had announced a curfew, but it wasn't being honoured outside the richer and heavily-garrisoned parts of the city. A number of street parties had broken out, the people dancing and singing in a manner that puzzled him until he realised it was nothing more than naked defiance. They didn't want to be under the government's control any longer. He grimaced as he spotted a pair of bodies dangling from makeshift nooses, twisting in the wind. Police spies? Loan sharks? Bankers? Or people in the wrong place at the wrong time? Who knew?

"Down here," Jean-Luc said. "Hurry."

Bruce gritted his teeth as they walked into a house, headed down into the basement ... and down a pit someone had dug into the sewers. The stench was thoroughly appalling, forcing him to breathe through his mouth. Jean-Luc lit a lantern and kept walking, the flickering light revealing pools of water – Bruce *hoped* it was water – and *things* shifting in the darkness. He tried not to think about stories of monsters lurking in the sewers under London or New York, stories that had always bothered him as a child. It wasn't impossible there were people living under the city, people who'd never seen the light of day ...

Jean-Luc paused and raised the lantern, revealing a ladder leading up into the darkness. It felt as if they'd walked for miles, perhaps under the river and into the upper-class districts of the city ... was that possible? Or ... Bruce stopped worrying about it as Jean-Luc passed him the lantern and scrambled up, then hissed for him to follow. The darkness ebbed and flowed around him, like a living thing, as he inched his way to the top. The shaft opened into a giant antechamber. He looked around as the lantern was passed up to them, frowning. There was one door – heavy metal, so solid he doubted it could be cracked easily – and no other way in or out. It made no sense, unless whoever owned the warehouse was doing some smuggling themselves. Having access to the sewers would make sense if they wanted to move things through the city without being spotted.

"Go to work," Jean-Luc said, indicating the door. "Good luck."

Bruce nodded coldly as he stepped towards the door and rested his hand against the cold metal. There was no obvious way to open the door from the outside ... a wise precaution, he supposed, given how easy it had been to get so far. Anyone with actual *permission* to be in the building wouldn't come through the sewers. He smiled at the thought as he pushed his magic through the door, parsing out the lock. It was surprisingly complex, to the point he wondered if it had been designed to sucker magicians. A regular Mover who tried to open the door might easily destroy the locking mechanism instead.

Interesting, he thought. Gwen had told him about Jack, the rebel Master Magician, who'd spent some time in France before returning to Britain to start a rebellion. *Did whoever designed this lock draw a few lessons from him?*

He hesitated, making sure he knew exactly how the lock worked, then reached out again to apply pressure in the right places. There was a click, loud enough to make him jump, as the first section undid itself, followed by the second and third. The door shifted and opened outward, nearly slamming him into the wall. Bruce jumped back, using magic to cushion the metal before it could make a noise. Perhaps there were no guards in the warehouse itself, but there'd be at least one person on the far side ...

Jean-Luc and his men hurried past him, into the warehouse. It was smaller than Bruce had expected, crammed with boxes of guns, ammunition and ... gemstones? Bruce stared at them in astonishment. He was no expert on gemstones, and he knew some gems were incredibly expensive, but ... why were they here? There were too many of them for him to believe they were worth *that* much. He picked one up and inspected it, turning it over and over to see how it glinted in the light. What was it?

"Help move the crates down to the sewers," Jean-Luc said. "And hurry."

Bruce nodded, putting the gemstone in his pocket for later inspection before setting to work with a will. The smugglers moved with practiced ease, picking up crates and carrying them to the shaft, then lowering them down to the sewers. Bruce had to admire their nerve, even as he wondered why so many guns and ammunition pallets had been stored in the warehouse instead of being distributed to the troops. Did the government think it didn't need to open the stockpiles? Or ... or what?

Incompetence, perhaps, Bruce thought. He'd seen enough of his father's administration to know a single incompetent official in the right place could do a hell of a lot of damage, particularly if he was well-connected enough to make it hard to get rid of him. *Or did they merely stockpile so many supplies they saw no need to open this particular dump?*

They worked for hours, transporting supplies down to the sewers and then whisking them along the smelly tunnels. Bruce silently gave Jean-Luc credit for working as hard as his men, remaining in the warehouse until the last of the easily-removed crates were picked up and stolen. Some of the supplies seemed worthless, others too large to be removed easily ... one giant crate was just too big to get out of the warehouse. Bruce wanted to poke around some more, but there was no time. Jean-Luc was already rigging up a bomb.

"When this is in place, we have to move fast," he said, shortly. "We won't be able to come back."

Bruce nodded, wordlessly. The blast would cover their escape. If they were lucky, it would be taken for an accident. If they weren't ... if nothing else, the explosion would set off other explosions that would conceal just how much they'd taken from the warehouse. He felt a twinge of hope as Jean-Luc finished putting the bomb together, then followed him to the shaft down to the sewers. The rebels would make good use of the weapons, even though the smugglers would charge an arm and a leg for them. Or at least hand them over in exchange for future favours.

He glanced at Jean-Luc. "Who put all those weapons in there?"

"I know a couple of filing clerks," Jean-Luc said, vaguely. "They told me the warehouse was taken over by the government."

He smiled, rather thinly. "They used to sell me goods in happier times ..."

The ground heaved. Bruce fell to his knees, nearly slipping into the sewage as the ground heaved a second time, then a third. A wash of warm air blew past them, eerie glowing lights flaring in the tunnels before fading back into nothingness. He tasted dust in the air and cursed under his breath, picking himself up and starting to run. The sewers were old, old enough to start collapsing ... it dawned on him, suddenly, that there might be pockets of explosive gas within the sewers. If it caught fire, they were dead.

He heard a rumble, followed by the sound of falling masonry, behind him. Jean-Luc muttered an oath in a language Bruce didn't recognise as they both ran ... it seemed unlikely a single blast could have brought down everything, but if it had set off a chain of explosions within the network ... a piece of flying debris passed overhead, too close for comfort. He grabbed Jean-Luc, throwing caution to the winds and flying them both down the sewer to safety. The crashing slowly died away as they reached the shaft the smugglers had opened into the sewers. Bruce hoped that meant they were safe.

"You can fly?" Jean-Luc sounded shocked. "Why ...?"

"It's a trick I wouldn't use unless I was desperate," Bruce said. "A magician could sense me, or kill me, if he saw me flying towards him."

Jean-Luc chuckled as they clambered up to the surface. "So you can't fly all the way to Antwerp and buy me some wine?"

"No." Bruce shook his head, although he wasn't sure if Jean-Luc could see him or not. "It has its limits."

The smugglers were already moving the crates, he noted. Half were gone, hurried to their next resting place before the police and the military tracked them down. Bruce knew the police had been reluctant to risk poking their heads into the underground, but now … if they worked out the warehouse had been looted, if they knew what had been stolen, they'd send an entire army to get the weapons back before it was too late. They had no choice. The rebels didn't have many arms, from what Bruce had seen. That was about to change.

"You saved my life," Jean-Luc said, once they were making their way back to the pub. "What can I give you, in return?"

"Just don't mention me to anyone, ever," Bruce said. He had no idea how much he could demand, and he didn't want to push it. Gratitude, in his experience, never went as far as it should. "And give me a little more room to work."

Jean-Luc studied him for a long moment. Bruce wondered what the smuggler was thinking. Bruce was … what? A rebel? A foreigner? A criminal in his own right, who'd fallen in with others of his kind? Or … Bruce sighed inwardly. He didn't dare tell the man the truth and he didn't dare risk a lie, not one that might be exposed at any second. And who knew what would happen then?

"Of course," Jean-Luc said. "Can I count on your services again? Later?"

"I certainly hope so," Bruce said. He glanced at the dark sky. It wouldn't be long until dawn. "But right now, I need to get some rest."

"So do we all," Jean-Luc said. "So do we all."

Chapter Twenty-Eight
Paris, France

aechel felt ... wrong.

It wasn't something she could put into words. It felt as if she was eying the world through a piece of tinted glass, as if the world was very slightly out of sync. She'd drunk too much Absinthe, she'd been told, and been very lucky to have been found by a doctor before the hallucinations put an end to her. Or she was found by someone with worse intentions. She wasn't sure that was true – her memories were a jumbled mess – but she had no other explanation. Her head felt as if she'd been slapped repeatedly, hard enough to knock her out time and time again. She wasn't sure she could swear to anything, beyond her name ...

She sat in her room, feeling weirdly lethargic. She wanted to get up and eat, or dance, or do something – anything – other than staying where she was, but she couldn't muster the energy to move. She wasn't sure how she'd managed to get dressed. She might be an aristocrat by blood, as far as the French Court was concerned, but she didn't rate a private maid. She hadn't minded – she'd have had no privacy at all, if she'd brought a maid into her rooms – yet ... her thoughts ran in circles. She really didn't understand what had happened. She didn't normally drink heavily, even when trying to be sociable. Irene had cautioned her drunkenness could easily lead to her saying something unfortunate – or worse.

If I had, she thought dully, *they wouldn't have returned me to my room.*

The thought made her smile, although she still thought something was wrong. What had happened? She had few illusions about what would have happened, if she'd got blind drunk in front of a courtier. She'd be lucky if she woke up in his bed, wearing nothing but her socks. And yet ... the doctor had found her ... her head ached as she tried to sort out what had happened. Had someone had his way with her, then called the doctor? It didn't feel that way.

Now you know why young women have to be careful about their drinks, her thoughts pointed out. They sounded very much like Irene. *You never know what someone might put in them.*

There was a tap at the door, which opened a moment later. Raechel knew she should have been alarmed – the door was meant to be locked – but it was hard to feel much of anything as Louis stepped into the room. His uniform was so gaudy Raechel would have snickered, if she'd been able to do more than offer a rather pained smile. She'd never felt so out of it, never felt as if she was watching her own body from a distance ... she wasn't even feeling threatened, with him so close to her and her in no state to say no. It was ... worrying.

"I came as soon as I heard," Louis said. He actually sounded concerned. "You drank a little too much ...?"

"I guess so," Raechel said. Her tongue felt furry and her voice ... she giggled, suddenly, as it dawned on her that her breath probably stank. No wonder he hadn't tried to kiss her! "I ..."

"You're coming to the Bastille," Louis said. "I'm allowed to have one guest and you're her."

Raechel blinked, her thoughts running in circles. It was hard to speak clearly, let alone coherently. Words slipped out before she could stop them. "The Bastille? Have I been a naughty girl?"

Louis chuckled, rather sardonically. "Have you, while I've been gone?"

Raechel bit her tongue. She was in no state to bandy words with him … with anyone. Louis wasn't the sharpest knife in the drawer, but if she said the wrong thing … she had no idea what he'd say or do, and she didn't want to find out the hard way. She tried to come up with something, but nothing came to mind. Except …

"What are you doing at the Bastille?" If she was any judge, Louis would love to talk about himself. "Are *you* in trouble?"

Louis smirked. "I'm special assistant to General Lafarge," he said. "I'm helping to coordinate the operations in Paris."

Oh dear, Raechel thought. *I did …*

Her memory blanked. She staggered, nearly falling off the bed. Louis put out a hand to steady her, his eyes wide with concern. Raechel gritted her teeth as her thoughts fragmented, then came back together … General Lafarge. She knew him, didn't she? And yet … she rubbed her forehead as she staggered to her feet. She needed water and some fresh air and a chance to think, without Louis babbling nonsense at her. But he was insistent and she was in no state to resist.

"I'll be happy to come," she said, trying to put on a light and breathy voice. "I can go shopping!"

Louis snorted, as if he thought she was overdoing it. "You'll have to stay close to me," he said, warningly. "The streets aren't safe."

"Of course I will," Raechel said. "Just give me a moment to get dressed."

She pushed him out of the room and closed the door, then leaned against the wood and tried to calm herself. She'd never got *really* drunk before, had she? The memories slipped around her, her head starting to pound every time she looked at them. If even Louis was concerned … it bothered her, although she was relieved he wasn't taking advantage and pawing her. He was normally so self-centred he barely gave any thought to anyone other than himself. She really *must* look a mess. She staggered into the washroom to undress and shower, then stumbled back into the bedroom to change into riding clothes. Her head hurt as she looked at herself in the mirror, twinges of pain stabbing at her …

You look ghastly, she thought, tiredly. She hadn't looked so bad when she'd been chased by the living dead. *What were you doing last night …?*

A wave of sickness sent her stumbling to her knees, banishing the thought from her mind. Was she ill? Or … or pregnant? She knew some women got sick when they were pregnant, but … was it immediately? She didn't know. She knew she couldn't have been pregnant for very long – her monthly cycles were very regular – if indeed she was … she retched again, then forced herself to stand. Whatever it was, she'd deal with it.

"You look wonderful," Louis said. He held out a hand. "Shall we go?"

Liar, Raechel thought. She was mildly surprised he hadn't taken one look and absented himself. *You know I look awful.*

Versailles seemed quieter, somehow, as they made their way down to the coachhouse. There were fewer people in the corridors and those she saw ignored her in favour of their companions. The gardens outside were nearly empty, save for a mass of soldiers drilling in formation … the ladies taking their ease, she noted to her discomfort, were almost completely gone. Versailles no longer looked like a collection of palaces, each one more striking and regal than the last, but a military camp. The officers might look like peacocks, but the weapons they carried were very real.

She glanced at Louis as he summoned his coach. "What's happening?"

"There was some trouble nearby," Louis said. "His Majesty thought it best to take precautions."

The coach arrived, the driver flanked by two armed men. Raechel clambered into the cabin and drew back the window curtain, staring out as the carriage rattled into life. Louis sat next to her, keeping his hands to himself. Raechel would have been concerned about his apparent lack of interest if her head hadn't been so sore, so unsure of itself. The fresh air helped, but there was a faint stench on the breeze that reminded her of Moscow. It hadn't been that long since she'd escaped by the skin of her teeth …

"When we reach the city, draw the curtains," Louis ordered, in a tone that made it very clear disobedience would not be tolerated. "No one is to see you."

Raechel felt a hot flash of anger overriding her common sense. Her aunt and uncle had always talked to her like that and she'd always tried to rebel, even when it had cost her. "Why …?"

"Because the rebels have been stoning carriages," Louis said, sharply. "You don't want them to see you unless you want to die."

Raechel swallowed. "I see."

She kept her thoughts to herself as they drove on, passing a handful of military checkpoints, followed by burnt-out villages, farmhouses and mansions. There was no one working the visible fields, as far as she could tell, no one on the roads or … the great slums around Paris, outside the walls, seemed to have grown in the weeks since she'd last passed through the city. She had no time for a proper look. Louis pushed the curtain closed, his face grim. Outside, she could hear people hooting and hollering …

Something hit the carriage. She jumped.

"Keep your head down," Louis said, as a second object rattled against the wooden box. "If they tip the coach over, hitch up your skirts and run."

Raechel nodded, ice washing through her mind as the racket grew louder. People were shouting and screaming, their words merging together into a single deafening racket. She couldn't pick out more than a handful of words, none of them pleasant. The carriage shifted, as if they had stepped onto a boat, then rattled onwards. She heard horsemen cantering alongside, followed by gunshots … silence fell, so quickly she thought every last shouter was dead. Louis reached for her hand and gripped it tightly as the coach picked up speed, long moments of silence passing slowly before the vehicle finally came to a stop. Louis risked a glance through the curtain, then opened the door. They had stopped in front of the Bastille.

It was hard not to feel a flicker of fear as Louis helped her to step down to the ground. The Bastille was a nightmarish symbol of tyranny, a reminder that – on paper – the French King was an absolute ruler, with the power to condemn his enemies to imprisonment for as long as suited him. She'd heard all the stories when she'd been preparing for the mission, all the tales of men and women being marched into the fortress and never being seen again, all the little horrors from men being executed to women being whipped and mutilated for petty little crimes against His Majesty. It mattered little that many of the tales were exaggerated, although there was a hard core of cold truth. Just being here, in the shadow of the place she could expect to be taken if they ever worked out who and what she really was, was chilling.

Louis held her arm possessively as they made their way through the courtyard and into the fortress. Raechel had to force herself to keep her eyes open, noting the hundreds of guards and open gunports threatening the city beyond. She couldn't see much of the city, but the plumes of smoke blighting the sky were a grim reminder the city was at war. A loud explosion rent the air, the ground shaking a moment later. The men around her didn't pay any attention. They just continued with their work.

She stuck close to him as they passed through a pair of checkpoints, the guards looking them up and down before waving them into the fortresses and up a long flight of stairs into a command room. General Lafarge was sitting on an elevated chair – it looked very much like a wooden throne – staring over a map of Paris and the surrounding environs. He didn't seem very concerned about her looking at it, she noted, although *that* wasn't too surprising. She'd encountered a *lot* of men who thought women couldn't read maps. Idiots. She would enjoy shoving that conceit down his throat, if she ever got the chance.

"General," Louis said. "You wanted to see me?"

Raechel was tempted to snort in disbelief. What was Louis playing at? Why had he even brought her to the Bastille? Did he know what she'd done? Or ... was General Lafarge playing with him? Or ... she put the thought out of her head and stared down at the map as the men talked, trying to put a gormless expression on her face. The map wasn't even *that* complicated. The purple sections marked friendly territory – the centre of the city and roads linking the centre to the walls – while the rest were various shades of red. She mentally compared it to the list of safe houses and dead drops Irene had given her and frowned inwardly. At least two of the latter were within the purple area ...

"I want you to assess the defences of the breeding farms," General Lafarge said, pointing to an icon on the map. "It is imperative the rebels don't capture or destroy the building."

Louis looked puzzled. "General, would it not be wiser to evacuate the breeding farm?"

Raechel shared his puzzlement. A breeding farm? She knew people kept backyard chickens and other small animals in London, raising them for food, and she saw no reason the Parisians wouldn't do the same, but ... something nagged at her mind, something she'd heard once. It refused to come into the light.

"Duke Philippe insists it cannot be moved," General Lafarge told him. "The magicians cannot be removed from their beds, not ..."

Raechel barely heard him. The mention of the duke galvanised something in her mind ... breeding farm? She'd heard stories – whispers, really – of a breeding programme for magicians, of women with magic being paid or forced to bear children ... Gwen had put a stop to it, from what she'd heard, but the French might easily have their own programme. There was no reason they couldn't and plenty of reason to do it, if you didn't give a damn about morality or decency or anything …

Her head swam. Her legs buckled. She almost collapsed.

"Poor girl," General Lafarge said. The amused condescension in his voice made Raechel's blood boil. If she hadn't been in such a state, she would have snapped at him and to hell with the consequences. "Such matters are not fit for feminine ears, I do believe."

"Yes, My Lord," Louis said.

"They are really too delicate for anything remotely masculine," the general continued. "The mere mention of blood makes them faint. Better they stay home with the children while the men go into danger."

I see my blood one week in every four, Raechel thought, so savagely the anger burnt through the haze. If the general wanted her to go down on him again, she'd bite. Hard. It was all she could do to keep from decking him. *And do you know how many women die in childbirth?*

"Give her some money, send her to buy a nice dress or something," General Lafarge said, in the same tone. "We don't want her wearing something *cheap* tonight, do we?"

"No, My Lord," Louis said. His voice was artfully flat. Raechel had the feeling he was annoyed too. Not that he'd have the nerve to do anything about it. He owed his position to the general and the only reason he'd got it had been that Raechel … her mind stopped, her thoughts hitting a brick wall. It should have bothered her. It didn't. "I'll see to it personally."

Raechel said nothing as he pulled her out of the room and hurried her through a maze of corridors. "This is my suite," he said, pushing open a door. "What do you think?"

"Nice," Raechel said. There was a surprising lack of chains, and torture equipment. It shouldn't have surprised her. The Bastille was like the Tower of London in at least one respect. Some of its guests were aristocrats who couldn't be locked up in dingy little cells, even if they'd committed treason. There might be locks and guards on the door, but otherwise their rooms could have come straight out of a fancy hotel. "I …"

"The general said you were to go shopping," Louis said. He passed her a small purse of coins. "Stay on the islands. Do not cross the bridges. The guards will let you out and then back in again, when you return. Don't stay out any longer than you absolutely have to and *certainly* not after dark. Do I make myself clear?"

Raechel said nothing for a long moment. She knew she should be angry – at General Lafarge for treating her like a brainless doll, at Louis for talking to her like a stern father – but it was hard to think clearly. Her head still felt … wrong. It felt like … she wasn't sure what it felt like, unless she was dreaming … the kind of dream that felt so real, she reflected, that it was impossible to be sure you were no longer dreaming when you woke up. And yet, it was hard to care. She knew where the dead drops were and she could get to them, ensuring Irene knew about the breeding farms. Something had to be done about them.

She swallowed, hard. "Yes," she said. It was no time for an argument, particularly one when he held all the cards. "I won't leave the island."

Louis nodded, then left. Raechel glowered at his back. She didn't have to leave the island. She just needed to reach the nearest dead drop. And then … Irene would do something about the farms. Raechel didn't know what, but she didn't care as long as *something* was done.

Dark eyes flickered at the back of her mind. Something was wrong. Something was very wrong. But she didn't let it bother her. It wasn't important.

Clearing her thoughts, she turned and left the room.

Chapter Twenty-Nine
Paris, France

wen looked down at the slip of paper, then up at Irene.

"The codes are correct," Irene said. "Raechel is the only one who knows them."

"And she somehow got the message into a dead drop on the other side of a heavily-defended bridge," Gwen said. "How?"

"They're doing their best to pretend everything is normal, on that side of the bridge," Irene said, shortly. "The shops are open – the prices fixed; the people ordered to show confidence that everything will soon return to normal, if they can't pretend everything is normal already. Never mind the hundreds of servants who have been ordered to live there, or pass a series of security checks before crossing the bridges and going to work ..."

She shrugged. "My sources tell me Raechel's young man invited her to stay with him at the Bastille. She probably didn't have much of a choice."

Gwen grimaced. She was all too aware a besotted young man could and *would* do something dangerous like inviting his lover into the middle of a war, or talk freely about things he shouldn't to a pair of ears connected to a very pretty body. And yet ... she shuddered, feeling a rush of sympathy and fear for her friend. Raechel might be lying back and thinking of her country, but still ... it was repulsive. The idea of passing from partner to partner ... she shook her head, putting the thought aside. They needed intelligence from the very heart of enemy territory ...

"Right," she said, slowly. "Do we have any independent verification of the message?"

"No," Irene said. "Nothing *direct*, at any rate. I did manage to get a look at the building she mentioned, and it was definitely guarded ... unobtrusively, true, but guarded nonetheless. My sources insist she's free to move around the fortress too, which would be unlikely if they suspected her. She could get a *lot* of intelligence for us."

Gwen made a face. The Duke of India had once – famously – cashiered an officer for bringing his mistress on campaign. It wasn't that he'd been opposed to romantic relationships, or so she'd heard; it was that he'd regarded the relationship as a distraction to a young man sent out to fight for his country. Gwen suspected the older man had a point. It was one thing bringing one's wife, when husband and wife knew and understood their duties, but quite another to bring one's lover. It was difficult to think straight when your lover was in the room.

Her eyes narrowed. It was hard enough to think straight *now*. A breeding farm ... she shuddered in disgust, anger powering her magic. She'd had no doubt the French had breeding farms of their own – a dispassionate term for a crime against humanity – and yet, she hadn't really *felt* it until one of their farms had been located. Her magic pulsed against her skin. The concept was simple, if horrific. Take a number of female magicians – common-born magicians – into the breeding farm, then pair them up with carefully-selected male magicians until they fell pregnant. And then ... her stomach heaved. She'd shut the British programme down, when she'd inherited Master Thomas's role, but the French would have continued their own. Of course. They'd had very little choice if they wanted to catch up with the British.

When the women give birth, take the children away and

have them placed with the right *sort of families,* she thought, coldly. *Raise them to be loyal to the king and his country, while the mother is sent back to the farms to be impregnated once again.*

"We have to check it out," she said, curtly. "And if it really *is* a breeding farm it needs to be shut down. Quickly."

Irene met her eyes. "Gwen, are you sure …?"

"Yes." Gwen couldn't turn away. Cold logic might insist the breeding farm wasn't an *immediate* danger – the women would be drugged, their babies taken away well before they came into their powers – but cold logic had no place in her decision. The breeding farm was an abomination. There was no way she could leave it alone and yet remain true to herself. "I have to go there."

"Right." Irene didn't look convinced. "The building *is* guarded."

Gwen swung around to look at the map. Paris was … her lips twitched in grim amusement. The government controlled the centre, and the roads and bridges leading into the heart of the city, but the rest of Paris had slipped out of government control. It wasn't *all* under rebel control – and half the rebel groups seemed more interested in fighting each other than the government – yet the government couldn't send troops outside the secure zones without heavy casualties. She suspected the government was playing a waiting game, hoping the rebels would starve or risk everything in a charge across the river … she was surprised, really, the government hadn't evacuated the centre and then left Paris to the mob. But then, losing control of the capital would be an unmistakable sign the empire was finished.

And then half the country will rise against them, she told herself. The countryside was in turmoil. Every day brought more reports of murdered officials, burnt churches and aristos chased out of their lands by angry mobs. The government didn't have the manpower to keep France under control, not if it wanted to deploy troops to Spain as well. *It will be the end.*

She put the thought aside and tapped the map. "It's nearly nightfall," she said. She had to move fast. Raechel was a good liar, and very quick on her feet, but the Bastille wasn't Versailles and there'd be far less room for mistakes. One sharp-eyed guard might be enough to get her friend sent to the dungeons under the fortress, the legendary – and nightmarish – chambers that housed prisoners the king wanted to see die in captivity. "Have the rebels mount a diversionary attack here, at the bridge, then fall back when the counterattack materialises. I'll get over the river and into the breeding farm."

Irene said nothing for a long moment. "As you wish," she said finally, in a tone that made it very clear she disapproved. "Are you sure this is a good idea?"

"Yes," Gwen lied. "The longer we leave the farm alone, the greater the chance they'll move the mothers out of the city."

She kept her face under tight control. Irene didn't need to be a mind-reader to know Gwen was coming up with reasons to justify her decision, rather than reasoning it out logically before deciding what to do. The men back home who insisted she was too emotional to make important decisions would laugh if they knew, although *she* knew the men were often just as emotional. They were just emotional about different things. Not, she reflected as she started to gather her supplies, that it mattered. The mothers *were* confirmed magicians or they wouldn't be there. If they were rescued, and given a few days to let the drugs work their way out of their bodies, they might prove very useful indeed.

"If you say so," Irene said, in the same tone. "Do you want me to come with you?"

Gwen shook her head. "Better I go alone," she said. Irene's talents were useful in her preferred role, but useless in a straight fight. She'd have taken Bruce, if he'd been with her ... she wished, suddenly, she'd fought harder to keep from having to send him to Spain. But the army needed him. "I get in, deal with the guards, and then signal the rebels to bring a boat for the mothers."

"I'll arrange it," Irene said. "Good luck."

She nodded curtly, then walked off. Gwen sighed inwardly as she reread the note for the umpteenth time, then finished gathering her supplies. It wouldn't be *that* hard to get into the breeding farm, given how few guards were clearly visible. The French wouldn't want to draw attention to the building by surrounding it with an army, although she was surprised they hadn't moved the farm out of the city long ago. But then, their British counterparts had kept *their* farm in London. Her lips twitched. From what she'd been told, it had seemed a good idea at the time.

Night fell slowly, darkness falling over Paris like a warm blanket. Gwen made her way up to the rooftops, tasting smoke and fire in the air. The city was restive, despite the curfew. The common citizens were hiding indoors, hoping and praying they'd see the next morning, while the rebels moved supplies under cover of darkness and prepared for the fighting to come. She winced as she heard shooting from the south, probably from the slums outside the walls. Government soldiers? Rebels? Criminals? It didn't matter. All that mattered was completing her mission and starting a civil war ...

Her heart twisted. *How many people are going to die, because of me?*

She shook her head as she levitated herself into the air and flew north, staying as low as she dared. It wasn't *her* fault. The French aristos had spent *years* grinding the commoners into the dirt, working and taxing them to death. Lord Mycroft had insisted there would be a revolution sooner or later, although even *he* had been unable to predict exactly *when*. She might be helping the rebels, she might be teaching them how to hide and take the offensive, but she hadn't piled up the dry wood. She was only lighting the match ...

The thought mocked her as she reached the embankment and peered over the slimy waters to the far side. There were no lights, save for a handful of streetlights; no troops marching along the waterside when they were desperately needed elsewhere. She cloaked herself in an illusion and settled down on the rooftop to wait, her eyes finding the breeding farm amidst the other buildings on the embankment. The mansion looked larger than any of the farms in London – she dreaded to think how many women might be imprisoned inside – and had its own jetty, allowing the enemy to bring people in and out by boat. No wonder it had been kept so secret. The rebels had never even had the slightest clue it existed.

A flash of lightning lit up the city, followed by a thunderous explosion that shook the ground under her feet. She glanced north and saw a fireball rising into the air, casting a baleful glow over the surrounding buildings. She could feel magic vibrating, pressing against her senses as the rebels attacked. The offensive wasn't intended to get across the bridges and into the wealthier parts of the city, but the defenders would have to assume the worst. The bridges were their sole advantage. They couldn't allow the rebels to seize a bridgehead on the far side or the city would be plunged into anarchy.

She stood and glided into the air, keeping the illusion around herself to hide her presence as she floated over the river. A guard stood on the rooftop, peering north. Gwen lowered herself to the ground, then reached out with her magic and crushed his skull. The body fell to the rooftop, landing in a pool of blood. Gwen felt a pang of guilt – a well-trained Mover could have killed the man by reaching into his head and *pinching* – which she rapidly suppressed. The man had been guarding a *breeding* farm. He had been, at the very least, an accessory to rape. And if he'd been a magician in his own right …

Disgust tainted her thoughts as she found her way into the building and inched down the stairs. There were no guards, something that surprised her. Very few people realised an attack could come from *above*, but magicians knew better. The government knew the rebels had magicians too now, magicians who could fly across the river … she sniffed the air, tasting the stench of human despair. It brought back memories she didn't want to admit existed.

The air was warm, uncomfortably warm, as she peered into a dorm. It was dark, but she could hear breathing and whimpering and nightmarish sounds she couldn't even begin to place. The darkness was so absolute it took time for her magic to pierce the shadows, to pick out the women lying on cots. It looked like a hospital, but hospitals didn't normally cuff their patients to the beds. Gwen's stomach clenched. Each and every one of the women were naked, with one hand cuffed to the bedrails. Escape was impossible even if one wasn't drugged.

Her eyes narrowed as something brushed against her mind, something *familiar*. A voice whispered something in the darkness, too quietly for her to make out the words. Alarm washed through her, sending her hurrying to the nearest bed. A young woman lay in it, staring up at her. Gwen's heart skipped a beat. *Simone?*

"Gwen," Simone said. Her voice was dazed, as if she was so tired she could barely think clearly. *"Run!"*

The wall behind Gwen shattered. Gwen ducked on instinct as *something* flashed overhead and landed further down the dorm. Two more followed, light pulsing around them as they lashed out at her. Gwen had a brief clear glimpse of Simone as the light banished the darkness – she'd been beaten by experts, battered into submission without any permanent damage – before a bolt of pure magic slammed into her. She warded it off, cursing under her breath. Simone was a prisoner and that meant …

She shoved the thought out of her head as the enemy magicians closed on her, their magic trying to trap her. The rooftop was crumbling – she split her attention, pushing them away even as she pulled on the ceiling and shoved pieces of debris at them. They shoved them away, heedless of the risks to the mothers. Gwen cursed under her breath. She dared not unleash her full power, for fear of hurting the helpless women, but the enemy had no such compunctions. They'd baited a trap and she'd walked right into it.

Magic punched at her, a wave of raw power strong enough to smash right through her defences. Gwen didn't try to push back – it would have been futile. Instead, she darted to the side and summoned light herself, trying to blind them. It didn't work ... she forced herself to think, her hand brushing against Simone's bare skin. She wasn't *good* at healing, but she could purge the drugs from her body. Simone threw up, violently, as Gwen's magic broke the cuffs and then raged on, freeing the other women. It wasn't much, but ...

An enemy magician yanked Simone's bed out from under her and threw it at Gwen with staggering force. Gwen had no time to dodge. Instead, she caught the bed and let it shield her even as it carried her right down the dorm. Her magic sparkled out, trying to save the other women. If she could free them all, perhaps they could help her ... a head spun overhead, blood flying in all directions. Gwen shuddered as she was slammed into the far wall, her magic barely cushioning the blow as the stone crumbled under the impact. The enemy magicians really didn't care about the mothers.

Idiot, Gwen told herself. *Of course they don't care about them ...*

A hand grabbed her upper arm and pulled at her. Gwen lashed out with her magic and stopped her would-be captor's heart, then threw his body at his friends. They stumbled backwards, giving her time to smash through the floor and drop into the lower dorm. If she could get out ... strong arms came at her from behind, wrapping themselves around her. She grunted in pain, trying to concentrate long enough to stop *his* heart too. The magic didn't work ... she braced herself as he pulled her arms behind her back, then pressed her hand against his chest and set fire to him. He howled in agony and shoved her away. Gwen tried not to scream herself as pain washed through her palm. She might not be able to hurt herself *directly* with magic, but indirectly ...

Move, she thought. Magic was sparkling around her, pressing down. The ceiling was caving in, rubble crashing down on the beds … she could barely muster the power to free the women and try to get them out. *Move, you idiot!*

The world exploded around her, magic crashing into her with staggering force. She squeezed her eyes shut as blinding light pulsed on the air, enough to render a normal magician completely helpless. Gwen concentrated on her senses, trying to find a path through the light and fog. They were coming down, apparently unable or unwilling to keep her from going *up*. Did they think her stunned and helpless? Did they know who she was? The magician who'd grabbed her *had* to know she was female – he *must* have felt her breasts – but he was in no state to tell the others. Simone could have told them, if they'd bothered to ask. There was no way to know.

She braced herself, gathering her magic. The mission had failed spectacularly and now all she could do was run. She hated the thought of retreating – she hated the thought of knowing whispers following her everywhere, of men telling her that *of course* they fully understood she couldn't have stayed to fight – but there was no choice. She'd been trapped and now all she could do was try to make her escape. She hurled herself upwards …

… And ran straight into a wall of magic.

Gwen fell, the force of the impact driving the breath from her lungs. She grunted, gasping for breath, just as someone landed on top of her and pressed a cloth to her lips. She couldn't help taking a breath, breathing in the drug. It was suddenly very hard to think clearly. Her magic sparkled away …

"Sleep," someone said. "Sleep."

Gwen closed her eyes. The darkness swallowed her.

Chapter Thirty
Paris, France

It had been an exciting night.

Jean-Luc had not – he'd said – known *precisely* what the rebels intended to do, but he'd known they intended to do *something* and he'd planned to take advantage of it. He'd kept his crew – including Bruce – running around the city from dusk till dawn, moving crates of supplies over the city walls and shipping them to various safe houses around the city. It had been surprisingly easy. The fighting near the bridges had raged for hours, keeping the troops from responding to sniping, bombing and any of a hundred other provocations designed to push them into a gross overrcaction. Bruce had done his bit, whenever he'd had a clear shot at an enemy soldier. The more troops who died on the streets, or just outside the walls, the fewer there'd be to stop Gwen when she made her move.

And yet, when he returned to the pub, it rapidly became clear that *something* had gone badly wrong.

"I thought you'd been captured," Jean-Luc said. "What happened?"

Bruce blinked, feeling ice in his stomach. *Nothing* had happened, certainly nothing that posed any threat to him. He'd launched stones at soldiers, and dropped a chamberpot on a policeman, and broken the legs of a man trying to force a woman to raise her skirts for him, but nothing *too* dramatic. And yet …

"Nothing," he said. He wondered, briefly, if Jean-Luc had set him up to be captured, then dismissed the thought a second later. Jean-Luc wouldn't last a day if word got out he'd betrayed one of his associates. The smuggler rings were held together by an odd code of honour – and silence – and they wouldn't hesitate to punish anyone who broke it. "Why did you think I'd been captured?"

Jean-Luc frowned. "I have a source over there," he said, waving in the rough direction of the Bastille. "They told me the government captured a powerful magician."

"No," Bruce said. A nasty thought crossed his mind. "It wasn't me they caught."

He turned and hurried out of the pub, pulling his cloak around him as he headed onto the streets. A powerful magician ... Gwen wasn't the only powerful magician in the city, let alone in the rebellion, but the average rebel magician would probably have his throat cut the moment he felt into government hands. It wasn't easy to keep a magician prisoner and there would be little to gain from trying, not when most rebels knew little more than what they needed to know. There was nothing to gain and quite a lot to lose by trying to torture the captives for information they didn't have. And yet ... if they'd captured *Gwen* ...

She'll be fine, he told himself. He found himself walking faster and faster, his mind barely noting the people on the streets. *Won't she?*

The uneasy sensation in his heart only grew worse as he approached the dressmaker's shop and paused outside the shuttered windows. The shop should be opening up – the government had ordered shops to remain open, despite the risks – and yet, the shop felt abandoned. Bruce hesitated, just for a second, then used his magic to unlock the door and slip inside. If Gwen was asleep, he'd take one look to confirm she was safe and then retreat before she realised he was there. If she was awake ... she'd be furious, but at least she'd be alive and free. If she wasn't there ... he swallowed, hard. He didn't want to think about it.

His senses prickled. Someone was touching his mind, trying to read his thoughts. It was a feminine presence, but it wasn't Gwen. It was so light and airy he barely sensed it, so faint it was easy to convince himself he was imagining it ... he gritted his teeth, tightening his shields as he unlocked the door into the backroom. Whoever was inside was hoping to slow a police raid for a few seconds ... Bruce suspected they were wasting their time. The door wasn't particularly tough. One good kick would bring it crashing down. The interior was dark, pools of shadow washing across the ground. He opened his senses, feeling a presence on the far side of the room ...

"Freeze," a voice said, in English. "Bruce?"

Bruce swore. It wasn't Gwen. "Who ...?"

"Irene," Irene said. "You remember me?"

"Vaguely," Bruce said. Gwen had introduced them, when they'd boarded ship to travel to England, but she hadn't been very clear on who or what Irene actually *was*. A Talker, obviously, yet ... what else? He concentrated on keeping his shields in place as he leaned forward, peering into the darkness. "Where is she?"

"She didn't come home," Irene said. Her voice was tightly controlled. "Something went very badly wrong."

"I'll say," Bruce snarled. A flash of anger shot through him. "There's a report someone was taken prisoner last night, someone important."

Irene muttered a word in a language Bruce didn't recognise. "Let me light the lantern," she said, her skirts rustling as she crossed the room. "Why are you here?"

"As I said, I heard about someone being taken captive," Bruce said. He cursed Lord Mycroft and the British Government under his breath. It would have been so much easier – and safer – if he'd been allowed to travel with Gwen openly. "What happened to her? Why did she ...?"

Irene lit the lantern. Bruce couldn't help noticing she looked older ... although, he reminded himself, it could easily be a trick of the light. "We located a breeding farm," she said, bitterly. "Either it was a trap, or the building had far more guards than we thought."

Bruce frowned. "A *breeding* farm? A breeding farm for *what*?"

"Magicians." Irene's voice was cold. "They take lower-class women and pair them up with male magicians until they get pregnant, then they take every care with the woman until she gives birth ... at which point, her children are taken away and given to aristos to raise, while *she* is sent right back to the breeding farm to get pregnant again. And so it goes until she is too old to have children ..."

"Shit." Bruce *knew* how Gwen would have reacted, when she'd been told about the farm. "Was it a trap baited for her?"

"I don't know," Irene said. "My ... my agent within the Bastille had codes she was supposed to use, if she was under any sort of duress. She didn't use them. I don't know if someone realised what she'd done and decided to take advantage of it, or if she was somehow turned against us, or even if we had a stroke of hellishly bad luck. Or ..."

"Or the women in the farm might have turned on her," Bruce said. "If they are magicians ... they might have decided they wanted to stay."

Irene gave him an icy look. "Do you think anyone *would*?"

"The streets out there are frightful for young women, particularly if they don't have fathers, brothers or strong husbands," Bruce said. He had no illusions about where the whorehouses – even the high-class brothels – found their staff. "They might feel that being perpetually pregnant is better than being on the streets."

"Maybe," Irene conceded, ruefully. "I *advise*" – her tone made it clear it was an order – "you not to say that to Gwen."

Bruce nodded. "Very well," he said. It wasn't important, not now. "Where is she and how do we get her back?"

"I don't know," Irene said. "Not yet."

"I ..." Bruce balled his fists. "We have to find her! And quickly!"

"I agree," Irene said. "But there is no way we can find her any *faster*."

Bruce glared, unwilling to admit she was right even though he *knew* it. Gwen had been missing for hours. The French could have taken her into the Bastille by now, or out of the city, or even simply slit her throat … no, he refused to even consider the possibility she might be dead. Or worse … she was a master magician and her children would very likely be masters too. The French might add her to their breeding programme … his stomach heaved at the very thought. It was horrific, all the more so because of the fools who'd blame her for being raped … he ground his teeth in silent rage, promising himself he'd bathe Versailles in blood if they so much as harmed a hair on her head. He'd burn the French Court to the ground and piss on the rubble.

And if someone dares tell me I should break the engagement because she was raped, I'll kill him, Bruce thought. *I'll torture him to the very edge of death and then heal him so I can torture him again and again.*

Irene cleared her throat. Bruce scowled, wondering how much of his thoughts she'd read. She'd recognised and accepted him on sight, despite the local outfit and overgrown stubble … she'd skimmed his mind, certainly enough to determine who he was. And yet … he concentrated on keeping his shields in place, all too aware there were memories in his mind he didn't want anyone to see. If Gwen didn't make it back alive, he was damned if he was letting anyone drag her reputation though the mud. Let them think she died a chaste virgin …

"I'll get in touch with a couple of other sources," Irene said. "And see what they tell me."

"We could attack the Bastille and get her out," Bruce said. The last thing he wanted to do was to sit down and wait. He was a man of action, as well as Gwen's lover. It wouldn't be *that* hard to get a rebel force across the river, particularly with magical help. "And then she'd be safe."

"If she's in the Bastille," Irene said. "We simply don't know …"

She broke off, holding up a hand. "Quiet!"

Bruce tensed. Irene's mental senses were far sharper than his. If someone was approaching with bad intentions, she might well detect them long before they realised they'd been spotted … his mind raced, considering their options. Gwen hadn't known he'd been following her. She couldn't tell her captors something she didn't know, no matter what they did to force her to talk. They wouldn't have prepared for him … his magic boiled, ready to teach the French a lesson. They'd be shitting teeth by the time he was done with them.

"Simone?" Irene glanced at him. "There's no one with her, as far as I can tell, but be wary."

"Right," Bruce said. Prudence suggested they broke contact and ran. He could no more listen to that part of him than he could simply abandon Gwen to her fate. "I'm ready."

He followed Irene into the shop as the door was pushed open and a young woman wearing a shapeless baggy dress stumbled inside. Irene sucked in her breath sharply. Bruce followed her gaze and understood. The young woman might have been pretty once, but it was impossible to be sure. She'd been badly battered, her face worked over by experts … judging by how she limped, it was quite likely the rest of her body had been battered too.

"I need to scan your thoughts," Irene said, as the girl stumbled to the floor. "Don't fight me."

The girl – Simone – made no attempt at resistance as Irene pressed her fingertips to Simone's face and touched her mind. Bruce shuddered, feeling a kernel of unease as he turned away. It just wasn't *right*. It wasn't. Simone wasn't naked, but she might as well be … Irene wouldn't let her keep any secrets, not even the simplest and most innocent. It was disgusting. He would sooner have killed the girl than exposed every last corner of her mind. And yet … what choice did they have?

Irene swore, again. "They did something to Raechel."

Bruce stared at her. "What?"

"The Duke," Simone said. Her voice was dry, as if her mouth were full of sand. Bruce poured her a glass of water as she struggled to speak. "He did something to her."

"Raechel," Bruce repeated. "What is she doing here?"

"We had her inserted in the French Court," Irene explained, briskly. "It was how we knew about Simone."

"Right," Bruce said. "And what happened to her?"

"We were caught exploring under the palace," Simone said, between sips of water. "The Duke … did something to her. I don't know what. I never saw her again."

Irene frowned. "They Charmed her?"

Bruce had a different question. "What happened to *you*?"

Simone shuddered. "They beat me, then drugged me, then … took me to the farm and …"

"She's a magician," Irene said quietly, echoing Bruce's earlier thoughts. "Her children will be magicians too."

"Shit," Bruce said. He'd grown up in a culture where husband and wife would negotiate a couple of children and then live largely separate lives, maintaining the fiction of being close even though they weren't, but even so … "Are you pregnant?"

Simone gave him a disgusted look. "I don't know yet."

Bruce gritted his teeth. "And what happened to Gwen?"

"I don't know," Simone said. "She did something to me, something to free me. I crawled away in the confusion and fell into the river and … a boatman pulled me out of the water and took me to the far side and … I had to … I had to get here and …"

Irene touched her shoulder lightly. "It's alright," she said. "You're safe now."

"Not for long," Bruce said. "Where *is* she?"

He stared down at Simone. "Where would they take her?"

"I don't know," Simone said. "I just don't know."

Bruce pressed harder. "What do they normally do with rogue magicians?"

"Kill them." Simone swallowed hard. "They can't hold them prisoner for long."

"Enough," Irene said, sharply. "She's in no state to talk."

Bruce scowled. "We have to get out of here," he said, sharply. "If they force Gwen to tell them where she was staying in the city ..."

"I'll take care of it," Irene said. She helped Simone to her feet, then half-carried her into the backroom. "Stay here and *think*. I'll do what I can for her."

Bruce nodded curtly, forcing himself to sit down. It wasn't easy. Simone had been brutalised and raped and God alone knew what else, which meant ... what the hell were they doing to Gwen? Did they even know who she was? How many of them had actually *met* Gwen? Bruce had seen a couple of Gwen's portraits, but none really captured the essential *her*. It was possible, he told himself, that the French wouldn't realise who and what she really was. But then, it was unlikely they'd assume she'd just sprung out of nowhere. They'd want to know everything about their mystery captive, from where and when she was born to who'd taught her magic and introduced her to the rebels and ... he felt his heart clench, painfully. They'd keep asking her questions, all the while drugging her or scanning her mind or ... given time, they'd break her. And then ...?

A wash of urgency ran through him. They had to get out – and fast. Gwen knew about the dressmaker's shop. She could be telling her captors right now. Bruce wanted to believe she could keep her mouth shut, but he knew better. Her mental defences could be ground down, one by one, until she talked or simply had secrets plucked from her mind ... Bruce cursed under his breath. Gwen wasn't *just* a powerful magician. She knew far too much to be allowed to remain in enemy hands.

And they sent her into danger, Bruce thought. *Did they expect her to be captured?*

He stood and paced the shop, his mind churning. The Bastille was supposed to be secure. There was a small army – magicians as well as soldiers – guarding the fortress. And yet, he was sure he could get into the defences and find her. Someone would talk, if he grabbed one of the officers and hurt the bastard until he broke. Someone could be made to talk … his magic shimmered around him, offering possibilities so horrific he would never have considered them if the situation hadn't been so dire. He could reach into someone's head and *twist* and …

Irene returned, looking grim. "I gave her something to help her sleep," she said, curtly. "She is in terrible pain."

Bruce nodded. He'd seen enough of Simone's bruises to be sure she'd been worked over by a pair of experts. She'd still been able to move, and presumably have children, but otherwise … he wasn't sure if it had been petty spite or if it served a deeper purpose. If the idea had been to break her to her new role, it had failed. He let out a breath, feeling worry gnawing at his vitals. Gwen was a prisoner and he … he could do nothing. Where *was* she?

"We'll find her," Irene said. "For the moment" – her eyes hardened – "I want you to help me pack a few things, before we go. This place isn't likely to be safe for long."

"No," Bruce agreed. "What … what did they do to Raechel?"

"I don't know," Irene said. "There are some … *techniques* … to assist someone to forget something, or even to convince them to do things they wouldn't normally. Magic could be used to assist this, if the duke is a magician … Raechel doesn't have magic herself, which makes her vulnerable if her defences get weakened or shattered. She wouldn't have willingly betrayed us, but her thoughts could have been twisted to the point she honestly thought she was doing the right thing …"

Bruce made a face. "Could they do that to Gwen?"

"I don't know," Irene said. "But we have to assume the worst."

She turned away. "Come on," she said. "We have to move."

Chapter Thirty-One
Paris, France

wen felt ... sick.

She swallowed hard, her entire body trembling as she wormed her way back towards the light. She'd drunk a little too much once, in a moment of teenage resentment and rebellion, and she felt drunk now, only worse. Far worse. Her body felt weak, as if she could barely muster the strength to breathe. It was hard to think clearly – her memories were a jumbled mess, her thoughts felt smothered – let alone feel any real sense of urgency. It felt as if she'd given up and accepted her fate and resigned herself ...

No!

She shuddered again, her body convulsing as her memories snapped back into place. She'd been tricked. She'd been lured into a trap and ... she'd been captured. Her magic ... she reached for her magic and felt nothing, save for a faint tremor at the back of her mind. Panic yammered at her, her heart starting to race as she tried to compose herself. She knew a few dirty tricks – Irene had taught her quite a few things she could do to defend herself – but she had few illusions. Her body felt weak, yet even if she'd been in peak health she'd be hard-pressed to defend herself. A strong man could overwhelm her with ease.

Her breathing slowed as she gathered herself. Her eyes

were closed … she kept them closed, even as she tried to listen to the world around her. The air was cool, but with a faint scent that worried her; something soft yet scratchy lay on top of her. She was on a bed … she swallowed, hard, as she realised she was naked. And that she wasn't alone …

"Well," a voice said. He spoke English with a French accent. "You may as well open your eyes. I know you're awake and thinking."

Gwen's eyes snapped open before she could think better of it. It might have been smarter to pretend she didn't understand English. The average Frenchman wouldn't speak English as a matter of course, certainly not if he wasn't a sailor, merchant or someone else whose duties brought him into regular contact with Englishmen. Hell, most *Englishmen* learnt at least *some* French and Latin during their schooling … she pushed the thought aside as she looked around, taking in the chamber surrounding her. It looked like an alchemical lab. A handful of glowing crystals, pulsing with eerie – and sickly – light were embedded in the stone wall. She could hardly stand to look at them. They were just … unnatural.

She turned her head slightly, trying to see as much as she could. She was lying on a bench, her hands cuffed to the railings. An older man sat at the end of the bed, his face … her thoughts twisted and fled, her eyes barely able to make out *anything*. He was … *unnatural*, so alien she couldn't force her eyes to make sense of what she was seeing. She'd seen circus freaks, poor unfortunates who had no place anywhere else, but this … it was all she could do to keep looking in his general direction. Her eyes kept insisting he wasn't even there.

"*Bonjour,*" the man said, with heavy irony. "Lady Gwen, is it not?"

"*Non, monsieur,*" Gwen said. "*Je m'appelle Jeannne.*"

The man let out a heavy sigh. "Your French is good, Lady Gwen, but it is clear you are not a native speaker. A common problem, amongst Englishmen who mistake schoolboy French for *real* French. Given time, you might have corrected your weaknesses, but ..."

He shrugged, expressively. "I am Duke Philippe, Kinsman to the King. It is a pleasure to make your acquaintance."

Gwen scowled, trying to think through a haze that threatened to descend on her thoughts and snuff them out. Who – what – was he? What had he *done* to her? To her magic? Could she stall long enough for her powers to regenerate? Or ... would he make sure to drug her and keep drugging her? Or ... what had he done to her powers? She'd never heard of a drug that dimmed a magician's power, not completely. The poor women in the breeding farms had been drugged out of their minds ... and they hadn't known how to use their powers, not really. She did. She was used to using very little magic to get things done. And yet, she was unable to so much as lift a needle.

"Really," Duke Philippe said. "There is no point in playing coy. We know Lady Gwen is no longer in England, and here you are – a young magician whose power and appearance matches hers perfectly. You *are* Lady Gwen, Royal Sorceress, aren't you? Who else could you be?"

Gwen gritted her teeth. "Jeanne de Valois-Saint-Rémy?"

"You're a little young to be *her*," Duke Philippe said. There was a hint of cold amusement in his tone. "And she was a terrible fabulist, not a magician."

He leaned forward. "You are my prisoner, Lady Gwen, if you like it or not. And if you refuse to cooperate, it can get very unpleasant for you."

"It's already unpleasant," Gwen said, sourly. "Do you make a habit of handcuffing your guests to their beds?"

"I find it helps them stay put," Duke Philippe said. His voice was so atonal Gwen couldn't tell if he was being sarcastic or not. "Do you know what I did to you?"

Gwen didn't want to think about it, but there was no choice. "Drugged me?"

"Not quite," Duke Philippe said. "Oh, yes; you were drugged into a stupor. That's how we captured you. But now? Tell me, how are we holding you prisoner?"

"A pair of handcuffs," Gwen said, dryly. "I feel sorry for your wife."

Duke Philippe showed no visible reaction to her sally. "You know as well as I do you could free yourself from handcuffs easily, if you had your powers," he said. "Why don't you?"

Gwen let out a breath. "What have you done?"

The duke seemed to smile. It was hard to be sure. "So … you don't know."

"No," Gwen said. "What …?"

Duke Philippe cut her off. "You are aware, of course, that magic isn't *really* magic. It isn't witches putting curses on poor unfortunates and dark lords running around the country making everyone miserable. Turning men into frogs and women into horses doesn't happen, certainly not on a regular basis. There are no fairies, no creatures from other worlds or higher planes … not even any angels or demons. They simply don't exist."

"I'm sure the Church will be delighted to hear you say it," Gwen said, sarcastically. "They might be so pleased to hear it they'll burn you at the stake."

"The Pope does what His Majesty tells him to do," Duke Philippe said, dryly. "His opinions don't matter."

He paused. "Magic, in short, is not *real* magic. It is, instead, an aspect of the mental arts."

Gwen made a show of raising her eyebrows. "How so?"

The duke waved a hand. "There have always been stories of men moving objects with the power of their mind … Movers, in other words. Rumours of telepathy … what are Talkers, if not telepaths? Charmers … is it a talent for understanding people and tailoring your argument to suit them or another mental art? Magic doesn't come from the heart, Lady Gwen, but from the head. It is just … something all humans could learn to do, given time."

Gwen was intrigued, despite herself. "If that is true, how come there are so few master magicians?"

Duke Philippe shrugged. "How much did you know about magic, before you were recruited?"

He went on before Gwen could answer. "Your teacher and his peers were all old enough to be your father, and they all grew up before the magical talents were carefully defined," he said. "Jack was raised by a man who recognised his potential and did nothing to limit it. You had almost nothing to use to guide your progress until you'd touched all the magical arts. How many master magicians do you know who were raised amongst other magicians?"

"None," Gwen said. Duke Philippe hadn't mentioned *Bruce* ... but Bruce wasn't an exception to the rules. His father hadn't been a magician. "If this is true, why aren't there more magicians?"

"Good question," Duke Philippe said. "We think it takes a certain amount of luck, as well as good breeding, to develop one's mental talents. But ..."

His voice seemed to shift, just slightly. "We discovered, partly by accident, that certain powers ... resonated with gemstones," he said. "We were lucky. It didn't seem a promising line of inquiry, back when we were desperately trying to catch up with you. If Versailles hadn't been going through a mesmerisation craze ... well, perhaps we wouldn't have worked out how gemstones can be used for magic. But we did."

Gwen turned her head to look at the glowing crystals. "You're using them to neutralise my powers."

"In essence," Duke Philippe agreed. "Put simply, the crystals resonate a field used to limit your powers. Placed into your body, they'd enhance them – or so we believe. The results are very difficult to predict."

Gwen remembered the super-magician she'd killed and shuddered. "That's what you did to your magicians, isn't it? You boosted their powers ..."

She paused. "But what happened to their bodies?"

"We're unsure," Duke Philippe said. "Our researchers

believe we are only scratching the surface of our potential. It's quite possible that we are … well, flexing one part of the mind while allowing other parts to atrophy, like a man lifting weights while neglecting the remainder of his body. It's also possible we are pushing bodies too far when we tamper with their minds, or … we simply don't know."

He cocked his head. "Did you not know anything about gemstones? And how they can be used for magic?"

Gwen hesitated, then realised it was pointless. "No."

"Odd," Duke Philippe said. "I heard sellers in London were offering magic crystals."

"To the credulous," Gwen said, before she could stop herself. "They are no more *magical* than anything else …"

She frowned as a thought struck her. "It isn't just gemstones, is it?"

Duke Philippe said nothing for a long moment. "What do you mean?"

"You don't just use gemstones to boost magic or you'd have an entire army of magicians by now," Gwen said. "And if you did, you'd have used it. Your empire is already coming apart at the seams. You need something else."

Understanding clicked, followed rapidly by horror. "You need a magician to empower the crystals, to infuse them with magic. Don't you?"

"Correct," Duke Philippe said. "For each of our empowered magicians, a trained magician has to die."

Gwen sucked in her breath as something else fell into place. Simone had clearly been marked for the farms from the moment her adopted father had been executed. She should have been sent to the hellish mansion at once, not … why had she been left to run around the court? She was easily old enough to bear children … had Duke Philippe known she'd make contact with the underground and kept an eye on her in hopes she'd lead him to more magicians, or … or what? Had she lured Gwen into a trap? It was possible, but unlikely. Irene would have spotted the deceit lurking in Simone's mind …

Perhaps, she thought, darkly. *Or perhaps she found a way to hide it.*

"So you need more than just magicians," she said. "You need someone trained to the point of actual usefulness, then ... you drain their power and murder them."

"Effectively," Duke Philippe agreed. "It doesn't always work, and we're not sure why, but it usually does."

There was an hint of a smile on his face. "It's theoretically possible to take an arm or a leg from one person and graft it on to another," he said. "I believe the Russians were experimenting with something similar, back before they had their ... unfortunate accident with your daughter. We just do the same with magic."

Gwen frowned. "You steal someone's magic and give it to someone else," she said. "How does it even work?"

"We think the magician's brain adapts to use the enhanced magic," Duke Philippe said, carefully. "How much of a medical background do you have?"

"Young women of my station are encouraged to be as ignorant as possible of such matters," Gwen said, dryly. It wasn't entirely true – her mother and maids had taught her a little, then she'd learnt much more after Master Thomas had taken her as his apprentice – but hopefully he wouldn't press the matter too far. "We are rarely taught anything useful, even the basics."

"A curious oversight," Duke Philippe said. "Our women are much more aware of how their bodies work."

He leaned forward. Gwen bit her lip. He was human and yet he felt ... different. He wasn't touching her and yet she felt as if she was being overshadowed by him ... she wondered, suddenly, if his enhanced magic was brushing against her awareness and scattering her thoughts. It was quite possible. And yet ... she shuddered.

"A human body is a machine," Duke Philippe said. "A very clever piece of machinery, to be sure, and so complex it makes an airship engine look simple, but nothing more than a piece of machinery, of ropes and wires and strings … we're all puppets of our own minds, if you want to look at it like that. There's a very inventive young man in my retinue, a fiction writer, who actually imagines we're on the way to evolving into creatures of pure brain and little else. We'll wind up looking like octopuses, perhaps not even that. With magic, who needs arms and legs?"

"Everyone," Gwen said, trying to keep him talking. She had a nasty idea where he was going – and what he had in mind for her. "There are limits to how much even the most experienced and powerful can do with magic."

"Given time, perhaps that could change," Duke Philippe said. "Your children, Lady Gwen, might be more powerful than yourself. Your grandchildren even more so."

"Perhaps," Gwen said. There'd been *someone* who'd insisted she was Master Thomas's bastard daughter. Her power had to come from somewhere, they'd said, and neither her parents nor her brother showed any trace of magic. Bastards. She was hardly the only magician to come from a magicless background, or to have siblings who lacked magic themselves. "And your point is?"

"Like I said, the human body is a machine," Duke Philippe said. "And we can use magic to craft new linkages between the implanted crystals and the brain. We not only attach a second pair of arms, if you'll excuse the analogy, but the connections that make it actually work."

"I see," Gwen said. She understood more, she thought, than he realised. "But it clearly weakens their bodies."

"Perhaps it does," Duke Philippe said. "Perhaps they just need time to adapt to it."

He leaned back in his chair. "And why do you think I'm telling you all this?"

Gwen made a show of pretending to think about it. "Because you want to gloat and there aren't many people you can gloat to?"

Duke Philippe snorted. "I'm Kinsman to the King," he

said. "Do you know what that means? I could talk about anything, from the care and feeding of honeybees to the local leather industry and people would pretend to listen and pay attention. There are no shortage of men and women eager to do anything, anything at all, in exchange for my patronage and favour. I could raise them high with my right hand and crush them with my left and they know it. No, Lady Gwen, I don't need to gloat. But I did want to talk with one of the few people on my level."

"I'm nothing like you," Gwen said. She peered into his obscured face, making out dark and dangerous eyes. "What have you done to yourself?"

"Interesting question," Duke Philippe said. For a second, she thought she saw a sadistic smile behind his mask. "I developed my magic."

"And then ..." Gwen had a nasty feeling she knew where the story was going. "How did you convince the king to support you?"

"The king isn't a fool," Duke Philippe said. "He is all too aware that, for all that he is cosseted inside his court, his kingdom is on the verge of collapse. He is also aware he can do little, not without making the collapse come faster. It would be easy, on paper, to solve the revenue shortfall by taxing the great estates and the church, but trying either one would lead to civil war. I offered him another choice. He'll let me do anything if I hold out the prospect of saving his throne."

"Lucky him," Gwen said. "You were a Charmer, weren't you?"

"In a manner of speaking," Duke Philippe said. "Charming and Talking are closely related. A skilled Talker should be able to Charm simply by posing arguments they *know* appeal to their victim. It was how *I* started ..."

He seemed to smile, again. "And now, do you know why you're here?"

Gwen scowled at him. "You're planning to steal *my* power."

"Quite," Duke Philippe said. He reached out and

patted Gwen's head. "Lie there. You don't have to do anything, but wait. Once you get weak enough for the collection … well, don't worry about it. It'll be over shortly. If you cooperate, you may even survive."

"I doubt it," Gwen said. She had to stall for time, although she feared it was pointless. She was powerless and chained and completely alone. "You won't let me live."

"Oh, I will," Duke Philippe said. He stood. "You have no idea how useful you're going to be."

Chapter Thirty-Two
Paris, France

aechel felt … odd.

It wasn't something she could put into words, but it was there. It felt as if she was part of her body and yet looking down on herself from high above, as if she was separated from the world by a pane of dirty glass. She felt mildly drunk, all the time, even though she *knew* she hadn't been drinking. And …

Louis paid little attention to her, when they were together. She was too far out of herself to find that odd, even though part of her *knew* that was wrong. Louis had been trying to get into her skirts for *weeks*. He'd been so adamant about chasing and catching her that it was hard to believe something as minor as a national crisis could possibly stop him from pulling her into bed. He'd gone to quite some trouble to have her with him, so he could impress her with his power and position and yet … Raechel's thoughts shied away from the question, whenever it crossed her mind. She was in no state to think clearly. The world was just a blur.

And yet, she could *feel* eyes on her. She was used to aristos looking at her, as she swayed around the dance floor or allowed certain noblemen to pay court to her while cutting others dead, but this was different. Men were watching her … she was aware of it, on some level, as she made her way back onto the streets, helping her lover to pretend everything was normal even though no one could possibly be fooled. The shops were open, but there was very little on the shelves and hardly anyone in the streets. If the king hadn't ordered the population to remain in place, and promised dire punishment to anyone who fled the city without permission, Paris would be depopulated. The sense of threat grew with every passing day.

Yesterday, the rebels tried to force the bridges, Raechel thought. She'd heard a lot of chatter about it, although – as a young woman – she'd been barred from the innermost councils of war. *Today ... who knows what they'll try to do today?*

Her thoughts spun around her as she made her way down the streets towards the shops. Paris really *was* a beautiful city. The palaces and government offices looked strikingly elegant, the streets were lined with trees and statues of the men – and a handful of women – who'd built France. There was an air to the city that was unmatched even by London, a sense of regality befitting the capital of a mighty empire ... odd, she supposed, given that the French Court had deserted Paris for Versailles long ago. But then, the bureaucrats who ran the empire still lived in Paris. So too did the many others. And anyone who was anyone maintained a residence in the city. It was one of the easier ways to tell who really did have power and influence.

Louis doesn't have a home in Paris, she reflected. Even a relatively small apartment in the upper-class districts would cost far too much for him. It would be cheaper to buy an estate well outside the city, but then he wouldn't be in *Paris*. *What does that say about him, I wonder?*

She felt the mist dropping over her thoughts, again, as she stepped into the high-class dressmaker's shop and looked around. There were only two outfits on display, both so expensive she knew she couldn't even *begin* to afford them. There would be no credit either, not now ... not ever, not for an aristocrat so far removed from the throne that no one outside her hometown had ever heard of her. A grim-faced woman nodded curtly to Raechel as she browsed, but otherwise said nothing. Raechel shivered. It was a disturbing sign. Normally, the shopkeepers competed to sell their wares to aristocrats who were so desperate to make an impression they cared nothing for their debts. Now ... she studied the dresses for a long moment, then turned and wandered on. The chocolatiers were empty. So too were the little cafes that, in happier times, provided seats for aristocratic women to gossip about their husbands or lovers. It was eerie. If there hadn't been a handful of waiters trying to pretend everything was normal, she would have wondered if she was alone in the world. None of them paid any attention to her.

Raechel sighed, turning away. There was nothing to do, no matter how much Louis and his patron wanted to convince the world everything was fine. She'd go back to the Bastille and then ... she didn't know. Perhaps it had been a mistake to let Louis take her to the city, even though ... her thoughts spun in circles, confusing her. Why *had* she let him take her? She didn't know. She hadn't been *that* desperate for anything ...

A man walked towards her, wearing an outfit that made him look like a nobleman. Raechel had no trouble recognising he was nothing of the sort. He strode with a purpose, so different from the aristocrats who affected a languid poise even when their superiors were ordering them to hurry. He was handsome, in a bland sort of way, and yet ... his eyes flickered over her, cool and calculating and somehow dangerous. Raechel barely had a moment to realise something was wrong before he caught her arm and yanked her into the shadows. She opened her mouth to scream, too late. A faint tingle ran through her body, her arms and legs suddenly turning to jelly. She stumbled and would have fallen if he hadn't held her upright. The world seemed to blur around her ...

... And then she was somewhere else.

She snapped awake, without ever being quite aware

she'd been unconscious. She was sitting in a chair, her hands tied behind her back, in a darkened room. Panic shot through her, driving away the haze that had covered her thoughts since ... since when? She forced herself to look around, spotting a middle-aged woman in mourning garb sitting in front of her ... she thought, although it was impossible to be sure, that there was also someone behind her. Her head pounded, her reality shattering ... she swallowed and retched, nearly throwing up everything in her stomach. The world was just wrong ...

No. It was *right*.

Raechel forced herself to speak. "Irene?"

"Raechel," Irene said. The mourning garb was odd for her, but it made sense. No one would disturb a mourning woman wandering the streets. All she had to do was pull down the veil and she'd be completely anonymous. "What happened to you?"

"I ..." Raechel retched again. "I ..."

"You went with Simone," Irene said. "You were caught. And then ... what?"

Raechel opened her mouth and *screamed* as the memories fell into place. The Duke ... he'd looked her in the eye and broken her mind and ... he'd made her talk and play a role and everything had been wrong and yet ... she retched again, her stomach churning so horribly she thought she was going to die. Irene picked up a glass of water and held it to Raechel's lips. She could barely take a couple of sips before retching again. Her head ... what had she done? What had she been made to do?

"Louis knew," she said. "Damn him – he *knew*."

Irene leaned forward. "What happened?"

Raechel found it impossible to put it into words. She felt like a child, trying a con trick that wouldn't fool the village idiot, except it *had*. Except it hadn't ... the village idiot had gone along with it, pretending to be fooled so the child could make a far greater fool of herself later on. And she'd thought she was so clever, listening to what her lover and her patron said and passing it on to her superior. She'd been so deeply under their influence that it had never crossed her mind, not once, that something was wrong. Her mind had been turned against her and ...

She retched again, then swallowed. She'd been raped. Not physically, but mentally. The duke could have made her say or do or believe anything and she *knew* it. She'd been utterly helpless against him ... worse, she hadn't even known she'd been under his control. She'd been sent back to her room with a slice gapped out of her memory, sent to play her role in a kabuki play she hadn't even known was staged. And if someone had told her ... she wouldn't have believed them. How could she? Her mind was compromised. Her thoughts and memories could no longer be trusted.

Tears prickled at her eyes. "He ... he made me his puppet," she said, finally. "I didn't even know something was wrong."

"And so you served as bait in a trap," a male voice said, from behind her. "What were you thinking?"

"She thought what the duke told her to think," Irene said, briskly. She'd have scanned Raechel's memories while she was unconscious. Normally, Raechel would have been angry at the thought, but now ... it felt a minor thing indeed, compared to the atrocity the duke had inflicted on her mind. "I don't know how he did it, but ... he did."

"And now Gwen is a prisoner," the male voice said. "Where is she?"

Raechel swallowed. "Gwen?"

"She's a prisoner," the male voice stated, coldly. "Is she in the Bastille?"

"I don't know," Raechel said. There *were* a number of captives in the fortress, but from what she'd heard the *important* prisoners had either been shipped out of the city or simply put on the block and executed. And yet, could her memories be trusted? "I didn't hear anything about her ..."

"Which is meaningless," Irene said, sharply. "They knew you were a spy."

"Yes," the male voice said. "So why leave her wandering the city?"

"Good question," Irene agreed. "They probably didn't want to disrupt her programming any further than necessary. She could be turned into an unwitting spy if they never gave her any reason to question her own actions …"

Raechel swallowed to keep from retching once again. "What now?"

"Now we find Gwen," the male voice said. "Where is she?"

"I don't know," Raechel repeated. "I just don't know!"

She forced herself to think. What would the French do with Gwen? Could they hold her prisoner for long? The smart answer might be to cut her throat as quickly as possible, before she woke up. And yet … her head ached as she remembered how easily the duke had put her in his thrall. He might be arrogant enough to assume he could do the same to Gwen, if he used a combination of drugs and mental manipulations to weaken her defences. And … her thoughts hardened. The duke needed to shore up his own position, as well as supporting his kinsman. There was a very good chance he might not have told anyone, not even the king, that he'd taken such an important prisoner.

"The duke won't want to let go of her in a hurry," she said, slowly. Gwen was *important*. "If he hands her over to the king, she'll be no further use to him."

"Right," the male voice said, sarcastically. "He's just going to keep her prisoner himself?"

"He might," Raechel said. She knew how the senior aristocracy thought. They put their own power and position ahead of anything else, including loyalty to their king and country. France could have solved half its problems by reforming and taxing the noble estates and yet … every time the scheme was proposed, the aristos closed ranks against it. The duke might be the king's kinsman, but that wouldn't make him *loyal*. "He has a home in Paris … a mansion. If she's held there …"

The male snorted. "Irene, is this another trap?"

"If it is, Raechel doesn't know it," Irene said. Raechel tried not to flinch at the reminder her mental defences no longer existed. "And no one knew you're here."

Raechel blinked. "Bruce?"

The man stepped around her, into view. "Yes," he said. "Didn't you recognise me?"

"No." Raechel gritted her teeth. "I think … how long has it been?"

"A day, more or less," Irene said. "There's no hint they took an important prisoner out of the city."

Raechel shrugged. That was meaningless. Gwen was tough, true, but the French could drug her and keep her drugged for quite some time. Probably … they could certainly keep her dazed for weeks, if they did it properly. And if they had a null to neutralise her magic … Raechel swallowed, hard. Gwen was her friend, one of her very few friends. Raechel didn't want to see her die, certainly not as a helpless captive.

"So they might have taken her to the duke's mansion," she said, slowly. It made a certain kind of sense. Sneaking a prisoner out of the city might lead to awkward questions being asked. Duke Philippe had no shortage of enemies who'd try to undermine his position, enemies who wouldn't hesitate to tattle on him to the king if they thought he'd compromised himself. "They'd certainly need to hold her *somewhere* while they figured out how to get her out of the city."

Bruce glared. "They control the city!"

"Not all of it," Irene said, quietly.

"Duke Philippe doesn't control every last officer in the city," Raechel pointed out. "The higher up they are, the more worried they'll be about protecting their own positions while undermining their superiors. He won't trust anyone who isn't completely and utterly *his* creature and if he moves to replace the current officers with his people, even for a few days, there will be resistance. It will end badly for him."

"Weird." Bruce shook his head. "Are you sure?"

"Of course not," Raechel said, dryly. "But I *do* know aristo politics are a snake pit of competing claims, precedences and endless battles for influence. Everyone seeks to build themselves up while tearing everyone else down. The country can go burn as long as the aristocracy survives."

"Charming," Bruce muttered. "They're insane."

"They honestly don't think they can lose," Irene corrected. "I know a handful of aristos who are thinking about reaching out to the rebels, on the assumption the rebels can help put them in office before obligingly turning their backs so their former allies can put knives in them. The king might be replaced, or rendered effectively powerless, but the aristocracy goes on and on. Or so they think."

Bruce made a face, then looked at Raechel. "Have you ever been in the duke's mansion?"

"No." Raechel shook her head. "I was never invited. Actually" – her eyes narrowed – "I don't know anyone who *was*."

"So what?" Bruce didn't see the point. "It means nothing."

"It means a great deal," Raechel said, quietly. "The aristos, particularly the ones who have nothing beyond a name, get ahead by putting everyone else down. If they were invited to a gathering at the duke's mansion and you weren't, you can bet your life they'd make sure you knew about it. The duke could tell them to keep it a secret and threaten them with death or worse and they'd *still* talk, because they need to make sure everything thinks they're important. And *no one* ever bragged of going to the duke's mansion. Not one."

"The mansion is in *Paris*," Bruce pointed out. "Not Versailles."

Irene snorted. "They're not *that* far apart," she said. "And while the aristocracy likes to pretend the slums don't exist, and keep their shutters down while they drive past them, they have no qualms about visiting the heart of the city."

"I'll take your word for it," Bruce said, reluctantly. "It's only a few short hours to nightfall. I'll go in once the streets are dark."

"Be careful," Irene said. "There'll be magicians on guard. *Strong* magicians."

"You need a diversion," Raechel said. "A big one."

"We don't have time," Bruce said. "And we can't get enough rebels over the river in time ... can we?"

He looked at Raechel. "What sort of magician *is* the duke?"

"I ... I don't know," Raechel said. She knew more about magic than most, thanks to Gwen and Irene, but neither of them had ever mentioned anything like the duke. "Just don't let him look you in the eye."

"I'll blind him first," Bruce promised. "And then kill him."

"Please." Raechel would have preferred to kill the man herself, but she suspected it wouldn't be possible. The duke wouldn't be entirely dependent on his magic. "But get Gwen out first."

"If she's there," Irene said. "We could be wrong."

Raechel scowled. It was guesswork – logical guesswork, to be fair, but guesswork nonetheless. They could be completely wrong – or worse. And ... she wondered, suddenly, what Louis would do when she failed to return to the Bastille. Would he think she'd been captured? Or mugged? Or simply slipped her leash and escaped ... hell, had someone seen Bruce take her off the streets? She didn't know.

"I can't go back," she said, reluctantly. "Can I?"

"Not now," Irene said. Her voice was tinged with regret. They'd gone to a lot of trouble to insert Raechel into Versailles, but there was no way they could keep up the pretence. "They know who and what you are."

"Stay here," Bruce said, firmly. "I don't want you anywhere near the enemy until I come back. Understand?"

Raechel scowled, but nodded. Bruce had a point. The duke could have planted quite a few commands in her mind, so deeply buried they could easily pass for her own thoughts and inclinations. She might go straight back to him, the moment she was untied, utterly unaware she'd been turned into an unwitting traitor. Again.

"You'll be fine," Irene said. "But right now you need to rest."

Chapter Thirty-Three
Paris, France

he mansion was smaller than Bruce had expected, he decided as he slipped up to the rear and settled down to wait for the signal, but large enough to mark its owner as a man of wealth and power. Duke Philippe might not understand the importance of surrounding himself with a circle of allies and clients, and making them feel respected and valued, yet it was clear he took no chances with his personal safety. Bruce had no trouble spotting the handful of guards patrolling the garden and he was fairly sure there were others, hidden away out of sight. It was what *he* would do. Bruce had never been *that* skilled at the mental arts, but he'd had no trouble confirming the walls were infused with magic to protect the duke from long-distance spying. He really *did* take his security seriously.

And yet, the estate could easily turn into a death trap, Bruce thought. The inner city was heavily defended, true, but the rebels could get across the bridges and through the checkpoints if they were prepared to soak up the casualties. *There'll be nowhere to run if they lose control of the roads and rivers.*

He pushed the thought aside as he waited, taking long breaths to calm himself. Every instinct demanded that he move at once, wrapping himself in a ball of pure magic and tearing through everything that stood between him and Gwen. The duke deserved to die and everyone who helped him deserved to die too, in a manner as agonising as possible, but … Bruce knew he wasn't invincible. He was strong and powerful and the French had no way to know he was in the city – he assumed they thought he was in Spain – yet they knew the rebels also had magicians. How many of the duke's private guardsmen were magicians too? There was no way to know, until he went on the offensive. And if they were strong and skilled enough to slow him down …

Gwen is in there, he thought, although he knew it was impossible to be sure. Irene had wanted to walk past the estate, and see how many minds she could read from a safe distance, but the outer layer of guards had turned her away before she could get close to anyone important. They'd been surprisingly rude about it too, a worrying sign in a world where being rude to a noblewoman was enough to get one flogged, exiled or even executed. *They wouldn't be so determined to keep everyone away from the house if they didn't have something inside worth guarding.*

He frowned, concentrating as he heard the sound of hooves clattering up the road. Paris was disturbingly quiet, the warm night air pregnant with the sense of looming violence and horrors on a scale unseen since the riots of 1789. Bruce could *feel* the violence brewing, the population readying itself for a brutal uprising that would bathe the streets in blood. He'd heard enough to know the rest of the country was on a knife-edge, to know that if the French lost control of Paris they were likely to lose everything … he wondered, suddenly, what the guardsmen thought of their position right in the heart of Paris. It really could become a death trap if the rebels crossed the river …

The hooves stopped. Bruce heard someone shout, followed by a shot. Too late. He ducked down and covered his ears, an instant before the cart exploded. The shockwave rattled and shattered windows, the blast shaking the ground; a fireball rose into the air, a mocking reminder to the aristos that there was no longer any safety, even in the heart of their capital. Bruce had no time to think about it. The guards were already running, hurrying to the front of the mansion. They had to be thinking the bomb had been intended to take out the gatehouse and walls, allowing the rebels to swarm over the river and into the mansion. They hadn't realised – not yet – that it was nothing more than a diversion.

Bruce scrambled up and over the wall, using as little magic as possible. He didn't expect to remain undetected for long – the guards would realise they'd been tricked soon – but he needed to get as far as possible before revealing his true nature. The French would realise who and what he was, the moment they saw him using multiple types of magic. The longer they remained in the dark, the better. He ran forward until he reached the back wall, then hopped up and through a broken window. A young woman gaped at him, her mouth dropping open. Bruce slapped her hard, sending her tumbling to the floor. It was hard not to feel a pang of guilt – the girl was a maid, hardly a valid threat – which he suppressed ruthlessly. She might not be a menace herself, but if she screamed she'd bring every last guard down on his head.

"Stay here," he ordered, putting as much magic into his voice as he dared. "Don't say a word."

He hurried to the door and peered outside. The hallway was eerily bare, compared to the palaces and mansions he'd seen elsewhere. Proof, if he'd needed it, that the mansion was more than just an aristocratic residence. He reached out with his senses as he hurried down the corridor, trying to get a sense of where the infused magic was strongest. It was hard to make out anything, beyond an ebb and flow that didn't feel natural. The magic was odd, odder than anything he'd sensed in his short career … he recalled Irene's warnings and frowned. The French really *had* found a way to make magicians more powerful and that meant … what?

A trio of guards appeared and ran towards him. Bruce cursed under his breath – he'd hoped to get further before they realised they'd been conned – and lashed out with his magic, ripping stones from the walls and hurling them at the guards. They barely had a moment to react before the stones smashed into them with terrifying force, tearing through their bodies like cannonballs. Two men fell to the ground, their bodies broken beyond all hope of repair; the third stumbled, blood pouring from a gash in his side. Bruce stepped forward and caught him by the throat, feeling warm liquid trickling down his legs and pooling at his feet. The wound was too deep for the man to survive, unless someone healed or bandaged him very quickly. Bruce had no time – or inclination – to try either.

He pushed his face as close to the guard's as he could. "Where is she?"

The guard stuttered, gasping for breath. Blood spewed from his mouth. The fear in his eyes was horrifying. It would have been enough to stop Bruce if he hadn't been so desperate to find Gwen. Instead, he pushed more magic into his voice, abandoning all pretence of being subtle. "Where is she?"

"Downstairs," the guard gasped. "She's …"

His head exploded. Bruce jerked back, spotting the magician further down the corridor. There was something wrong with his face … Bruce barely had any time to notice as he gathered his magic and threw it at the magician, a battering ram of pure power that should have spattered the bastard against the wall. Instead, the magic ran into an unbreakable shield and bounced off, shredding the walls on either side. The entire building shook … Bruce cursed under his breath, shaping an illusion of himself as the magician struck back hard, his power shaking the building a second time. Bruce smirked as the riposte missed its target completely, shattering walls behind the illusion, then drew his dagger and darted around the advancing magician and shoved his way right into his magic. The magician's warped eyes seemed to go wide, an instant before Bruce shoved the dagger under his chin and into his brain. The sense of something alien vanished as he collapsed, revealing a face that looked horribly mutated. Bruce felt sick as he turned away, sensing two other magicians hurrying towards him. They were wrapped in light …

Die, he thought, hurling more pieces of debris ahead of him. The magicians barely had a second to react, nowhere near long enough to save themselves. They were remarkably strong, their power threatening to burn through his magic, but not strong enough to make a difference. *Just die.*

He reached the stairwell and directed streams of fire upwards, setting the mansion ablaze. It would keep the guards busy – and hopefully they'd think he'd gone up too – while he headed down into the darkness. The shadows seemed to pool around him as he flew down, relying on his magic to guide him to the bottom. A guard sprang out of nowhere, pistol raised, as Bruce came into view. Bruce yanked the pistol out of the guard's hand and smashed the guard into the stone wall with all the power he could muster, leaving him little more than a bloody dripping mess. Two more guards appeared, wrapped in their own magic. There was no room to be clever. Bruce threw himself at them, screaming charmed words even as his magic bored into theirs. They weakened, just long enough for him to break and kill them both. He crashed through their shattering magic and landed on the far side of the basement hallway. The stone was so heavily infused with magic he suspected it was effectively unbreakable.

Keep moving, he told himself. *Hurry.*

The air grew colder as he made his way through the corridors, eyes snapping from side to side. One chamber was crammed with workbenches, laden with gemstones; another looked like a butcher's shop, with human body parts hanging from hooks … Bruce stared at it, shocked beyond words. He'd seen battlefield hospitals, and the aftermath of bloody fighting and wars, but this … he shook his head, forcing himself to keep moving. A man appeared at the far end of the corridor, his eyes wide and staring. Bruce blasted him down without hesitation and jumped over his body, then stopped to study it a little closer. He looked more like a doctor than a guard, or an aristocrat ...

He cursed as he felt something explode overhead. He might have made a mistake. The flames wouldn't slow him down, nor would the mansion collapsing into a pile of rubble, but the infused walls were another story. If the building collapsed completely, he might be trapped ... there were techniques to drain infused magic, from what he'd heard, but it was hard to be sure they worked. He gritted his teeth as he picked up speed, throwing open door after door as the corridor sloped downwards. A large metal door blocked his way, reminding him of the one he'd opened for Jean-Luc. He shoved the thought out of his mind as he pushed the door open and peered into a brightly-lit chamber. The light was so ... *wrong* ... it made his head hurt. It wasn't that it was bright. It was that it seemed to burn right into his mind, driving his thoughts away.

Someone swore, in French. Bruce blinked, half covering his eyes as he struggled to see through the light. It was hard to make out anything, but ... Gwen was lying on a table, surrounded by eerily-glowing gemstones, a young woman standing beside her. Bruce blinked, the scene so *wrong* it felt more like a dream than anything else, then reached out with his magic. It didn't work. The power just ... faded.

The woman stumbled backwards. Bruce forced himself forward and punched her in the chest. She folded, coughing as she hit the ground. Bruce barely noticed as he stared down at Gwen. She looked ... dazed, yet ... her eyes barely seemed to focus on him. Bruce gritted his teeth, resisting the urge to kick the woman as he pulled back the blanket. Gwen was cuffed to the table ... he stared at the gemstones, then picked up the nearest one and smashed it against the others. The light dimmed, his thoughts clearing ... as if they'd been a fog over his mind he hadn't known existed. He smashed the rest of the glowing gemstones, his magic returning the moment the last one was gone. Bruce picked the handcuffs, freeing Gwen, and helped her to her feet. He tried not to notice she was naked.

"Here," he said. At least her captors had given her a blanket … he picked it up and wrapped it around her, then reached out with his magic to scoop up the woman. She struggled against him, trying to resist the invisible force surrounding her. "We need to move."

Gwen coughed, then went limp as Bruce wrapped all three of them in his magic and flew out the chamber. He lashed out, throwing bolts of raw magic or tongues of fire into each of the chambers as they passed, hoping to burn the entire nightmarish basement of horrors to the ground. The coldly logical part of his mind wanted to think the duke would never be sure what had happened, or why; the remainder knew he just wanted to destroy everything, to take his rage out on the nearest target. He saw a guard screaming as flames licked his skin, his entire body catching fire a second later; two more fled, chased by tongues of fire that seemed drawn to them. Something exploded behind him, the blast shaking the entire complex and sending pieces of debris dropping from overhead. Bruce hesitated, feeling the complex shake again, then reached out with his power and sent himself flying straight up. They weren't *that* far underground. He punched up and into the mansion …

A wave of raw power crashed down on him. Bruce barely saw the four magicians charging him, wrapped in a haze of magic. He – somehow – held the field together long enough to get clear, rather than let them punch him back down into the complex. The mansion was collapsing … he reached out to grab at the falling debris, shoving it at the magicians before they could escape. One of them was struck in the head and sent sprawling to the ground, unconscious or dead; the others shielded themselves in time. Bruce started to steer the way out of the falling mansion, then kicked himself for being an idiot. There was no point in trying to hide, not now. The mansion was collapsing and burning and the underground explosions had probably been felt right across the city … if the entire army wasn't on the way, he'd be very surprised. Irene had hinted the rebels might do something, but unless they got across the river in force Bruce doubted their diversion would work. The duke's mansion would be the army's priority.

Darkness washed around him as he flew up and out of the wreckage, then across the river and down into the darkened alleyway. Exhaustion threatened to overwhelm him as he hit the ground, nearly dropping Gwen and his captive. He'd pushed his power as far as it would go and … he swallowed hard, feeling hungry and tired and utterly drained. Irene was supposed to be nearby, waiting for them … Bruce hoped, prayed, she was on her way. They'd had to leave Raechel in the safe house – he tried not to feel guilty for insisting she be tied up, just in case – and there was no one else who could help them. Jean-Luc was probably wondering what had happened to him. Bruce knew he couldn't go back to the smuggler now.

His heart hurt, a stabbing pain that brought him back to his senses. A wash of panic ran through him. A heart attack? It wasn't likely, was it? He was young … most men who had heart attacks were old, old enough to be his father. And yet, the pain was growing worse, a knife digging into his guts and twisting deep inside …

"Stop," Gwen said, staggering to her feet. Magic – weak, but present – sparkled around her fingertips. "Stop, or I'll kill you."

The woman scowled, then slumped. Bruce felt the pain vanish, as if it had never existed … it hadn't, he realised dully. The woman was a healer – a *dark* healer. He'd heard stories of the healing talent being perverted and yet … he swallowed hard, recalling the warped and mutilated magicians he'd fought. Had the woman used her talent to help make them? What had she done to Gwen? She'd certainly tried to kill Bruce!

Irene appeared, followed by a pair of rebels in workman's clothes. "Who's this?"

"She's a prisoner," Bruce managed. "She's also a healer and …"

Irene nodded, produced a handkerchief from her pocket and pressed it against the prisoner's mouth. Bruce snuffed the air, tasting the chloroform. The prisoner would be unconscious for hours and then … he didn't know, but he felt it wouldn't be hard to keep her a prisoner. If she had more than one talent, she wouldn't have been wasted serving the duke. Her power could have taken her to the very top.

"We need to move," Irene said. Her assistants picked up the prisoner, then helped Bruce to stand. "They'll be coming after us."

Bruce nodded, curtly. The duke's mansion was burning brightly, so brightly it was clear he'd hidden *something* unnatural under the building. He hoped, with a flicker of vindictive glee, that the duke had to answer some very hard questions from his kinsman or the rest of the aristocracy. He'd look weak and foolish and if anyone worked out just *who* he'd been holding captive …

He might think Gwen broke out on her own, he thought, as they made their way through darkened streets and alleys. It wouldn't be long until daybreak and they had to be in the safe house by then. *And that might make him rethink everything.*

Chapter Thirty-Four
Paris, France

wen woke, half-convinced the last two days had been a dream – or a nightmare. It was hard to be sure of anything. She'd been captured, she'd been drained of her power and then Bruce had come to rescue her ... if she hadn't woken up in a strange bed, her hands and legs unmarred by handcuffs and manacles, she would have suspected she really *was* dreaming. The French had drugged her, she thought, and she'd seen things ... she swallowed hard as she sat upright, feeling her magic crackling around her. Whatever the duke had been trying to do to her – copy her powers or steal them – it hadn't worked.

She breathed a sigh of relief, then reached for the clothes someone – Irene, she hoped – had piled beside the bed. If she'd lost her powers permanently ... she wondered, idly, if she'd be allowed to retain her position for even a second or two, after the government worked out what had happened. Lord Nelson had been allowed to retain *his* post well after his tactical skill faded, and his love affair with Lady Hamilton had become a national scandal, but *he* was a man. Gwen knew better than to think *she'd* be allowed to remain in her post. The government would promote Bruce into the role and expect her to go home and stay there.

Her thoughts hardened. Bruce ... what was he *doing* in Paris? He was in Spain ... why had he come to Paris?

How long had she been held captive? It was hard to be sure, but … she checked her hair, noting it hadn't grown any longer. She hadn't had her period either … she couldn't have been a prisoner for more than a few days at most, which meant …? She scowled as she stood and dressed, gritting her teeth as she worked it out. Bruce *couldn't* have been summoned to Paris from Spain, not in a hurry. It would take at least a week for him to reach the city and, if anything, that was optimistic. And that meant he'd been in the city before she'd been captured.

The door opened. Simone stepped into the chamber. "Lady Gwen?"

Gwen scowled. She didn't want to see Simone right now. She didn't really want to see *anyone* right now. And yet, she knew she had little choice. She had to know why Bruce had been in the city, and why he'd never told her and … cold anger, mingled with an odd kind of despair, boiled through her mind. She was all too aware of men who thought women shouldn't trouble their pretty little heads with anything important, that young girls should place their trust in their husbands, but she'd thought Bruce was different. She'd thought …

"It was my mistake," Simone said. The bruises on her face hadn't healed. Gwen didn't want to think about the bruises everywhere else. "I'm sorry."

"You were in the farm," Gwen said. "What happened?"

"We got caught," Simone said. "I was sent to the farm."

Gwen shook her head. She knew she needed to hear the whole story, and work out what had happened so it wouldn't happen again, but she couldn't muster the interest. Her emotions were spinning out of control, making it impossible to think clearly … black rage burned through her mind as she realised the *last* time she'd felt so conflicted had been just after she'd slept with Bruce for the first time. It had been wonderful and she'd wanted to do it again and yet she'd known the risks were just too high … now, she wondered if their relationship was going to end before they even married. She snorted in bitter disgust. Perhaps she'd be wiser not having a relationship with anyone. It would certainly make her life easier …

"Tell Bruce I want to see him," she ordered, finally. "Now."

Simone nodded and left the room, closing the door behind her. Gwen lowered her eyes, trying to control her thoughts. It was hard to calm herself, not when she felt so betrayed. It was one thing to put up with condescension from elderly men who saw her as a child, or younger men who made sly remarks just to see them anger her, but quite another to deal with mistreatment from her future husband. And the fact most people wouldn't even see it as mistreatment … her anger boiled again, before calming herself. She needed to get the facts. She needed to hear what he had to say for himself. She needed to *understand* before she did something she might regret later …

Easy to say, she thought, as the door opened. *Harder to do*.

Bruce stepped into the room. He'd made some effort to look like a common labourer – the sort of worker who rarely had a steady job, and spent what little money he had on drink – but he couldn't disguise himself from her. His face was unshaven, giving him an odd look compared to the clean-shaven or bearded men she worked besides; his hair was oddly unkempt, something that should have irritated her, but she had to admit it made him look attractive. Or perhaps it was just the awareness Bruce was *Bruce*. Her body was suddenly reminding her of just how long it had been since they'd so much as kissed.

"Bruce." Gwen bit down hard on the impulse to kiss him. It was tricky enough to keep the accusation out of her voice. "Why … why were you in Paris?"

A conflicting series of emotions flashed across his face, coming and going before she could properly grasp them. Bruce was American, not British, but it was never easy for a man to be questioned so bluntly by a woman, even a wife. She knew how many of her subordinates resented her discussing their mistakes with them, chafing at lectures they would have taken in good part if they'd come from an older man. And yet ...

"Lord Mycroft told me to shadow you," Bruce said, finally. "He feared your enemies might have sent you to die."

Gwen hesitated, suspecting there was more to the story than that and yet fearing what she'd hear if she pushed further. Lord Mycroft was one of the very few men she trusted completely, but ... why had he overridden the government's orders and sent Bruce to Paris? There would be consequences, particularly if the army suffered a defeat that might have gone the other way if Bruce had been there. Lord Mycroft might wind up in very hot water indeed.

Anger flared through her. "And you never thought to come tell me you were near?"

"He told me to remain unseen, unless you ran into real trouble," Bruce said. "I had to keep my distance. I didn't even realise you'd been captured until I heard rumours about ..."

Gwen cut him off. "And do you know how it will look, back home, when they find out you went running after me?"

"You have enemies," Bruce said. She heard a hint of anger in his voice and sensed more. "Do you think they'd shed a tear if you went into that torture chamber and never came out again?"

"My enemies are my concern," Gwen snapped. "You could have undermined me ..."

"I also saved your life," Bruce snapped back. "You'd be dead – or worse – if I hadn't been there to save you!"

Gwen gritted her teeth, putting firm controls on her anger. Cold logic told her Bruce had a point. So had Lord Mycroft. She *knew* there were things that had to be kept from anyone going into enemy territory, for fear they'd be captured and forced to talk. But she couldn't help feeling as if she'd been betrayed. They were *engaged*, for crying out loud! He should have told her he was in Paris and …

She felt her heart sink. The Duke of India would be furious. Lord Mycroft would bear the brunt of his anger, she was sure, but there'd be plenty left for her. He'd insist Lord Mycroft wouldn't have withdrawn Bruce from the army if Gwen had been a man and he might be right. Gwen couldn't recall anyone being sent out with an unseen guardian, certainly not someone like *her*. No matter the outcome – no matter the simple fact Bruce really *had* saved her life – it wasn't going to end well. There were already too many people who thought of her as nothing more than a little girl-child, wearing her father's clothes. How many would join them when they heard what had happened?

Bruce went on. "They picked their moment well," he said. "I had no time to talk to you privately. No time to tell you what Pinfold said."

Gwen blinked. "What?"

"He told me that I should take your place," Bruce said. "And that I'd find support if I tried."

"What?" Gwen stared at him, torn between shock and anger. "Pinfold?"

Her mind raced. Pinfold wasn't the kind of man who did anything on his own. He didn't even have the nerve to make snide – and deniable – remarks. Gwen had heard his wife ruled the roost, in his house, even though he was technically the head of the household. And that meant … someone had put him up to it, but who? Her lips twitched in bitter amusement. Her enemies were so desperate to replace her they were willing to accept an American with a very questionable heritage …

"They must be desperate," she teased. It wasn't really amusing. "Why didn't you come to me?"

"I had no opportunity," Bruce told her. "What would people have said?"

Gwen muttered a very unladylike word under her breath. People had talked about her being alone with Master Thomas, even though he'd been old enough to be her grandfather. It was lucky they'd never quite realised how alone she'd been with Sir Charles Bellingham. And if they'd realised she'd been alone with Bruce … she ground her teeth in rage. Perhaps it would have been wiser to go straight to Gretna Green, get married and dare anyone to say anything. No one could have said a word if they were actually married …

Of course, they would have started whining about me giving orders to my husband, she thought, savagely. *Or insisting I stepped aside for him.*

"I would have told you, if things had gone otherwise," Bruce said. "But …"

Gwen tried to keep her face under control. He didn't understand. How could he? Bruce was a man. No man, not even Lord Mycroft, could really understand what it was like to be a young woman, to be treated with amused condescension at best and blatant and rude dismissal at worst. Or to have a single rumour destroy your life so completely you had to go into *de facto* exile and never return. He had saved her life, and yet he'd done it in a manner that would have significant personal and professional repercussions for her … even if Lord Mycroft took all the blame. Even if she hadn't been captured, it would have made her look bad. Or weak. Or powerless.

Queen Elizabeth's servants defied her constantly and justified it to themselves by insisting they were only doing what she would have ordered them to do, if she'd been a man, she thought, savagely. *How often does it happen to me?*

"I wish you'd told me," she ground out. Oh, there was no way it was going to end well. The grim awareness she should be relieved didn't make it any easier. "I wish …"

"I couldn't let you go into danger alone," Bruce said. "Gwen, I …"

"If I'd been a man," Gwen snapped, "would you have shadowed me?"

"If you'd been a man, I would not have been in love with you," Bruce said, bluntly. "But if I'd been ordered to shadow you, I would have done so."

Gwen felt her lips thin. She *knew* Bruce. He wasn't one for cool reflection or forethought … he prided himself, like so many others she knew, on being a man of action. She suspected he might have shadowed her anyway, even if Lord Mycroft had explicitly ordered him not to do anything of the sort, out of fear and protectiveness and everything else she found infuriating even though it sometimes worked in her favour. He certainly wasn't as emotionally tied to the country as herself. He might not see anything wrong in putting his lover ahead of his nation. And yet …

"I'm glad you rescued me," she said, finally. She was fairly sure he would have shadowed her anyway, but she didn't want to know. "And, at the same time, I wish you'd told me."

"I'm sorry," Bruce said.

Gwen sighed, feeling tired. Her feelings were still a mess. She wanted to kiss him, to pull him to the bed, and yet she wanted to tell him to go away and … she shook her head, all too aware she was in an untenable position. What should she do? What *could* she do? The walls looked very thin … she wondered, sourly, how many people were listening to their frank exchange of views. Irene was an experienced spy, Simone had grown up listening at doors and … who else was there? Gwen didn't know.

"I need a moment to gather myself," she said, hoping he'd take the hint. "I'll be out shortly."

Bruce nodded, then leaned forward and kissed her forehead gently before turning and leaving the room. Gwen kept her feelings under control until the door closed behind him, then buried her head in her hands. It was a mess. It would be so much easier if she'd been just another aristocratic girl, entering a match with both sides well aware of what was expected from them – and their partners. She would stay at home and run the household and bear her husband's children and …

She shook her head, forcing herself to stand up. It

would be a predictable life, barring foreign invasion or rebellion or natural disaster, but it would be boring. She would have nothing beyond running a household and bearing children and working her way through the ranks of High Society ... having the rules enforced on her until she was in a position to enforce them herself. It wouldn't suit her and she knew it. And if that meant having to deal with problems caused by being a woman in a man's world, she'd deal with them.

Pinfold really wouldn't risk approaching Bruce on his own, she thought. It had been a risky step. Bruce could have reacted *very* badly, perhaps by dragging Pinfold to Gwen to explain himself. *Who put him up to it and why?*

The thought nagged at her mind. It was possible her enemies were simply reluctant to serve under her command. And yet, Bruce was a largely unknown factor as far as the rest of the corps was concerned. He might turn out to be worse ... her lips twisted into a bitter smile. If they knew about Bruce and the Sons of Liberty, they'd have a collective heart attack.

Perhaps it really is petty spite, she thought, although she doubted it. Pinfold perhaps, but whoever was behind him might have something grander in mind. *What is the point?*

Her mind spun. Bruce couldn't displace her, not without a fight that would shatter their relationship beyond repair. Even if he tried to blackmail her ... she shook her head. It made no sense, unless ... perhaps the intent was to break them up. They were both powerful magicians and their children would be powerful too, particularly if the duke was right about magic being a mental talent rather than true magic. And yet, even that made no sense. What was the point of the whole affair?

She stepped over to the washbasin and splashed water on her face, silently forgiving Bruce. Mostly. She wished he'd come to her sooner, before she'd set sail, or at least before she'd been captured. If they'd fought together ... a thrill ran through her at the thought. They were partners, working together with an intensity that dwarfed anything else she'd ever felt. And yet … she put the thought out of her head as she checked her appearance, then opened the door and headed outside. It felt like early afternoon, but breakfast was still on the table.

"Gwen," Raechel said. She sat at the table, her face grim. "I'm sorry for …"

"It wasn't your fault," Irene said, turning from the stove. "Don't beat yourself up over it."

Gwen nodded, taking a seat and accepting a cup of grainy coffee. "How long was I a prisoner?"

"About a day," Irene said. "We were lucky to track you down so quickly."

"I know." Gwen frowned as Irene returned to the stove. A day? It had felt longer. Much longer. "Did the duke get killed in the fighting?"

"Impossible to say," Raechel said. "I haven't been back to the Bastille or to Versailles since you were captured and …"

"They'd keep it quiet," Simone said, softly. "He's close enough to the king that his death will have a meaningful impact on the line of succession. They'll want to keep his death a secret until they can inform everyone, in hopes of ensuring a smooth transition. But I don't think he'd die so easily."

Gwen frowned. "He was very talkative," she mused. The duke had told her far too much for her peace of mind. Had he been gloating, taking pleasure in her suffering, or had he been trying to mislead her? "How much of what he told me was actually true?"

"Our captive has had some interesting things to tell us," Irene said. "But she can wait until you've had something to eat. And then you can listen to her and decide what you want to do next."

Chapter Thirty-Five
Paris, France

ruce felt ... conflicted.

It was hard to put his feelings into words. He'd done the right thing – he thought – and yet he *knew* Gwen wasn't happy. He wanted to tell himself she was being silly, like so many other young girls he'd met, but he had too high a regard for her intelligence to believe it. She was smart and pragmatic and not afraid to speak her mind and ... it was impossible, no matter how hard he tried, to convince himself she was wrong. Lord Mycroft really *had* gone behind her back, as had Bruce himself, and Gwen had every reason to be unhappy about it.

She would be dead – or worse – if I hadn't shadowed her, Bruce thought, as he paced the room. *She can be angry at me because I freed her from captivity.*

He sighed, inwardly. There were hundreds of thousands of cheap novels with the same plotline. The male hero – the stiff upper lip or dashing rogue – rescued the fair maiden and married her. The maiden didn't try to free herself ... hell, she didn't even get herself into trouble! She was innocent and virginal and everything else that existed only in the minds of writers trying to get their books past moralistic censors. The idea of a woman having agency was alien to them, particularly if the woman's agency was what got her into trouble in the first place. He'd thought those books little more than trash –

it was easy to predict the outcome, no matter how many plot twists the writer threw in – but Gwen had to find them maddening. They treated women as caged birds … and he'd dived in to rescue her, as if she were one of those maidens and he a dashing male heroine. And …

The thought made him smile, humourlessly. It wasn't really funny. The books glossed over everything that could – and did, in real life – happen to young women who were kidnapped off the roads or locked up by their evil relatives or simply found themselves terminally short of cash. Gwen had been hooked up to a torture bench – or whatever – on the verge of suffering a ghastly fate when he'd crashed into the room to free her. Let her be angry at him if she wished. At least she was alive and reasonably healthy. If they'd killed her, he would have bathed Paris and Versailles in blood to avenge her.

He paced the room, unwilling to relax. He was just too keyed up. God alone knew what was happening outside, now the sun was high in the sky. Did Duke Philippe know he'd saved Gwen? Or did he think Gwen's body was lying under the pile of rubble? Or … Bruce wondered, numbly, just how many people had seen his desperate flight across the river. If they'd reported him … he shook his head. They were far enough from the riverbank to ensure they had warning, if the French sent a small army after them. The only *real* threat was flying magicians, dropping in without warning. But there were enough rebel magicians in the area to make such a gambit very risky indeed.

Of course, the French might not know it, he thought, sourly. *They've cut so many lines of communication their spies might not be able to get in touch with their superiors.*

The door opened. Irene stepped into the room. "Bruce," she said. "The prisoner is ready."

Bruce nodded, curtly. Irene had told him to be patient, hours ago. Gwen would understand once she calmed down and she wouldn't calm down as long as he was agitating her. Bruce wasn't sure what he thought about *that*, although he had to admit Irene probably knew Gwen better than *he* did. And she was a woman … he wished, suddenly, that he'd known more girls socially, as friends rather than prospective wives or lovers. Everyone said it was hard to understand how women thought …

But they said that about the tribes too, he reminded himself, as he followed her down into the basement. The early settlers had regarded the natives as irrational savages. *Once we started spending time with them, we started to understand how they thought.*

He put the thought aside and schooled his face into a mask as she led him into the basement. The prisoner sat on a chair, her hands tied behind her back and ankles firmly bound to the chair. Bruce couldn't help thinking Irene had been excessively paranoid, although there was no way to be *sure* the prisoner couldn't escape. There might be ways for her to use her talent to wear down the bonds, or even convince her captors to free her. He tightened his mental defences as Gwen and Raechel joined them, the former looking grim. Raechel's expression was unreadable. She'd been tied up herself only a few short hours ago.

Just like the girls in those trashy books, Bruce thought, feeling a flicker of amusement mixed with annoyance. *And in those books, it is almost romantic.*

Gwen's voice was very cold. "We can do this the easy way or the hard way," she said. "If you lower your mental defences, so we can verify you're telling us the truth as you answer our questions, we won't hurt you. If you try to resist, we will use drugs and violence to break your defences and rip your mind to shreds, then hand whatever is left of you over to the rebels. What's it to be?"

Bruce shivered. He was no stranger to torture – he knew prisoners had been compelled to talk, he knew even his mild-mannered father had ordered rigorous interrogations from time to time – and yet, hearing Gwen speak like that was chilling. Women shouldn't be involved in interrogations … he bit down on that thought *hard*, reminding himself it was the last thing she needed to hear. The idea he could spare her delicate sensibilities ... no, she'd never forgive him for suggesting anything of the sort. Besides, no amount of insisting that women shouldn't see horrible things would keep them from happening to women anyway.

The prisoner scowled. "If I talk, I die," she said, in an oddly-accented voice. Her French was perfect, but ... Bruce couldn't place the accent. "He'll kill me."

Gwen met her eyes. "If you talk and cooperate, we can take you with us when we go," she said, calmly. "If not, and we have to force you to talk, we can hand you back to the duke and his men instead."

There was a long chilling pause, long enough for Bruce to wonder if that was what the prisoner wanted, before she slumped against her bonds. He felt a sudden stab of sympathy, mingled with the wry awareness he'd never have felt so sorry for a *male* prisoner. It didn't feel *right* to keep a woman tied to a chair, let alone threaten her with naked violence to force her to talk. And yet ...

The prisoner slumped. "What do you want to know?"

Gwen smiled, then started bouncing questions off her. Bruce rapidly found himself growing bored. Gwen jumped from topic to topic as if she were scatter-brained, then jumped back again to force the prisoner to answer the same question – if slightly differently worded – time and time again. He supposed it would make it harder for her to tell a consistent series of lies ... he glanced at Irene, who's eyes were half-closed. It was harder for her to be *sure* the prisoner wasn't lying, not when she might be skilled enough to lower her mental defences without dropping them completely. But if she had to concentrate on a coherent story while maintaining the defences ...

"So ... you helped his test subjects survive his procedures," Gwen said. "Why ...?"

The prisoner snorted. "Do you think I was given a choice?"

Bruce shook his head. The duke was apparently a sadist, a man who – if the rumours were true – had started dissecting small animals as a child and moved on to humans as he grew older. He'd heard *stories* about aristocrats – and grave-robbing doctors – who told themselves their experiments were nothing more than research, but the duke had taken it past the point of sanity. The experiments were bad enough, yet he'd been doing them in the heart of Paris … Bruce was mildly surprised very little had slipped out, although the combination of power, prestige, money and the duke's own magical talent had probably kept whispers to the bare minimum. It was astonishing how much could be covered up if one had the money and connections to do it.

And he became close enough to the king to be one of his trusted advisors, he thought. *No wonder everyone kept their mouths firmly shut.*

"So he wasn't entirely telling the truth," Gwen said, slowly. "He needs a healer to complete the process."

Bruce frowned. He hadn't been able to follow any of the technical details. Charged gemstones, implanted in a magician's body … he wasn't sure it made any sense. If he hadn't seen the super-magicians, he wouldn't have believed the prisoner even if Irene insisted she was telling the truth. A lie could pass undetected if the person speaking thought they were telling the truth … he shook his head, then followed Raechel back up the stairs to the sitting room. A handful of men had arrived, hard-worn men in hard-worn clothing. He tried to keep his expression blank as he spotted Jean-Luc.

"I knew there was *something* up with you," Jean-Luc said, before Bruce could think of a cover story. "I'm glad to see you're on our side."

"You had ample time to test me," Bruce said, as Simone passed out coffee. It tasted foul, but he drank it anyway. He hadn't had anything like enough sleep since rescuing Gwen and returning to Irene. "I'm sorry I couldn't tell you everything."

"Oh, it's quite understandable," Jean-Luc said. "I didn't tell you everything either."

Another man, one Bruce didn't recognise, cleared his throat. "Whatever happened last night seems to have stunned our overlords," he said. "Many of our sources on the far side of the river have dried up, but what few have remained in touch have been able to inform us that the aristos are running around like headless chickens. Some seem to want to recall the army and fight us in the city, others want to evacuate and leave the population to starve. Either way, we have to act and act now."

"Or someone else will act for you," Simone said, quietly. She moved with exaggerated jerky motions as she sat down, bearing mute testament to the beating she'd taken. "If you are not in control of the uprising, the results will be absolute chaos."

Bruce nodded, curtly. The mood on the streets, even in the upper middle class districts, was ugly. Policemen and soldiers went out in small groups or they didn't go out at all, all too aware they'd never return if they did. There were fights over bread and water, housewives looting bakers and butchers only to discover there was very little food to be had. It was just a matter of time before something exploded and all hell broke loose, plunging the city of lights into madness. And if the rebels weren't on top of it ...

"The problem is getting across the river," he pointed out. He'd seen the guardposts. They were more like blockhouses than simple checkpoints, designed to allow a relatively small number of men to slow or even stop an army. Half the river crossings had been closed completely and the remainder were heavily guarded, stopping and searching anyone trying to cross. He doubted it would be possible to sneak guns and powder into the upper-class districts now. "How do you intend to get past the guards?"

Jean-Luc smiled. "I have a plan," he said. "But it might not be feasible."

Gwen joined them, her face grim. "According to our friend, there were roughly thirty super-magicians," she said. "We don't know for sure how many have been killed. There's also a number of *natural* magicians who might stand in our way."

"And someone else might have started making their own super-magicians," Raechel put in.

"Doubtful," Simone said. "If they knew how to do it, the story would have leaked a long time ago."

Bruce wasn't so sure. Aristos – British and French alike – weren't good at keeping secrets, unless they had a very good reason to keep their mouths shut. In this case … the duke had excellent reason not to share anything with his peers, while anyone else would be trying frantically to build up their own magical corps before the duke turned on them or something else happened. Who knew *just* how far word had spread? The duke might be a sadist of the first order, but he was hardly unique. The stories from Russia suggested he wasn't the only one pushing the limits of magic as far as they could go.

"We need to move quickly," Gwen said. She looked at the man Bruce didn't recognise. "When can we start?"

"Tomorrow," the man told her. "I don't think it can be held back much longer …"

"Something will happen," Simone agreed. "Or it will be made to happen."

"And we have to take the Bastille," Jean-Luc said. "If we do, the entire country will rise."

"They know it too," Gwen said. "It will make them desperate."

Bruce nodded. France was a tinderbox, ready to catch fire. The simmering anger demanded release. There'd already been flare-ups all over the country, each one barely put down before it could spread out of control. If Paris went up in flames, if the streets and the fortresses fell to the mob, the country would collapse into utter chaos. He hoped the aristos didn't have time to run before the mob swept over them, extracting revenge for decades upon decades of utter humiliation. The French Empire would be ruined beyond all hope of repair.

And if the rebels take power, they might even be grateful, he thought. *We don't have to be enemies for the rest of time.*

He sat back and watched as the small council hashed

out the plan. Gwen *was* good, he acknowledged, and the French seemed willing to follow her lead. He doubted *that* would last for long, once the old government was destroyed and the new took power, but for the moment … he snorted to himself. The French rebels couldn't afford to be seen as British puppets or their nation would turn against them. They'd be lucky if they ended up like the Jacobites … his lips quirked in cold amusement. If King Louis ran fast enough, he might flee to Britain and find refuge there, just in case the new French government proved as much a bane as the monarchy. But if half the stories about King Louis were true, Bruce doubted he'd be able to mount his own version of the Forty-Five.

But his son might have a chance, Bruce thought. *Might*.

"Tomorrow, then," Gwen said, bringing the meeting to an end. "We'll be there."

Bruce sat back, suddenly unsure of himself as the room emptied. What was he going to say to her. What *could* he say? He wanted to suggest they left the matter until after the return to Britain, but he didn't know if they *would* get home. And even if they did … he made a promise to himself to track down Pinfold and *shake* him until he told Bruce *precisely* who'd put him up to undermining Gwen. And then …

He blinked as he realised they were alone. Irene had taken Raechel and Simone as soon as the rebel leaders had left … he wanted to stay and yet he also wanted to run, as if he didn't want to face up to what had happened. Perhaps it would have been wiser to tell her he'd decided to shadow her, rather than try to keep her in the dark. The truth would have come out eventually. He doubted she would have been any happier about it even if she hadn't been captured and threatened with a fate worse than death.

"Bruce," Gwen said. "You should have told me."

Bruce bit down on the urge to argue, or to point out she'd be dead – or worse – if he'd gone to Spain. If she'd known he was there … he sighed, remembering how many of his friends had insisted it was impossible to win an argument with a woman. He was starting to wonder if they were right. He *had* saved her life, but it had come at a cost.

"I'm sorry," he said, finally. "I … I didn't want you to die."

He saw a hot flash of anger in her eyes. "I have been risking my life for *years*," she said, sharply. "Even most women … do you think they are safe, just because they stay at home while the men go to war? Do you know how many women die in childbirth?"

Bruce flushed. "Too many," he said. "I think your enemies earmarked you for the mission because they hoped you'd die. And I was *not* going to let that happen."

"No," Gwen agreed. The anger in her voice was bad enough, but the pain was worse. "And you are *not* to do it again."

Bruce crossed his heart. "I won't."

"Good," Gwen said. She leaned forward and kissed him, quick and sharp. "And now we need to get some rest. We're both going to be needed tomorrow."

Bruce wanted to take her in his arms and kiss her, then do more. Much more. It might be their last night… he quashed *that* thought quickly, even though he was sure Irene and the others wouldn't say a word if Bruce and Gwen spent the night together. No. They had to get some sleep.

"Goodnight," he said, quietly. "I'll see you in the morning."

Chapter Thirty-Six
Paris, France

READ, BREAD, BREAD!"

Raechel could *hear* the shouting as she hurried towards the bridge, clutching her papers in one hand and a purse in the other. The mob had spilled onto the streets at daybreak, and marched up and down the road – daring the soldiers to intervene – before turning and advancing straight towards the bridge. She wasn't the only person running for her life, hoping and praying the guards would let her through and then keep the mob from crossing the bridges. A handful of soldiers stood on the far end of the bridge, backed up by a clearly-visible pair of cannons and a single massive blockhouse bristling with visible guns. Raechel suspected it was designed more to intimidate than protect the crossing, although it was hard to be sure. The designers had *known*, hadn't they, that sooner or later all hell was going to break loose.

"BREAD, BREAD, BREAD!" The chanting grew louder. "BREAD, BREAD, BREAD!"

She shuddered. Behind her, the looting had already started. Carefully-organised teams were smashing their way into upper-class houses and shops, forcing the owners to flee. More and more people would be joining the mob too, pulled into the human tide and steered effortlessly towards the bridges. Panic was already spreading ... she saw a small girl, wearing an impractical dress, get knocked to the ground and barely yanked out of the path of a man on horseback before it was too late. Her lips twitched as her eyes swept over the crowd. They were aristos – not *quite* aristocratic enough to have a home on the far side of the river – and merchants, successful enough to have money and yet not permitted to climb to the top. Her smile grew wider as she realised there were almost no servants amongst the mob, not even governesses or nannies. Had they been left behind, she wondered, or had they deserted their posts? Either way, the aristos would have to take care of themselves for once.

The guards held up a hand to stop her as she crossed the bridge. Raechel shoved the papers into the nearest guard's hand, careful to lower her eyes and bend slightly to expose her cleavage. The guard looked too nervous to pay much attention – his eyes were on the far side of the bridge, not looking at her – but she found it hard to care. Louis was an idiot, and she cursed the day she'd convinced his new superior to give him a place at the Bastille, yet even *he* would have noticed she'd been missing for two days. Raechel had tried to think of an explanation, but nothing remotely convincing had come to mind. The duke would certainly ask questions, even if Louis didn't. She'd just have to play it by ear and hope for the best.

She saw the guard twitch as the shouting grew louder, the mob coming into view. He gave her back her papers and waved her through the checkpoint as his commander started barking orders, directing the guards to lower the barricades and prepare to defend themselves. Raechel felt a flicker of sympathy for the refugees caught between the troops and the mob – they no longer had anywhere to run – as she headed through the checkpoint and joined the stream of people heading further into the district. They'd let themselves be caught, she told herself, trying not to remind herself that she was in the same predicament. The roads were already blocked. The only way out of the city was by boat and even that …

The ground heaved. She looked back, just in time to see a massive fireball rising into the air. The rebels had driven a cart onto a bridge and detonated it … she'd been told it was a diversion, targeted on a bridge that had already been rendered impassable, but she couldn't help wondering how many innocents had been caught in the blast. The French aristos and bureaucrats and soldiers might be upholders of an evil regime, and therefore had to be targeted, but there would have been women and children close to the blast too. She wondered how many, then shook her head. No matter what happened, there would be entire oceans of blood on the streets by the end of the day.

And there's no hope of a peaceful surrender, she thought. She'd seen the nation, from the highest to the lowest; she'd seen the attitudes that led the aristos to think they could do anything and seen the hatred simmering on the streets, just waiting for the chance to burst free and burn the entire rotten structure to the ground. *Even if the aristos wanted to surrender, it would never be accepted.*

The chanting behind her grew louder – again – even though she was hurrying towards the Bastille as fast as she could without actually running. She wasn't alone – upper-class women were hurrying to the gates, while their husbands, brothers and sons were joining the soldiers as they prepared for war. Raechel hadn't had a chance to overhear their plans – in hindsight, it was clear she'd only been allowed to see what they wanted her to see – but she could guess. The river was a perfect natural barrier. As long as they held the bridges and kept boats from crossing the water, they'd be safe while their supplies held out.

And the army can hack its way through the streets to save them, Raechel thought. It wasn't a good plan, as far as she could tell, but it was probably the only realistic option. *As long as they can hold out …*

The guards seemed more alert, checking papers carefully before waving the women into the fortress.

Raechel braced herself, hoping the guards didn't look *too* closely. She'd changed her appearance as far as she could, and stolen papers belonging to a high-class courtesan, but the guards might have seen her when she'd first arrived, seemingly a lifetime ago. Hell, they might have been ordered to keep a quiet eye on her. Irene had said most guards weren't particularly subtle, but the Bastille was one of the most important fortresses in France. The guards would be amongst the best in the business ... and yet, with so many people fleeing into the building, they barely had any time to pay attention to anyone. The guard glanced at her, his lips twisting in a mixture of disgust and envy, then shoved her through the gate and into the fortress. Raechel smiled inwardly as she joined the line heading inside. The guard wouldn't have been so disgusted if *he* had been able to hire a high-class courtesan.

"Move downstairs," a burly man bellowed. He walked up and down, barking orders at the woman and children. "Keep moving ..."

Raechel silently thanked her lucky stars for the tour as she slipped past the man and headed up the stairs instead. The war room was right at the top of the fortress, just below the battlements ... if she was any judge, they'd be so many people coming and going that she wouldn't attract any attention until she tried to get into the war room itself. Messengers ran everywhere, followed by soldiers, waiters and cooks, shouting and screaming as they tried to be heard over the din. From what she'd heard, the organised chain of command had been breaking down for weeks as more and more aristocratic officers had been moved in or out of the city. It was unlikely Louis and his fellows had been able to fix the problem before it was too late.

The ground heaved again. She heard someone scream, further down the stairs. The rebels had been tight-lipped about precisely how many people they had in the district, or how much they could do to keep the soldiers busy, but it was clear they'd done *something*. She put the thought aside as she reached the war room, breathing a sigh of relief that there was only one guard on duty. He eyed her sourly as she approached, his eyes lingering on her chest. She was almost grateful. It made the mission a great deal easier.

"I need to speak to the general," she lied, holding out her papers. They wouldn't get her through the door, but they'd distract the guard for a few vital seconds. She drew the dagger from her sleeve and braced herself. "I need …"

She stabbed forward, burying the dagger in the guard's chest. He staggered, his mouth opening to gurgle before he fell. It was risky to use a poisoned blade, and she was fairly sure the knife had pieced his heart, but she'd seen no choice. She had to take him down before he could raise the alarm. She pulled the dagger out, wiped it on her dress, then reached into her pack and found the pistol. Nine shots. It would have to be enough.

The door was unlocked. She pushed it open and peered inside. The room was busy, junior officers updating the giant map on the far wall while their superiors talked and argued and made decisions only to change their minds a few moments later. Raechel looked for Louis and spotted him standing right next to General Lafarge, the latter holding court and pretending he knew what he was doing. She wasn't fooled. The old goat looked like someone on the verge of panic, someone who knew he was going to get the blame for everything even if he won. Raechel knew better as her eyes flickered from officer to officer. The general wasn't going to live long enough to be blamed for anything.

She lifted the pistol and fired. The room seemed to freeze as the general tumbled to the floor, utter horror pervading the room. They'd assumed, she figured, that the Bastille was completely impregnable. They'd assumed no rebel – or anyone – would ever enter the fortress. Raechel had no time to enjoy their shock as she shifted aim, shooting Louis and five other officers, one a complete stranger. The rest of the room dived for cover, the quicker amongst them grabbing swords and pistols. Raechel fired one last shot – aimed at the lamp – and then turned and fled, slamming the door behind her. If she was lucky, the officers would inadvertently shoot the men coming to save them ...

Run, she told herself. She had no idea how far the sound had carried, but she had to assume the guards outside were already alert. She tossed away the pistol and her wig, then tugged at her clothes to make them look different. It wasn't much, but if she could get out before they sealed the fortress she'd have a very good chance of making it clear. *You have to get out before it's too late.*

Behind her, she heard the sound of utter chaos.

***

Gwen stood on a rooftop and watched the angry crowd thronging around the bridges, shouting and screaming. Rage boiled in the air, demands for food and jobs nearly drowned out by screams for violent revenge on the aristocracy. The guards on the far side were fingering their weapons nervously, all too aware of what would happen if – when – the order came to fire on the crowd. They'd kill hundreds, but there were hundreds of *thousands* of people on the streets. She raised her eyes, scanning the sky for magicians. They had to be on their way.

Unless they were withdrawn to Versailles, she thought. The duke hadn't been seen since his mansion had been destroyed, which meant ... what? She dared not assume he was dead. *The duke needs to protect the king ...*

Bruce caught her eye. "Is it time?"

"Nearly." Gwen glanced at the rising sun, then forced herself to wait for the signal. The plan had too many moving parts for her peace of mind, but as long as *her* part in the plan went off without a hitch the rest shouldn't matter too much. "We have to be ready ..."

She broke off as the ground heaved, again and again. The earlier bombings had been nothing more than test runs and diversions, probing attacks to keep the enemy jumpy. Now … she heard shooting as guards panicked and opened fire, only to come under fire themselves from rebel sharpshooters. Emplaced guns started barking a moment later, shells crashing down amidst the crowd. She shuddered, trying not to think of how many people had died in the first horrible moments. They were lucky the defenders didn't have any heavy naval guns to turn on the crowd.

"Now," she said. "Get them up here."

Bruce turned and barked orders, summoning the rebel magicians onto the rooftop. Gwen let out a breath as the leaders went to work as planned, wrapping the magicians in a bubble of magic. The guns on the far side of the river might be relatively light, but they'd make hash out of the entire building if the defenders recognised the threat in time to react. She glanced at the rest of the magicians – male and female, young and old – then turned back to stare at the river. It was all that stood between the mob and its target …

"All together now," she said, bracing herself. No one had *ever* tried anything like this before, not as far as she knew. "Focus … and *push*."

Magic boiled around her and flowed down – and into – the river, forming an invisible dam. Her magic blended with other magics, pulsing together into a single force; the river seemed to shudder, then fell rapidly as the dam grew bigger and bigger. The defenders seemed to stop and stare, just for a second, watching in disbelief as the riverbed came into view. Gwen spotted a nightmarish vision of dead bodies, ruined boats half-buried in the mud and long-forgotten structures, then forced herself to concentrate on the magic as the crowd ran forwards, outflanking the defenders. They'd assumed any attackers would be bottlenecked by the bridges and the lack of boats, not …

"It's working," Bruce said, as the shooting intensified. "It's working!"

Gwen barely heard him. The water pressure was

growing rapidly, water flooding into the city as it sought a way through – or around – the invisible dam. The rebel teams knew what to do – they were already laying down boards to help the mob cross the river, then target the blockhouses from the rear – but their time was running out. Gwen felt the dam waver as a handful of magicians fainted, unable to maintain the magic any longer. She gritted her teeth, all too aware of just how *many* people were flooding across the riverbed. They'd all be swept away and drowned when the dam finally broke …

She fell to her knees, closing her eyes as the pressure grew ever-stronger. She could *feel* the water flowing around the dam, flooding more and more buildings and breaking into underground basements and sewers. The city was going to have real problems cleaning up the mess, no matter who won … she heard another explosion, far too close for comfort, followed by a series of shots. The dam started to shudder, as if it were being pushed backwards by the sheer weight of water bearing down on it. Gwen felt as if she were being pushed too.

"It's going to break," she said. She couldn't hear herself speak. The air was juddering around her, as if she were caught in a particularly nasty storm. She felt as if the building was on the verge of collapsing, as if she'd set off something she didn't quite understand. "It's going to break …"

Bruce started to shout a warning, telling everyone to run, but it was too late. The dam shattered, the last remnants of the magic flickering and dying as water poured down into the riverbed and rampaged down towards the sea. Gwen nearly fainted – if she hadn't been on her knees, she was sure she would have collapsed – as her head threatened to explode with pain. The world was dark … she was so dazed she feared for a moment she'd gone blind, before realising her eyes were screwed tightly shut. She had to force herself to open them, as if her body had forgotten how to do it. The waters below her were boiling as they raged onwards. She remembered all the netting the aristos had put in place, to make sure no one could sail in or out of the city without permission, and smiled. It wouldn't survive the tidal wave smashing towards it.

She stood on wobbly legs and glanced around. The rebel magicians looked shattered. Some were unconscious, some were bleeding from their noses and ears … a handful, a very few, looking ready to continue. Gwen hoped they'd have the sense to wait and rest long enough to restore their powers, but feared they'd insist on crossing the captured bridges with the rest of the underground. The rebel uprising had been a long time in the making.

Bruce held out a hand to help her stand upright. "They took the bridges," he said. "The way to the Bastille is open."

Gwen nodded. The sight before her was wondrous and terrible and … she scowled inwardly, all too aware she was woozy. Her magic was dimmed … she silently congratulated herself on insisting Bruce didn't add his power to hers. He'd be able to look after her, at least for a while … the ground heaved again, a fireball rising up from somewhere near the edge of the city. The rebels were attacking the walls too …

"Raechel is in there somewhere," she said, softly. She needed to eat and rest before the enemy magicians arrived. "Go help her."

Bruce kissed her forehead, lightly. "Let me get you downstairs first," he said. The rebels were already arriving to assist their comrades. "And then I'll go after her."

Gwen was too drained to argue.

Chapter Thirty-Seven
Paris, France

ruce had always been in awe of Gwen, when he'd realised just how capable a magician she truly was, but he'd never expected her to hold back an entire *river*. Even with the help of twenty other magicians it had been one hell of a gamble, a gamble so wild Bruce had privately feared it wouldn't work. It was easy to think water was soft, but the sheer power of a river flowing down to the sea was incalculable. And Gwen had held it back long enough for the rebels to get an entire army across the river.

He kept his eyes open as he strolled across the bridge and through the remains of the blockhouse. The soldiers who'd manned the complex were dead, their bodies torn to pieces or simply dumped into the raging waters below, after being stripped of anything useful. A steady flow of rebel fighters were crossing beside him, their eyes flickering from side to side as they hurried towards the Bastille. The rebels appeared to be in control and yet ... he scowled as he saw a handful of men break out of their formation and run into a mansion, waving their weapons around in a manner that threatened their allies more than their enemies. The plans had been to loot *after* the Bastille had fallen, but ...

Too many opportunists amongst the rebels, Bruce reflected. It wasn't really a surprise. The rebel and criminal undergrounds had been closely interlinked, the latter often supplying the former in exchange for later considerations or simple money. There was little to be gained by supporting the government instead, not when the government couldn't or wouldn't give the criminals what they wanted. *The looting is going to take place if the leadership likes it or not.*

He did his best to avoid it as he hurried to the sound of the guns. Shops were being looted, crates of food and drink carried out by victorious looters and hastily shipped back to the bridges ... Bruce felt his heart twist in disgust at just how much had been held back to keep the aristos fed while the rest of the city starved. A handful of shopkeepers were marched outside and lynched, their bodies left to rot; he saw a pair of young women, fleeing a gang of looters, and reached out with his magic to trip the men up. The girls would have a chance ... not much of one, the bitter part of his mind noted, but better than many others. There were very few places to hide now, yet if they managed to keep their heads down long enough for Jean-Luc and his allies to take control ...

The atrocities grew worse as he made his way onwards. Expensive shops looted, then burnt to the ground; expensive apartments ransacked, a handful of desperate owners and guardians tossed out of windows to certain death; bureaucratic offices searched, the papers dragged out and burnt in the middle of the streets. That, at least, had been planned. The rebels wanted to destroy all records, from taxes and tithes to police and government files. Even if they lost, they'd noted, the government would need to rebuild everything before it could start taxing the people again. Bruce suspected there were copies somewhere, but who knew? Perhaps the copies could be wiped out too.

He paused as the shooting grew louder, then turned the corner. The Bastille was a looming and ugly fortress, the kind of building that simply didn't exist in America. He'd expected something akin to the Tower of London, but the Bastille somehow managed to look even less inviting, although it shared the same ominous mien that suggested anyone who went into the building wouldn't come out again. The gatehouses were barred, the soldiers on the rooftops keeping their heads down as they fired into the crowd. He saw a handful of faces briefly visible in the slits, people glancing out and vanishing again before the rebel sharpshooters could take them out. He cursed under his breath. Could they get into the Bastille before reinforcements arrived …

"Bruce," a voice called. He looked up to see Jean-Luc, standing next to a young man Bruce vaguely recalled seeing in the pub. "We have them pinned down, but they're refusing to surrender."

"Offer them safe conduct?" Bruce suspected it was pointless, but he had to ask. The rebels held most of the city and the entire country was on the verge of exploding. The garrison might think they were dead anyway, no matter what they did. If they decided to sell their lives dearly … "If they surrender without ado …?"

"No answer," Jean-Luc said. "They fired on our messenger, even though he was under a flag of truce."

Bruce made a face. The gatehouse and walls were strong. He could feel magic woven into the stonework, making it harder for him to break them down with naked force. The guards were clearly armed and ready to fight, which meant they'd have to either expend hundreds of lives in storming the building or sit down for a prolonged siege. Bruce cursed under his breath. The Bastille was the symbol of everything wrong with the regime, a building that embodied the fear that kept the population from rising up to claim their freedoms. It *had* to fall.

And Raechel is in there, somewhere, he thought. He didn't know Raechel that well, but she was Gwen's friend and she wanted Raechel safe. She would have made herself known to the rebels if she'd escaped, wouldn't she? He didn't want to consider what might have happened if she'd run into the rebels and been killed by accident. *I have to get her out.*

"We have heavy guns on the way," Jean-Luc said. "We captured a bunch of them from the walls, along with shells, but that would kill everyone in the building."

Bruce glanced at him. "How many prisoners are inside?"

Jean-Luc gave a very Gallic shrug. "Impossible to say," he said. "They rounded up a lot of people once the war started going badly, none of whom were ever seen again. We'd like them back."

If they're still alive, Bruce thought. The Bastille was big, but it wasn't *that* big. The government might give the prisoners a cursory trial before sentencing them to exile or death, or it might simply kill them out of hand and pretend they'd never been arrested. *We might already be too late.*

He made up his mind. "I'm going to fly up and land on their roof," he said, finally. "Can you gather a squad to accompany me?"

Jean-Luc nodded. Bruce sighed inwardly. God alone knew what would happen when the shooting stopped. The rebel factions might start to splinter, the rebel leaders becoming warlords ... warlords entirely dependent on their troops to stay in power. It would be one hell of a mess ... he put the thought out of his mind as Jean-Luc's men gathered around him, readying themselves for the flight. He reached out with his mind, trying to sense any other magicians, but drew a blank. The Bastille seemed to have no magical defenders at all.

And that means they're somewhere else, he thought, coldly. He wasn't fool enough to assume they'd all been killed. *Where are they?*

"Get the sharpshooters to sweep the roof," he ordered, quietly. "Make them keep their heads down."

Jean-Luc turned away and barked orders. Bruce braced himself, then gathered his magic and lifted himself and the squad into the air – he heard one of them swear in a dialect he didn't recognise – as the sharpshooters opened fire, expending ammunition recklessly to force the soldiers to duck. Bullets snapped past him, bouncing off the fortress's walls, as he rose higher and higher. He shaped his magic, lashing it out like a whip as he rose above the battlements, throwing a pair of men out into empty space. They dropped out of sight, falling to the ground. There was no time for sympathy.

"Get into the fortress," he snapped, hurrying to the battlements. "Move!"

He peered down. The guards at the gate looked up at him, their eyes wide. He summoned fire and directed a tongue of flame into the gatehouse, hoping they'd have stowed something explosive within the structure. The guards ran in all directions, an instant before something exploded. It wasn't enough to bring the entire gatehouse tumbling down, but it blew open the doors and allowed the rebels to break into the fortress. He didn't have to hear Jean-Luc barking orders, again, to know his men were being ordered to charge. The Bastille was vulnerable now. It had to fall.

Bruce looked over the edge of the battlements, towards distant Versailles, then turned and hurried into the fortress. It wasn't over yet.

***

"You ..." Raechel braced herself as her captor drew back his hand to strike her, then thought better of it. "You ... what have you done?"

Raechel made a show of shrugging, even though she knew it might lead to him actually carrying out the unspoken threat. She hadn't managed to get out before the guards slammed the door, or to hide amongst the ladies ... she wondered, sourly, just what had given her away. Perhaps they simply hadn't recognised her. She hadn't lived in upper-class Paris even before her cover had been thoroughly blown, leading them to think she was the murderer. Or something. It hardly mattered. She'd been caught and that was all there was to it.

At the very least, I kept them from mustering a proper response, she told herself. She had no idea how long it had taken for the French to determine who was in charge, now General Lafarge was dead, but it had ensured they didn't have the chance to keep the rebels from storming the centre of the city and marching all the way to the Bastille itself. *Paris has fallen. France will follow.*

"Well?" Her captor glared down at her. "What have you done?"

Raechel studied him thoughtfully. He was young ... probably a young aristo promoted well above his competence. It was far from uncommon, in the French Army ... he would normally have an older and wiser sergeant assigned to him, to make sure he didn't do anything *too* foolish through incompetence or ignorance, but there was no sign of anyone else. The men who'd grabbed Raechel and dragged her to him were gone. Judging from the shouts she'd heard, they'd hurried back to defend the wall.

"There's no way out," she said, quietly. "The king isn't coming to help you."

The officer started to draw back his hand again, then stopped. Raechel smiled inwardly. A very young man then, not one given to either casual brutality or wielding authority. And probably not someone here by choice. She knew the type. She could work on him. If she could make him doubt himself, and his loyalty ...

"You are trapped here, you and your men," she said. A shudder ran through the vast fortress, pieces of dust falling from the ceiling. "What will happen, when the howling mobs storm the walls? The Bastille will fall."

The man glared at her. "Shut up!"

"You will die here," Raechel said, calmly. The shouting was growing louder. "You will die here, for nothing. Your body will never be found."

"Shut up!" The threat was back in his voice, but this time it was undermined by fear and a hint of pleading. "What ... what else can I do?"

"You can surrender," Raechel said. She met his eyes, silently daring him to look away. "All you have to do is run up the white flag. Order your men to stand down."

The young man swallowed. "My family ..."

"... Is already planning to flee," Raechel said. She was

morbidly sure of it. The moment they realised the king had lost control of much of the country, the aristos would start heading for the nearest exit. She wondered, idly, where they'd go. They wouldn't be particularly welcome in Britain, to say the least, but it might be the safest possible destination. "You have been left here to die."

"At least I'll die with honour," the young man said. It was strikingly unconvincing. She could tell, just by his voice, that he knew it. "My family will not be shamed ..."

The fortress shook again. Raechel heard shooting in the distance ... no, it had to be close if she could hear it. The Bastille's walls were thick, thick enough to make the prisoners below feel utterly isolated from the world around them. Louis had told her even the luxury suites were isolated. The prisoners were meant to understand it was only through the king's grace they'd ever see freedom again.

"Surrender," she said, quietly. If the shooting was that close, the mob was already within the walls. "There's nothing left to fight for."

The young man sighed and closed his eyes. Raechel almost felt sorry for him. He'd been raised to be stubborn, to obey orders from his social superiors or die trying ... he was, in his own way, as pigheaded as his British counterparts, the young men who would sooner die than fall back and live to fight again. He was loyal and yet his loyalty had been abused and he'd been cast away ... not, she supposed, that he'd ever been *meant* to take command of the garrison. She killed his superiors ...

"Hurry," she advised. "You need to decide now."

***

Bruce charged down the corridor, leaving the rest of the squad behind as a billowing wave of raw magic swept ahead of him. The enemy had outsmarted themselves, he noted absently; they'd infused the walls with so much magic they were actually making his power more dangerous to anyone who happened to run into him. A pair of guards and a footman appeared out of nowhere, only to be shredded the instant they brushed against his power. Bruce had no time to feel sick as blood and gore splattered in all directions. He rushed onwards, mentally putting together a map of the prison. Where *was* she?

He plunged down a staircase, his power raging out ahead of him. There was a hint of resistance as he encountered a door, infused with magic, but he picked the lock almost effortlessly and pushed on. He'd expected more guards, although he suspected many of the fortress's soldiers had been assigned to guard the riverbanks to keep the mob as far from the fortress as possible. The Bastille might be heavily defended, but the fortress would be easy to besiege once the rebels took the inner city. Jean-Luc had been talking about bringing up guns, after all, and they'd pound the Bastille into scrap. A lone man stared at him, then ran. Bruce blasted him in the back and carried on over his smoking corpse. There was no time to do anything else …

Another man, wearing a fancy uniform, stepped out and threw up his hands. Bruce stared at him, barely stopping himself from tearing the man to pieces. The Frenchman stood his ground, despite his obvious terror. Bruce slowed to a halt, magic shimmering around him. If it was a trick or a trap, the French officer in front of him would be the first to die.

"I … I want to surrender," the officer said. "And I want safe passage out of the city for my men."

Bruce scowled. It was probably a little too late to demand *that*. The rebels had tried to negotiate a surrender, after all … he cursed under his breath, wondering what Gwen would do. If the enemy surrendered, it would make life so much easier … but he feared he would have problems convincing the rebels to honour the surrender. He didn't *know* what was happening below, but he feared the worst. The rebels had every reason to brutally slaughter every prison guard and soldier they met.

"Very well," he said, finally. It was worth a try. "Order your men to surrender – now – and then to come to the upper levels. We'll try to organise safe-passage once the city calms down."

He directed the man downstairs, then glanced into the office. Raechel sat on the floor, bound hand and foot … Bruce rolled his eyes, then freed her and looked her up and down. She looked tired and worn, but otherwise fine. It was difficult to see why Raechel and Gwen were friends. Raechel looked … he wasn't sure he could put it into words. But it was there.

"I convinced him to try surrendering," Raechel said, quietly. "He was left in command – all on his own."

Bruce nodded, curtly. The sounds from below were slowly dying away. He kept his magic at the ready as soldiers started to trickle upstairs, looking as if they expected to be torn apart at any moment. They might not be wrong, Bruce reflected. The rebels had told him they intended to free the prisoners first, then mete out justice. If the prisoners were dead …

Jean-Luc stepped inside, looking grim. "Who gave you permission to offer terms?"

"The war isn't over yet," Bruce said. It was a difficult question to answer. Gwen had very limited authority over the rebels and he had none. "If they'd fought to the last, they could have delayed matters until reinforcements arrived."

"There are none," Jean-Luc said. "There's been no sign of movement from Versailles. The troops haven't moved an inch."

"Yet," Bruce said. "The senior officers are dead. The junior officers and men … they're not to blame. If you start slaughtering them all, they'll refuse to surrender in future."

Jean-Luc snorted. "Don't say that to Henri," he said. "Really, *don't*. He wants everyone who ever donned a royalist outfit executed."

"I won't," Bruce said. He wasn't sure which of the rebel leaders was Henri. They'd been careful not to use many names in front of the foreigners. "And now, on to Versailles."

Chapter Thirty-Eight
Versailles, France

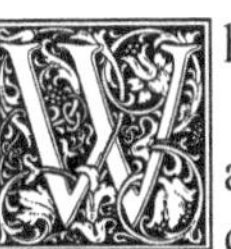here had it all gone wrong?

King Louis sat on his chair, in the elegant – and empty – war room, and asked himself the question he'd been asking ever since the war had started to turn against him, ever since it had started to threaten the monarchy itself. Where had it all gone wrong? What had he done that was so wrong?

He'd inherited a mess, no doubt about it. The French Empire had been in a desperate state even before it had tied itself to Spain, an act akin to shackling oneself to a corpse. There had been no way to boost revenue, not without taxing either the nobility or the clergy ... and both had steadfastly refused to be taxed, bringing so much pressure to bear that Louis had had to send one Finance Minister into exile and another to the Bastille, then to the block. They hadn't deserved their fate, he knew, but there'd been no choice. The survival of the monarchy was paramount and yet ... right now, the survival of the monarchy itself was in doubt.

The reports were clear. The Bastille had fallen. The revolts in the provinces were gathering steam. Spain was effectively lost – he cursed himself for agreeing to send much of his army south – and the rest of the empire might well follow, if the rebels weren't stopped in time. A strong king might have accomplished much, but Louis had few illusions about himself. The simple fact much of the aristocracy had already left the court was clear proof they were putting their own interests ahead of his … not, he supposed, that it mattered. If the unconfirmed reports were accurate, very few of them had any estates left. The nasty cynical part of his mind suspected they were heading straight for the ports instead and going directly into exile. They wouldn't put their lives on the line for a king whose time had come.

He glanced up as Duke Philippe stepped into the room and bowed. Louis was mildly surprised the duke had stayed, even though he still had at least *some* troops – and sorcerers – under his command. Louis wasn't even sure the Royal Guard would stay loyal for much longer. He'd picked their commander for blood rather than competence and the man simply wasn't up to the task. The guardsmen were already deserting, or so he'd been told. They saw no reason to fight and die for him either.

"Your Majesty," Duke Philippe said. "The carriage awaits."

"I will stay," Louis said. There was no way *he* could go into exile, certainly not in Britain. Better to die in his palace and leave the throne to his son. "Send the others away."

Duke Philippe nodded, curtly. "The rebels are advancing," he said. "If we can defeat them in the field, we can still save the empire."

Louis studied his kinsman thoughtfully. There had always been disturbing rumours about him – but then, there'd been such rumours about everyone. Louis himself had been accused of incest with his sisters and he knew for a fact that wasn't true. The rumours about his wife had been much – much – worse, to the point they'd been physically impossible. And yet, there had been something about the duke that had bothered even the hardened courtiers …

He cocked his head. "You'll lead the troops into battle?"

"Yes," Duke Philippe said. "I'll be there."

Louis had his doubts. Duke Philippe had never been a renowned soldier. He'd never led troops on parade, let alone into battle. He hadn't even bothered to acquire the rank and posts that should have come to him by right, as a kinsman of the king. And yet, at least he was trying. It was more than could be said for anyone else. Versailles was almost empty. The majority of the servants had fled hours ago.

He stood. "I'm coming with you."

Duke Philippe blinked, surprised. "Your Majesty?"

"I can die here or I can die on the field," Louis said. If he led the troops to victory – or was at least present on the field – he could turn himself into a strong monarch and save his country. He could crush the rebels *and* teach the aristocracy to respect him, clipping their wings to the point they could no longer challenge his power. "My son will not be ashamed of his father."

"As you wish," Duke Philippe said. "Should I send the convoy away now?"

"Yes," Louis said. There was no time to bid farewell to his wife. The thought hurt him more than he'd expected. He didn't love her, not really, but he was fond of her. "And then we'll go to the front."

***

Where, Gwen asked herself, *are the magicians?*

She hung in the darkening sky, looking down at the rebel army as it flowed out of Paris and made its way towards Versailles. The scene looked chaotic – the rebels had had no time to organise cavalry flankers or supplies or anything else a regular army needed as a matter of course – but she couldn't help finding it a little intimidating. Many rebels carried flaming torches as well as weapons, lighting up the twilight as they marched onwards. It would take around four hours to reach Versailles, she'd been told, but the rebels looked ready to march for days. Their blood was up. The time had come, their leadership insisted, to finally take their revenge. Gwen half-hoped the French Court had had the sense to evacuate Versailles before the mob arrived. She saw no mercy in their eyes.

Her eyes probed the darkness, searching for … *trouble.* Where *were* the enemy magicians? She'd expected them to attempt to save the Bastille, or at least keep the rebels penned up in Paris, but they hadn't so much as *tried.* Gwen didn't understand it. The rebels might talk of cowardly magicians in one breath, and assert they'd already killed all the magicians the next, yet Gwen knew better. They hadn't accounted for *all* the enemy magicians. She wanted to think they were fleeing – the reports suggested the aristocrats were running for their lives abandoning their estates and regiments in a desperate bid to escape the country before it was too late – but she doubted it. They would be as brash as their British counterparts, she thought, and they wouldn't run without firing a shot for the honour of the flag. Where were they?

And we know what their master did to create them, Gwen thought. The interrogation had been chilling. She knew what the Russian Tsar had done, in a desperate bid to ensure he lived forever, but Duke Philippe had done worse. Much worse. No wonder he'd been so willing to gloat to her. He'd probably wanted to gloat for a long time, yet forced himself to keep his mouth shut. His peers might not have seen his experiments as anything other than the monstrous atrocities they were. *How many of his creatures are left?*

She scowled, inwardly. The duke had been right about one thing. They'd barely scratched the surface of what magic could do. She hated the thought of turning their captive over to the Royal College, of letting them push for experiments of their own, and yet … she wondered, numbly, if she should arrange an accident for the prisoner. She knew too much and there would be people trying to take advantage of her knowledge, telling themselves the experiments had already been carried out and they might as well try to benefit from them …

The chanting grew louder as the army flowed onwards. It was slightly more organised now – the rebels had stewards in place, directing the crowd towards Versailles

– but it still looked as though a whiff of grapeshot would be enough to stop it in its tracks. Gwen shuddered at the thought as she looked up, her eyes seeking the distant French Court. Versailles was shrouded in darkness, the complex invisible even to her. There wasn't a single light. She glanced back at Paris and shivered. The mob had set fire to large parts of the city. As far as she knew, no one was even trying to put out the flames.

Bruce floated up to join her, his face grim. "No sign of the enemy," he said, quietly. "The king has to try to stop us, doesn't he?"

Gwen nodded. King Louis was a weak man, according to Raechel and Simone, but even a weak man *had* to try to slow the rebels. He could run, of course, yet it would leave his reputation in tatters. No one would follow him; no one would see him as a credible monarch capable of returning to his country and reclaiming his throne. He'd be – at best – the French Edward I or Richard II ... she wondered, idly, if any French monarch had ever been deposed by his own people. She couldn't recall. French history had never been her forte ...

She waited, feeling the night growing darker as the hours wore on. The mob never stopped, although she could see a handful of people falling out and slipping into the shadows. She could understand, better than she cared to admit. The mob was bent on bloody revenge and it didn't much care if it had to trample over its own people to get it. She shook her head tiredly and peered into the darkness. What was the king doing? Was he preparing to make a stand? Or was he running for his life?

"We'll be there shortly," Bruce said. The mob was already passing through small towns and villages, their populations – wisely – having fled long ago. "Perhaps they simply fled ..."

"Perhaps." Gwen doubted it. Versailles had been the French Court for nearly two hundred years. In its own way, it was as symbolic as the Bastille. The French could no more abandon it without a fight than they could abandon their own capital city. They might lose the coming battle – they would, unless they had more troops on hand than she knew – but they couldn't refuse to fight. It would just put another nail in the monarchy's coffin. "We'll see."

She glanced at him, feeling an odd little thrill of anticipation. It had been far too long since they'd fought side by side, their powers blurring together until they were wrong. She was almost looking forward to it, despite the risk of being killed. Her lips twisted into a grim smile. Her enemies would be pleased, no doubt, if they died together. If they completed the mission while dying, their enemies would even find some nice things to say about them afterwards. She had no intention of giving them the satisfaction. It would be so much better to force them to praise her to her face.

They have to show themselves soon, she told herself. *Don't they?*

***

Louis wished, not for the first time, that he'd been allowed to spend more time with soldiers during basic training, if not campaigning. As the heir to the throne, there had been no way he could put his life at risk by leading from the front, yet he could have done more – surely – than just wear a fancy uniform and pretend his rank had been honourably earned. The guardsmen around him were working frantically, digging trenches and emplacing guns, but he didn't have the slightest idea if they were doing the right thing. Half of them kept glancing in his direction, their expressions so unreadable he *knew* they were contemplating treachery. If the duke hadn't been there, he feared they would have put a bullet in him and then deserted. Or simply left him alone.

He heard the mob before it came into view, a crowd chanting a revolutionary song that had been banned long – long – ago. Men and women had been lashed, in the old days, for even mouthing the words. Now, their singing was an act of open defiance, binding the mob together as it marched towards him. His heart pounded erratically as the faint light grew stronger, his legs threatening to turn to collapse under his own weight. The mob was every last one of his nightmares given shape and form. It was the end of his society, the end of a system in which everyone knew their place and stuck to it …

Louis shivered. It was the end of the world.

"There are two flying magicians," Duke Philippe said, pointing into the dark sky. Louis couldn't see anything in the darkness. "There will be others, down on the ground."

"Send your men to confront them," Louis ordered. The duke had held his magicians back, pointing out their mere presence upset the troops. "If we can take them out …"

"Not yet," Duke Philippe said. "We have to let them walk into the trap first."

Louis scowled at his kinsman. Which of them was *really* in command? He was the king and yet the duke had a remarkable talent for convincing people to do as he wished. The rumours … Louis glanced at the guardsmen and scowled. Their commander had vanished and they were taking orders from the duke, as if he was their true master. Louis forced himself to mentally step back, keeping his face expressionless. They couldn't afford to argue in front of the men. There would be time to sort out the matter later.

"Prepare to fire," Duke Philippe ordered. "And fire constantly until I countermand the order."

The mob came closer. Louis fancied he could see individual faces, contorted in hatred, as they neared. He asked himself, bitterly, why they couldn't accept their place in life. He hadn't wanted to be monarch – he hadn't been asked to be born. Why couldn't they be happy with what they had? And yet … he shook his head. It didn't matter any longer. The rebels had to be stopped or they'd tear down everything, leaving the country in ruins.

Perhaps it would have been wiser not to fight the war at all, he thought, sourly. *But the only other option was watching helplessly as the British became a superpower, condemning us to permanent subordination.*

"Fire," Duke Philippe ordered.

The guns boomed, the sound so loud Louis almost lost control of his bowels. The riflemen fired a second later, spraying bullets into the crowd. The people recoiled, torches falling to the ground as they were blown away; Louis saw a man, his head blown off his shoulders by a passing shell, stumbling onwards … for a horrible moment, he thought the man had become an undead monster, before realising the body was being shoved forward by the weight of the crowd. He felt a moment of savage exultation as he saw the crowd staggering under his fire, heard the screaming rising over the booming guns. That'd teach them. Perhaps they'd flee back to Paris, cowed and broken. Perhaps … they'd never dare raise a hand to their social superiors again …

Light flared. Louis barely had a second to realise what was happening before bolts of brilliant magic started flashing towards him. Duke Philippe knocked him to the ground as light darted over his head, some splattering uselessly against the makeshift earthworks and others vanishing into the darkness. The ground heaved as pieces of debris were picked up and hurled towards him – he saw a young guardsman literally *disintegrate* as something struck his chest with enough force to slam right through his body – then settle as the guns resumed their pounding. There were bodies on the ground, hundreds of bodies, but they didn't seem anything like enough. The howling was growing darker …

Louis shivered. The people wanted blood. His blood.

"They're trying to flank us," Duke Philippe observed. "Wise of them. We don't have the manpower to defend the entire complex."

"So stop them," Louis barked. "Hurry!"

He gritted his teeth. The mob was bleeding, but it wasn't down. He could hear shots from all directions, feel bullets whistling through the air overhead. The assault had clearly been carefully planned … he wondered, suddenly, which of his aristos had helped the rebels plan their offensive. It was impossible to believe the commoners could have done it on their own. Perhaps it was the Guises. They'd always had delusions of grandeur that had required careful politicking to keep in check, without pushing them into open rebellion. The bastards had never been on anyone's side but their own. He was mortally certain they were looking at the chaos and trying to determine how they could put their family on the throne, rather than planning how to save the country ...

"Soon," Duke Philippe said. "Let them get a little closer ..."

Louis felt the ground heave again. He was no expert, but he'd reviewed the defences in the last desperate hours. If they were outflanked, they'd be surrounded and trapped within the hour ... he wondered if he should hurry to the stables, find a horse and gallop into the distance, then shook his head. There were no more horses. He'd sent them away as escorts for his wife and family. His hand dropped to his sword. Perhaps he could sell his life dearly ...

"Now," Duke Philippe said. He raised his hand, sending a signal. Light flared, summoning the magicians. "Now we will see."

Louis nodded, muttering prayers. The gunners were starting to waver, all too aware they were on the verge of being surrounded. A handful of men had vanished ... dead or deserted, it hardly mattered. He glanced back, then drew his sword as the magicians flashed overhead. They could slash through the mob and then turn their attention to their peers ...

He blinked. What were they *doing*? They were heading up, not heading into the mob ... why? They needed to destroy the mob before it was too late ... they needed ...

"What ...?"

He turned to look for Duke Philippe. But the duke was gone.

Chapter Thirty-Nine
Versailles, France

wen felt sick as the enemy magicians charged.

It wasn't just the carnage below, although it had taken all her will to keep from diving down to obliterate the defenders before they could fire another round. It was the sheer *wrongness* of the enhanced magicians, the aura of pure *alienness* that surrounded them as they flew. She had no trouble sensing them, but her mind seemed to skitter over their presence as if it refused to believe they even existed. They were just too *wrong*. Their mere presence poisoned the air, making her feel sick to her stomach. She feared Bruce felt the same way.

The magicians opened fire, bolts of raw magic lighting up the air. She saw their faces, twisting and bulging in unnatural directions; she saw their eyes, glowing faintly with the power they'd been given. One of them had a gemstone mounted in his eye socket – she had no idea how he'd survived the procedure, even with a healer's help – and another had a gemstone in his palm, somehow directing the magic he was tossing at her. A third ... she caught a glimpse of his arm and shuddered helplessly, unable to avoid the sense someone had taken an adult's arm and grafted it to a child. Whatever Duke Philippe had done to them, it was profoundly unnatural. The energies they'd unleashed were tearing their bodies apart.

Which is how to stop them, she thought. The healer had

been clear on that, when she'd been interrogated. *Make them burn themselves out.*

She felt her magic blur into Bruce's as the enemy magicians attacked. There was no technique to their moves, as far as she could tell; no hint they'd ever had proper training in the use of their new powers. Two were skilled Movers, suggesting they'd originally had those powers before Duke Philippe started adding others; three threw burst after burst of magic at her, trying to batter down her – their – defences. Gwen shielded while Bruce slapped back at them, knocking one out of the sky. Another came at her, gemstone glowing in the palm of his hand, only to lose it as she formed a razor-sharp line of magic and sliced off his hand. He screamed and dropped, his concentration broken. He had no time to save himself before he hit the ground.

Bruce chuckled, then reached out again to disrupt their magic. The French were strong, yet they weren't trying to use their powers to best advantage. Gwen kept her and Bruce ducking and dodging, refusing to let the French pin them down and shove them into the ground. She could feel unseen hands brushing against her shields, searching for weaknesses … it would have worked, she thought, if she'd been alone. She could tighten their defences while letting Bruce do the fighting, then …

She smiled, despite herself, as they fused together, their magic blurring into one force. Bruce shaped a needle of raw power and shoved it into a flying magician, punching through his magic and straight into his head. Another tried to copy the trick, only to have his needle blunted on Gwen's defences. Brilliant lightning flashed, but she closed her eyes and trusted in her senses to guide her. The French magicians were easy to spot, even if her mind *did* try to slip away from them. Bruce kept up the attack as she moved them around, forcing the French to chase them. How long could they keep it up?

Gwen gritted her teeth as an enemy sorcerer slammed into her shields, trying to break them down through sheer force of will. Her magic drew on Bruce's and shaped a single command – NO MORE MAGIC – and slammed it into his head. He might have survived if he'd had better shields, but he had no time. His powers failed and he fell, landing in the mob below. Gwen had no idea if he'd survived the fall, but it hardly mattered. The mob trampled him before he could rise.

A blast of raw magic slammed into her shields. They were thrown right across the battlefield and straight into a large apartment block, smashing through walls and crashing through abandoned bedrooms and suites. She had a brief glimpse of a young woman lying on a bed, utterly unmoving, before the entire building started to come apart. Bruce acted on instinct, shoving the debris at the French magicians as they swooped after them. Gwen thought she saw one of them fall and drop out of sight … dead? It was hard to be sure. Their dead bodies still felt fundamentally wrong.

Something shifted, and exploded. The force tore them apart, sending her spinning away from her lover. Gwen caught herself, wrapping magic around her protectively as she crashed into another building and landed in a large sitting room. A French magician came after her, his eyes glowing with eerie light and his face … she felt sick, just looking at the sight. It looked as if there were worms, crawling under his skin. He raised his hand …

I'm not here, Gwen thought, pushing the compulsion at him as hard as she could. *You can't see me.*

The enemy magician paused, just for a second. He'd have seen her vanish right in front of his eyes … no, he'd have thought, for a moment, she'd never been there at all. The flicker of confusion was just long enough for her to gather her power and split it in two, driving a beam of pure force into his chest and a much smaller one into his brain. He stopped the first blow – the most obvious thrust – but missed the second. Gwen felt a pang of guilt as she tore his head apart, despite the grim awareness he would have killed her – or worse – if she'd let him live. His face had been a twisted nightmare …

She stopped, dead, as she saw a magician catch fire in

mid-air, the heat so intense she could see buildings and trees igniting as his body hit the ground. She hadn't killed him … had Bruce? She glanced around, unable to see her lover. Bruce had been knocked in the other direction … she felt a flicker of hope as a second magician exploded, the blast knocking down another building. The enhanced magicians were burning out, their powers spinning out of control! She took a moment to gather herself, then flew back into the air. The mob was storming the complex, crashing into the palaces and mansions that made up the inner court. There was almost no resistance now. A magician stood in front of a building and tried to slow the mob, only to be crushed by a handful of rebel magicians. Gwen allowed herself a tight smile. They'd won. There was no way to stop the civil war now …

A pair of magicians crashed into her, one carrying the other as he lashed out with his magic. She couldn't tell if they were enhanced, although she supposed the lack of visible warping was proof they weren't. They were certainly more practiced than the enhanced magicians, although too few in number to make a difference. She reached out and yanked them apart, then let the Blazer fall to his death while holding the Mover in place. The Frenchman was surprisingly strong, his magic nearly battering through her shields. She darted forward, melted right through *his* shields, and pulsed magic into his neck. He was dead well before he hit the ground.

Bruce joined her, his face tired but happy. "Mine caught fire on me," he said. "I think we won."

Gwen hesitated, looking down. The palace was on fire now, as the mob stormed the buildings and looted everything it could. There were no more defenders, as far as she could tell; there was no sign of King Louis or Duke Philippe or anyone else who could order a surrender. She scowled, studying the bodies below her. Was the duke dead? Or had he fled, ordering his magicians to cover his retreat? It was quite possible. The magicians could have turned the tide if they'd strafed the crowd first and *then* challenged Bruce and her.

"We need to find the duke," she said, finally. "Or at least his body."

***

Louis wasn't sure what had hit him, as the lines broke, but *something* had knocked him to the ground and left him dazed. He'd blanked out for a second – perhaps longer – and then recovered in time to see the mob charging past him, screaming and shouting as it crashed into apartment blocks, mansions and the royal palaces. He shuddered, unwilling to even think about the commoners ransacking the palace – his palace – and carrying off the artworks of France, perhaps even burning them to light their homes. It was all he could do to stand and look around, trying to spot the duke. Where had he gone? Where ...

He swallowed, hard. Had Duke Philippe fled? Or ... or what?

Someone shouted. Louis turned, just in time to see a middle-aged woman charging towards him. She carried a sword ... no, a long knife, perhaps the sort of blade he'd use to cut his meat. It was hellishly intimidating ... and, behind her, there were more and more people coming for him. He felt his legs turn to ice, his hand refusing to pick up his sword. He wanted to open his mouth, to plead for his life, to promise anything – anything at all – if they let him keep his life, but he couldn't speak. What could he say? She wanted him dead and there was nothing he could do about it.

His thoughts started to wander. Did she know who he was? He might be wearing a fancy uniform, but otherwise he looked nothing like his official portrait. She might know she was killing the king or ... he sighed as he met her eyes and saw the hatred burning bright within her. She might not know who he was, but she hated him. She drove her knife into him with astonishing force, pushing the blade into his chest. Weirdly, it was almost painless. He had a moment to wonder if he'd really been that bad a king …

… And then the darkness rose up and swallowed him.

***

Bruce watched Gwen's back as she walked the palace corridors and made her way down into the hidden complex under Versailles. The district was in utter chaos – half the buildings were on fire, the remainder were being looted – and no one, Jean-Luc nor the rebel leaders Gwen knew, appeared to be in charge. It was easy to imagine them lying dead on the ground, their bodies buried under a pile of other bodies. They'd have to be cremated soon, he told himself, before they started to decay. He wasn't sure the rebels were organised enough to do it.

The scene felt curiously anticlimactic as they made their way down the stairwell and into the secret tunnels. His eyes narrowed as he realised the doors had been left open and there were no guards. The entire underground complex felt as cold and silent as the grave. Gwen moved on, glancing into room after room; Bruce swore under his breath as he spotted the signs of a hasty evacuation. Some compartments had been hurriedly emptied, others had been blasted with magic. One room, very clearly a prison cell, was strewn with dead bodies chained to the walls. Their throats had been cut.

"They took everything they could," Gwen said, tiredly. She hadn't had anything like enough sleep after she'd dammed the river. If Bruce had had his way, she would have stayed in Paris to rest while he went to Versailles. "And what they couldn't take they destroyed."

Bruce nodded. He was familiar with evacuating underground lairs, although he was a little surprised the French had bothered to come up with an evacuation plan, let alone put it into action. They couldn't really have expected the uprising, could they? Perhaps they were just paranoid or … he frowned. The French Court was wilder than London and New York, if half the stories were true, but even *they* had their limits. Duke Philippe might have planned to evacuate in a hurry if his peers realised what he was doing.

He kept that thought to himself as they checked the rest of the compartments. There were no documents, no charged gemstones ... nothing, save for two more dead bodies, both with no obvious cause of death. Magic? Or poison? They might have simply outlived their usefulness ... he shuddered, remembering what the duke had done to Raechel. If you had the power to turn someone's mind against her, could you convince someone else's mind to simply shut down? He shuddered. Duke Philippe was clearly a very different kind of magician, his talent previously unknown. What else could he do?

"We'll have to have this place searched thoroughly, and quickly," Gwen said. "I don't know how long we'll be welcome here."

Bruce nodded. "They'll kick us out within a day," he predicted. "They won't want us around any longer."

Gwen said nothing, but it was clear she agreed. The French Underground wouldn't want to give the British any credit. Wise of them, Bruce thought, but irritating. There was even a reasonable chance the French would try to stop them leaving, just to keep the truth of the affair buried. Would they risk continuing the war with Britain in the midst of a civil war? Or would they gamble Britain wouldn't seek to avenge their deaths? Or ...

He followed her back up the steps and into the palace. The looters were running wild – some grabbing paintings, others carrying artworks and candlesticks – and the rebel leadership wasn't making any attempt to control them. Bruce suspected that was common sense. The quickest way to destroy your authority was to issue orders you knew wouldn't – or couldn't – be obeyed. The looters wanted to ransack everything and woe betide anyone who got in their way. The rebel army couldn't stop them. They *were* the looters. His lips twitched as he passed a pair of men carrying a carpet, as if it were a priceless artefact. Did they intend to put it in their homes? Or were they just trying to make sure they took something before the complex burnt to the ground.

Jean-Luc waved to them as they left the palace. Bruce wasn't surprised to see a handful of familiar faces carrying looted goods back to Paris. He wondered, idly, if they'd be worth much of anything in the months and years to come. There'd be a glut of stolen goods on the market, while there was still a massive shortage of food. He hoped someone had the sense to put guards on the wine cellar before the looters broke in and started drinking. The situation was quite bad enough already.

"We found the king," Jean-Luc said, cheerfully. "His body was hacked to pieces."

"Charming," Gwen said. There was a twinge of regret in her voice, as if she'd have preferred to take the king alive. "And Duke Philippe?"

"No sign of him," Jean-Luc said. "We know a bunch of horsemen galloped off as soon as we started to break through the defences, so it's possible he's halfway to Dunkirk by now. Or trying to hide in the countryside. We'll hang him when we find him."

"Please," Gwen said. "What happened to the others?"

"Back in Paris, trying to figure out what to do next," Jean-Luc said. "The king is dead, the aristos fled" – he giggled – "and the country is on fire. What about you?"

"We'll go back to Paris long enough to collect our things, then be on our way," Gwen said, simply. If she was irritated by his attitude, she didn't show it. "And then we'll hopefully meet again in better times."

Jean-Luc shrugged and turned away. Bruce eyed his back, then shrugged himself. The smugglers weren't idealists, for all they were happy to work with the rebels. Jean-Luc probably had a dozen fallback plans, for everything from a total rebel victory to their total defeat. Bruce wouldn't be surprised to discover he had ties to the aristocracy – there were things forbidden even to them, which was partly why they wanted them – as well as links to the army, the navy and even the clergy. Jean-Luc was no idealist ... he wondered, idly, if the rebels wouldn't be wiser to put him in charge. Idealists had their place, but it wasn't in power politics. The underground would need a strong and decisive leader soon, if it didn't already. It wouldn't be long before the aristocrats started planning their return.

There were no horses. They settled for walking back to Paris, following hundreds of looters carrying their wares to the city. The air was warm, but heavy with the stench of smoke and dead bodies. Bruce could hear people singing and dancing, celebrating the fall of the monarchy, and yet ... what would happen, he asked himself, when the people realised they hadn't solve all of France's problems? The rebels had had no trouble pointing out all the problems, but solving them would be a great deal harder. What would happen if the average person's life didn't get any better? When food remained scarce, and jobs remained rare, and taxes started to rise again ...?

But that was what our government wanted, he reminded himself. They'd had their orders. They understood the reasoning behind them. *A France riven by civil war is a France that cannot continue to fight us.*

He wondered, numbly, if they'd done the right thing. The super-magicians had been a threat. Given time, they might have won the war for France. And yet ... God alone knew how many Frenchmen were going to die in the weeks and months to come. It was going to be a nightmare.

They'd won. But it felt almost as if they'd lost.

Chapter Forty
Dover, England

wen hadn't been sure what sort of welcome to expect, as they sailed under false names from Dunkirk to Dover. It was bad enough that she'd had to leave Irene and Raechel – and Simone – behind to keep an eye on matters in France, all too aware they might be caught up in the brewing civil war and killed before they could escape. The ride to Dunkirk had been dangerous and the voyage even worse, as elements of the French Navy seemed to have turned pirate and were attacking everything leaving French ports. She had no idea what the *Royal* Navy was doing, but she thought it had orders not to engage. The British Government would be profoundly embarrassed if hundreds and thousands of French aristos arrived, begging for sanctuary. They might quietly prefer to have them lost at sea.

She glanced at Bruce as the crew ran down the gangplank, then shrugged and led the way onto dry land. The message she'd sent ahead had noted her planned return and arranged for a carriage to take them straight to London. Lord Mycroft would want his debriefing … she sighed, inwardly, unsure what she was going to say to him. On one hand, he *had* undermined her by sending Bruce to shadow her; on the other, he'd probably saved her life and Bruce's career. If Bruce had deserted the army and set off to Paris on his own …

"Home sweet home," Bruce said. "Should we head straight to Gretna Green?"

Gwen smiled, despite herself. They'd wanted to kiss – and do other things – after their return to Paris, but they'd had almost no privacy. The ship hadn't been any better. She told herself they could kiss in the carriage, perhaps even ... she put the thought out of her head as they passed the guards at the gate, then headed straight for the horse-drawn coach. They'd be back in London soon and then ...

We should go home first, she thought. The government ministers might want to see her at once, or so she assumed, but she needed a wash and a change of clothes first. The only person who'd ever walked into the council chamber looking as if he'd just marched off the battlefield was the Duke of India, who had the prestige to get away with it. Her lips twitched as she recalled their faces. *They couldn't believe what they saw.*

Her smile vanished as she peered into the cab. Lord Mycroft sat inside, taking up one of the benches. Gwen blinked in shock. She could count on the fingers of one hand just how many times she'd seen him outside his offices, his club or his lodgings. His brother was the active one of the family, not him ... the idea of him coming to Dover to *meet* her was just unthinkable. And yet, he was right in front of her.

"Lady Gwen," Lord Mycroft said. He looked older somehow, as if all his years had suddenly caught up with him. "Please. Join me."

Gwen scrambled up into the carriage, Bruce right behind her. The coachman – he looked surprisingly familiar – closed the door, casting the interior into shadow. Gwen took her seat and braced herself, hearing the coachman scrambling into place and cracking the whip. The coach rattled into motion, heading down the road. Gwen felt vaguely confined. The two men took up an awful lot of space.

"I'm sorry to surprise you like this," Lord Mycroft said. "Unfortunately, there have been developments."

Gwen shivered. "Developments?"

"Lord Liverpool died two weeks ago," Lord Mycroft said. "The war was still on, so it was kept very quiet as the ruling party struggled to choose a successor and present him to the king. There was, as you might expect, a great deal of horse-trading and favour-calling and everything else that goes into selecting a new Prime Minister. It was only yesterday that a final decision was reached."

"I heard nothing about it," Gwen said. She wasn't sure of her feelings. Lord Liverpool hadn't been a bad man, and he'd been an effective war leader, but he'd had his limitations as a thinker. Being conservative wasn't a bad thing, yet there were limits. "The French had no idea."

"We didn't tell the country," Lord Mycroft said. "Whispers got out, of course, but nothing solid. Nothing anyone could use as a base for policy. That said ..."

He paused, his face grim. "Sir Edmund Hellebore will be formally announced as the new Prime Minister later today."

Gwen sucked in her breath. "Sir Edmund?"

"I'm afraid so," Lord Mycroft said. "Sir Edmund has already started recognising the cabinet and associated departments. My official title hasn't been altered, but I have been told to consider myself on effective leave for an indeterminate period. The Duke of India may be advised to step down, when he returns from Spain, and several others have either been shuffled around or told to seek employment elsewhere. Sir Edmund has started bringing in his own men to replace them."

"Oh," Gwen said. It was hard to imagine the government without Lord Mycroft. Or the Duke of India. And ... she tried not to swallow as it dawned on her Sir Edmund might try to undermine her too. "What about the Royal College? And the Sorcerers Corps?"

"I believe he has yet to come to any decision," Lord Mycroft told her. "You are not easy to replace."

He looked at Bruce. "I took the liberty of filing orders for you to go to France instead of Spain," he said. "I certainly *intend* to convince Arthur" – it took Gwen a moment to realise he meant the Duke of India – "that you were operating under my instructions, although he will still be unhappy. That said, it isn't clear how matters will play out. Sir Edmund thinks I concealed important information from the cabinet. He may be right."

Gwen scowled, unsure how she felt. She didn't *like* Sir Edmund. She feared he'd try to undermine her ... was *he* the one behind Pinfold? He certainly had the nerve his agent conspicuously lacked, as well as the power and position to shield Pinfold from Gwen's rage if – when – she found out what he'd been doing behind her back. And yet ... if he was the legal Prime Minister, reshuffling the Cabinet was his right as well as his duty. He had every legal right to put his supporters in key places, rather than risk his enemies undermining him from within the Cabinet itself. Hell ... if he didn't, he'd make himself look weak. The Opposition would certainly be quick to take advantage, now the war was effectively over.

"You do your duty," Lord Mycroft told her. "And you make it harder for him to replace you."

Bruce leaned forward. "Is he likely to be a real problem, or is he just another over-ambitious politician with delusions of grandeur?"

"It's hard to say," Lord Mycroft said. "He's ambitious. He wouldn't have risen so high if he lacked ambition. He's also ... not common-born, not in any real sense of the word, but lower down the social scale than many others. He cannot command the respect those of higher birth can ..."

He shook his head. "I may be jumping at shadows, but I fear Sir Edmund's ambitions will lead the nation into troubled waters."

Gwen shivered.

Lord Mycroft leaned back against the wooden box. "France is at war with itself," he said. "And our war with the French is effectively over."

"Yes," Gwen said, flatly. "It will take some time for a clear winner to emerge."

"And whoever wins will find it impossible to put the Bourbon Empire back together," Lord Mycroft said. "Portugal has been liberated. Spain has effectively freed herself, although the country may fragment into several smaller states ... right now, it's impossible to be sure. Italy is in chaos and the Vatican has been sacked ... given time, the various states might unite into one, either through conquest or cooperation. And the wars spreading across Latin America ... Sir Edmund will have plenty of opportunity to cause trouble, if he wishes."

"Or he might find himself too busy here to cause problems elsewhere," Gwen said. "Right?"

"We can but hope," Lord Mycroft said. "I've taken the liberty of directing the coach to the Royal College. The cabinet will be too busy to meet with you, at least until tomorrow. The two of you can have a rest, and recuperate from your journey. After that ... we'll see."

Gwen nodded, wordlessly. They would see ... she wondered, sourly, if Sir Edmund would ask for her resignation immediately or if he'd wait to hear her report before he asked her to step down in favour of Bruce. Or someone. There were no other Master Magicians, as far as she knew, but ... it wasn't a *law* her post needed a Master. It was just tradition. And not a very long-standing tradition either.

She shivered again, closing her eyes as the coach rattled on. Perhaps she was overthinking it. Perhaps she was worrying over nothing. Perhaps ... but deep inside, she feared things were about to get worse. She could feel the ground shifting under her feet ...

... And who knew what would happen, in the days and weeks to come?

Epilogue

o not worry, Captain," Duke Philippe said, careful to maintain eye contact. The naval captain had a strong will, but few men could bear to disagree with him for long if he met their eyes and drew on his power. "The British will not harm us."

The captain turned away, shouting orders as the tiny corvette slowed to allow the British sailors to board. Duke Philippe watched him for a moment, just to be sure, then turned his attention to the rowing boat coming up alongside his ship. The corvette could have blown the boarding party out of the water with ease, but the cruiser keeping her distance could return the favour within seconds – and would, if she saw any reason to open fire. Duke Philippe had insisted on sailing straight for the Royal Navy's blockading squadron, rather than trying to make it to Toulon or flee into the Atlantic. There were few other places to go, certainly nowhere the British – or whoever took power in France – couldn't find him, if they wanted him. He'd considered sailing for the Far East, but he'd stand out a mile. And he didn't speak the language.

He calmed himself as the British sailors scrambled up the ropes and onto the decks. The leader was one of their famous boy sailors, surprisingly young for his rank; Duke Philippe wondered, idly, if one of the enlisted men behind the boy was actually the one in charge. He'd certainly be an advisor ... the smarter boys would know to listen and follow his advice. He'd be strong-willed too, too strong for the mesmerising trick to work reliably. And he'd have an audience …

The leader glanced at him. "What is your business with us?"

Duke Philippe was almost impressed. His outfit was hardly a naval uniform, but the lad had picked him out as the true leader right from the start. The men behind him kept their hands close to their weapons, taking care to make it clear they could draw them in a moment. The French crew could probably rush the British, but it would only get the ship sunk when the cruiser realised what had happened and opened fire. Besides, Duke Philippe didn't want a fight. He wanted – needed – an escort to Britain.

"I'm Duke Philippe, Kinsman to the King," Duke Philippe said, calmly. He bit down on the urge to use his magic. The boy would have to be talked into helping him the old fashioned way. "And I have a vitally important message for your government …"

And he smiled.

End of Book V

Elsewhen Press

delivering outstanding new talents in speculative fiction

Visit the Elsewhen Press website at elsewhen.press for the latest information on all of our titles, authors and events; to read our blog; find out where to buy our books and ebooks; or to place an order.

Sign up for the Elsewhen Press InFlight Newsletter at elsewhen.press/newsletter

Bookworm series by Christopher G. Nuttall

Bookworm

Elaine, an inexperienced witch in Golden City, has her life turned upside down when she triggers a magical trap to end up with all the knowledge in the Great Library stuffed inside her head. Avoiding the Inquisition she tries to understand what has happened to her. But she is a pawn in the dark plans of one who wants the Grand Sorcerer's power.

Bookworm won the Gold Award in the Adult Fiction category of the 2013 Wishing Shelf Independent Book Awards.

ISBN: 9781908168320 (epub, kindle) / 9781908168221 (368pp, paperback)

Visit bit.ly/Bookworm-Nuttall

Bookworm II – The Very Ugly Duckling

Not every ugly duckling becomes a swan ...

In the wake of the disastrous attack on the Golden City, Lady Light Spinner has become Grand Sorceress and Elaine, the Bookworm, has been settling into her positions as Head Librarian and Privy Councillor. But any hope of vanishing into her books is negated when a new magician of staggering power appears in the city, one whose abilities seem to defy the known laws of magic.

ISBN: 9781908168382 (epub, kindle) / 9781908168283 (432pp, paperback)

Visit bit.ly/Bookworm2-Nuttall

Bookworm III – The Best Laid Plans

Elaine and Johan prepare to leave Golden City, with Daria and Cass, to search for the Witch-King. But Elaine is arrested on the orders of a new Emperor, puppet of the Witch-King. She must escape and destroy him. Privy Councillors and Heads of the Great Houses have bowed to the Emperor. Only Elaine and her friends can prevent an all-out war.

ISBN: 9781908168764 (epub, kindle) / 9781908168665 (400pp, paperback)

Visit bit.ly/Bookworm3

Bookworm IV – Full Circle

Until now the Witch-King had remained hidden as a lich. But Elaine was intent on his destruction. Bonded to the unknowingly powerful Johan, she was the only other magician who understood the deeper layers of magic. As they slowly made their way towards the catacombs in Ida where his lich was hiding, he had to rely on the new Emperor to stop them.

ISBN: 9781908168948 (epub, kindle) / 9781908168849 (416pp, paperback)

Visit bit.ly/Bookworm4

Now available as audiobooks from Tantor

The Unwritten Words series by Christopher G. Nuttall

The Golden City has fallen, the Empire is no more, ancient magic threatens the land. In *The Unwritten Words*, Christopher Nuttall's story-telling mastery weaves a new epic which follows on from his bestselling *Bookworm* series and is set in that same world.

I – The Promised Lie

Five years have passed since the earth-shattering events of *Bookworm IV*. The Golden City has fallen. The Grand Sorcerer and Court Wizards are dead. The Empire they ruled is nothing more than a memory, a golden age lost in the civil wars as kings and princes battle for supremacy. And only a handful of trained magicians remain alive.

Isabella Majuro, Lady Sorceress, is little more than a mercenary, fighting for money in a desperate bid to escape her past. But when Prince Reginald of Andalusia plots the invasion of the Summer Isle, Isabella finds herself dragged into a war against strange magics from before recorded history …

… And an ancient mystery that may spell the end of the human race.

ISBN: 9781908168311 (epub, kindle) / 9781908168212 (416pp, paperback)

Visit bit.ly/ThePromisedLie

II – The Ancient Lie

After the campaign in the Summer Isle, Isabella rides out the winter storms by studying the godly magic under Mother Lembu, in the process learning about the origins of the old gods.

Crown Prince Reginald receives word that his father the King, is ill while his sister Princess Sofia, acting as regent, is imposing a regime that is strangely similar to what had been happening on the Summer Isle – nobles killed, temples smashed, enforced public worship of old gods. Concerned that his family, and indeed his homeland, are in danger, Reginald is determined to return home. But the storms are still raging with what appears to be unnatural force, making any attempt to return to Andalusia too risky for the Prince and his men.… unless Isabella can somehow use the new rituals she has learnt to placate the powers behind the storms and navigate the fleet safely home to face whatever has taken control of the kingdom.

ISBN: 9781908168397 (epub, kindle) / 9781908168292 (352pp, paperback)

Visit bit.ly/TheAncientLie

III – The Truthful Lie

Reginald, now King, is struggling against the rising tide of the Old God entities. He knows that his army alone cannot defeat them, even with cold iron that can contain them and free enslaved humans. But as cities burn and farmland is devastated, the people have been easily convinced by cultists to turn to the Old Gods.

In a neighbouring kingdom the weak young ruler, fallen prey to an entity that promised him the world, starts his campaign to fulfil that promise, adding to the threats heading towards Andalusia.

Reginald's best hope is that Isabella, his sorceress Queen, and Princess Silverdale, his talented sister, can learn enough about the entities and their relationship with the human realm to find a magical way to defeat them. But, as time is running out, shattering news arrives from the Golden City…

ISBN: 9781908168502 (epub, kindle) / 9781908168403 (352pp, paperback)

Visit bit.ly/TheTruthfulLie

Series available as audiobooks from Tantor

Existence is Elsewhen

Twenty stories from twenty great authors including
John Gribbin, Rhys Hughes
Christopher G. Nuttall, Douglas Thompson

The title *Existence is Elsewhen* paraphrases the last sentence of André Breton's 1924 *Manifesto of Surrealism*, perfectly summing up the intent behind this anthology of stories from a wonderful collection of authors. Different worlds... different times. It's what Elsewhen Press has been about since we launched our first title in 2011.

Here, we present twenty science fiction stories for you to enjoy. We are delighted that headlining this collection is the fantastic **John Gribbin,** with a worrying vision of medical research in the near future. Future global healthcare is the theme of **J A Christy's** story; while the ultimate in spare part surgery is where **Dave Weaver** takes us. **Edwin Hayward's** search for a renewable protein source turns out to be digital; and **Tanya Reimer's** story with characters we think we know gives us pause for thought about another food we take for granted. Evolution is examined too, with **Andy McKell's** chilling tale of what states could become if genetics are used to drive policy. Similarly, **Robin Moran's** story explores the societal impact of an undesirable evolutionary trend; while **Douglas Thompson** provides a truly surreal warning of an impending disaster that will reverse evolution, with dire consequences.

On a lighter note, we have satire from **Steve Harrison** discovering who really owns the Earth (and why); and **Ira Nayman,** who uses the surreal alternative realities of his *Transdimensional Authority* series as the setting for a detective story mash-up of Agatha Christie and Dashiel Hammett. Pursuing the crime-solving theme, **Peter Wolfe** explores life, and death, on a space station; while **Stefan Jackson** follows a police investigation into some bizarre cold-blooded murders in a cyberpunk future. Going into the past, albeit an 1831 set in the alternate Britain of his *Royal Sorceress* series, **Christopher G. Nuttall** reports on an investigation into a girl with strange powers.

Strange powers in the present-day is the theme for **Tej Turner,** who tells a poignant tale of how extra-sensory perception makes it easier for a husband to bear his dying wife's last few days. Difficult decisions are the theme of **Chloe Skye's** heart-rending story exploring personal sacrifice. Relationships aren't always so close, as **Susan Oke's** tale demonstrates, when sibling rivalry is taken to the limit. Relationships are the backdrop to **Peter R. Ellis's** story where a spectacular mid-winter event on a newly- colonised distant planet involves a Madonna and Child. Coming right back to Earth and in what feels like an almost imminent future, **Siobhan McVeigh** tells a cautionary tale for anyone thinking of using technology to deflect the blame for their actions. Building on the remarkable setting of Pera from her *LiGa* series, and developing Pera's legendary *Book of Shadow*, **Sanem Ozdural** spins the creation myth of the first light tree in a lyrical and poetic song. Also exploring language, the master of fantastika and absurdism, **Rhys Hughes,** extrapolates the way in which language changes over time, with an entertaining result.

ISBN: 9781908168955 (epub, kindle) / 9781908168856 (320pp paperback)
Visit bit.ly/ExistenceIsElsewhen

THE MAREK SERIES BY JULIET KEMP
1: THE DEEP AND SHINING DARK
A Locus Recommended Read in 2018

"A rich and memorable tale of political ambition, family and magic, set in an imagined city that feels as vibrant as the characters inhabiting it." **Aliette de Bodard**

You know something's wrong when the cityangel turns up at your door

An agreement 300 years ago, between an angel and Marek's founding fathers, protects magic and political stability within the city. A recent plague wiped out most of the city's sorcerers. Reb, one of the survivors, realises that someone has deposed the cityangel without replacing it. Marcia, Heir to House Fereno, stumbles across that same truth. But it is just one part of a much more ambitious plan to seize control of Marek. Meanwhile, city Council members connive and conspire, manipulated in a dangerous political game that threatens the peace and security of all the states around the Oval Sea. Reb, Marcia, the deposed cityangel, and Jonas, a Salina messenger, must work together to stop the impending disaster. They must discover who is behind it, and whom they can really trust.

ISBN: 9781911409342 (epub, kindle) / 9781911409243 (272pp paperback)

Visit bit.ly/DeepShiningDark

2: SHADOW AND STORM

"never short on adventure and intrigue... the characters are real, full of depth, and richly drawn, and you'll wish you had even more time with them by book's end. A fantastic read." **Rivers Solomon**

Never trust a demon… or a Teren politician

The new Teren Lord Lieutenant has an agenda. A young Teren magician being sought by an unleashed demon, believes their only hope may be to escape to Marek where the cityangel can keep the demon at bay. Once again Reb, Cato, Jonas and Beckett must deal with a magical problem, while Marcia tackles a serious political challenge to Marek's future.

ISBN: 9781911409595 (epub, kindle) / 9781911409496 (336pp paperback)

Visit bit.ly/ShadowAndStorm

3: THE RISING FLOOD

"Fantasy politics with real nuance … a fantastic read" **Malka Older**

Hope alone cannot withstand a rising flood

A darkness writhes in the heart of Teren, unleashing demons on dissenters. Marek's five sorcerers with the cityangel can expel a single demon, but Teren has many. Storms rampage across the Oval Sea. Menaced by the distant capital, dissension from within, and even nature itself – will the rising flood lift all boats? Or will they be capsized?

ISBN: 9781911409984 (epub, kindle) / 9781911409885 (392pp paperback)

Visit bit.ly/TheRisingFlood

4: THE CITY REVEALED

"Eminently satisfying epic fantasy" **Juliet E. McKenna**
"An absorbing fantasy set in a richly imagined world" **Una McCormack**

Independence brings self-determination but also threats

Marek is newly-independent. Teren's expelled Lieutenant threatened to return with soldiers & war sorcerers. The common folk of Marek demand representation. Marcia, Fereno-Heir, agrees with them. She and sorcerer Reb, her lover, must convince the Council of the truth of magic, whilst her sorcerer brother, Cato, rushes to build some sort of defence.

ISBN: 9781915304315 (epub, kindle) / 9781915304216 (344pp paperback)

Visit bit.ly/TheCityRevealed

The Avatars of Ruin series by Tej Turner

Book 1: Bloodsworn

"Classic epic fantasy. I enjoyed it enormously"
– Anna Smith Spark

"a stunning introduction to a new fantasy world"
– Christopher G Nuttall

It has been twelve years since the war between the nations of Sharma and Gavendara. The villagers of Jalard live a bucolic existence, nestled within the hills of western Sharma, far from the warzone. They have little contact with the outside world, apart from once a year when Academy representatives choose two of them to be taken away to the institute in the capital. To be Chosen is considered a great honour… of which most of Jalard's children dream. But this year, their announcement is so shocking it causes friction between villagers, and some begin to suspect that all is not what it seems. Where are they taking the Chosen, and why? Some intend to find out, but what they discover will change their lives forever and set them on a long and bloody path to seek vengeance…

ISBN: 9781911409779 (epub, kindle) / 9781911409670 (432pp paperback)
Visit bit.ly/Bloodsworn

Book 2: Blood Legacy

The ragtag group from Jalard have finally reached Shemet, Sharma's capital city. Scarred and bereft, they bring a grim tale of what happened to their village, and a warning about the threat to all humanity. Some expect sanctuary within the Synod to mean an end to their hardships, but their hopes are soon dashed. Sharma's ruling class are caught within their own inner turmoil. Jaedin senses moles within their ranks, but his call to crisis falls mostly on deaf ears, and some seek to thwart him when he tries to hunt the infiltrators down.

Meanwhile, Gavendara is mustering its forces. With ritualistically augmented soldiers, their mutant army is like nothing the world has ever seen.

The Zakaras are coming. And Sharma's only hope of stopping them is if it can unite its people in time.

ISBN: 9781911409991 (epub, kindle) / 9781911409892 (474pp paperback)
Visit bit.ly/Blood-Legacy

Book 3: Blood War

Coming soon

The Magic Fix series by Mark Montanaro

The Magic Fix

**The Known World needs a fix or things could get very ugly
(even uglier than an Ogre!)**

"Did we win the battle?" asked King Wyndham.

"Well it depends how you define winning," answered Longfield, one of the King's royal commanders.

In fact, the Humans are fighting a losing battle with the Trolls. Meanwhile the Ogres are up to something, which probably isn't good. Could one flying unicorn bring about peace in the Known World? No, obviously not.

But maybe a group of rebels have the answer. Or perhaps the answer lies with a young Pixie with one remarkable gift. Does the Elvish Oracle have the answer? Who knows? And, even if she did, would anyone understand her cryptic answers (we all know what Oracles are like!)

The Known World is in danger of being rent in twain, and twain-rending is never good!

Did I mention the dragon? No? Ah… well… there's also a dragon.

ISBN: 9781911409731 (epub, kindle) / 9781911409632 (240pp paperback)
Visit bit.ly/TheMagicFix

The Enchanting Tricks

The Known World is still not fixed… and things <u>have</u> got ugly

In the Goblin realm, Queen Afflech was doing remarkably well considering the circumstances. She had seen her husband die, and both her sons killed within the space of a couple of weeks. That kind of thing does tend to bring you down a bit.

Losing three kings in a few days looked rather careless. But of more concern to the Goblin warlords was whether it looked weak to their enemies. They suspected the Humans were behind one death and the Ogres behind another. The Pixies were no threat, the Trolls would probably soon be killing one another again, and the Elves were irrelevant (or, to be precise, just annoying).

Meanwhile, King Wyndham wanted to show the Goblins that Humans were not to blame (apart from the two that might be to blame). Petra, the most famous Pixie in the Known World, knew exactly who was to blame and wanted to rescue them. Lord Protector Higarth was determined to help the Goblins with their predicament, whether they wanted Ogre-help or not.

But on the plus side, the dragon's gone; and there are still plenty of unicorns… maybe they can somehow solve everything?

ISBN: 9781915304193 (epub, kindle) / 9781915304094 (270pp paperback)
Visit bit.ly/TheEnchantingTricks

The Vanished Mage

Penelope Hill and J. A. Mortimore

A vanished mage…

A missing diamond…

The game is afoot.

"From Broderick, Prince of Asconar, Earl of Carlshore and Thorn, Duke of Wicksborough, Baron of Highbury and Warden of Dershanmoor, to My Lady Parisan, King's Investigator, greetings. It has been brought to my attention that a certain Reinwald, Master Historian, noted Archmagus and tutor to our court in this city of Nemithia, has this day failed to report to the duties awaiting him. I do ask you, as my father's most loyal servant, to seek the cause of this laxity and bring word of the mage to me, so that my concerns as to his safety be allayed."

The herald delivered the message word-perfect to The Lady Parisan, Baroness of Orandy, Knight of the Diamond Circle and Sworn Paladin to Our Lady of the Sighs. Parisan's companion, Foorourow Miar Raar Ramoura, Prince of Ilsfacar, (Foo to his friends) thought it a rather mundane assignment, but nevertheless together they ventured to the Archmagus' imposing home to seek him. It turned out to be the start of an adventure to solve a mystery wrapped in an enigma bound by a conundrum and secured by a puzzle. All because of a missing diamond with a solar system at its core.

Authors Penelope Hill and J. A. Mortimore have effortlessly melded a Holmesian investigative duo, a richly detailed city where they encounter both nobility and seedier denizens, swashbuckling action, and magic that is palpable and, at times, awesome.

ISBN: 9781915304186 (epub, kindle) / 97819153041087 (212pp paperback)

About the author

hristopher G. Nuttall has been planning sci-fi books since he learnt to read. Born and raised in Edinburgh, Chris created an alternate history website and eventually graduated to writing full-sized novels. Studying history independently allowed him to develop worlds that hung together and provided a base for storytelling. After graduating from university, Chris started writing full- time. As an indie author he has self-published many novels, this is his latest fantasy to be published by Elsewhen Press, the much-anticipated fifth in the popular *Royal Sorceress* series. The first was *The Royal Sorceress*, followed by *The Great Game*, *Necropolis* and *Sons of Liberty*. *The Revolutionary War* continues Gwen's story. Chris is currently living in Edinburgh with his wife, muse, and critic Aisha and their two sons.